THE CLOUD PEOPLE

To: Aunt Carrie Hudson;

I am a member of two great families;
from Father's side, the Golden Clan, and from
my wife's Mother's side, there are the Bryants.

Because of you, I feel just as loved and accepted
in the Bryants Clan (In-Laws) as I do from my own
birth clan (The "Golden's")

At this point in my life I can truly say that
I have just one living aunt left... and it's You

I Love You

MC

M. Samuel Golden

NEWMAN SPRINGS PUBLISHING
320 Broad Street
Red Bank, NJ 07701

First originally published by Newman Springs Publishing 2021

All scriptures are taken from the King James
translation of the Holy Bible.

ISBN 978-1-63692-418-2 (Paperback)
ISBN 978-1-68498-160-1 (Hardcover)
ISBN 978-1-63692-419-9 (Digital)

Printed in the United States of America

To my late grandmother, Mrs. Lillian Golden, while she lived, she was an angel upon the earth. Like Polly to her mother, I miss you, Grandma, and cannot wait to see you again.

CONTENTS

PART 1

The First Cloud (1933)

And the LORD came down in a cloud, and spake unto him.

—Numbers 11:25 (KJV)[1]

Wherefore seeing we also are compassed with so great a cloud of witnesses.

—Hebrews 12:1, 2 (KJV)

That they may be one, as we are.

—John 17:11b (KJV)

What doesn't kill you leaves you scarred, crippled, and bitter.

—Benjamin "Buck" Riser

CHAPTER 1

Vulcan's Anvil

The winds swooped down upon us like bandits, but unlike bandits, they stole from us, much more than insignificant baubles or meaningless currency. The winds took from us our land, stripping it away, layer after agonizing layer, leaving us with no crops, no livelihood, no dignity, and no hope. It also left a good many of our neighbors with no home, as Vulcan's Anvil hammered away their last desire to remain on lands held by four generations of hardy homesteaders. They simply could not take it anymore. And so, they left. They packed up everything they could carry and walked away from everything else.

Unknowingly we ourselves were collaborators with the very thieves who made off with our way of life. Our mechanized plowshares, greedy to transform the sparse grasslands of Western Kansas into arable crop-producing land, ultimately produced the opposite effect. The grasses' roots were no match for the metal claws, which pillaged and plundered their shallow purchase. This left the soil with no anchor and with no protection from the Aeolian processes that followed the worst continuous drought in our nation's history. *Aeolian process* is a scientific term referring to wind-induced land erosion. However, it didn't take a scientist to know that the process caused an already-poor quality of soil to be reduced to absolute desolation. Then reminiscent of the clouds of dust kicked up by the hooves of bandit-ridden horses, clouds consisting of millions of metric tons of dirt, which were newly liberated, formed a plague of blinding choking fury that blazed a murderous swathe, all the way to the East Coast of the United States.[2]

Even before the advent of the phenomena history would refer to as the black blizzards,[3] the town of Garden City in Finney County, Kansas, bore little resemblance to its namesake. During the Great Depression of the 1930s, it was hard enough to coax a meager living from the reluctant earth, much less to indulge in an impractical pursuit of an utterly vain horticultural aesthetic. That was what Grandma Molly always called "picking wildflowers." She would often chide her granddaughter, Polly, saying, "Lord knows, child, if God had wanted his flowers to be picked, he would have made them to grow in pretied bundles, like hay."

Notwithstanding she would always relent to her grandchild's persistence. "I suppose, child, it's better to have you picking flowers in the field than to have you underfoot and meddling where grown folks are trying to work."

In the end, that was precisely what Polly happily spent the better part of her morning doing. Now with a trophy of wildflowers in hand, her slender legs propelled her toward her family's farmhouse and to the loving embrace of her mother.

As Polly neared the house, the familiar aroma of greens cooking on the stove, and of biscuits baking in the oven, greeted her from the kitchen and filled her with joy. It always had. All the things she loved most in life were right here, in the roughly nine square miles that was Garden City, Kansas.

Getting closer, she could see all the people she loved so well. There was Grandma Molly and Grandpa Clemmons. There was her father, Benjamin. There was even Reverend Knowles. In fact, it seemed as if everyone was there, except for Penelope, her mother.

"Hi, Reverend Knowles!" Polly shouted, coming closer to the group. It seemed strange to her that they were all standing around something near the back of the house; something she was still too far away to make out. "Hey! What's going on?" Whatever it was, she thought, it could certainly wait. She had to give the flowers to her mother.

Suddenly a feeling of dread began to mercilessly probe her stomach.

"Mom!" she screamed, even as the preacher leaped from the others to bar her way to the house. His efforts came too late.

When the tractor was new, it was the envy of everyone in the small cluster of farms that made up Garden City. Now, though small and rusting, it was still large enough to perform all the tasks required of it on the farm. However, it was not quite large enough to conceal the lithe broken figure pinned underneath the overturned vehicle.

The flowers, discarded and forgotten, lay in mud made from her tears.

*****

Polly Riser, Age Twelve

The economic crisis known as the Great Depression seemed of no concern to those of us in rural Garden City, Kansas; it only affected the fancy-mannered fancy-dressed folks in the financial centers back East. We felt isolated, somehow immune to their troubles. We were so wrong.

Soon one by one, Eastern banks began to fail, and monies farmers depended on to buy seed and other essentials petered out like a dry creek. That's when one farm after another was declared in foreclosure by banks that had newly found themselves bankrupt.

Pa felt he was blessed by God, though, and would loudly declare his thanks to him each Sunday. Where others had no seed to plant, our barn had barrels of seed, put aside each harvest by Grandpa Clemmons. With it, we were able to grow subsistence crops but not enough to be sold at the market commercially. Still we ate, and Pa took pride in his ability to provide for his family.

Then the rain stopped falling. We waited and prayed for its life-giving return. But it did not return. For years it did not return.

That's when Pa started praying to a different god—an idol— one not made of gold but of fermented and distilled corn. He began to drink something fierce, and it seemed to me as if his love for the "shine" was much greater than his love for our Savior had ever been.

Sunday after Sunday, Ma and I would go to church without him. At first, people in the congregation would stare at us with puzzled looks, as Pa's usual seat with the other deacons, on the front pew, remained empty. I wish that someone—anyone—was straightforward enough to talk to us directly about it instead of gossiping among themselves. I guess they were all too timid to talk to us. Even so, it was easy for anyone to see that something was terribly wrong. The embarrassing truth was Pa's love for God (as well as for his family) was being swept away, washed away by the baptism of booze.

Soon Pa's new god made him begin to hurt Ma. He would even come after me sometimes. It only took one look at me to make him roar and snort like a crazed bull, then charge me. That's when Ma would jump in between us, which would make him even madder and more violent.

And now, Ma was gone.

"Dear God, let Pa love me so that we can be a family again."

*****

Space—outer space—was once believed to be a vast unending expanse of nothing apart from stars and the planets and planetoids that orbit them. However, even as the universe was expanding, so too was man's understanding of it. No longer a great emptiness, it has long been known that the sky beyond our world is, in fact, teeming with a plethora of objects and phenomena, with more discovered seemingly every day. More in common with one of Earth's oceans, space abounds with its own variety of flotsam and jetsam, carried about by gravitational pulls, solar winds and eddies, and even by other cosmic forces yet unknown.

Meandering between solar systems of a spiral galaxy scientists designated as the Milky Way was one such phenomena: a nebula, a cloud of dust, gases, and other cosmic particles, its amethyst hue contrasted against the darkness of space as if lit by fires from within. Appearing a mere two light-years from Earth, astronomers would have been hard-pressed to call it a true nebula whose size would normally be between one and ten times the distance between the Earth and its sun.[4] This purple pygmy, however, was no larger than the distance between Earth and its moon, Luna.

Astronomers recorded it as a dwarf nebula and gave it no further thought. That is until the year 1933, when the nebula's familiar brightness increased almost imperceptibly. However, what was most striking about the incident was that the object had inexplicably moved out of its known orbit. No longer moving within the confines of the cosmic current it had occupied, its trajectory had altered, along with its relative velocity. Alarm, like an epidemic, permeated the world's astronomers, as the dwarf nebula's new course and speed were calculated. Unless it changed its coarse again, within a mere two years, it would illuminate Earth's night sky.

*****

Polly knew she was expected to be with the others at her mother, Penelope's, internment. Instead she sat alone in Pastor Knowles's 1929 Model A Ford sedan, savoring the scent of a lace-bordered handkerchief. It had been infused with one of the only luxuries her mother had owned, a small bottle of Chanel No. 5 perfume. The fragrance of the kerchief brought unchecked tears to her eyes, as the pain of her mother's loss washed over her anew. Even so, it brought a small measure of comfort to the girl. It was Mother's scent; now it was a precious part of her that Polly could cling to.

Benjamin "Buck" Riser stood by the excavation and took yet another gulp from the steel boot-flask he was never apart from.

"Why ain't that stupid heifer here?" he asked no one in particular, pointing a meaty thumb toward the car at the top of the hill. "It was her mother, for crying out loud!"

"Now, Buck," Pastor Knowles began, putting a conciliatory hand upon the man's shoulder. "We've all been hurt in one way or another by Penelope's untimely passing. Let the poor child grieve for her mother in her own way."

"I'll show her some grieving." Buck growled as he noisily gulped down another swig from the flask and began to stomp his way up the small hill, toward the car.

Grandma Molly flashed an alarmed look to her husband, Saint Peter Clemmons. Though silent, it was enough to spur her husband to act.

Polly was unaware of her father's approach until a meaty fist pounded on the passenger-side window. Polly nearly jumped out of her skin.

"D-Pa," she stammered as Buck Riser's face pressed against the window. The little girl could easily detect his threatening mood, even before the man had spoken. When he did speak, his words filled the little girl with terror.

"Get your narrow ass back there and show your mother some proper respect!" He said the words clearly despite the steady amount of homemade booze he had consumed since late last evening. It was now noon.

Somehow the reference to her mother emboldened her to protest. "But, Pa, I want to keep Ma alive in my heart. I want to remember her the way she was when she was alive, not dead."

The girl's timid plea caused Buck's familiar alcohol-imbued complexion to turn absolutely crimson with rage. He leaned his six-foot-ten-inch frame against the car, flung open the door, and snatched the frightened child out.

With one hand clutching her slender quivering throat, he hefted the hapless child up, her feet dangling off the ground. His other hand was clenched in a massive fist, which he menacingly raised, preparing to strike.

"I don't take sass from a scrawny little brat like you," he said as his bludgeoning fist began its terrible arc toward the child.

Suddenly its path was stayed by another equally massive fist.

"You want some of this too, old man?" Buck growled, starring down at the shorter stoutly built form of Grandpa Clemmons.

"No!" Clem said calmly as he raised his old Colt .45 semiautomatic pistol, bringing it directly between Buck's eyes. "And neither do you!"

By now, Polly was all but forgotten by Buck. His attention rested entirely upon his aging father-in-law and upon the barrel of his old Colt M1911, both left over from the Great War. Buck's hold on the girl's throat lessened. She slipped from his grip and fell to the ground.

"Run to the house, Polly!" Grandpa Clemmons ordered over his shoulder, as his grandchild scurried away. Deftly his thumb pulled the hammer back. A loud click announced the weapon was now cocked and ready.

"She's my bloody kid!" Buck bellowed drunkenly. "Mine! You hear me?"

"I know how you've been treating that sweet innocent child, and I'm telling you this, if you ever hurt MY little girl again...EVER... I'll finish this. Now get the hell outta here."

Like a dog with his tail stuck between his legs, Buck scrambled away from his father-in-law, down the hill, and the dirt road leading to town.

Grandma Molly breathed a loud sigh of relief as she rushed to put her arms around her husband's neck. "My hero!" she exclaimed, as she planted a wet kiss upon his cheek.

"More like a con artist, I'd say," Clemmons said as he removed the gun's magazine and showed it to his wife.

"Why, Clem, it's empty!" Molly gasped. "What if Buck decided to call your bluff? What if next—"

"Next time," he interrupted her. "Next time, and from now on, it's going to be loaded." He pushed the clip back into the pistol's grip, and without another word between them, the two held hands as they walked together toward the house and their unfortunate grandchild.

*****

Though it was only two hours into the afternoon, the sun's eternal quest to unite with the beloved silver goddess caused long shadows to trail from every object below in somber salute of Apollo's passing. Polly felt that it was far too early for supper but offered neither protest nor resistance as she was escorted to a long table just within the entrance to the barn near her family's house. The emotional demands of this day conspired to rob her of any reserve she might have otherwise possessed. Even had she the desire to voice complaint of her family's barn being converted into a (temporary) banquet hall by the women's auxiliary of her church, she was unable to. The rustic aromas emanating from the open door of her kitchen, instead of stimulating her, acted as an ether to her already-spent mind. The cacophony produced by those in the crowded "beehive" equally had no effect upon her.

Polly sat despondently between her grandparents at a special table reserved for the bereaved family and officials, where Pastor Knowles sat at its head (her father, Buck, was nowhere to be seen). She watched with complete disinterest as the sisters began to bring in plates laden with her favorite foods. Polly's table was served first, and the servers worked quickly and efficiently to set individual plates before all those seated there. Still it took no effort for her to sense the impatience of those at the other tables.

Eventually every table had been served; but before they could eat, Pastor Knowles beckoned all to rise as he offered to bless the repass with a quick word of prayer. Stomachs growled loud enough to be heard in unison with the barely muffled complaints of the congregation, while the Free Methodist minister was converted to Southern Baptist at the worst possible moment.

Mercifully the prayer ended, and every one of the congregates experienced their own conversion as well into ravenous beasts, once starved, now released to form a feeding frenzy. Everyone, that is, except for Polly, who had not so much as lifted her fork but stared blankly at her plate.

Grandma Molly was first to notice the child's reticence. Putting her utensils down, she placed a reassuring arm around the girl's slender shoulders. "What's ailing you, child? I thought these were supposed to be all of your favorites."

"I know, and I'm sorry," Polly said as she slumped further down in her chair. "I guess I just don't feel much like eating."

"Oh, Molly!" Grandpa Clemmons said between mouthfuls. "Leave the girl be. For crying out loud, she's just lost the only real parent she's known. Believe me, she'll eat when she's of a mind to.

Meanwhile why don't you take Polliwog back to the house and get her ready for bed. Biddy—I mean, Bedelia—you go with them. I want to borrow your husband a moment."

"All right, Saint," Molly said dutifully. Then like two conspirators, the two aging lovers exchanged knowing glances, and without another word between them, Molly and company were on their way into the farmhouse's foyer, then up the long stairway.

Clemmons gazed through the farmhouse windows to follow Molly's ascent, transfixed by the rhythmic sway of her full hips, until she had disappeared from the room. He shook his head thoughtfully, as an adolescent's mischievous smile spread over his grizzled face. "Even now," he mused. "Even now..."

It didn't take Clemmons long to locate Pastor Knowles. He was at the rear of the barn, leaning against a well-rusted but still-functioning tractor. Knowles stared up into a cloudless sky, the stem of an empty pipe clenched in his teeth. Occasionally the pipe was removed, its stem pointed upward, gesturing like an orchestra leader's wand, while its master mumbled, seemingly to himself.

"He's praying," said Clemmons and waited patiently for the prayer to end before sidling up to the pastor. "Molly and I are heading home in the morning, and we're concerned for Polly's welfare."

"Take her with you," Knowles said, not taking his eyes from the sky. "Heck, her old man will be happy to unload her. Besides it's best she be with her kin."

Clemmons stared at the ground to avoid the pastor's eyes. Slyly he said, "I couldn't agree more. But there's kin, and then again, there's kin...kin she may not even know she has."

"I'm not following you," Knowles said, finally taking his eyes off their vigil of the sky to look directly into the old man's pleading face.

"You probably wouldn't have to do it forever. You can petition Judge Lynch to grant you and Biddy—oops, I mean Bedelia—temporary guardianship until something more suitable comes along."

This time, Knowles had no trouble understanding what Clemmons hinted at. No trouble at all, and its meaning suddenly filled him with dread. "I thought you loved her," he protested. "Polly should be with her grandparents up north, near Topeka."

"I'll grant you that," said the old man, who had already anticipated Knowles's move. Like a skilled chess player, he immediately countered, "However," he replied gently, "she should be with people who are able to take care of her. Molly and I love that little girl, more than life itself. That's why I'm coming to you. Molly and I are simply too old, too worn out to properly care for her full-time. No, that girl needs something more…she needs you."

Clemmons paused to allow the cleric to offer further argument. When none was offered, he decided it was finally time to play his endgame. Carefully, like a hunter, he moved in for the kill. Quietly, almost under his breath, he said, "Besides, Reverend, if rumors in this town have any meat to them, I know you'd love that little girl… love her as if she were your very own flesh and blood."

"Damn!" Knowles said quietly, hoping the older man had not heard him. Clemmons had heard him just the same. A wry smile formed on his lips, a subtle gesture of his victory. However, when next he spoke, he deliberately sounded as if Knowles had emerged the victor of their contest instead of himself.

"I believe, son, it's time to pass the baton."

With this, Clemmons produced from his back pocket something carefully wrapped in a woman's bandana. He handed it to the cleric.

Knowles accepted it without comment. He found that it felt somewhat weighty in comparison to its size. Curiosity gripped him as he slowly unfolded the kerchief. A deep furrow appeared on his brow.

"It's a souvenir from the Great War," Clemmons said matter-of-factly. "I took it from a German officer who no longer needed it."

The fissure that, of late, had been on Knowles's forehead became a chasm as the perfectly maintained Luger automatic pistol was revealed.

"You know how to use it?" Clemmons asked.

Knowles released the magazine. It was full of nine-millimeter cartridges. Returning it to its housing, he nodded and simply said that he did know how.

"But could you...would you use it...you being a man of the cloth and all?"

Knowles slowly but decisively replied, "Yeah, old man. For her, I believe I could."

Clemmons scrutinized the younger man's face, as if he could see into Knowles's very soul. Satisfied, he began to return to the house. Over his shoulder, he pronounced the benediction, "If you ask me, I say the wrong Riser died."

As Clemmons disappeared into the house, Knowles stood alone, thoughtfully turning the weapon in his hand over and over. Cold sweat ran down his back as he became fearful he might have to use it against another human being. Then he thought of Penelope that night, her naked rain-soaked body held close to his, shivering more from her injuries than the coldness of the rain.

He felt as if he stood outside himself and watched his trepidation change into something hot and menacing. The feeling brought back the fear, causing him to raise his hand, preparing to throw the abominable object away, ridding himself of the temptation toward taboo. However, when he thought of Polly, all his fear burned away by a new resolve. Knowles lowered his arm and tucked the gun into his pants pocket. Then with eyes reddened by anguish and pain, he turned them toward the heavens and said, "Amen to that, old man... Amen to that."

CHAPTER 2

A Matter of Discipline

It was often said of Benjamin Bucannon Riser (and rightly so) that he possessed only three friends in the entire world: corn liquor and the Sweeny brothers, Douglas (the elder by three years) and Collier (whom everyone had called Budd for so long, no one remembered his real name anymore).

Buck was busy keeping company with all three of them in a booth, in the darkest corner of the only speakeasy in town.

"I hate that old man Clemmons," Buck said, thoroughly inebriated. "I can only take so much from him. I swear, someday he's gonna push me too far...him...and his high-and-mighty ways."

Doug Sweeny put down his cup of coffee, annoyed his friend had not passed out by now, giving him some peace and quiet. However, years ago he had painfully learned never to interrupt Buck when he was on one of his drunken tirades. So he patiently waited (just outside of arm's reach) until the storm subsided.

Buck took a long drink from a half-empty bottle of cheap whiskey. "He got no call to in...inter..."

"Interfere!" Doug said impatiently.

"Right, inter...inter...whatever you just said. A man's got a right to discipline his own kid, ain't he?"

"Yes," Sweeny said, sounding as if for once he agreed with Buck's point of view. However, Buck's triumph was short-lived when Sweeny added, "But she's Clemmons' child as well...or rather grandchild."

"That don't make no never mind," Buck said as he slammed the bottle on the table with such violence, the elder Sweeny brother was sure it would shatter. "A father's rights come before a grandfather's, and I got me a God-given right to discipline her as I sees fit."

"Well, what you call discipline, the law will see as abuse of a minor or child endangerment. Speaking of which, I haven't seen the 'stain' around in quite a spell. You lock her in the closet again?"

"Yeah, I did," Buck admitted, as an evil smirk formed on his drunken lips. "But only till the brat's attitude improves."

Exasperated, Sweeny asked, "And how long is it going to be this time? Two or three days on bread and water?"

"More like four an' without the bread."

*****

The road leading out of Garden City was little more than a wide compression trail, packed down and hardened by many an automobile which had passed down its bumpy uneven length for the last thirty years. Each imperfection on its surface jolted the old Ford pickup truck, aggravating a lumbar which had been overused by Saint Peter's family's moving business, then abused by years of service as a doughboy during the Great War to end all wars. Saint Peter Clemmons (Clem) grimaced from every dip and bump in the road; not so much from the pain it caused his back, as from the deeper darker pain of a tortured mind. Molina (Molly) Clemmons patiently listened, while her aging husband medicated his pain, through her sympathetic ear.

"You know, Moll?" Clem said through clenched teeth. "I often blame myself for what happened between Buck and Penny. I mean, I was the one who introduced him to her when he came to Garden City, looking for work. I didn't know him from Adam's off ox, but like her, I was moved by how big and handsome he was. Later I started to see that Buck would become violently angry whenever he became frustrated. I tried to warn Penny, but she married him anyway."

The old man paused as tears began to well up in his already-blood-shot eyes. Molly remained silent. She had been here with him many times and knew that it was best not to interrupt. Whenever her husband became somber like this, she had learned through experience that Clem was only talking to an audience of his own inner demons named guilt, shame, and regret.

The old man continued, "Then the land began to dry out, and whole crops would fail. That's when Buck began to drink…constantly, and to beat Penny…constantly."

Molly suddenly became pensive and melancholic, as her husband, like a necromancer, resurrected memories what could never fully be laid to rest; of how they had questioned Penny about the black eyes and bruises that frequently presented themselves. She would always say that she had fallen down the steps or something—anything but the truth.

Tears cascaded freely down her face when she recalled that terrible night. Penny flew out of the house, naked and screaming, as she took off down the road to town with Buck in close pursuit. Fortunately coming up the road were Pastor Knowles and Sheriff Pucket, who interfered with the butt of his revolver. By the time Buck woke up, he was safely in Puckett's custody and Penny was safely in Knowles'.

Months later, Penny left Pastor Knowles parsonage and returned home. Things were quiet for a while, and it seemed that Buck was mellowing out. Soon Penny announced that she was expecting. Every day she carried that baby, Buck looked angrier and meaner but somehow managed to keep a lid on his temper. That was until the baby, Polly Quashi'miuoo ("vibrant, sparkle" in Gaelic)[5] Riser was born. All at once, Buck seemed to turn his anger from his wife and shift it to the baby. To be sure, he wouldn't beat Polly like he did Penny, but he was cruel and abusive just the same.

Now the funny thing was that Penny could be real patient and forgiving when Buck hurt her, saying that she still loved him despite everything. However, when it came to the child, her love for her husband seemed to come in second place to her love for Polly. One day, following a night of beating and screaming, he was at his favorite watering hole, getting drunk. She called Pastor Knowles. He and Bedelia helped her throw a few things into an old carpetbag, then put the two of them on a bus heading to Topeka and her parents. Buck hadn't bothered to hunt them down.

A whole year passed in safety and quiet when Penny said that, despite everything, she was going back home to her husband. When they reunited, it seemed that Buck had become a changed man. But like always, it didn't last. Soon the violence began anew.

Then the tractor overturned, and Penelope was gone. Immediately Buck's abuse of the child intensified. Unnecessary beatings (for no good reason) became common, as well as slaps in the face. He would even lock her in an upstairs closet for days on end without food. Buck never gave a reason for his animosity toward Polly; however, he wore his hatred for her on his face, like a cattle brand.

Molly gave out a deep sigh, as more tears cascaded down her careworn face. She would have taken the girl in herself long ago, if she could. But she was too old and too sick to be able to provide for the child properly. She felt so helpless.

Clemmons noticed the gesture, and while he kept one hand on the truck's wheel, he used the other to fumble around his pants pocket.

"Ah!" he said as his efforts produced an odd piece of cloth resembling a large quilting square.

In fact, it could have been just that. Cut from his daughter's favorite blanket when she was a toddler, he had kept it ever since. Now its once-bright-green luster had long ago faded to an indistinct hue, and although it was clean, it was becoming too threadbare for him to repair. The old man knew he should have discarded the rag long ago; but it was precious to him. However, it was not so precious as the woman seated next to him.

He handed the tattered remnant to Molly, who used it to dry the tears in her eyes. Then Clem placed a reassuring hand on her shoulder and said, "Not to worry, my love. I took steps to make sure that Polly's taken care of in our absence. Judge Lynch is an old friend. I spoke to him earlier yesterday before I had spoken to the good reverend. She should be—"

His pronouncement was cut short by a sickening thud as the truck's windshield transformed into a shower of stiletto-like shards, heralding the arrival of a broken bleeding mass that, of late, had been a perfect twelve-point buck.

The three were spotted the next morning by a passing state patrolman.

Clem and Molly were still holding each other's hand.

*****

News of the Clemmons' death spread through Garden City almost as fast as a foreclosure notice. The news came far too close on the heels of Penny's death that Polly had no time to recover from one pain before a new devastating event arrived. With the death of her mother, Polly grew increasingly depressed and despondent. Now in the wake of the deaths of both of her grandparents, the girl was inconsolable.

Indeed, the untimely deaths of the Clemmons produced a general feeling of melancholy among Garden City's citizenry; however, the feeling of loss was not quite unanimous. In the small speakeasy, located in the southeast corner of town, three men held a different darker, more sinister wake.

"Y-you goin' to the funeral to-tomorrow?" Budd asked the imposing figure to his right.

"Hell no!" the man exclaimed, taking another drink from the well-worn metal cup held tight in his meaty fist. I ain't had much use for him."

"But, Buck," the man protested. "He was your father-in-law. For crying out loud, you were married to the man's daughter."

Buck took an infuriatingly long time to answer as he took another drink from his glass. "So what?" he said, bringing his mug down onto the splintered table with a loud thud. "I ain't have much use for her neither, except for—"

"Yeah, we know." Chimed in Doug Sweeny with a sly grin, seated on Buck's right. Of the three, he was the only one not drunk.

"No, you don't," said Buck, with only a hint of annoyance in his voice. "So I'm going to tell you."

As Budd struggled to remain conscious, his older brother, Doug, listened with rapt keenness, as Buck told of his former father-in-law's mistrust of traditional financial institutions, choosing instead to keep all his money in a thick heavy metal box, resembling an army foot-locker. The case boasted of having a locking mechanism that was impossible to open in any manner, other than with a special key kept in possession of his daughter, Penelope. Unfortunately since her passing, the location of the key was unknown, as well as the location of the strongbox. Both Penny and her father's deaths happened too fast to allow for the information to be passed to another.

Buck ended his narrative by drinking long and deep from his glass, even as Budd's head noisily crashed onto the well-worn table.

Doug Sweeny listened to the rhythmic, though labored, breathing. Rubbing a deeply furrowed brow (always an indication of his being deep in thought), he said, "Since the old man never believed in using banks, I figure that he'd probably keep the stronghold either in the old farmhouse or somewhere close by it. I reckon, we can look for it undisturbed, it being so isolated and all. But once we find it, what about the key?"

"Clemmons would have to keep it close as well. Don't worry, we'll find it all in time and then—"

"Then"—Doug Sweeny chimed in enthusiastically—"we can leave this place, with its failed crops, its failed banks, and its failed way of life far behind. I say we don't stop until we get to Rio. But what about the brat?"

"Forget that skinny sawed-off cuss!" Buck said, his voice becoming dangerously loud, even in this dark place of secrets. "That stupid kid wouldn't be worth nearly half the trouble she'd cause. She... she..." Buck's voice trailed off, as his mind began to finally show signs that it was succumbing to the amount of alcohol he had abused it with.

Doug Sweeny gratefully watched as his friend's head dipped below half-mast.

Suddenly the head unexplainably resurrected itself long enough for its owner to cryptically announce that, "Besides that...that...b-b-brat ain't none of mine."

Buck's head finally sank beneath the waves of consciousness, leaving his companion to ponder the disappointment of his own torpedoed hopes.

CHAPTER 3

The Road to Cimarron

Sheriff Pucket's patrol car noisily bounced up and down with every imperfection in the road; and there were many. At first, Polly squealed with delight whenever the car hit a bump, propelling the girl upward to strike the clothed roof of the Ford Model A police car. It was fun at first, but soon the child developed a headache, which changed her usually effervescent disposition to one exhibited by whininess and complaining. It was a rare mood of hers, which was new to Reverend Knowles, one which he knew he would never become used to.

"But why do I have to leave you?" she grumbled. "It makes me feel like I've lost both my parents, an orphan who is being shuffled off to one place or another."

In response to this challenge, Reverend Knowles pinched the bridge of his nose to massage a growing headache of his own. The gesture was noticed by Sheriff Pucket, who was concerned his friend would show an inexpedient side of him, one in which a man of the cloth may never live down.

To save the pastor's image, the sheriff answered Polly's question for him. "I know being moved around is rough for a little girl who's just lost her mother," Sheriff Pucket said reassuringly. "But sometimes, change can be a good thing, Polly."

A puzzled look invaded the girl's face, momentarily displacing the upset one she had previously worn. With her temporary silence, Pucket decided to drive his point home.

He repeated, "Yes, Polly, sometimes change can do us a bit of good."

"How?" the little girl said, fighting back a sob.

"Well, you've always been around adults. But where we're going has a bunch of kids around your age for you to relate to. You might even make a friend or two."

Pucket knew he had lost his advantage as, all at once, the girl's continence changed back to the upset and inconsolable one she had worn before. "But you don't understand," she said, giving way to a torrent of tears she could no longer hold back. "I don't need to make friends with other kids. All I need is for Pa to love me so we can be a family again."

With this, Polly collapsed onto the bench seat, burying her face in her trembling arms.

"Polly," Reverend Knowles said calmly, belying anything he was feeling at that moment. "You know you'll only be with them for a short while, just long enough for Biddy—oops, Bedelia—and me to get the parsonage ready for you to live in. At the most, it should take us till the end of summer to open up an unused room and turn it into a proper bedroom."

Polly seemed to calm down somewhat. "Until the end of summer," she said in between sobs. "You promise?"

"Yeah, I promise."

Following Knowles's reassurance, Polly straightened up and sat quietly, patiently, in the back of the car. With the emotional storm subsiding, Knowles leaned toward Pucket and whispered, "I know how inconvenient this trip is. Believe me, I appreciate it. Judge Lynch is a good man, but I don't quite trust his restraining order… not where Buck Riser is concerned. I just can't risk that animal finding her, at least not until I have prepared Fortress Parsonage to ward off a possible siege."

"Well, for what it's worth," Sheriff Pucket said, "I think you're doing the right thing. He'll never bother looking in such a remote place as the Russell family homestead, just south of Cimarron."

"Thank God for that!" Reverend Knowles said as he leaned back in his seat and tried to relax for the remainder of the trip.

Sheriff Pucket's patrol car made its way down the dusty bumpy road in relative silence. The peace and quiet gave the sheriff time to ponder all the myriad of times he was called by one citizen or another, all complaining about Benjamin Bucannon Riser. In fact, it felt as if his whole job consisted of little else than policing the town bully. Time after time, he would throw the ruffian into the municipal jail for upward of thirty days. He usually relied on the help of his "favorite deputy" (the hardwood butt of the .38 long-barreled revolver tied cowboy style, low on his right hip). Each time the polished walnut handle came crashing down on the big man's skull, Sheriff Pucket hoped that he was knocking some sense into Buck's hard head. Of course, it never did, making the sheriff wish that he could, just once, use the proper end of the pistol.

Just then, Polly awoke from her slumber. Yawning, she said, "Sheriff Pucket, you must be thinking of Pa again."

Pucket let out a loud exasperated sigh and said, "So now the girl is psychic?"

"No, sir," she replied with another yawn. "I looked in your rear-view mirror. You have that same frowny face you always have whenever you're around Pa."

Pucket laughed, then became pensive for a moment. When he spoke again, his voice was quiet, almost a whisper, not wanting to wake Reverend Knowles. "Polly, I heard you talking in your sleep. You were praying about him again."

"Yes, sir," she answered shyly. "I pray for Pa every day, that God will make us a family again."

"That'll never happen," he said under his breath, instantly regretting that Polly had heard him.

"How can you say that?" she asked indignantly. "Don't you believe that God can do anything?"

The little girl's challenge forced to the surface thoughts and feelings he had long ago buried. Thoughts of his wife who lay in a comma for three days following a head-on collision with a drunken driver. For three days and nights, he prayed for God to spare her. Never leaving her side, he maintained his vigil, until the morning of the fourth day when doctors announced that she had passed, taking their unborn child with her.

Bitterly he replied, "What's possible with God and what's probable are two separate things, girl."

Finally awake, Reverend Knowles wasted no time in jumping in to quickly resolve this new verbal conflict. "I've discovered over the years that faith seems strongest in the young."

With this, Pucket decided to change the direction of the conversation. "Now don't think I don't believe in miracles because I do believe—I have to. Both the Reverend and I are old enough, we've both seen things that can only be attributed to the intervention of God in the lives of men."

"In fact," Reverend Knowles said, "we're headed to one of those miracles right now."

"That's right, Polly," Sheriff Pucket said, not allowing the preacher to tell the story. "Polly, we're headed to the Russell's place. They're a young couple with twelve…that's right, twelve kids. And that's not all, Polly. They're also taking care of the wife's aging parents and the husband's mother."

"Now the miracle is this," Knowles said anxiously, regaining control of the report. "As tough as times are for all of us, and as crowded as their house is…when we asked them to be foster parents and take in one more child, they did not hesitate to agree to take you in WITHOUT question. And the amazing thing is, they were happy to do it. They even insisted on you going to live with them, with no compensation from the state."

"They wouldn't even discuss the county paying them but dismissed the idea entirely. As the wife said, 'THE LITTLE GIRL JUST LOST HER MOTHER, AND HER FATHER IS A REAL SON OF A… WELL, HER FATHER ISN'T QUITE UP TO THE TASK OF TAKING CARE OF A SWEET YOUNG LADY. SHE NEEDS US, EVEN IF IT'S ONLY FOR A LITTLE WHILE… SHE WILL KNOW WHAT IT'S LIKE TO BE LOVED AND CARED FOR PROPERLY.'"

Polly thought hard for a while, then said, "If taking me in will be such a hardship, maybe I can stay with Reverend Knowles and

Biddy—oops, Bedelia. I'm such a flibbertigibbet. I could help them get the parsonage ready for me?"

"Not a chance, Polly," Knowles said firmly but kindly. "Judge Lynch issued a restraint order against Buck. There will be no contact between you two until Buck gets help to control his temper, or until I and the parsonage are ready to deal with him."

"But that's not fair." She whined as tears began to flow unchecked. "How can my miracle happen if we can never ever be together again? You're blocking my miracle."

Before Sheriff Pucket could speak, Pastor Knowles broke in, trying his best to sound authoritative and reassuring. "No, Polly, we're not blocking your miracle. We're just trying to keep you alive in order to receive it. When God decides to move, no power on earth can effectively resist his will. Remember your Sunday school lesson, 'No good thing will he withhold from them that walk uprightly'" (Psalm 84:11 KJV).

"Oh, thanks, I'll try and remember that."

She turned her head away from him and sounded both sullen and unconvincing. Knowles decided the girl can tell him all about it later. He figured he had been in enough arguments with her for one day.

Presently Polly raised her head and said, "Well, if my going to the Russells is unavoidable..." The pastor noted that it was a question, almost pleading. Gently he nodded his head, and the girl continued, "Then my going there will be a further hardship for them... no matter how Mrs. Russell will say otherwise."

She paused and waited for her pastor's conformation. He nodded again and she continued, "Well," she said slowly, thoughtfully, "as you know, Grandpa never trusted banks, and so, when the banks failed, he still had all his money, hidden in a strongbox somewhere around the house. Shortly after Ma and Pa were married, Grandpa told Ma where he had hidden it. He even gave her the key to it and told her never to use it or even expose it, except for dire need. Then after Pa started drinking and...a-and..." Her voice trailed off as tears choked her into silence.

"We understand, dear," said Pastor Knowles. "And what happened next?"

"Ma told me where the box was hidden and gave the key to me, along with the same warning that Grandpa had given her." She stopped and looked up at the two men and waited, waited for any sign that told her she hadn't done wrong in breaking her mother's confidence.

"Whew!" Pastor Knowles said, letting out a long sigh. Slowly a thin smile pushed its way onto his lips. "So you've known where the money was hidden all this time?"

"Yes, sir," Polly said cautiously.

"And had the key to it all along!" exclaimed the sheriff, rubbing his shock of thinning hair.

"Yes, sir!"

"That sly old man!" Chuckled Knowles. "Thank God he never trusted the banks. We all used to think he was crazy, not keeping his money safe in a bank and earning interest."

"Yeah!" Chimed in Sheriff Pucket. "We thought your grandfather was crazy all right…until the banks went belly-up, and everyone lost all of their money, everyone except for him."

"Then…," she said, "could we not use some of it to help the Russells…to maybe pay for my room and board there?"

Knowles thought for a moment, then said, "Lord love you, girl. Of course we can use some of your inheritance to help the Russell family, if you've a mind to."

"Then after that," she said enthusiastically, "couldn't we use the rest to help the townspeople…just until the banks recover?"

Sheriff Pucket asked, "Wouldn't it bother you to give away your whole inheritance and have nothing to show for it?"

"Biddy—oops, I mean Sister Bedelia—always said that, 'You can't beat God giving.' God has always taken care of me…even with the money hidden, we've done all right."

"Well," said Sheriff Pucket, pointing down the road, "if we're going to do it, you have to decide now. Your house is coming up quick."

Polly became excited as she asked, "Oh please, can we stop and get the box? Please?"

"We might as well do it now," said Pastor Knowles. "Sheriff, can we pull over and—"

"I'm way ahead of you, Reverend," said the sheriff as he turned the wheel sharply and pressed hard on the brake pedal, bringing the car to a dusty sliding stop in front of the old farmhouse that was Polly's home.

"Come on!" squealed the girl with delight. "I'll show you where it is," she said as she flung the back seat door open and dashed out, heading as fast as her slender legs could carry her toward the house.

As she rounded the building's corner, ushering her into the backyard, she suddenly stopped; her feet and her heart instantly became frozen as she looked into the bloodshot, hateful, venomous eyes of her father.

CHAPTER 4

An Ax to Grind

Benjamin Bucannon Riser was nothing if not doggedly persistent. In fact, once he put his mind to something, he could shut out everything around him, as if there were only two things in the entire world: Buck Riser and the object of his pursuit. So it was with his single-minded quest to find Grandfather Clemmons's hidden treasure. He had arrived at the deserted farmhouse four days ago and spent the entire first day riffling through every corner and cupboard of the house, to no avail. For the next three days and nights, he neither ate nor slept but tirelessly dug one hole after another in the backyard. At first, he had dug up and around every concealed and covered area in the yard, with no success. Then he remembered what the old man had said to him, while they were busy hiding Easter eggs for the children's hunt, "Folks will look in absolutely every nook and cranny for something while almost always ignoring things that were in plain sight."

Buck looked around the yard. "Where haven't I looked yet?" he asked himself, scratching his sweat-matted hair. Then he saw it. In the very center of the yard stood an old water trough, which was now being used as a flower planter. He stood over it and probed it with the curved blade of the pickax he was carrying. He discovered that the soil was shallow, barely enough to support the vegetation it contained. The soil's roots were wrapped throughout the length and breadth of an old burlap sack, which in turn rested on a wood-framed double chicken-wire grating. He cautiously stuck the pickax blade through the grating and listened as it struck something both metallic and hollow.

Anxiously he lifted off the flowerbed facade to reveal the five-by-three-foot steel footlocker/strongbox. Only when he had lifted it from its sarcophagus, noting the strange heavy padlock on its front, that he suddenly heard the patter of running feet. Looking up, he was startled to see Polly, who stared at him with a stricken frightened look on her face.

"WHAT ARE YOU DOING HERE?" they both said in unison as the girl stopped in midstep, her feet suddenly unable to move. Then he chanced to see the tiny heart-shaped locket, worn like a choker around her throat.

"You!" he said, pointing the pickax in her direction. "Come 'ere, you little brat!"

Polly merely shook her head, terrified and unable to either run or to scream for help.

"I said come 'ere, brat," he said menacingly as he rose and quickly headed for her. That's when a terrible scream burst from her lips as Polly's legs moved like pistons to distance herself from the crazed man who pursued her.

"Gimme that blasted key, you little brat!"

As Polly frantically continued to run toward the front of the house, suddenly she saw Reverend Knowles and Sheriff Pucket hurrying toward her. However, Buck was still too far behind the girl to see the approach of the two men.

Just before Polly rounded the corner of the house, Buck, like a true lumberjack, reared his arm far up and behind him, then explosively threw it forward, launching the pickax murderously toward the fleeing girl.

Had Buck seen the other two men approaching, he might not have thrown the ax at Polly. As it stood, they had just come into view as the deadly missile was released. It quickly reached the girl, handle-first, it struck between her knees, causing Polly to trip and fall down; however, the ax head continued its spinning momentum, tearing deeply into her right thigh, in plain sight of the sheriff and pastor. They saw her writhing in agony, and then, they saw Buck, looking like a wild man, bearing down upon the helpless girl.

"Stop, Buck!" demanded the pastor, too late to prevent the madman from reaching Polly.

Sizing up the situation, Puckett knew it was too late to block Buck from reaching his victim. "Oh, hell!" said the sheriff as he quickly drew his Colt .38 revolver and pulled the trigger.

In the stillness of the all-but-deserted farm, the gun report sounded like canon fire. The cacophony caused a flock of crows, seated atop the old farmhouse, to take to the air in fearful flight.

Like his namesake during hunting season, Buck cried out in pain and anger as the bullet shattered his right femur, just above the kneecap. Buck went down like a sack of coal, so close to Polly and her locket, an outstretched hand clutched at the hem of her blood-spattered sundress.

The sheriff wasted no time in dragging Buck by the collar, away from his hapless victim, whom he left to the pastor to attend. The sheriff quickly reached the waiting patrol car, and after handcuffing Buck to the rear bumper, he produced a large commercial first-aid kit from the trunk. While Buck howled like an animal, Pucket proceeded to dress his wound, while Pastor Knowles tended to Polly's.

With Buck's injury heavily bandaged and splinted, Sheriff Pucket stood up from his work, stretched, and gazed down on his prisoner, who struggled like a madman against being so roughly handcuffed to the bumper of the patrol car. Pucket took a dirty handkerchief from his trouser pocket and wiped the sweat from his head and neck, saying, "You shouldn't fight against those shackles like that, you might get a new injury, like cutting off your hand or something. Then again, it's your nature to fight against everything, ain't it?"

Buck howled with pain and rage but somehow managed to bellow, "I don't know how long…but no matter how long it takes, lawman, you better know… I'm gonna get you for this. You can bet on it."

Sheriff Pucket took little offense at Buck's threat. After all, he had heard so many of them from so many prisoners (including

Buck). He paid little notice of them. He was a man who preferred to live in the present, and after the myriad of threats against his life, he was still here.

Instead he returned Buck's look of anger and disgust and said, "You've gone way too bloody far this time, Buck! I don't know what that booze-soaked brain of yours was thinking…or if you were thinking at all, but you attacked that child with an ax and in front of witnesses. You'll be lucky if you're let out by the end of this decade."

He then radioed for two deputies to come and transport Buck to the hospital for treatment, then to the jail to await trial by Judge Lynch, while he and Knowles continued with Polly to the Russell homestead.

CHAPTER 5

Of Homesteads and Hoosegows

Sheriff Pucket couldn't remember the last time he had driven this fast, even in pursuit of a suspect. The dust and dirt from the road behind the patrol car took on the semblance of Roman candles. The roar from the car's engine helped solidify the image. Unfortunately with increased speed came much more bumps from the road, transmitted unerringly to the cabin of the car.

Pastor Knowles, who cradled the little girl on his knees, might normally have complained with words like, "My god, man, can't you slow down? The ride is killing the child as much as your driving." However, the precious burden he carried left no time for either arguments or sloth. Instead he shouted to the driver (for the fourth time since their frantic race began), "Can't this bloody thing go any faster? I thought you could drive? This is a police car, isn't it?

"I could speed up, but on this loose dusty road, we could overturn the car, and none of us would make it to help."

Just then, Polly gave out an eerie moan, which emphasized to all the urgency of the situation.

"I... I-I'm s...so...c...c-cold. And so...sleep...sleepy." Her voice trailed off as Polly began to fall asleep and fall and fall.

Instantly alarmed, Reverend Knowles sat the girl up. "Don't do this to me, kid. After we reach the homestead, you can sleep for days, if you've a mind to. But not now...not yet."

"Pa, p...please don't slap Ma and me," Polly said sleepily, as Knowles delivered a series of sharp open-handed strikes to the side of the child's face.

"Stay with me, Polly! Stay with me! Stay awake, just until we reach the Russells place. We'll be there very shortly, baby..."

"P...promise?" she said so dreamily through chattering teeth.

"Oh, yeah, kid, we're almost there." He paused to flash the sheriff a concerned look, as if to say, *Please don't make me a liar.*

To this, the sheriff nodded his approval, saying, "We should be there in about another minute."

Just then, the pastor noticed Polly's eyes were half-closed, and her pupils had rolled up into her head as her head slumped over to the side.

"No, no, no, no, no!" he quickly prayed, then prepared to strike the girl again. However, he suddenly had another idea. Placing the little girl again on his lap, he said, "Look, Polly! We're almost there. Count with me, girl, count with me, Polly," he said as he secretly prayed again, with the same plea he had made to the sheriff—that is, *Please don't let me be a liar.*

"Okay. Polly, count with me, girl. Count with me! Thirty... Twenty-nine... Twenty-eight... Twenty-seven..."

Somehow Polly had managed to come around as she partially opened her eyes, looked through the car window, and weakly counted down with her pastor.

"Eighteen... Seventeen... Sixteen..."

Knowles felt that the girl's heart was keeping in unison with his own heart's excited pace.

"Six... Five... Four... Three... Two..."

Sheriff Pucket's patrol car slowed down and turned to head down a dusty dirt road that gradually leveled out into a long winding well-packed-down trail.

The change in the car's momentum caused Polly to become wide awake. Immediately the stabbing throbbing pain in the back of her right leg torturously returned. Every bump in the road caused the pain to intensify and threatened to exacerbate the wound's hemorrhaging. Seated next to the girl, Knowles took advantage of his long arms to reach under her thigh, to apply enough pressure to control the bleeding. The move caused her to scream, but she was otherwise patient.

"That's my good girl," said the pastor, as he tried to reassure her that the trip was almost at an end.

"Promise?" Polly said through gritted teeth, as she turned her head and cradled it in Knowles's arm.

"Yes, girl," he said, keeping pressure on the injury, making Polly cry out with the renewed pain.

"How…much…longer?"

"Oh, I'd say, just…about…now."

All at once, the narrow service road opened out into a large farm.

Polly was quick to notice a humungous farmhouse they were rapidly approaching. However, what really excited the young girl were the people standing in front of it. Immediately Polly could see two young adults she assumed were the Russell parents; and standing close behind them, according to age, stood the Russell kids. Standing behind the children, she noticed three elderly grown-ups she thought had to be the grandparents. Then she saw him—a tall thin man, wearing a long white robe or gown, and atop his head, he wore an old-fashioned genuine beaver-skin top hat.

"Polly," said Pucket, answering her unspoken question." This is Dr. Henry Goodwell, from Saint Catherine Hospital back in Garden City. I managed to get ahold of him after I radioed my deputies to go pick up your father."

"Such as he is," whispered Reverend Knowles, as he got out of the patrol car, carefully cradling Polly in his arms.

"Excellent!" said a gravelly voice coming from a relatively young man. "You made good time getting here, Constable. The Lady Russell has graciously allowed the use of her kitchen table. We're already set up, so let us convene there, posthaste."

*****

Buck Riser grimaced as a young physician examined his leg.

"W...W... Where am I?" he groggily asked.

"Hi, I'm Dr. Lyndon Mattock," he said, while chewing a wad of gum as big as a golf ball with his mouth open. "You're at the dispensary at Leavenworth Federal Prison. Geez, young man, it looks like you were shot with a canon. We worked on you for six hours straight and still almost lost the leg. There were so many bone fragments to find and secure. Half of them were so tiny, we had to leave them for your body to deal with. Who shot you anyway, a jealous husband?"

Just then, the head of surgery came and gently took Dr. Mattock aside.

"Hello, Dr. Pike! What's up?" Mattock asked as the other man handed him a note to be placed in Buck's record. Dr. Mattock's eyes narrowed, and a deep furrow developed between them as he silently read the short missive. He looked up at his department head and asked, "Dr. Pike, if we were almost anyplace but Leavenworth, I'd dismiss this as some intern's hoax. Is it really true?"

"Darn right it's true, Lenny," Dr. Pike said to his colleague. "That fella over there was shot by the sheriff over in Garden City, while attempting to kill a twelve-year-old little girl with an ax."

"My god!" Lenny said, incredulously shaking his head. "You mean to tell me, I've just spent the last six hours doing a job which will cost the federal government thousands of taxpayer dollars, all for that anal orifice who doesn't deserve it?"

Dr. Pike spoke up, "Lenny, whether he's worthy or not is not for us to judge. We took an oath to heal without prejudice. After all, Lenny, this is Leavenworth, for crying out loud. What kind of clients did you hope to see?"

Dr. Pike walked down the hall to continue his morning rounds, leaving Lenny to ponder the note a moment longer.

Meanwhile Buck's head began to clear from the influence of the anesthesia. He could almost wish it hadn't, for instantly, the foul aroma of bodies stifling in the sweltering heat, of various and sundry chemicals and drugs and of dried urine, assailed his nostrils.

"Leavenworth... Leavenworth..." he said over and over to himself, trying to remember. Suddenly the trial came into focus, and Judge Thaddeus Lynch was speaking.

"*Before this court passes judgment,*" he said to the defendant (Buck), "*we would like to say this. For years, we've waited for you to stand in front of this bench, for something other than a mere misdemeanor… something warranting a stay someplace other than Sheriff Pucket's county jail. Knowing that, for a man with your personality and temperament, it was just a matter of time before you proved us right. And here you are. The prisoner will stand to hear the judgment of the court.*"

"*But, Your Honor,*" protested Buck's state-appointed attorney, "*the accused's leg is broken.*"

"*Looks like you're going to have to wrinkle that suit of yours and help him up,*" said Judge Lynch, thoroughly enjoying the predicament that the defendant was in. "*After all, we must maintain tradition and protocol.*"

In response, the young public defender allowed Buck to keep his injured leg off the floor by leaning on his lawyer's shoulder. It was with great difficulty, but the two managed to stand upright.

"*Now, Mr. Benjamin Bucannon Riser, for the charge of assault of a minor with intent to kill, we find you…not guilty.*"

Judge Lynch waited for the commotion from the court spectators to cease before continuing. "*Your argument as to the mitigating circumstances of the assault shows sufficient evidence to dismiss the charge of attempted murder. Now having conceded that point, however, it must be pointed out that though your brutal attack on the child lacked the intent to kill, the desire to hurt, harm, and even maim this child, in a flash of mindless fury, was clearly demonstrated.*

"*Furthermore, the method of your assault, though not intended to kill, exhibited a callous disregard for the life and welfare of the child and of society. In addition, a review of other convictions shows a clear and constant pattern of violence, abuse, and neglect perpetrated against this child in occurrence almost since the moment of her birth. It is clear from these findings that every moment you retain unrestricted custody of her, the child is in constant mortal danger and that you are patently unfit to remain her custodian.*

"*We had entertained a petition to grant temporary guardianship with limited visitation rights being retained by you. We hereby dismiss that petition and order Sheriff Pucket to immediately remove the child from the home and place her in protective custody. Further, this court grants immediate, full, and permanent custody of the child to the Knowles.*

"Finally we find that the defendant lacks self-control, as well as exhibits a complete lack of respect for others. In and of themselves, this is no crime. Neither is it within the charter of this court to provide the basic teachings of socialization. That job rightfully lies with parents. We can only hold one accountable, should their lack of parental training lead to a violation of society's laws, as you, sir, most certainly have. And though we are by no means your parents, and you certainly are no child, still you, sir, need a serious time-out. Therefore, we hereby sentence you to fifteen to twenty years' incarceration at the maximum-security federal prison in Leavenworth, Kansas."

"But you can't send me there!" Buck bellowed as the bailiff approached. "That's for military types."

"Well, the commandant there is a close friend who assured me that his Marines can guard anyone, and that his 'hotel' has an extra room all waiting for you. So, Bailiff…remove the prisoner."

Suddenly Buck's remembrances were interrupted by a searing pain in his right leg, as Dr. Mattock released his grip on Buck's injured leg. "Ah, yes!" he said, pretending to write in the patient's chart. "Neurological test complete, leg reflexes strong and normal. See you in the morning…and every morning this month until you're released to your cell."

CHAPTER 6

The Russell Sprouts

Polly had awakened to the driest throat she had ever known in her life. Her tongue felt like it was covered with dust as it clung to the roof of her mouth. She began to rise from the kitchen table when two wiry but strong arms prevented her.

"You just lie there and relax, Polly," said Mrs. Russell. "Anything you need, child, we'll bring to you. And try not to move around so much, dear, you might tear your stitches."

Dr. Goodwell, who had just finished washing his hands, came over to Polly's "bed" and said, "Your throat feels like that because of the ether we used to put you to sleep. Young lady, you are extremely fortunate the hamstring tendon was only partially severed. We were able to repair it and then to close the surrounding tissue. It was relatively a clean cut, considering it was done with an ax. Now if we can keep the edges of the laceration together, it should heal quite nicely, even though there will be a scar. For now, our biggest concerns are to prevent renewed hemorrhage and to ward off any possible infection."

When he had finished speaking to Polly, Dr. Goodwell turned to the Russell parents to give them further instructions. "Thanks for calling me, Sheriff. It was an interesting case, though I admit, I'd like to get my hands on the guy who would hurt a child in that way."

"Don't worry about that," said the sheriff. "We've got him locked away good."

Dr. Goodwell said his farewells to all and then departed as quickly as he had arrived.

Likewise, when Reverend Knowles had placed a bulging envelope in Mr. Russell's hands, he and Sheriff Pucket said goodbye to all and prepared to leave. Though Polly had uttered neither sound nor syllable of protest, her eyes spoke volumes to Pastor Knowles. They virtually screamed at him, *Please...don't leave me.*

Quickly he went over to the kitchen table/bed and sat next to her. He had no intention of reprimanding the girl. Instead he spoke quietly and gently as he said, "Ah, my little Polly, don't be sad. We've already talked about this. You should consider this a great adventure. You're going to see places you've never been to before. You might even form close relationships with people your own age."

Polly's gaze never strayed from his as she said, "Remember your promise!"

To which he replied, "Just until the end of summer... Promise." He warmly kissed her upon her forehead, and just like that, he and the sheriff were gone.

Polly was almost successful at holding back her tears when the Russell parents came over to her bedside and sat on either side of her. "Polly, dear," began Mrs. Russell, "we were so busy fixing you up that we didn't have an opportunity to introduce ourselves. I'm Louise Randcine 'Randie' Russell, and this is my husband, Randolph."

"Your name is Randolph Russell?" Polly asked, choking back the urge to laugh.

"Oh, it gets worse," replied Mr. Russell. "My full name is Randolph Russell Russell."

Polly laughed despite herself and was about to comment, when Mrs. Russell seemed to read her mind, saying, "I thoroughly agree, dear. His parents did lack a degree of imagination."

"Anyway," said Mr. Russell, "I'd like for you to meet our kids." He paused as their twelve children lined up according to age outside the kitchen door. "Presenting the fabulous Russell children, or like we always call them, the 'Russell Sprouts.'"

"Come on in, children," said Mrs. Russell. "Say hello to our guest."

First to enter was the oldest, who smartly marched into the room to take up position next to his father. "Hi, I'm Randal, and

I'm fourteen years old," announced a light-brown-haired youth, who extended a hand in welcome.

"Hello!" Polly answered, taking the proffered hand in hers.

Next came a beautiful blond-haired girl, who also marched in to stand next to her brother. "My name is Rhonda, and I'm thirteen."

Mrs. Russell said proudly, "She was born in February, exactly one year and one month after Randal."

"In fact"—chimed in the father—"somehow all of our children managed to be born one year and a month behind the previous sibling. I'm convinced it's a miracle."

"Me too," declared a curly red-haired boy. "I'm Ricky, and I'm twelve."

"Hey, so am I," said Polly, showing genuine enthusiasm.

"My name's Rochelle," said a bright and cheery dark-haired girl, who quickly made her way to the table to give Polly a warm hug. "I'm eleven years old, and I just know we're going to be best friends."

Next to come into the room were a boy and a girl who looked so much alike, Polly thought they were twins. They practically skipped over to the table, introducing themselves as Raine (the boy), age ten, and Rainie (the girl), age nine.

The procession seemed to have no end as one by one, the Russell Sprouts appeared to greet the girl who would be part of their family, if only for a while. In came Rusty, then Rachelle, Ronald, Ronnie, Robert, and finally, Roberta, who was a mere three years of age.

With all the smaller children sitting on the bed (being careful not to lean against Polly), and the older ones jockeying for position around the table, the room felt claustrophobic. Even so, the tight quarters only served to make all present feel close and intimate.

"Hello, everyone," Polly said, extending her arms to include them all. "My name is Polly Quashi'miuoo Riser, and I'm happy to meet all of you. I do so hope that we can all be friends."

"Kids," said Mr. Russell, "Polly comes to us from Garden City, where she has spent most her life, having precious little experience dealing with children around her own age. Our family should be the ideal place to help solve that little matter."

All at once, the room erupted into laughter and applause as all the children voiced their approval and consent; and it was certain that each of the Russell Sprouts felt that the new girl would prove to be more than just friends but that they had just met another cousin or sibling. And so did Polly. Everyone was so excited about the new girl coming to live with them, everyone, that is, except for Rusty, who stood apart from the others with his arms crossed over his chest and facing the wall.

Both Polly and Mrs. Russell noticed the boy's withdrawal. After exchanging puzzled looks, Mrs. Russell decided to leave the matter to Polly. When she had left the kitchen, Polly immediately gestured for the boy to join her upon the table. Rusty shyly shook his head *no*, and when asked why, the boy replied matter-of-factly that, "Girls have cooties."

Polly could have flatly denied the accusation. Instead she said (without taking offense), "That's because boys give them to us."

"No, we don't!" Rusty protested.

"Sure do, and I'll show you...come on over."

This time, the boy did not hesitate but immediately left the corner and came to the edge of the table. There he struggled with his baby legs to scramble up the side of the bed but without success. "I can't climb up," he said, frustrated to near tears.

"Really?" she asked, thoroughly amused. "I thought all boys could climb. I see them all the time, climb trees back home."

"That's...that's because trees have limbs to climb up with," he said as he renewed his efforts, only to fall straight on his backside on the kitchen floor.

They both laughed until their sides hurt. Polly was glad the boy could laugh at himself. For her part, she could not remember laughing since her mother, Penelope's, funeral. Carefully she rolled over to the side of the bed, facing Rusty, and extended a hand for him to use. When he was safely nestled next to her, Polly began to use her lithe fingers to sift through the boy's thoroughly unruly hair.

As she rummaged around, Rusty said, "Quash...i...m...m..."

"Quashi'miuoo," she said, never ceasing from her scrutiny of Rusty's head.

"Thanks a lot…" Rusty said, his words trailing off as he thought deeply for a moment.

A moment later, he began to rub his head, his fingers getting in the way of Polly's endeavors.

"That Quashi-mi-jig is too hard. Ain't you got a nickname or something?"

"Umm, let's see. Stupid Useless Girl?"

"Nah, that won't do. Dad says that a nickname should be something special to remember something special you did."

"Like what?" Polly asked as her search through Rusty's hair finally uncovered something, and she began to tug at it.

"I don't know, but when it happens, I hope I'm there to see it and give you a proper one—oww!" Rusty cried as whatever it was became dislodged, along with almost an entire lock of hair. Triumphantly she presented it to him, hair and all. "Oh, that," he said, almost embarrassed. "Rachelle threw her chewing gum at me."

The two laughed uncontrollably until all the Russell Sprouts came to see what the matter was, only to join them in their merriment.

*****

Almost four whole weeks passed before Mrs. Russell felt that Polly's leg had healed enough for her to be allowed out of bed, to sit almost stationary upon an old chair that the Sprouts had thoroughly padded with blankets and pillows. The younger ones considered it a game, as their parents directed them in taking care of Polly. Another week passed, and Polly was finally permitted to walk short distances outside and to play with the other kids (though she was always careful not to reinjure her leg. Yet one more week passed before Dr. Goodwell arrived for a follow-up visit. He closely examined her wounded leg, evaluating her degree of healing and looking for any evidence of infection. Satisfied, he removed what remaining sutures that had not dislodged and fallen off on their own.

"Young lady," Dr. Goodwell said as he redressed her wound with a dry sterile dressing. "It's a miracle…indeed, a miracle that your wound has healed as quickly as it has…and with so little scarring, it looks more like you were injured in a fall at the playground instead of with a pickax."

Finally after declaring that Polly was now fit to resume normal activities (within reason), he gently kissed her on the forehead, said farewell to everyone, and then sped away, back to Saint Catherine Hospital in Garden City.

All the children were more than ecstatic to welcome her into their regular routine, while Polly felt as if she were just released from prison. The thought reminded her of her father, far away in Leavenworth. She prayed, "Lord, thank you for my healing and for my freedom. Please bless my pa so that whenever he gets out of jail, he'll be changed and that we can be a family again. In Jesus's name... Thank you, Lord... Amen."

*****

Polly was happy to help the other kids clean up the kitchen after breakfast. After Mr. Russell had inspected their work, he declared that it was a far side cleaner than they would surely be when they returned home.

And then they were off to explore around the farm and to play. The children frolicked until the early afternoon when Polly's leg grew tired after weeks of inactivity and confinement. She sat down in the shade provided by an abandoned barn's door.

It had not taken long before the others noticed her absence. It also had not taken long before their search for her proved successful. Immediately the youngest child rested comfortably in her lap, while the two next in line to her were cradled in her arms, excited to have found her.

Suddenly the bright afternoon sun darkened, as if a giant curtain had been drawn across it. Frightened chatter indicated the near-panic-stricken state of the children, until Randal urged them all to silence. "Shh, everyone, listen."

Obediently they all became quiet, forcing their ears to pierce the living darkness. And then it came, far in the distance, the sound of a steam locomotive was heard. But somehow, it was different. The sound seemed to be coming from all points in the western sky. And it was barreling down on them quickly.

"Guys, let's go!" said Polly as she picked up the three children who were closest, while the older children struggled with the rest. Carry and shepherd, carry and shepherd, the band began the hopeless rush to get back to the house. All at once, their parents, driving an old Ford Model A pickup truck, came skidding to a halt in front of them.

"Hurry!" Mr. Russell shouted as their world erupted into blinding, choking fury.

CHAPTER 7

Adventures in Stoney Lonesome[6]

If it ain't one bloody thing, it's another!
—Benjamin "Buck" Riser

Benjamin Bucannon ("Buck") Riser sat alone in his cell on the second floor of a cellblock reserved for those whom Warden "Sir" referred to as "problem children," that is, the most violent and therefore most dangerous inmates in the United States Penitentiary in Leavenworth, Kansas. Being so labeled marked an inmate for a greater degree of gratuitous violence administered by overly sadistic guards. It was amusing how Warden Sir had gone out of his way to personally welcome Buck to general housing. This not-so-subtle gesture informed Buck that he would be "getting it" from his fellow prisoners, as well as from the guards.

Though the warden's pronouncement offered occasion for neither mirth nor merriment, Buck smiled, as he thought of the utter hypocrisy of the prisoner's code. Though inmates would not tolerate anyone who was sent there as a "fink" (an informant), a rapist, or a child molester, most prisoners on the first night of their arrival could expect a visitation from the welcome wagon to rape and sodomize them.

At first, Buck had wondered why they had neglected him for so long. That was when an inmate assigned as a hospital orderly introduced himself. He said that everyone called him "the Weasel."

He was short overall, though he possessed an unusually long waist (a childhood accident of being run down by a horse and carriage had resulted in his legs being permanently stunted, like the French Impressionist painter Henri de Toulouse-Lautrec).[7] In addition, after awakening from a monthlong coma following the accident, it was discovered he had full and immediate recollection of anything that he saw or heard. This curious condition gained him useful employment in his uncle's gambling house. It also awarded him an inmate status when the aforementioned establishment was raided. It also made him quite useful disseminating rumors and gossip among his fellow cons (and occasionally to sir).

"So there you have it," said the Weasel matter-of-factly, as he settled in the lower bunk in Buck's cell. "No one's laid so much as a paw on you because Sir has you reserved for 'Bull' Bettermann's pleasure."

"What's a 'Bull' Bettermann?"

"Not what but who," Weasel replied, his voice unmistakably tinged with fear. "Every prison has one con whom all the other cons, and even the guards, step aside for. He's the one who really runs the joint, and Sir's just a figurehead."

"Oh, I see…thanks," said Buck thoughtfully.

"That ain't all," Weasel said, leaning in close so that he couldn't be overheard by the other prisoners. "He's the one had Sir put you in general housing and ordered hands-off to the others until you're fully healed. You gotta understand, you a big guy, almost as big as the Bull. And you come in here with a reputation. So he naturally must prove himself all over and make you an example for everyone to see." He paused to study the grim look on Buck's face before adding, "My advice is, don't make it worse than it's gonna be. He gets around to everyone, sooner or later."

Buck noticed an unchecked tear escape from the small man's eye to run freely down his cheek. "You too?" Buck quietly asked.

"Hell, I think I was his first. I belong to him. After the first month here, I got tired of winding up in the infirmary, beaten and banged just the same. It was gonna happen anyway, so eventually… I stopped resisting. Now don't give me that pitying look. At least none of the others can lay a hand on me anymore."

Buck listened to the man's sobs from the lower bunk. In a moment, he lit down from his perch with an agility that belied his great size. He gently covered the man's shoulders with his own blanket before whispering in his ear. "Old man, I want you to spread a rumor tomorrow that you despise your cellmate and that any man that would harm a child ain't a man at all but is yellow through and through."

"But, Buck, that practically guarantees he'll be after you."

Buck offered no answer to Weasel but allowed his statement to hang in the air, while he climbed up into his bunk and contemplated his next move—and Bettermann's.

*****

There are tests, and then again, there are tests. Some tests are used to gauge one's academic prowess. The world of the "Big House" was far removed from the world of academia. Some would judge that it was removed from any viable tenant of civilization. Here in this vile repository of human refuse, in this man-made hell, even here resided a test of sorts, one used to gauge a man's physical strength, as well as his strength of character.

Day after day, Buck Riser was administered this test. Without warning, an inmate would approach him and, without provocation, would lash out in assault, pummeling him until he lay helpless on the floor. Day after day, Buck refused to offer defense to his assailant's attack or to the subsequent derision and disdain heaped upon him.

"Come on, man, get up...get up and fight me, damn you. You big enough to terrorize little girls but ain't got guts enough to stand up to a real man. You disgust me...you little punk!"

The melee would continue until a whistle sounded, and a cadre of guards would appear to restore order and usher the combatants to neutral corners; the aggressor would end up in "the hole" (solitary confinement), while Buck would invariably be taken to the infirmary.

"What in hell do you think you're doing?" demanded Buck's cellmate, as he tended to the big man's wounds. "You're just letting everyone make you a punk! Why, Buck, why?"

"Hey, keep it down," Buck said as Weasel applied gauze dressings to the sutures the doctor had just placed. "You done good, making everyone think I'm nothing but a coward, afraid to fight. Now I'm just waiting until the right fish takes the bait. I won't waste time with the guppies. Only the big fish will do."

"But what if Bettermann don't think you're worth it? What if he never comes after you?"

"Relax!" Buck said with a calm demeanor that belied anything he was feeling. "My butt's too tempting a target for him to pass. It's just a matter of time before he bites."

"But what happens then?" Weasel frantically asked as he finished up his work.

"Wait and see, old man. But no matter how it turns out, at least he'll be too busy with me, he won't have time to bother you."

CHAPTER 8

A Storm unlike Any Other

In the moment it had taken the kids to arrange themselves like sardines on the truck bed floor, the "monster locomotive" overtook them, turning their surroundings as dark as if a seventeen-year locust plague had arrived. Randal (the oldest) looked up to feel the sting of a thousand angry bees attack his face and hands, though there were no bees present. The smaller children, curious as always, also raised themselves, like submarine periscopes, above the transom of the truck, only to come crashing back down and rubbing their face and hands. In truth, every area of exposed skin was instantly assailed, not by bees and not by locusts or cicadas.

"What is it?" the Russell Sprouts asked their father in unison.

"The entire state of Kansas, I think," answered Randolph, their father, who was closer to the truth than he could have possibly imagined.

Polly, who, up until then, had used her own body to cover the four smallest children (Ronald, Ronnie, Robert, and Roberta), was now totally absorbed in using her slender fingers to comb through the youngest child's hair. "I think..." she said to everyone. "It is only dirt, dust, and sand."

"But where..." the mother said incredulously to her husband, Randolph, "where could it possibly have come from?"

Randolph thought for a moment before answering. "I think it's coming from everywhere around us and from everywhere the wind comes from."

The father's explanation seemed to satisfy everyone and the children began to settle down.

That is until an already-darkened sky suddenly took vengeance upon any remaining light—and extinguished it.

Frightened sobs filled the rear of the truck. There was a time when such commotion would prompt the mother to quiet the children down, saying that it was a distraction to their father and could cause him to lose control of the vehicle. There was no need to bother, for just then, the dust and other particulates, which choked the light from the sky, now choked the truck's engine, causing it first to sputter, and then to peter out entirely.

Even with the light all but gone, Mr. Russell could almost feel the frightened look on his wife's face. Indeed, the same look could be had of all the children as well. Their voiceless expressions spoke louder than any words.

"Pa, do something!"

The Russell family's situation grew more desperate with each beat of their racing hearts.

"Guys, listen up!" Mr. Russell said, forcing himself to sound braver and more focused than he knew he felt at that time. "The bad news is that, we can't hunker down here in the truck until this storm subsides. I'm afraid we'd all suffocate within the sand dune growing outside."

He waited for any contrary opinions. Satisfied that none were forthcoming, he continued, "Even worse, to reach the shelter of home, we must face exposure and suffocation." Still no dissent, so he said, "Right, Randal, there are two large tarps in the truck bed's cargo box, along with a jug of water. Break them all out. Ricky, give your brother a hand, please. As for the rest of us...start tearing your undershirts into rags but leave your outside clothes intact...we're gonna need the protection."

When all preparations were completed, Mr. Russell separated everyone into two groups, in possession of a tarp apiece. He then instructed everyone to interlock their arms with the persons on either side. "Now!" he ordered. "Thoroughly wet your rags and hold them over your nose and mouth. Older kids, help the younger ones. Keep your heads down, and don't let go of each other...FOR ANY REASON!"

After all was ready, and they were in formation, Mr. Russell said a quick prayer and took the lead, assuring them that the house was not very far away, and that he could lead them there blindfolded—*literally*.

Windblown dirt and debris bit at every unprotected part and threatened to expose even more. Though all fought the constant urge to let go of an arm to massage a smarting arm or leg, no one did, for fear of becoming lost in the storm (as if they weren't already lost in the storm). Three times, Mr. Russell fell to his hands and knees, beaten down by the invisible force which seemed to move the whole earth to assail them. However, still he struggled. Still he fought his way back to his feet. Still he pressed on.

Though fear of the dangers of walking where one could not see gripped them all, paradoxically fear of the daggers that swirled all around gave them enough motivation to endure. On and on they plodded, like newborn geese behind their mother, one tarp-covered group following the other.

Suddenly, the forward edge of the second group's tarp was violently torn from Randal's hands. Then like dominoes, the grip of one child after another failed as the rapidly increasing weight of newly liberated canvas ripped itself away from everyone—everyone except for little eight-year-old Rusty, who was bringing up the rear.

Determination flooded the lad as he refused to let go. Like the tail of a dragon, the wayward sailcloth whipped back and forth, up and down, and even corkscrewed. Whipping round and round, the unruly cloth fought against the lone little boy. Deep blisters formed on Rusty's palms and the back of his knuckles, and these, in turn, instantly ruptured and bled. The blood then made the portion of the tarp he had too slippery to continue to hold. Painfully the sailcloth released itself from his grip. The tarp, however, refused to relinquish the boy.

Once freed from all semblance of human control, the tarp, agitated and flapping in all directions, somehow managed to wrap itself around the helpless youth, trapping him in its coils like some impossible constrictor. It then began to tumble, end over end, quickly distancing itself from the others. From deep within the bowels of what should have been their protection from the gale, Rusty's desperate pleas for help were carried away with the wind.

Instantly, order in the trailing second group disintegrated as the older children broke formation to pursue the runaway canvas, and rescue their brother Rusty. They were heedless of the fact that the gale-force winds had churned, troubled, and blown aloft the loose earth until nearly the entire sky had been wiped from view. They were heedless of the fact that they could only effectively see their hands, probing along in front of them. They were heedless of any danger, so they plunged on, not so much as following where they saw the monstrous tarp was headed and certainly not from following their brother's faint cries, lost in the cacophony of the storm. They pressed their way in desperate blind faith.

As the children maintained their reckless pursuit, Polly silently prayed, "Oh, gracious Lord, please ease this storm and help us find Rusty. He may be injured, so please, Lord, help us to find him quickly. In Jesus's name… Thank you."

Like cattle in an Old West stampede or like children engaged in a game of follow-the-leader, all the Russell Family which comprised the first (leading) group were preparing to dash away like the others; however, they were constrained by Mr. Russell to keep this last group intact and in formation. He had told them that, "They have quite enough folks down there bumping into each other without you guys adding to the confusion." Then silently, secretly, he prayed that those searching below already would indeed be enough to find his son, even in this storm.

The passage of time is always torturous when you are anxiously awaiting something. From the birth of a baby to the arrival of Christmas Day, it is all the same. So then, for all those standing by in the first group, each passing moment felt like a belabored lifetime.

And then the quite unexpected happened—the blinding, choking, devastating dust storm shifted, changed its heading abruptly and proceeded on a southeasterly course toward Oklahoma. No longer borne by the hot gale-force wind, dust, dirt, sand, and other debris settled back down upon the ground. Then like the morning sun burning off a thick fog, visibility was restored, and the children in the second group could now easily spot the errant tarp.

When the storm had ripped the tarp from the others, Rusty saw himself as an anchor, keeping the tarp under control and within easy retrieval distance of his siblings. However, the gyrating undulating cloth was, at first, dangerous but, with only himself holding it, became an instrument of potential maiming, mauling, and death. He could have let it go. He should have let it go. But he continued to "hold the tiger by the tail" and immediately regretted it. All the newly liberated mass of canvas tarp, when stimulated by the windstorm, acted as a whiplash, transferring its force through the rough cloth into the soft eight-year-old hands. No matter how determined he was to be one of the big kids, he was far outweighed and outgunned by the forces generated by the windstorm.

And so for as long as Rusty held onto the tarp, it whipped, turned, and twisted him around like the boy was part of it, repeatedly bumping and banging into the ground before snapping back up. Massive blisters formed in the deep tissues of his hands. These quickly ruptured and hemorrhaged, making his portion of the tarp too slippery for him to continue holding. The final snap of the sailcloth launched him up into the storm, which carried him downhill to land at the beginning of a small grove of tree stumps. Though his separation from the tarp had been painful, he was happy that he was, at last, free.

His rejoicing was short-lived, however, as the tarp, now free of the boy's weight, turned and twisted in the air like a Chinese kite, blew directly toward the boy. Rusty had his face covered to protect it from the stinging onslaught that was the windstorm. As such, he could not see the returning tarp, much less prevent his being swallowed into its folds for a second time.

Rusty had almost forgotten that he was claustrophobic, uncontrollably afraid of tight closed-in spaces. However, being trapped deep inside the old musty tarp brought it all back with interest. Fear and pain worked in tandem as the boy was both slammed over and over onto the ground as well as being suffocated.

Suddenly the winds subsided, and the sailcloth prison came to a violent stop against a rundown abandoned toolshed. Though the boy's exterior environment was at rest, his interior environment remained chaotic, turning and churning the contents of his stomach into a storm in its own right. Rusty threw up.

"Praise God!" Polly exclaimed as she reached the writhing mass first and began to pull apart its labyrinth of folds to finally liberate the bruised, battered, and befouled boy within. She then used the hem of her sundress to gently expose Rusty's soiled nose and mouth.

"So," she asked, as she slowly raised the black and blue puke-streaked face. "What's my nickname now?"

"A...An... Angel!" Rusty gasped. "ANGEL!"

CHAPTER 9

Adventures in Stoney Lonesome (Continued); Buck versus the Bull: Round 1

Weasel had informed Buck that the evening meal was the time when the greatest number of prisoners would be present in one place. Buck chose then to dangle his "bait" for all to see. He had arranged with Weasel to remain in the infirmary until the majority of inmates were present and seated with their trays of slop. That's when Buck made his entrance. As he slowly made his way to receive his tray, he deliberately exaggerated the limp from his now-healed gunshot wound to his right knee.

With tray in hand, he slowly, laboriously crossed over to one of the first tables, one that uncoincidentally could be seen by most everyone in the room. As he approached the table, all those seated shifted to the farthest end or moved to a different table altogether. No one desired to be seated near him, especially today. As Buck plopped his nearly seven-foot frame onto the bench seat, he secretly scanned the room and discovered that very few guards were present. Buck knew that the absence of a majority of COs (correction officers) meant that whoever oversaw what was about to happen, there would be no interference from them.

Buck lowered his head to hide a mischievous smile as he remembered the reaction of the duty cook to his request that morning. He was only too eager to give Buck a handful of salt and an equal measure of red pepper to be used in a contrived repentance ritual. Being the father of four (adorable) little girls, the cook was full of pompous pride for his role in preventing the abuse of even one more child.

Buck scrutinized the contents on his tray. The cook had indifferently placed each item too close to, and even on top of, others until each menu item was indistinguishable from any other. In addition, the cook had slathered everything with gravy, transforming the tray into a homogenous mess resembling pig slop, vice anything fit for human consumption.

Buck only made a pretense of eating, absentmindedly fidgeting with his meal, which was now as jumbled as his own thoughts. Buck was in his third attempt to sort out and marshal those thoughts, when suddenly, he became overshadowed, as if by a tremendous storm cloud. The "cloud" emanated from a great ogre of a man, who, despite Buck's considerable size, nearly dwarfed him. As suddenly as he appeared, a truly massive hand shot forth from him to strike Buck's tray and send it careening against a nearby wall. Then reminiscent of Moses being addressed by the burning bush, a booming bass voice resonated throughout the entire chow hall.

"You're sitting at the wrong table. In fact, you're sitting in the wrong chow hall. We don't allow no child-molesting little coward like you to sit and eat with real men like us."

Until now, Buck hadn't looked up from the table, even when his tray was slapped from his hands. However, Buck chose now to slowly turn and face the mountain standing before him and said, "But it's all right to let in an ass-popping fudge-packing sodomite like you."

Everyone in the room could see Bull Bettermann rise to his full height of eight feet (a full head and shoulders taller than Buck). Everyone could clearly see Bettermann's distended neck veins as well as the deep-red patch on his neck, all indications of a build up for a massive outburst of hatred and rage.

So intense was the spectators' morbid anticipation of what Bettermann would do next, no one saw Buck reach into his opposite-facing pants pocket to clutch at whatever was carried within.

"Get up, you sorry excuse for a man," Bull Bettermann bellowed like his bovine namesake. "Get up and face me, you bastard!"

"Look, Bull!" Buck said in a voice that was calmer than anything he felt under the circumstances. "I don't want no beef with you. All I want is to do my time in peace and quiet."

Now Buck had known from his earliest days of Sunday school that, the Bible says, "A soft answer turneth away wrath; but grievous words stir up anger" (Proverbs 15:1 KJV). However, it had the opposite effect on Bettermann, driving him further into madness.

"I said, face me, blast you," he said as his hands reached down, like a benediction of doom, to grab Buck under one arm and by the scruff of his neck, snatching Buck from his bench seat to suspend him, legs dangling like an infant, above the ground. "I was going to be polite and wait to do this in private. But you deserve to have everyone see me pop your can right here, right now."

The chow hall erupted in cheers for their Goliath. Some cheered out of pure excitement for the event. While others were relieved that Bettermann's attention was on someone else. Absolutely no one voiced any sort of genuine comradery for the Bull. He had no friends, only victims. Even his closest followers, his henchmen, had decided that it was far better to be a banger than the banged.

Suddenly before anyone could see that his hand concealed anything, it snapped forward in a near-perfect roundhouse. Too fast for the Bull to either block or to otherwise avoid, Bettermann braced himself for the inevitable. However, he was surprised when instead of impacting his face, Buck's fist stopped short, opened, and released what it had concealed up until that moment.

The cheers from the chow hall crowd immediately became astonished silence as the tortured scream that filled the room emanated not from their champion's intended victim but from Bettermann himself. He screamed a most terrible scream as a wreath consisting of finely ground red pepper powder and salt encircled his head, invading every orifice it touched.

Eyes, which had slammed tightly shut, could not hold back the torrent of tears that gushed from them in a failed attempt to purge the fires in them. Immediately the pepper raised blisters on the whites of his eyes, which were immediately "medicated" by the salt. Was it his imagination, or were his very tears causing the burning to exacerbate?

It took a truly Herculean effort for Bettermann to hang onto Buck while in such torturous pain and anguish. However, as the next assault of pain stabbed and burned every mucous membrane in his head, Bettermann could hold onto Buck no longer. Now freed, like a child who had fallen out of bed, Buck plunged to the floor below. However, like a cat, Buck landed unhurt onto all four limbs.

As soon as he touched the floor, Buck brought his knees up and, for the briefest moment, crouched on the floor with Bettermann looming over him. Then like a frog, Buck extended both legs, rising off of the floor and leaping into the air—directly toward Bettermann's abdomen. Then like a switchblade, Buck's elbow snapped forward, held in place by his other arm. With a thud loud enough for the guards loitering in the hallway to hear, Buck's elbow collided with the Bull's groin with enough force to shatter walnuts. Then before the larger man could collapse on the floor, Buck leaped off the table's bench chair, making him a full two heads taller than his gargantuan opponent. Again a mighty roundhouse punch streaked toward the Bull, making full contact. A great cracking sound, reminiscent of a genuine Louisville Slugger propelling a stitched leather orb out of the park, echoed throughout the hall. Someone (perhaps Weasel) yelled *timber* as Bettermann's eyes rolled into his head, just before he hit the floor, as stiff as a lumberjack's felled tree.

Slowly, reverently, all those inmates present gathered to their fallen "champion."

"God, man!" exclaimed one man. "Look at his mouth. Should it be open that wide?"

"And it's so crooked," said another.

"Hey! Is he even breathing, man?" asked the first.

All of a sudden, a single whistle sounded, and like birds calling and answering each other in the morning, first, one whistle blared in answer to the original one's call, then another, and even another, until the whole wing was full of harsh painfully loud whistle calls, accompanied by the sound of many leather boots racing to the chow hall.

Soon Buck found himself surrounded by guards who painfully handcuffed him and even slapped on leg manacles for good measure. Then as he was led out of the hall, he was approached by Warden Sir, who took him aside from the guards.

"Officially, Riser," he whispered, "I'm reminding you that anytime you start something here, I've got to throw you in the hold. However, unofficially, I owe you a thanks. And to show you my gratitude, I'll make you a promise concerning the Bull. Every time you knock that bastard's block off, I'm going to knock six months off your sentence."

*****

Tributaries pour into streams, which eventually become rivers, which empty into oceans. Similarly days inevitably grow into weeks, which, in turn, accumulate and become months. During his first months residing in solitary confinement, Buck discovered that he greatly preferred his own company to that of his fellow convicts.

Few, if any, believed Weasel's report that Buck had flatly declined to take up the mantle of alpha prisoner, following the crushing defeat of the Bull, which resulted in an immediate vacuum in the perceived prisoner power hierarchy.

"But, Buck," Weasel pleaded. "Even when he gets out the infirmary, he may never be able to be the lead dog ever again. Think about it, man. The guy who is in for murdering a cop just got nailed by a guy in for felony assault of a child. He may never be able to live it down. Believe me, Buck, you really pissed him off."

"Weasel," Buck said thoughtfully. "I'll let you in on a little secret. I'm not half-done pissing Bettermann off yet."

Fear flashed through Weasel's eyes as he said, "Buck, are you out of your mind? I work in the infirmary and have to listen to him.

Even with his jaw wired shut, he has a lot of choice mumbled words for you. If I were you, I'd lay low for a while."

"I can't, Weasel. I haven't made Bettermann mad enough yet."

Weasel looked incredulous. "Just how mad is mad enough to suit you?"

Buck looked tired, as if all this talk was a strain for him. Finally he said, "Weasel, you must understand, Bettermann would have come after me sooner or later. It was inevitable. So I decided to strike first. But once you start something like this, you can't stop until it's all over."

"After what you did to him, I thought it was a done deal. I mean, you hit him just two times...only two times, and it was over. And what two blows they were. The first one permanently collapsed his left testicle. And the last one dislocated the man's jaw, and if that wasn't enough, you completely shattered his lower mandible. Even after he returns to his cell, his jaw will still be pinned up for many months to come. Irvine will have to fight every new street tough who comes in looking for a quick reputation."

Buck replied, "All the more reason he must come at me again. He wants to—no, he needs to get me in order to get his status back. I can't control when or where he does it, but before it happens, I want him to be so mad at me, he won't be able to think about anything else except what he's gonna do to me. I want to rile him so bad it'll drive him crazy."

"But why, Buck? Why enrage him so?"

"Because, Weasel, when you're mad—really mad—you make mistakes. And when Bettermann comes after me again, I want him to be so blind with rage, he'll make that one fatal mistake. So to make this happen, I'm going to hurt him again...and again... In fact, I'm going to lay into him every time I see his ugly face." Buck paused and noticed the troubled look on Weasel's face, then added, "What can I say, I like the hole."

CHAPTER 10

Another Great Depression

Enjoying a precious reprieve from the dust storm, Mr. Russell looked around and saw their stalled truck, not more than a hundred yards from where they now stood. He then looked further down the direction they were headed. With their farmhouse clearly visible only a short quarter of a mile away, he began to thank God that he had made the truth out of the half-truth he had told his family when they abandoned the truck to begin the dangerous trek on foot to the shelter of home. That he had tried to assuage their fears by his confidence that he knew exactly the way home and could lead them to it blind-folded was not entirely true. In truth, he had only a general notion of where home might be. Once again, Mr. Russell loudly thanked God for making what he said to come to fruition. And though he had repented to the Lord for his well-meaning wrongdoing, deep down, he knew that it would be a long time before he felt that he could tell his family of it—*if ever.*

With Rusty finally extricated from the "monster," the Russell family continued to prod and trudge their way to the comfort and safety of home. Both parent and child alike were thankful to cross the threshold, to enter the Victorian-styled estate.

"Wow!" exclaimed Polly as she saw the long ornate hallway for the first time. "I've never seen a house so big and so beautiful. But what about the house I stayed in first? Are they all a part of the same farm?"

"Oh, the old farmhouse," Rusty said. "That used to be the servant's quarters. But this…" He waved his arms all around for emphasis. "This is where we really live."

Rusty excitedly explained the curious history of their home, sounding every bit like a real estate salesman. He informed her that though the house was built sometime in the early 1910s, the eccentric owner had a love for the long-past Victorian era. So he built this tribute to the era as a gift to his aging mother (who had actually lived back then). Designed to be one of the largest residential structures in the area, it was the envy of all who had seen it and was even featured in the social registry. However, shortly after completion, the mother passed away, having never spent a day in the house. Grief drove the owner into a terrible depression of which he never recovered. He completely withdrew from life, including his business obligations. When he died, he had left a substantial property tax debt. With the collapse of Wall Street, no one had money enough to concern themselves with the rundown farm and its houses. Sadly the house remained vacant until the county threatened to auction it off.

"That's when Dad and the rest of us were passing through, looking for a place to raise such a freak show of a large family. That's when we saw this house with its surrounding acreage, and it was the old saying, 'love at first sight.' Well, Pa had a sizable inheritance in steel and oil—domestic refineries. So we rushed to city hall, where he paid all of the assessed back taxes before the auction began. And that's how we came to be here."

"Oh, my!" said Polly, genuinely exhausted from the hunt for Rusty. "All of that for a compliment of the hallway."

They all began to laugh when Mrs. Russell said, "Let's go to the kitchen and see if there's any injuries other than Rusty's bruises. You too, Polly. You did an awful lot of running today."

Polly fought back a moment of pride that tempted her to say that she had beaten everyone else to get to Rusty. Instead she obediently replied, "Yes, ma'am."

As they prepared to leave the hallway, they heard a commotion coming from the kitchen just ahead. Mr. and Mrs. Russell looked at each other in puzzlement as the noise sounded like children frolicking on the beach during the summer. Peering into the kitchen, the couple was shocked to see that the room had, in fact, somehow been transformed into a beach of sorts.

"Hey! It's my turn to go down the sand!"

"No, you come after me, and you'd better hurry. Here I go. WEEEEEEE!"

"I can build a better castle than you can."

Even as it seemed Louise's precious kitchen had been transformed into a giant sand dune, so too it appeared as if Louise had been turned into a ghost. Like water draining from a sink, all the color suddenly drained from her head to the knuckles of her hands, which now trapped her husband's arm in a death grip.

"RANDOLPH!"

His wife's scream caused Russell's heart to freeze in midbeat. Without removing the torturous appendage entrapping his arm, he turned his head and took a lightning-quick inventory. Sure enough, all the five youngest children (Roberta, Robert, Ronnie, Ronald, and Rachelle) were there.

Drained of energy, as well as pallor, she hesitated to move or even speak, apart from the loud gasp which had escaped through the fingers of her other hand covering her mouth. The truth was, she was afraid to move, afraid to enter the chaos that had been her favorite room in the house. Eventually her husband's gentle coaxing prevailed.

For the rest of their lives, the Russell Sprouts would share an inside joke among themselves, how their mother looked when she saw the mountain of dirt and sand which obscured the view of everything else in the room. From ghostly pale to bright lobster red, that's how the kids would describe their mother as she sat upon the mound in the kitchen and remained deadly silent.

Polly and Rusty were just returning from a nearby kitchen-support closet, bringing with them an old broom and dustpan.

"Kids," Russell declared as the two stood before him and his outstretched arms placed on each of their shoulders. "I love your initiative. However, you are going to need greater firepower and a heck of a lot more personnel.

By more personnel, Russell meant that the upcoming project was to be an all-hands evolution (which is to say *everybody*). And by "firepower," he was referring to a cache of large wide-bladed deep-bowled shovels used to feed large amounts of coal into even larger coal-hungry steam engines, such as the ones used by trains and ships. No one could say how a shipping crate containing twenty-five industrial/military-grade shovels, packed in grease, ended up at the entrance to an abandoned forest ranger firefighting shed. Atchison, Topeka, and Santa Fe manifests indicate shipment was paid for and delivered (to the abandoned ranger station) but subsequently never picked up by the purchaser. Randal discovered it while on a hike, and after notifying appropriate authorities and waiting the prerequisite number of days, the shipment was his (his father always wondered what a boy was going to do with all those shovels).

Even with all hands armed with a spanking-new Coal-Thrower 3 ultimate shovel, it took until that evening for the kitchen to be sufficiently clear for basic meal preparation to resume.

By the following afternoon, the living room was almost finished. However, bedrooms were not tackled; mattresses and cots were set up in the living room at night.

On the third day, Mr. Russell separated the two oldest children, Randal and Rhonda, as well as Polly, for detached duty, which entailed putting up storm shutters and then boarding up every opening or vent not closed with shutters. When finished, they stood back from the house to inspect their work.

On the fourth day, a dust storm even larger than the first tore away every shutter and every boarding plank and flung them so far away, it became impossible to retrieve.

In the house, three to four days of hard work were reduced to an exercise in futility. Not only was the interior of the house coated from floor to ceiling in dirt and sand, but the human occupants as well were no longer composed of flesh and bone but had been so permeated by the filth that they now seemed one in substance. No longer people, they had become golems. Even in spirit, did their base humanity surrender to the futility. Humanity and hope had all been beaten, pulverized, and swept away by the winds.

*****

Dirty faces greeted one another. Dirty hands and dirty feet performed what little chores that could still be done in this bleak desolate homestead. Dirty bodies embraced and said good night.

For the three oldest family members, the good night would be permanent, as their dirty bodies were consigned to the dirty ground that formed it. And not-so-few dirty minds employed their not-so-few dirty mouths to curse the winds, the drought, the economic depression, and especially the God they felt responsible for it all.

The stereotypical maternal practice of utilizing their own saliva to spot clean their children's faces had long been abandoned by Louise Russell. What was the use? In the current drought conditions, the spittle could not be spared. What was the use? She could no longer protect those faces from the grime that clung to them like her own feelings of inadequacy. Everything was useless. Keeping a house clean, keeping clothes clean, keeping children clean, keeping herself clean, everything was useless.

Randolph Russell had lost much when Wall Street crashed, when the drought came, when the dust winds blew. But he had been genuinely thankful for all he had left. For his family, for his farm, and for the life he felt blessed to have with them. He was also thankful for one important lesson he had learned in life—that is, times change, and though it was impossible to escape the bad times, he knew that they could not last forever. Therefore, he had always believed that good times would come again, and that life would one day return to the land. His greatest hope and prayer was that, when life returned to the land, that it would return to his wife, Louise, as well.

CHAPTER 11

Adventures in Stoney Lonesome (Continued); Buck versus the Bull: Round 2

"Battling Buck" (a name given him by his fellow inmates) had many flaws in his character: He drank too much, he was loud, belligerent, and often violent. He was cunning, conniving, and crafty. In fact, he had so many personality issues, it would be almost impossible to name them all here. However, for the sake of expedience, further listing will be curtailed. Suffice it to say that Buck was considerably above average in his contemptibility and his mendacity. However, despite all this, it has never been said of Buck that he was a liar. Quite the contrary, long before he had come to Leavenworth, he religiously clung to the saying that "a man is only as good as his word." Consequently to his all-too-few friends, he had proven himself to be both reliable and steadfast. However, to an ever-growing list of enemies, Buck had shown a marked propensity for holding grudges and for seeking revenge, even for minor provocations.

So it was that, shortly after being released from solitary confinement, Buck had persuaded Weasel to give him Bull's prognosis and discharge date.

Now that Buck knew when his prey would be available, he found that his days and nights were filled with the boredom that comes from anticipation. Yet eventually, that day did arrive (as all days do indeed arrive, in time).

Though Weasel didn't believe it was possible, Buck successfully managed to convince one of Bull's recent victims to trade cleaning duty schedules with him. Warden Sir was only too happy to approve the exchange, saying, "This ought to be rich," as he signed the request.

Finally Buck was at work with the prisoner cleaning crew, in the passageway between the infirmary and the prisoner cellblock. He kept his head lowered while he busied himself swabbing the deck in order to subtly observe the position of the guards.

How clumsy of them, he thought. *How supremely overconfident they are. None of them are alert, and all of them are too far away to prevent what's about to happen.*

Buck kept himself busy swabbing the deck and waited, listening for the approach of his intended prey. Suddenly Buck's vigil was interrupted by the prisoner supervising the work detail.

"Hey, new guy," he said as he propped himself against the passageway wall, his hands stuffed in his pockets. "You're doing a real bang-up job, but you been at it only two hours, and have done more than the rest of us who have been here since this morning. You're making the rest of us look bad. Why don't you let me relieve you for a breather?" he said as he reached for the well-worn mop.

"Nothing doing," Buck said as he drew the swab away from the other's reach. "I'm having too much fun. And besides..." Buck's speech trailed off as he thought he might have heard something down the distant passageway.

"Besides what?" the other man said as he positioned himself to reach for the mop again.

"Shoosh! I'm trying to listen."

"There ain't nothing to listen to. Now give me the bloody mop!"

"I said hush up!" Buck said as a massive hand flew out from him to cover the other man's mouth (and darn near most of his face) and pin him against the same wall he had just occupied, his feet dangling an entire foot above the floor, futilely struggling to regain their purchase, even as the hapless prisoner struggled to regain his breath.

A thin triumphant smile came to Buck's face as once again, he was able to concentrate and continue his vigil. Then he heard it, much clearer than before—the sound of footsteps, several footsteps—rapidly approaching. With remarkable reflexes, he turned his back to the coming footfalls, shielding one victim from view of another. With one hand, he continued to stifle the now-desperate struggles of his captive. With the other hand, he kept the mop pressed to his side, making a pretense of mopping the floor.

Closer and closer, the footsteps continued to bear down on his position. A bead of icy sweat cascaded down his back as he contemplated what he had devised as his next move. All at once, there was no longer time for the luxury of thought as through the corner of his eye, he could now plainly make out the oncoming party.

Four guards surrounded a much-larger man. Larger, yes, but not quite as large as he had been two short months ago. Then he saw the reason (though Buck was hardly surprised). Thin metal pins openly protruded from his mouth, weaving their way through a metal structure resembling a suspension bridge, which covered most of his head.

As the detail drew near, Buck slowly rotated his body to hide his face, as well as his own prisoner. The first guard passed him without incident. Buck's muscles tensed to the point of producing pain, as the man in the center of the escort came directly in line with him. Then even through the latticework of his jaw brace, Buck could see the man's eyes widen with recognition; his mouth struggled against their restraints to raise alarm. As crimson rivets appeared throughout the lower half of his face, along with the sound of twisting metal, snapping bands, and of chipping bone, a single word spewed forth from deep in Bettermann's hellish soul.

"*RISER!*"

Faster than even he would have thought possible, Buck released his now-unconscious prisoner to turn toward the startled guards. Twirling the mop like a deranged parasol, Buck easily brushed aside the guards closest to his intended victim, and while the others scrambled to gather their wits and close with the attacker, there developed an unimpeded line between Buck and Bettermann. Then raising the handle of the mop like a javelin in the hands of a jousting knight, Buck charged his opponent.

Before anyone could offer defense, the tip of the weapon found its well-rehearsed mark. Deftly it struck, parting the space between Bettermann's body and his right arm. Buck swung quickly around, using his own body to lock the poled weapon at the level of Bull's elbow. Then quickly, mercilessly, Buck continued to turn his own body to put more and more pressure on the tortured joint. It was anyone's guess which sound was louder—Bettermann's scream or the sound of his shattered elbow.

Bettermann writhed in pain and anguish. "You're a dead man, Riser! You hear me? You're a dead man…" he somehow managed to say, even as a dark patch rapidly spread from the lifelessly hung limb to collect in a puddle on the newly mopped floor.

Buck offered no resistance to the swarm of deeply shocked guards, as both handcuffs as well as heavy leg irons were roughly applied. Then as orderlies arrived to convey the injured man back to the infirmary, Buck was conveyed back to solitary confinement.

*****

It was dark, hot, and humid in the hold without any comforts or amenities. Yet as its sole entrance creakily opened to allow his being pushed inside by the guards, Buck could barely make out that he was not alone.

"Bloody hell, man, you're really complicating my life. Why him? Why this sudden campaign against Bettermann?"

"Let's say I'm doing it for a friend. Besides I like it down here, no one to bug me. By the way, that's now one year off you owe me."

"I know how much I owe you, dag-nab-it! I don't need you to remind me."

Buck became quiet for a moment, as he moved as close as possible to the warden, as far as possible from the door so as not to be heard, before cautiously asking, "Warden Sir, just how much do you owe Bettermann? How deep are you in for? Just what has he got on you!"

A long period of silence ensued between them, and Buck wondered if the warden would answer him at all. At length, however, he did answer, and the tale he told caused even Buck to experience a rare emotion—*fear*. Buck began to wonder if maybe he might have taken things with Bettermann way too far.

The warden spoke of how Braniff Irvine Bettermann was not an ordinary inmate, more even than the head of the various small-time crime gangs of the prison's underground. Bettermann was the self-styled czar of a criminal network which specialized in the use of blackmail for the seduction, corruption, and ultimately the recruitment of select officials in the corporate, law enforcement, judicial, and even local and state politics.

The warden paused from his narrative, and Buck took this opportunity to ask, "If he owns people in the judiciary, how did he end up here?"

"Well, the simple answer would be that he murdered a cop, a police detective who was investigating his emerging criminal empire. But it gets complicated. The truth is, that detective he killed had been on Bettermann's own payroll for quite some time. However, after Bettermann corrupted him, he became greedy. He demanded more payoff money and threatened to expose his boss if he didn't get it."

"That's when Bettermann killed him?" Buck asked.

"Yeah… Bettermann broke his spine in half, with his bare hands no less. As for the judges he owns, Bettermann had them put him in here…on purpose. This way, he avoids police retaliation while being able to run his business, unimpeded, all the same. Unimpeded, that is, until you got here."

"I know," Buck said thoughtfully. "Now I've 'impeded' him twice and in front of witnesses. I wonder what he'll do to get even?"

"Buck, he's going to have to kill you. Hear me good…he's going to have to kill you. It's the only way he can regain his status. I don't know how he plans to do it or when he'll try it. So you better start watching yourself."

Again Buck grew silent, as he became lost in his thoughts. Presently he said, "Thanks for the warning, sir. I'll be sure to watch myself. However, you still haven't answered my question…what's Bettermann got on you? How is that oversized punk controlling you?"

The warden kept his eyes focused on the cold concrete floor, avoiding the other man's scrutiny. "I won't say who, mind you, but there's a guest here that worked as an executive clerk for one of the top financiers in the country. Shortly before all those banks collapsed, he has this dream where the biggest men in finance were discussing that collapse…BEFORE IT ACTUALLY HAPPENED.

"That very day, our clerk is asked to set up a meeting between his boss and the very men who were in his dream. Dutifully our clerk obeys. However, just before the meeting begins, he is ordered to take the rest of the day off. Instead of leaving, he hides in the wardrobe and listens in as these 'captains of industry' discuss the very thing he has dreamed about. One would think they would agree to raise an alarm and save the country, but no. They all conspire to liquidate their bank holdings and convert them to gold. And in order to prevent the federal government from confiscating all that lovely gold, they hide it…some in the States and some of it overseas."

Buck listened with more patience than what he considered himself capable of exhibiting. However, before he could tell the warden to cut to the chase, the narrative changed.

"That is when our clerk's life went down the toilet. He sneezed, interrupting the somberness of their meeting. Then another sneeze, and then another, all betraying the hiding place of the hapless little clerk who had overheard everything."

Even before the warden began to tell of his own involvement, Buck had easily deduced it. In order to properly deal with the wayward Mr. Weasel, the fix-it-man Bettermann was consulted, and evidence was manufactured implicating Weasel for embezzlement.

Next one of the judges he owned convicted him and sentenced that poor soul to Leavenworth in order for Bettermann to keep an eye on him.

"And as for you, Warden Sir," Buck continued, "you knew that Weasel was innocent but agreed to receive him here because the stock market did indeed crash, just as predicted. You had lost everything and felt what Weasel carried in his head was a way to recoup your losses."

"You can't judge me, Riser," the Warden said, as his face flushed red to match the rising anger in his voice. "Don't sound so sanctimonious with me. You've done more than enough to that little girl to deserve being sent here."

"Let's get one thing straight, right here and now!" Buck said, as he suddenly stood as tall as the diminished dimensions of the room would allow. "I'm not your bloody judge, Warden, and I'm neither your priest nor your confessor. Whatever you've done, you're going to have to look Weasel in his eyes and live with yourself."

Afterward an uneasy moment passed between the two men, in which neither man had spoken to the other. At length, the warden stood and prepared to leave. However, after he had called for the guard, Buck called out to him.

"I'm still in the dark about all that overgrown punk has got on you. What I have seen is this, no matter how he blackmails and manipulates you, you are still basically a good man. Unlike Bettermann, you have not made a conscious decision to live in the dark. There's still time left to turn around. But know this...time is running out."

As a corrections officer slowly opened the cell door to allow the warden to pass through, he thought of Buck's last sentence, *But know this...time is running out.*

"Buck, what did you mean by that last crack...'time is running out'?"

"I don't know what you mean, Warden Sir. I didn't say anything."

*****

It was late that evening, and most of the warden's charge rested in Orpheus's embrace. However, no solace could be found there for him, but rather those of self-rerecriminations, self-revilement, and of self-hatred. Was it over a lifetime of blunders and failures (like many in his custodial care)? Or was it as open and unobscured as a single moment of weakness in an otherwise sterling record of a life of public service? Yes, that was it—one misstep, one mistake, one lie. Was it right that one lapse of judgment should now threaten that otherwise sterling record of service?

Large beads of cold sweat decorated a troubled brow, marking the latest round in an often-fought always-lost battle against a most cunning, ruthless, and even merciless opponent, who thought it nothing to take the warden's most intricately planned arguments and then change the outcomes into no-win scenarios that portended doom for himself.

Was it right that one mistake, one lie should bring ruination to a good man's career and reputation?

Was it right that *your* one lie should falsely convict an innocent man and condemn him to the violence and terrors of prison life?

Though alone in the private sleeping quarters attached to his office, shame of his own actions inadvertently bringing destruction to another overcame and prevailed over the conscience of a man who maintained the personal delusion that in spite of everything, he was still "one of the good guys."

But goodness is as goodness does. Besides it wasn't for one little mistake. It was only one little mistake, at first. But that one was soon joined by a myriad of others, spurred on by a man of corruption who used the fear of revelation to entrap and control.

"Until it was he, Bettermann, a convict, who was really running this prison," the warden said, as his face finally rose up to confront the other one framed in his bathroom mirror.

"If you would be free of him, then know that there is a price to pay."

"I know, the price is losing the very reputation and position I went into bondage trying to protect."

"When it becomes time to pay, don't bear that burden alone!"

"Please, I-I don't understand. H-How can I—"

"Confess your faults one to another...that you may be healed" (James 5:16 KJV).

"'Don't pay the cost alone...and confess, that ye may be healed.' Now I'm confused."

"'But ye shall know the truth, and the truth shall make you free.' Know this…there is a truth that will topple your enemy's entire kingdom. Think on this… Think on this… Think on this…"

When the warden opened his eyes, he was alone, except for his reflection in the bathroom mirror.

CHAPTER 12

Hasenpfeffer

Eleven-year-old Rochelle maintained a death grip on Polly's arm, impatiently towing her charge along toward the back of the house and its many half-plowed and never-plowed rows of otherwise vacant land, baking, as if on a spit, under a merciless summer sun.

"All right, Rochelle, I've seen them," Polly said with somewhat less enthusiasm than her partner.

"Oh, that!" said Rochelle dismissively. "That's not what you're here to see. No family can live on all that barren land."

"Well, what then?" Polly demanded, irritated as much with Rochelle as she was with this incessant heat.

"Here!" Rochelle said proudly, as they passed the edge of the house and followed the cobblestone walkway leading to the back.

In order to cheaply warm the house, it had been built with its front porch facing the noonday sun. However, in order to take full advantage of the evening's coolness, the back porch was built to face the setting/twilight sun. So as the girls came into the shade of the backyard, Polly saw it. Just off the porch, but still within its shadow, someone had built what looked to be a horse stable for a Shetland pony. However, building a stable so close to the house seemed utterly ridiculous. So it couldn't be a stable. Furthermore, as they got closer to it, they could see that it was transparent; that is, they could see right through the thing. And they saw what was in it also—something quite large and quite furry.

"Oh, it's a doghouse," said Polly, as if she had just emerged the winner at a dinner theater. "But why can we see through it?"

"Aha!" exclaimed Rochelle. "Because it's not a doghouse, and that's not a dog. Look closer, Polly."

Even before she was told, Polly began to walk slower, cautiously approaching the—whatever it was. At first, it appeared to be a gray-ish-brown mass, moving back and forth in the enclosure. However, as she crept ever closer to the thing—*suddenly*! She could see it clearly; she could see it plainly; she could see it astonishingly.

Polly tried to speak but found that she could not. Instead she tried to think of a word to properly describe the magnificence and sheer size of the thing, but she could not. "That... That's a rabbit!" she finally managed to say, pointing at the thing.

"Yeah, it is," said Rochelle, laughing at and certainly with her friend Polly. "But not just any rabbit. Oh no, girl. By now you should know that nothing can live on this farm except it's a freak, like us."

"All of you are freaks?"

"Absolutely! With twelve of us, we can't be anything else."

Polly suddenly become quiet and pensive again. "What about me, Rochelle? Am I a freak?"

"The biggest and best one of all. Don't you understand, you could not have survived this long, with a father like yours, if you were just an ordinary girl. But as things stand, believe me, Polly, you ought to be a sideshow attraction."

With that, they both laughed until their stomachs began to hurt, and their tears began to fall. Finally and with great effort, Rochelle managed to compose herself and say, "Polly, introducing, Hasenpfeffer. She's a Flemish giant rabbit, the largest breed of rabbit on earth."

"I can believe that," said Polly.

"Officially she's Roberta's pet, but we all take turns taking care of her."

Polly was thoughtful for a moment. "If I remember right, *Hasenpfeffer* is a German word for 'rabbit stew.'"

"Shhhh!" said Rochelle, waving her arms frantically. "We don't use the word STEW when we're around her."

Bewildered, Polly began to ask, "Then why, for crying out loud, would anyone in their right mind name their pet rabbit that?"

"It's all Randal's fault," Rochelle confessed, as she waved her hands helplessly in the air. "To cut down on the arguments, the oldest child, Randal, was given the job of naming the new pet. It was supposed to be a joke, but the parents loved it. Even us kids always get a laugh when anyone says that name—everyone that is, except for—"

"Yeah, I get it," said Polly

"And she's smart too," confessed Rochelle. "She gets upset whenever she hears her name spoken or the word *stew*. Worst of all, whenever it becomes Randal's time to take care of her, she tries to bite him whenever he comes near."

"Wow! That's incredible—sad but incredible."

"Yeah, I know. By the way, Polly, I have to clean her house today. Would you help me and hold her while I play housemaid?"

"Yes, I'd be delighted to," she said, not being entirely truthful. "How much does she weigh?"

"About fifteen to twenty pounds."

"Thanks."

"You're more than welcome." She paused to hand Polly a handful of carrots, then unlatched the door to the rabbit's enclosure.

Hasenpfeffer took one look at where the gold bullion of the garden had been laid and instantly became enthusiastic about Rochelle removing her from the enclosure.

"Hey, Rochelle, I didn't know that rabbits could walk on air."

Polly was thankful that all she had to do was allow Hasenpfeffer to sit on her lap, as she offered the horse in rabbit's disguise, one carrot after another, after another after another. In fact, before Rochelle had finished cleaning the enclosure, Polly's supply of carrots was becoming dangerously thin, along with Polly's confidence that the bottomless pit on her lap wouldn't consume her as well. However, her confidence in God's timing was reinforced, for as soon as the final carrot had been aggressively grabbed from her hands, Rochelle's hands reached down to relieve Polly of the gnawing wonder.

*****

Intelligence among animals has been measured by, and subsequently ranked on, a hierarchy based on the quality as well as the quantity of problems solved. Ideally each problem solved (or obstacle traversed) brought the test subject closer to obtaining the reward (or the object of desire).[8] Now suffice it to say that whatever degree of intelligence that Hasenpfeffer possessed, it allowed her to overcome a major obstacle to achieving her goal. Instinctively (if one wished to call it that) her several periodic naps throughout the day had gradually convinced the Russell family that she shared their day/night-activity pattern. They had been fooled, for Hasenpfeffer maintained the day/night-activity pattern she shared with her fellow rabbits; that is, she was nocturnal (active at night). This fact gave her time to overcome her next obstacle—getting out of her cage. One day, she had observed the family's Border collie dig its way under, and then outside of, the fence separating the backyard from the front yard. And so one night, she used the memory of the dog, coupled with rabbits' natural ability to burrow, in order to dig her way underneath the wall of her enclosure. After this, she received the reward—that is, she finally got into the family's main vegetable garden to gorge herself until the early dawn. Her degree of intelligence had one last test or problem to solve. When she returned to her enclosure, in the early morning, she used her hind feet to kick the dirt that had been displaced by her digging back into place. The Russells never suspected that she had ever been out of her house.

When the mother, Louise Russell, discovered that, her vegetable garden (used to produce a subsistence crop for the family) had been rifled through, trampled over, and indiscriminately munched upon, she became upset, beyond the philosophical boundaries of the term—*she was livid!* Shouts were heard; accusations were made; names were called; God's name was called upon in vain. In the end, the order of business for that day was changed, and by that evening, certain subtle alterations to the Russells' homestead had taken place.

That very evening, when the family had gone to bed, Hasenpfeffer, motivated by hunger and armed with both intelligence and experience, slipped out from under her habitat wall and crossed over to Louise's garden. She paid no attention to the fine layer of talcum powder sprinkled liberally throughout the yard (after all, it was not within her experience) Nor did she pay much attention to the funny, circular decorations that had been hung on the fence of the garden, except that they had a metallic scent, not unlike blood. It alarmed her at first; however, since it posed no obstacle to the reward, she eventually ignored it to fit through the slats in the garden fence and, once again, gorge herself on the garden's delights.

Dawn approached, and it was time to leave. But she had eaten too much and was now bloated and sluggish. She struggled, turning herself from side to side until she reached the funny-smelling gate. Though it allowed her to easily enter the garden, the many almost-invisible lines of fine barbed wire snagged her wonderfully soft fur. They then twisted and turned with every effort she employed to escape; each endeavor only served to drive the barbs deeper into her fur and then painfully into her hide. Now exhausted and hurt, she lay upon the ground between the forgotten pleasures of the garden and the safety and security of her enclosure and awaited the arrival of one predator or another. In the early morning, the incessant barking of the dog heralded the arrival of a superpredator—a bipedal primate female named Louise Russell.

That very morning, evidence was presented in a one-sided trial, which took more time to fill up the courtroom/kitchen than it did to arrive at a verdict. Being caught red-pawed at the scene of the crime usually did not bode well for the accused. In addition, footprints / paw prints left in the talcum powder sprinkled throughout the yard presented incontrovertible evidence that only further pointed to the accused. Finally with the verdict having been given, and the judge's reiteration that the subsistence garden was their primary source for food during the drought, it was then announced that sentencing would take place, without further pronouncement, upon Judge

Louise Russell's discretion. However, there could be no misinterpretation of the look in Judge Russell's hazel eyes, which promised—Hasenpfeffer would finally live up to her name.

For the rest of the morning, and far into the afternoon, all the Russell Sprouts employed themselves in lying low, being scarce, and staying out of their mother's way. It was not that they were off somewhere plotting to affect the prisoner's escape. For one thing, there simply was no place to go where Hasenpfeffer could survive on her own, having been raised by the children since she was born. For another thing, their mother, Louise, was right when she said that because of the drought, and the current economic status of the country, that this rabbit of a monstrously huge breed could quite literally eat them all out of house and home. There was no way around the fact that Hasenpfeffer had to go—and go in such a way that would cause her to make good all the things lost from Mother's subsistence garden. All the Russell Sprouts had known this to be true. From the oldest child, Randal, at age fourteen, all the way down to the youngest child, Roberta, at age three—all of them knew in their heads that their mother was right. However, that did not keep their hearts from breaking.

Sometime during the midafternoon (and following much prayer and meditation), Polly excused herself from the other children and quietly went downstairs into the kitchen. Sitting at a corner of the table, she asked, "Is there anything I can do to help?"

Mr. and Mrs. Russell flashed a peculiar look toward each other, as Russ said, "Oh, oh, Lou. It's been my experience that whenever a child asks if they can help you, it usually means they're about to ask you for something."

Polly tilted her head down and away, and covered her mouth, in order to hide her blushing face. "I know it had to be hard for you to make the decision you did."

"Russ," Louise said as she busied herself preparing a marinade. "Beware of Greeks bearing gifts."

"Quite right, dearest," Russ said to his wife. Then turning to Polly, he asked, "Okay, young lady, out with it. What do you want?"

"Well, to Mrs. Russell," Polly began shyly, embarrassingly, almost apologetically, "Ma'am, I'd like to ask that when you cut up Hasenpfeffer, that you please..."

Polly was grateful that Louise listened to her without interruptions or criticisms, but nodded her head at each point; not to indicate that she agreed but that she thoroughly understood what was being asked of her. When Polly was finished, Louise said, "Well, Polly, since I haven't started to 'operate' yet, I don't see why not. PROVIDED...you will be here to help me out...in plain sight of the other kids."

"Yes, ma'am, I can be here to help you. After that, I must complete the other part of the mission with Mr. Russell and come right back."

"And just what is OUR part of the mission?" Russ asked.

"Well, sir, last year, I saw a banner, advertising an exhibition and opening of...in the next town over. If we go there, I'm sure I can persuade the owner to..."

Again Polly was grateful that Russ listened without saying anything, such as no, no way, not a chance, or the always hope-crushing final words of judgment—you must be out of your cotton picking chicken plucking mind! Instead he looked very thoughtful and said, "Well, young lady, if that's what you want to do with your money... let's leave as soon as Mom finishes her part before I have time to change my mind."

*****

For nearly the entire drive to the town of Dodge City, very little was spoken between Polly and her foster father. However, there was almost a constant discourse between Polly and her Heavenly Father. In fact, she was just ending her prayer when Russ pulled into a general parking yard across the street from a small shop nestled between two larger edifices. Polly became excited when she read a sign above the white French doors that read "The Living End: Taxidermists Shoppe and Gallery—Serving the Nobility of Europe—Endorsed by the National Museum of Natural History in France." Once inside,

Randolph wasted no time in telling a clerk that they would like to see the proprietor.

While they waited, Polly had the opportunity to walk around and view the displays (so long as she promised not to touch anything and to remain in sight of Russ always). Many of the items shown, Polly recognized from books she has read on exotic animals. Other displays depicted creatures that only existed in fantasy stories. She identified gryphons and unicorns, rocs and dragons. At length, she happened upon a creature that she could not readily identify. From its waist to its feet, the thing resembled an eagle. But from the waist up, it looked to be so much more than mere mortal beauty could hope to compare. No mere earthly woman—an angel maybe, or perhaps a goddess?

The item, unlike the other displays, exhibited no tile with the creature's name. She stood before it, mesmerized by its beauty, as she pondered what it could be.

While she stood there, transfixed, the only other gallery patron sauntered up to her.

"Do you know what it is you see, girl?" Came the gravelly voice of the man next to her. It was only then that she became aware of his presence. And what a presence; at once he seemed to her to be nearly as old as some of the animals shown. Despite the heat, the old man was covered from head to toe in black (trousers, ruffled puffed-sleeve shirt, shoes, and cloak, topped with a slouch hat atop his long silver-haired head). Lastly the man's hands looked quite remarkable as well. They were withered to a far greater degree than his face, she could scarcely believe they were from the same being. And then there were the scars; they were from burns of a sort, but certainly not from fire. The only item the man wore that was not black was a long white silk scarf he wore loosely draped over his neck, without twists or turns.

It took Polly a moment before she could answer the man's query. "I'm not sure. She's way too beautiful to be what I first thought it was."

"And that would be?"

"I-I thought at first that it was a harpy. But then, I thought not. Harpies are supremely ugly hags."

"Not necessarily." The old man chuckled. "And not always. In fact, their visage denotes the spirit within them."

Presently Russ came to her other side, along with another man, not much older.

"Polly, this is Mr. Nicklaus Koe. Sir, this is Miss. Polly Riser... and she has something to ask of you."

Nicklaus Koe gestured for the two to follow, and he led them to a small workroom at the end of an even smaller passageway. He then nodded toward her and listened without comment as she told of the creature that had of-late been Hasenpfeffer. She talked of her beauty, her gracefulness, her intelligence. But mostly, she told of the great love her family had for her. At times, her narrative was interrupted as she fought back tears. However, as soon as her tale was at an end, so was her composure.

Handing her a kerchief, Koe asked, "And so, good lady, what may I do for you?"

Polly fought back a last wave of sobs and placed a tightly bound bundle, made of rough butcher paper on top of a workbench.

Nicklaus Koe carefully, ever-so gently, removed the package's bindings to gaze with raised eyebrow upon what it had concealed. Then a half-smile showed itself through his heavy beard, as he brought the photograph from the other artifacts to scrutinize it at eye level.

"You believe I am able to do this thing but—"

"But," Polly respectfully interrupted, "it is too expensive a work for such a little girl in these days in Kansas. It will take impossibly too long to accomplish, and it could not be done with such poor remains. Did I miss anything, sir?" She addressed this last question to Mr. Russell, who shook his head. "However," she continued, "the very fact that you, as a master taxidermist, have produced subjects from absolutely no remains whatsoever but, are in every respect, artificial constructs, as is the case of your fantasy animal showings. Further, we do indeed possess the funds to procure your expertise. And finally, in about one month from now, I must depart the area.

There will be a fifteen percent bonus in addition to your other fees, if delivery is received before I leave. To show that we are in earnest, we are prepared to pay you forty percent now, followed by the remainder, including bonus fees, upon delivery."

Trying to conduct business as an adult was taking its toll upon the little girl.

"Are there any other concerns, Mr. Koe?" Randolph asked while he applied gentle pressure to ease the shaking in the girl's slender shoulders.

Nicklaus Koe stroked his beard, while his eyes moved back and forth from the photograph to the remnants in the butcher paper to the pleading eyes of the little girl before him.

*****

The return drive to Cimarron proved more relaxing; the conversation more congenial; the laughter, warmer and more genuine. Suddenly Randolph grew quiet, and Polly began to wonder what the matter was. A moment longer, and Polly began to feel self-conscious and question whether she was the cause. Her concern was turning to trepidation when Russ reached out to place an arm around her shoulders, and then gently stroked the back of her head.

Though Randolph continued his silence, Polly enjoyed the touch of his hand; its warmth and its gentleness alone brought her peace and contentment.

"Polly," Randolph finally managed to say. "I am so very…very godly proud of you."

"Thanks, sir," Polly said, genuinely relieved as she snuggled closer under Russ's arm.

"The way that you conducted yourself at The Living End showed great maturity, as well as a demonstration of tremendous self-control."

As Randolph spoke, Biddy's—oops, Bedelia's—Sunday school lesson on honesty pricked at her delicate conscience as a cattle prod. "Even though you don't say an outright lie, if you know something to be true concerning yourself, to omit telling the truth in order to deceive another is still a lie." Now Polly very much loved receiving praise from others (especially from someone she cared about and respected, like Randolph Russell), the thought of him thinking less of her was something her twelve-year-old self was not prepared to wrestle with. Yet wrestle with it she did until she made the decision to tell the truth, no matter what the consequences were to herself. While Mr. Russell went on about her self-control and courage, she forced herself to interrupt him; though it felt as if the words were to surely tear open her throat and damn her in her foster parent's eyes.

Large tears began to well up in her own eyes, as she suddenly blurted out, "But, sir, you don't understand. I'm not brave, and I didn't have self-control back at the shop. I was scared, and I was shaking inside the whole time."

Randolph Russell looked down upon her tortured features and held the child closer, while he smiled, then quickly returned his concentration upon the road. "Oh, Polly," he said, giving her shoulders a warm squeeze. "It is you who do not understand. To be brave and courageous doesn't mean that you are without fear, but rather that you possess the determination that your fear won't prevent you from doing what you know to be right. Yes, you were frightened, but that is precisely how true courage is shown."

They drove on for the rest of that afternoon, engaged mostly in small talk with an occasional question or observation of a more serious note from Polly. One such occasion came when Polly blurted out, "You know, I'm very thankful that God has blessed me to be a part of your family, even if it's just for a little while."

"And what part do you especially feel blessed by?"

"Well," she said thoughtfully, "you're a pa."

"That's very true."

"And...you have twelve kids."

"Again no argument there. But, dear, what's the point?"

"Well, sir, the point is, you're a good dad, aren't you? I mean, you love your kids and all, and they love you too?"

"Okay, I think I know where this is going," Russell said as he lifted his well-worn hat to wipe away the sweat underneath. "Yes, Polly, I like to think that I'm a good father to my kids. With the

Lord's help, I've always tried to do right by them. But you have to know…no one's perfect…not even big Ben Riser."

"If you know my dad, then you DO understand," Polly said as tears, once again, began to fill her eyes. "Because I've been blessed to know you, now I know what kind of pa for God to make him into."

"Whoa there, little girl—"

"But I know he can do it! I just know he can… I've been praying everyday…"

Even as he watched his distraught foster child, Russell inwardly prayed, *Dear God in heaven, Lord of all, your sweet daughter has questions that only you can answer…and she needs to hear from you now, oh Lord. Therefore, have mercy upon her right now, Lord, and use me now, oh Lord… Speak a word to her soul…"a word spoken in due season" (Proverbs 15:23 KJV) oh God, and grant to her the peace and comfort that can only come through you…in the precious name of our Lord and Savior, Jesus, who is the Christ… Amen.*

"So you see, I believe so hard, and I've prayed so hard… I WANT MY PA BACK!"

"Beloved child!" Russell said, though the voice, somehow, seemed not to be his own.

"Beloved child!" he said again, and all crying and hysteria ceased.

"Beloved child!" he said thrice, and the girl's whole attention was squarely focused on him. "Do you pray for my perfect will to be done in your life, or do you pray that YOUR will be done. Will you trust in me and my purpose for your father, or will you have respect only for your idea of the perfect father? Know this, oh girl, I have created all people, and each one is unique, with strengths and abilities and even weaknesses, and all to accomplish my will in the earth. Where you and most people only see your father as a town bully, his aggressiveness is really a strength of character, which will avail itself in time. Your foster father has qualities that are not as edgy nor as effective for that time. All are made after my design, and you must accept them and love them for who they are…as they are. I am the potter. I create, I unmake, and I remake as I choose. But know this, child, your earthly father's life will not be taken until his name has been added to my kingdom. And you, beloved daughter, will not be called home until you have seen it with your own eyes. Have I not said it? Shall I not bring it to pass? 'For I know the thoughts that I think toward you, saith the LORD, thoughts of peace, and not of evil, to give you an expected end'" (Jeremiah 29:11 KJV).

The rest of the return drive to the outskirts of Cimarron was done in complete silence. Not that Polly lay asleep, for she remained wide awake for the remainder of the trip. Awake, yes, but she dared not utter a single word, for the thought that it might disturb her spirit from what had already been said.

Finally the two arrived back home thoroughly exhausted physically; however, they were both thoroughly excited and exuberated spiritually over what they had heard.

*****

Suppertime and the Russell family had gathered around the dinner table. On the table, the fare this evening would be relatively simple, except for one covered ceramic croc in the center of the table. There were greens (a mustard and turnip green mix), crowder peas, and the ubiquitous platter of biscuits (Louise's mother-in-law's award-winning bread recipe was present at almost every meal).

By now, it was no secret as to the contents of the centerpiece dish. And so, Randolph Russell had finished his Baptist-style blessing of the table, and while everyone was taking a seat, Polly quietly escorted every child under the age of eleven (Raine, Rainie, Rusty, Rachelle, Ronald, Ronnie, Robert, and Roberta) to the only upstairs bedroom that was practically free of dirt and sand and thus was livable again. Once there, tears that had, for too long, been in check now flowed both freely and unashamedly.

On a corner of the bed, Polly sat with the head of the youngest Russell Sprout (three-year-old Roberta) cradled gently on her lap. The two formed a sort of nucleus around which the rest of the children were lying, strewn about without order. They had all refused to eat so much as a single morsel of the family's fine-furred friend.

Oh, how they cried and cried. Fueled by the pangs of their empty stomachs, their collective lamentation (like the "national razor" of the French Revolution) descended and pierced through the floorboards, the ceiling, and finally through the hearts of those at repast below.

Slamming his knife and fork onto his plate, the oldest child, Randal (age fourteen), angrily asked, "Do we have to listen to those babies all night? It doesn't necessarily have to be Hasenp—rabbit stew. We can send up some greens or crowder peas or biscuits or something. Anything just to shut them up."

Now it had always been the custom of the family for Dad to exercise his role as disciplinarian whenever there was an emotional outburst among their children. Tonight, however, tradition and protocol had gone the way of a Flemish giant rabbit named Hasenpfeffer. Rising to her feet, Louise Randcine Caulfield Russell fiercely gazed into the eyes of all those present and said, "For young folk like them, a pet is another member of the family and a best friend. And so... they have the right to grieve for the loss of their friend, in their own way."

"And in their own time," Russell added. "One night without supper won't kill them. So for now..." He nodded toward his wife.

Louise returned her husband's gesture and continued, "So for now, we're just going to let 'em all be. Kids, when you clean up, leave THE REST of the biscuits on the table, in case they get hungry."

For Randal Russell, there could be no doubt what his mother's emphasis of *the rest* meant and that she had primarily directed it at himself. So without further comment, he inwardly (in his own way and own time) lamented the loss of the golden nuggets, while he and his siblings set about cleaning up the kitchen.

CHAPTER 13

Adventures in Stoney Lonesome (Continued); Buck versus the Bull: Final Round

It had taken the warden quite some time to come to a conclusion concerning "don't pay alone" and "there's a truth that will topple your enemy's kingdom." Not so much as he didn't know what they meant, but that he knew full well what they meant and for what they portended were he to follow through. However, one phone call to a friend in the state capital, and the plan was set.

On the morning of the next day, Warden Simon "Sir" Sherman waited nervously as he looked out of his office window, which afforded an excellent view of the entire parking lot. Nervousness notwithstanding, he felt remarkably composed (perhaps resigned might be closer to the truth, he thought) for a man about to destroy his own career and to hang himself on his own political gallows. He had not been waiting long when, at the far end of the parking lot, his executioners were arriving. Two federal marshals' cars were followed closely by two black state limousines and a large flatbed truck, whose cargo platform contained two portable office trailers.

The party wasted no time in exiting the vehicles, and just as quickly, the warden's secretary had ushered them all into the warden's office. There a slightly built man with eyeglasses nearly the size of his entire head came over to the warden and offered to shake his hand.

"Better take the hand, son. It may be the only pleasantries to be had until this party is over. Horace Pettibone, Federal Office of the Inspector General, at your service."

"Simon Sherman, warden and soon-to-be resident. I'm glad you're finally here, it's been long overdue."

"My goodness, assistant to the inspector general himself here, with armed federal marshals with arrest warrants filled out before the audit has even begun, along with the need for absolute secrecy... sounds a bit overly dramatic to me. I doubt if it could be as bad as all that. Who do you suppose those warrants are addressed to?"

"Believe me, Mr. Pettibone, the situation is worse than even I would have dreamed. As for those warrants... I'll wager that one of them is for me. Now please excuse me, while I spring our little trap," he said, as he crossed over to his secretary, taking the large microphone from his hand.

"Now the inspector general's audit team has arrived. All inmates are to be in lockdown status. That is, all inmates are to be in lockdown status. All staff not actually on watch are to muster in the main chow hall."

*****

In the brief hour since lockdown, Braniff "The Bull" Bettermann had been desperately pacing back and forth in his cell. He resembled more an animal in a zoo exhibit than an alpha prisoner. Indeed, in the three years since the judge he had "owned" sentenced him to this facility, it was only now that he felt himself every bit the convicted inmate. He may be the head prisoner in the prison of his choosing, but he was no longer in control. And it was all Warden Sir's fault. In Bettermann's world, he ruled his subjects through the fear that what Bettermann had on them was worth keeping it out of public scrutiny. Maybe he had pushed the warden too far. Maybe he pushed the warden for far too long. In any event, he had chosen to be free of his blackmailer in the worst possible way—a way which guaranteed to topple Bettermann's enterprises while sacrificing the warden's own career. Calling for a long-postponed federal audit was the one move that assured both outcomes. Now Bettermann was trapped, and he knew it. How ironic that in this facility with a fake sentence, he should now find himself threatened by actual entombment/incarceration with no avenue of escape, unless—

"Where in hell is that bloody fool guard," he said angrily, and almost as soon as he had spoken, a tall prison guard with a blank unintelligent facial expression appeared at the cell door.

"He made it...he made it! Despite a scheduled world tour to promote the virtues of aglets and grommets, he has pressed his way to us, the little people...in order to—"

"You wanted to see me, Mr. Bull?" said the prison guard, the blank facial expression never wavering.

"Ah, Mr. Javier Dumas, ever the unsophisticated, unpretentious one. Truly sarcasm is wasted on you." Again the blank stare. "Auditors from the inspector general's office will surely destroy all we have labored to build...unless..."

"Yes, Mr. Bull?"

"Mr. Dumas, tonight, there will be a fire in our cellblock, followed by a prison break. I have something very special for you and your BAR to do during the prison break. Do it well, and this will finish your obligation to me, and any and all pictures, along with their film negatives, of you and your kid sister will all belong to you."

*****

"I'm telling you," the Weasel pleaded to two very skeptical men. "I don't know why I'm allowed to 'know things.' I don't begin to consider myself anyone special. Some tell me it's a gift from God. I don't call it no gift if it keeps me in here...it's more like a curse. What I do know is that Bettermann's built an empire holding people's secrets over their heads, but he can't afford to have his own exposed. And the warden calling for an audit threatens all that Bettermann has worked so hard to accomplish. Believe me, he's not about to give it all up without a fight."

"That term *accomplish* is very dubious," Buck said. "Whatever Bettermann has done was only possible through the lives of those he was leaning on. Trust me, the feds can shut it all down, and you won't hear me complain. But I am concerned over what he plans to do about it."

"But that's the main point I overheard. He's going to make it happen sometime tonight…a fire will be started as a diversion, and then, Bettermann and other armed prisoners will stage an escape… and all this, just to have us shot by a guard with a bar, whatever that means."

"Not a 'bar,' Weasel." Chimed in the warden. "But a BAR. It stands for Browning Automatic Rifle and is the nasty big brother to the Thompson submachine gun."

"Is it called a submachine gun because it's used on submarines?"

"Good guess Weasel," continued the Warden, "but a submachine gun uses smaller-caliber pistol ammo, but the BAR uses the larger rifle rounds[9] spewed out at such a high rate, it can literally cut a man in half."

"Oh, well that makes a lot more sense. You know, Bettermann said that if that fed guy discovers anything, he'll have him murdered during the escape as well."

The meeting of the doomed counterconspirators seemed to go on and on unendingly. Finally the warden looked at his pocket watch and announced, "It's getting late, and this party should be starting soon. What if I simply lock everyone in my office until the morning? It's pretty nigh impregnable, and we should all be safe here. What do you all say about that?"

Once again, it was the Weasel who spoke without thinking. "Sounds great to me. I'm all set to spend a very noisy but otherwise safe night, and in the morning, we can have that bastard picked up. I'm all for that."

"Excellent! And what of you, Mr. Riser?"

Buck stroked his clean-shaven face, as if it were covered in a full beard, and thought for a brief moment before saying, "If we all hide out here, it will alert Bettermann of our discovery of his trap for us… giving him time to try again later. However, should we sacrifice our brief advantage, we can turn his trap for us into assured destruction for Bettermann instead."

The warden looked at Buck incredulously before saying, "You know, Mr. Riser, when you haven't been drinking booze, you're a completely different man. Where did you learn such wisdom?"

Without a moment of hesitation, Buck responded, "From my father-in-law, Mr. Saint Peter Clemmons, while we were on good terms…before I started drinking…before I started beating my wife—his daughter and grandchild."

There was a long thoughtful pause before the warden asked what the particulars of the plan were.

"No, Warden Sir, it's best that the particulars remain with me until the time we strike. If we appear natural, he'll have no suspicions raised until it is too late, and he'll be ours for certain."

*****

Benjamin Bucannon "Buck" Riser was not at all surprised by the insomnia which had plagued his mind since last evening, robbing him of desperately needed slumber. Nor was he disturbed by the fact that in spite of his calm and self-assured demeanor, while discussing upcoming events with his counterconspirators, inwardly his anxiety level felt close to panic. No, what Buck found truly surprising was that despite of all of this, his mind had clouded over in brief periods of restless dreamless sleep, just the same.

At just before dawn, Buck's all-too-precious respite became invaded, shattered, and violated by the irrepressible scream of every emergency alarm in the entire cellblock suddenly coming to life in frantic, desperate warning.

Was he hallucinating or had the door of his cell suddenly unlocked and swung noisily open? No hallucination, no dream, for as soon as the door was remotely opened, his cell became instantly inundated with blinding, choking smoke.

Suddenly the stock of a twelve-gauge shotgun was slammed painfully into his chest, causing him to gasp the more from the acrid smoke. "All right, Riser, on your feet! We're evacuating this entire cellblock."

Buck swallowed his mounting anger at the rudeness of the corrections officers' and quickly complied with the guard's demand to join an ever-growing mass of fellow inmates being assembled in the passageway and surrounded by armed guards.

Buck thought that ordinarily, the prison environment, in comparison with the outside world, seemed strange and surreal. However, amid the dense smothering smoke and the guards following emergency protocol, the prison was now transformed into something totally otherworldly, devoid of any familiarity.

Surrounded by the smoke, sirens, and guards barking orders, Buck's mind struggled to remember something important. But what could it be? Then as the group began to be quick-marched from the stricken cellblock, another sort of alarm hammered at his still not-quite conscious mind—*where were the others?* Where were his fellow counterconspirators: the Weasel, the warden, or even the government auditor? They were nowhere to be seen. Buck wanted very much to ask where they were but resisted the urge, knowing it would alert the guards of his foreknowledge of their plan.

As they marched along, Buck noticed that all distinguishing features of the once-familiar cellblock were now lost in the chaos of the fire. There were no more rooms. There were no more adjoining corridors and passageways. In fact, even in the very hallway where they marched, all but the immediate two to three feet surrounding them seemed to no longer to even exist, effectively erased by the not-too-distant conflagration.

Suddenly two pairs of arms shot out from one of the no-longer-existent passageways to grab Buck and roughly snatch him out of line. A disembodied gravelly voice said, "Out of line, Riser, you're coming with us!"

"Where are we going?" The words burst forth before Buck could stop them.

"Don't ask questions, just do as you're told!" came the harsh response, followed immediately by an even harsher blow between his shoulder blades from the stock of the same weapon used to stir his slumber.

Following this, Buck was manhandled more than marched, as he was directed down two more corridors, all as dark as ones encountered before it. Without warning, the group turned down a third hallway, and to Buck's surprise, this one was brightly illuminated and was free of the blinding, choking smoke that seemed to permeate the entire wing of the facility.

It took Buck's eyes a few moments to become readjusted to the bright unrestricted visibility conditions where he now found himself. A few moments later, and happily, there they were. A loud sigh of relief came from Buck as he greeted the Weasel, Warden Sir, and even Mr. Horace Pettibone of the Federal Office of the Inspector General. All here and all safe—so far.

It was then that Buck recognized where they were—in the last back corridor leading to the large exercise quadrangle, which was overseen by the nearby guard tower. There was someone else there as well. His mirthless laughter confirmed his presence, while his celebratoryless handclapping confirmed his purpose.

"Ah, yes!" Bull Bettermann said. "This looks like a family reunion." He pointed to a large black equipment box on the floor. "This smoke machine comes on loan to us from a fire chief who is heavily indebted to me. Just the thing to use when you want a simulated cellblock fire to disguise a prison break...which, in truth, is a kidnapping made to hide an execution."

"An execution," said Mr. Horace Pettibone over the top of his black horn-rimmed bifocal glasses, never pausing from work on his adding machine. "Whose execution?"

"Why, Mr. Pettibone, your own, of course, among others."

The ceaseless drone from the adding machine abruptly ceased.

"As newly hatched chicks beg their parents for food, your stricken face begs me for an explanation... For the last three years, whenever the subject of an audit for this facility would arise, agents of mine would immediately readjust Mr. Pettibone's schedule with higher-priority targets."

"Oh, I see, now," said Mr. Pettibone gravely. "Even when I was winning awards for most audits completed, for three consecutive years, your Mr. Bull has been breaking records as well—most money laundered, most amount embezzled.

"You've forgotten some," Bettermann said proudly. "Number of judges or other officials bribed, blackmailed, or outright bought. And we have a new category—number of judges or other officials 'rubbed out' for crossing me. Which brings us now to all of you."

"Before you begin," Buck spoke up, trying desperately to sound more confident than the loaded twelve-gauge pump-action shotgun pointed at his face would allow, "let me be an informant for once. You see, despite your size, your ambition, and your leadership skills, you're here, Bettermann, hiding from all your rivals and enemies outside. Everyone here trembles whenever your name is spoken, while you feel yourself safe from everything else. Well, those days are over because I've spent all last night writing letters to the major families and syndicates, letting them know where you're hiding out. Now tell me, Bull, if you couldn't handle one Kansas sodbuster who ain't afraid of you, how in hell are you going to deal with a dozen or more trained and dedicated assassins. If I were you, I'd make this false prison break for real and get the hell out of here, for real."

Bettermann seemed confused and indecisive for a moment, but it took only that brief moment for his resolve to be restored, the murderous grimace he wore for all of them returned, and the muzzle of the shotgun releveled onto Buck's unflinching face. "I think you may be right. It is time to leave, and you're going through that door first."

"What's so special about that particular door?" asked Mr. Pettibone with growing trepidation.

Bettermann was preparing to give a lie for an answer, like, "The door to ultimate freedom." However, Buck (maintaining his calm, courageous demeanor) forced himself not to flinch away from the barrel of the twelve-gauge pump-action shotgun but to gaze its length, into the malevolent eyes of the man who wielded it, said, "That door leads directly onto the exercise quadrangle and a chance to escape this hellhole. However, what he won't tell you is that the entire yard is overseen by a guard tower. The supervisor of that tower is Corrections Officer Javier Dumas, using the very same automatic rifle he rated Expert on in the Marines. Mr. Bettermann has ordered him to gun down anyone who comes out that door during his staged prison break, making our assassination appear in the line of duty. Now did I leave anything out, Mr. Bull Bettermann?"

"What you left out was that, once outside that door, if you all move fast and scatter, there's a chance…a bloody slim chance…that one or more might make it out alive. But if you think you can stay safe in here… I swear to God, I'll kill every one of you bastards… right here, right now. Now you got anything else to say, sodbuster, before we get this bloody party started?"

Prior to this night, both inmates and staff entertained themselves contrasting the two men (Bettermann and Riser). Aptly named, the Bull was a bully in an environment of bullies and victims, both inmates and guards alike. However, it was quickly seen by all that the more intimidating Bettermann would become, the more Buck would refuse to be intimidated. Buck's quiet strength, though seldom seen in civilian life, became a dominant character trait within a couple of months following his arrival. This phenomenon always had the effect of pouring grease on the other man's hot coals. Invariably this generated an out-of-control flare-up in the leading prisoner's life, exposing the truth that while Bettermann was a master of controlling others, he was rarely in control of himself. A fact that his diametrical opponent exploited with fanatical glee.

Buck waited an infuriatingly long moment before he answered the man with the shotgun, the man in charge, the man who controlled their fate. However, when he finally answered, Buck watched carefully to see how each well-chosen verbal arrow would strike.

"Well, Bull, I have only one last thing to say to you…my 'parting shots,' if you will. Afterward there is little doubt that we will never set eyes on each other again…in this life or the other."

"You're dang-gummed right, we won't." Bettermann hissed like a cobra, and just as menacingly. "Speak on and have done, you sorry bastard."

"You or Mr. Dummy out there may succeed in killing all of us, but in the end, it won't matter…not one bit. Because no matter what you do in the next moment, the truth is, I've beaten you. I promised Weasel I'd nail you for him, and I did just that. I've put you in the infirmary twice, and I did it in front of everyone. Your friends and followers wanted to hail me as the new Bull, but the position you coveted so much, I wouldn't touch. It's a useless title now. The real power in this joint is back in the hands of the new warden, whoever that may be. Your empire is finished for good, and for the rest of your life, you'll remember that a 'sorry sodbuster' was the one who brought you down."

Anger, like vomit, welled up from Bettermann's gut, but he just managed to keep it in check.

"And what good has it done you?" Bettermann spat the words out. "Where did all that get you but here, about to die? And for what? Because I leaned on your little cellmate? Tell me, was it worth it, sodbuster?"

"Not because you leaned on a cellmate. Because you hurt my friend, a man you're not worthy to even look in the eyes. What you did to him made you feel big and powerful. But the truth is, as small and slight as he is, Weasel is a bigger man than you are, a better man than you'll ever be."

Animal rage, like fire, flashed through Bettermann's eyes as he brought the barrel of the shotgun down hard against Buck's forehead. Immediately Buck collapsed to one knee, as a jagged line of red appeared on his scalp. The sight of his victim's blood inspired the sadistic side of Bettermann's already twisted personality. Without pause, the shotgun barrel repeated the path of the previous blow, driving its victim facedown upon the cold hard floor.

Blood streaming down into both eyes could not hide the look of defiance from Buck as he raised his head and said, "Is that the best you got? You're supposed to be the Bull here, but you hit like a bloody punk. Didn't I piss you off worse than this?"

"What in hell are you playing at, son?" Warden Sherman said silently to himself. "Keep this up, and you can forget about our one chance to make it through that door. He's going to kill us all, right here."

"Bloody right you did," said Bettermann, as he swung the butt of the gunstock hard to the side of Buck's head. "I'm the Bull here! I'm the Bull here!" Each time he said it, he brought the gunstock back across Buck's face. "Who in hell do you think you are?" he continued. "You come here, trying to start a beef with me because I busted your small weak cellmates can. But what are you in here for? What are you in here for?" He spat the words out in pure hatred as he continued to mercilessly punish Buck with the gunstock, as if he were playing golf. "You're here for abusing your little girl...someone smaller and weaker than you. You're a blasted hypocrite, you hear me?"

This last blow sent Buck sprawling on the floor some distance from his attacker. Pushing with his feet in a vain effort to stand, he then kicked at the ground frantically, desperately trying to get farther away. In the end, Bettermann caught up to his prey. Using one arm, he scooped his victim from the ground, only to throw him against a wall a short distance away. By some miracle, Buck managed to scramble to his feet, even as his opponent slowly advanced for the coup de grâce.

From his vantage point a few feet away, Warden Sherman watched the two opponents as if he was looking at a single image through the lens of a camera. Even though the barrel of the shotgun was pointed directly at Buck's head, for some reason, Bettermann was still advancing on the other man. Only then did the warden see what Bettermann, in his fiery rage, had failed to. That is, throughout the two men's entire exchange, Buck fought until the last calculated moment to keep his fingers curled against his wrists and his elbows slightly bent. This gave the illusion that Buck's arms were much shorter than they were. Finally Bettermann missed Buck's feet subtly shift from side to side, almost imperceptibly inching his way forward, closing the distance between them until the trap was set, and there was now no hope of escape.

"Now what else you got to say, you sodbusting bastard...before I get you off my back for good?" said Bettermann, his eyes narrowing as his fingers began to put pressure on the trigger.

"The last thing is, my father-in-law always taught me…if you're going to shoot someone, don't waste time throwing a tantrum… Just shoot them…LIKE THIS!"

Suddenly Buck's previously concealed hands shot forward, his fingers transmuting from bone and flesh into stone around Bettermann's trigger fingers. First alarm, then understanding, followed by fear, flashed through the gunman's eyes, as Buck's suddenly added weight forced the butt of the shotgun down, its barrel swung wildly up and up, even as Buck's hand around his forced the Bull to pull the trigger.

Bettermann's screams were lost in the roar of thunder, even as his left ear (along with much of the upper-left side of his face) disappeared in a flash of fire and lightning. Blood and bone fragments poured through the ragged gap opened into his upper and lower dentition and down his throat.

Choking and gasping caused his grip on the shotgun to relax. The moment was not lost on Buck, who twisted his body to the side, throwing Bettermann off balance and across his back to land completely disarmed on the floor at Buck's feet. With the shotgun now in his possession, Buck drove the stock of it hard into Bettermann's chest, over and over until he could feel ribs break under the onslaught and see a bloody froth ooze from his opponent's mouth. A final blow of the gunstock was redirected to Bettermann's unguarded cricoid cartilage of his throat with perfect accuracy and devastating effect.

"Shoot him, Buck, shoot him now!" Cried Weasel, on his hands and knees on the floor, on the verge of hysterics.

"Yes, Mr. Riser." Came the voice of one of the two guards in the hallway. "You deserve your victory, sir."

The other two guards, in the heat of the fight, Buck had all but forgotten them. Just as well, Buck thought as he saw their guns resting by their sides.

"Was he blackmailing you too?" Buck asked. They both nodded in the affirmative. "Well, the victory wasn't for me, and I'm not going to shoot him. I've got a much better idea. Weasel, are you familiar with Haman in the book of Esther?" Without waiting for an answer, Buck continued, "The evil he had planned for someone else—Mordechai—was how he met his end. That's called poetic justice. Now you two guards…you mind letting the warden hold your guns for a while? I got something for you to do."

The two liberated corrections officers were only too happy to relinquish their weapons to Warden Sherman. Then Buck instructed them to open the door leading out into the recreation quadrangle, and then for everyone else to stand way back of the door. Afterward Buck stood over prisoner Braniff "the Bull" Bettermann, who writhed on the floor, unable to take a decent breath, who, by now, was as weak as a newborn, his skin ashen gray, like a corpse.

Bettermann's mind was being tortured, as well as his body, to a degree he had never known. For though he knew full well of Buck's intentions, he was unable to offer more resistance than to shake his head in protest. It was a subtle but futile plea for the mercy he had never shown another.

As Buck grabbed Bettermann by the back of his collar and dragged him toward the door, Warden Sherman asked, "You look tired, son, you need any help taking out the garbage?"

"Much thanks, Warden, but no," answered Buck, handing his shotgun to Sir. "I owe this to myself."

"Right! Well, you be real careful then. I hear there's a hell of a strong wind outside."

Buck nodded his head in acknowledgment. Quickly hefting the Bull from the floor, Buck used the last of his waning strength to hold the barely conscious Bettermann in a bear hug, supporting his helpless victim beneath the armpits. Like Haman on his own gallows, Bettermann's feet dangled uselessly beneath him, then twisted back and forth, as Buck extended his arms to their fullest, shoving his opponent well outside the door and into the recreation quadrangle.

"Hey, dummy!" Buck yelled as loud as he could manage despite the beating he had suffered. "Officer Dummy, we're leaving now."

Warden Sherman grabbed Buck's jacket collar and snatched him back inside, then slammed the door shut. Even as the Bull's intended victims scrambled to distance themselves from the entry, Buck's challenge was answered by the staccato of thirty-odd-six caliber brass-coated lead fingers reaching for the sound of the voice, at

500–650 rounds per minute.[10] Beams from the searchlight probed their way through several holes that had just appeared in the heavy steel door.

It took only seconds for the forty-round magazine (used only in war against enemy aircraft[11] to empty, giving the horrific impression that a giant fairy-tale ogre had chewed up the Bull, swallowed him, only to vomit him forth again, to lie in a heap on the quadrangle pavement—unrecognizable as having ever been human.

Then too exhausted to do otherwise, Buck collapsed ignobly onto the hallway floor. Only then did Weasel gasp in fear and astonishment, as he pointed to two red streaks that appeared from Buck's upper arm and lower right side of his chest, which competed to race to an unseen finish line upon the hallway floor.

*****

Shortly before dawn, Kansas State Police arrived to restore order to the prison, only to embarrassingly find that order had already been restored by a simple announcement by Warden Sherman:

THE BULL IS DEAD! FURTHERMORE, HIS CACHE OF INCRIMINATING EVIDENCE AGAINST INMATE AND STAFF ALIKE HAS BEEN DISCOVERED BY MR. WEASEL AND SECURED. ANY AND ALL WHO HAVE BEEN UNDULY INFLUENCED/VICTIMIZED BY THE BULL ARE URGED TO SUBMIT TO AN INTERVIEW WITH THE WARDEN, WHO IS AUTHORIZED BY THE GOVERNOR TO GRANT AMNESTY TO THOSE WHO COME FORWARD PRIOR TO NOON TODAY.

AT NOON, THE ENTIRE CONTENTS OF THAT FILE SHALL BE DESTROYED BY FIRE IN THE QUAD-RANGLE. CURRENTLY LOCKDOWN STATUS IS STILL IN EFFECT. DURING THEIR ROUNDS, GUARDS WILL SCHEDULE INTERVIEWS FOR ALL INMATES INTER-ESTED IN THE WARDEN'S AMNESTY PROGRAM.

Though Weasel had not signed up for the amnesty interview, at precisely eleven o'clock, Officer Dumas escorted him to Warden Sherman's office, where he was warmly greeted by the warden, Federal Inspector General Auditor Pettibone, and the two federal marshals.

"Why—why am I here?" he stammered, confused by the presence of so many officials. "I didn't request an interview."

"No, son, you didn't," said Warden Sherman. "However, I'm here to be interviewed by you. The others are here as witnesses."

"But—but I don't understand," Weasel said with mounting panic. "Who am I to interview you? I'm just a convict. I was accused with having stolen over a billion dollars in vital company information, which resulted in a run on the banks, causing a wholesale collapse of the nation, and later, nearly the entire world's financial institutions."

"Falsely accused is more like it," chimed in Warden Sherman. "When the richest most powerful businessmen in the country discovered that you had overheard all their criminal plans, they panicked and arranged to have you shut away on trumped-up charges. Then I secretly asked the judge to have you convicted and sentenced to here, in the hopes that you might be persuaded to reveal where they had hidden their offshore gold reserves."

Warden Sherman paused to wipe the sweat from his brow, while he gestured to the auditor and the marshals that more was to come.

Weasel observed that the warden seemed to be in a physical struggle, as if whatever he wanted to reveal next fought to remain hidden, buried in the past.

"Go on, Warden Sir," assured Weasel. "It's too late to stop now. Besides whatever it is, it can't be that bad compared with everything else that has happened."

"But you don't understand!" exclaimed the warden, as he buried his head in his hands. "The worst of it is this…of all the wardens who clamored to have you sentenced to their facility… I was the only one…the only one that…knew you were completely innocent and that the charges were all false."

Torrents of tears burst unchecked from Weasel's eyes and nose, as his body shook uncontrollably. A marshal rushed over to hold up the poor man as his knees collapsed under him. "You mean that… all of the beatings…all of the sodomising…was because of you? My wife divorced me because of you. She said she just couldn't live with a criminal who did to the country what I was convicted of. For god's sake, WHY? WHY?"

Warden Sherman spoke slowly, deliberately, as if he were walking to his own execution. "Because this bloody Depression was affecting everyone…everyone…even public officials. I succumbed to a moment of temptation…and of greed…hoping that prison life would force you to reveal the location of the hidden gold."

Weasel's words were indistinguishable between laughing or crying as he said, "You fool, don't you know…immediately after my arrest, the moguls changed the location of all the stashes. I haven't broken down and talked because I have absolutely no knowledge of where those stashes are. You wasted your time and my life. May God have mercy on whatever you use for a soul."

The marshals nodded to each other but did not make a move to take the warden into custody, while they interrogated the other inmates concerning Bull Bettermann and his reign of terror. After all, the marshals could afford to take their time. There was nowhere for the warden to escape.

In the morning, they discovered Warden Sherman hanging from the ceiling of his office. A hastily scribbled letter on his desk simply read, WEASEL, FORGIVE ME…PLEASE!

CHAPTER 14

The Breathing of Life

Days come, and days go, so progressed the summer. And Polly (along with most of the state of Kansas) wished that the days would not include those awful blinding windstorms, with their inescapable and inexhaustible dust and dirt. However, the dust storms came anyway; not every day, to be sure, just enough to smother farms, towns, and hopes. It also smothered the resolve of those foolish enough to cling to the notion that their efforts could somehow sweep away the dust and dirt that invaded edifices, both public and private, to rob those within of any sense of safety or security.

Days come, and days go until it was midsummer, and in Polly's mind, the passage of time was marked by the mother's worsening temperament, and this grew to trouble the girl greatly. Without knowing why, for the entire last week of July, Polly had felt compelled to stay close to Aunt Louise (who asked that Polly call her that after the girl had revealed her plans for Hasenpfeffer) on the pretext of helping her with her housework. One day, while the two were preparing lunch, Polly suddenly asked, "Aunty Louise, are you depressed?"

For a moment, Louise looked as if she couldn't breathe. She quickly recovered and said, "Land sakes, child, the things that go through that head of yours. Why would a little girl like you be so concerned with grown folks' issues? Where in the world did you hear that word anyway?"

Polly quickly explained that last year, she and Sister Bedelia Knowles (I said that right...for once) were at the Garden City

Reference Library, looking up a word they had heard on the radio—
psychology. "I told Biddy—oh, darn… Bedelia… Bedelia!—that the
first part of the word sounded like *cycle*. She said to me, 'No, dear,
that's PSYCH, and they do sound very much alike, and in a way, they
both help get you where you're trying to go, sort of, and they both
even go around in circles.

"Anyway," Polly said, "there were other words that went with
psychology. That's why I asked if you were depressed."

"What would you know about depression?" Aunt Louise asked,
her voice sounding low and menacing, like a guard dog.

Boldly Polly observed that at the beginning of summer, Louise
was full of smiles and laughter. But now, she always seemed sad and
irritable. Polly had even heard her mumbling to herself, "I hate this.
How can anyone live in all this filth?"

At first, it looked as if Louise was going to be quite cross with
her as she noticed her aunt's lips suddenly tightened, and her eyes
reddened behind large pools of tears. Instead Aunt Louise took Polly
by the hand and sat the girl upon her lap at the kitchen table. There,
with her head pressed firmly on the back of Polly's neck, she moved
back and forth, as if she sat on a rocking chair. Then Polly noticed
that the rocking was keeping time to the song she could barely be
heard to hum "Great Is Thy Faithfulness." Quietly Polly sang the
lyrics:

> Great is they faithfulness, Oh God my father
> There is no shadow of turning with thee.
> Thou changest not, thy compassions they fail
> not.
> As thou hast been, thou forever shalt be.
> Great is they faithfulness; Great is they
> faithfulness.
> Morning by morning, new mercies I see.
> All I have needed thine hand hath provided.
> Great is thy faithfulness, LORD unto me.

When the chorus was finished, Louise continued to rock back and forth, with Polly on her lap. After a while, she quietly addressed the bundle on her knees. "So, Polly, I believe that 'Great Is Thy Faithfulness' was your mother's favorite hymn."

"Oh, it was!" said Polly. "D-did you know my ma?"

"Yes, I did, child," Louise answered thoughtfully. "She had taught me that song when she was my choir directress. Since then, it's become my favorite one also."

With that, a silence ensued between them, making Polly think that their discourse was over. Finally Louise spoke up, "To answer your question...YES... I believe I am somewhat depressed. You see, I take a great deal of pride in seeing that my house is as clean as possible. It was the one thing in life that I thought I could control. Now those dust storms have taken all that away."

Polly looked thoughtful for a moment before saying, "Days come...and days go..."

She had said it so low that Louise was about to ask her what she had said. Suddenly Polly flew off her knees. "It was the last thing my Grandma Molly said to me, on the day she died, 'Days come... and days go...all days...every day...even the bad days. Like a single breath, a day comes to us, and then, almost without noticing it, it is gone.' She was talking about people's lives...her life"—sniff—"But then, while sitting with you, it suddenly came to me..."

"What did, child?" asked Aunt Louise, taking a genuine interest.

"Why the dust storms, Aunt Louise. The dust storms are like— NO! The dust storms ARE a breath. Don't you see, Auntie? 'Days come...and days go...' The dust storms blew in...they're going to blow out again. They MUST...they MUST. The dust storms are as much a part of the rhythm of life on the earth as our own breathing is. We breathe in, we breathe out. Those dust storms are like the earth breathing. In and out. Here today and—"

"Gone tomorrow," Louise finished for her." Days come...and days go."

While they were talking, eight-year-old Rusty (Russell Russell IV) knocked on the French doors leading to the kitchen. "Hey,

Mom! I don't know how urgent this is, but a letter was just delivered for Polly."

"How wonderful," said Aunt Louise "Please, come on in." Rusty entered and placed the message into his mother's outstretched hand, then stood next to her, opposite Polly. After a precursory scan of the envelope, she said to her son, "Ah, yes! Steamed, I should think. Rusty, what does it say?"

The boy had turned beet red from embarrassment before answering. "The big kids, they—"

Suddenly his mother interrupted, "Now, now, Rusty, nobody likes a tattletale."

"Yes, ma'am," he said as she handed the message to Polly and then promptly left the room.

After taking a moment to read the letter, she said, "It's from Reverend Knowles and Bi… Bedelia—whew! They say that room in the parsonage is ready for me. They also say that it has been a long summer—they're telling us—and that they'll be here to pick me up the afternoon of the first Friday in August, sometime after breakfast. It also says that they have contacted my friend in Dodge City at the library. They say that the book I ordered on Egyptian embalming and mummifying practices, along with my new library card, is scheduled for delivery to correspond with the arrival of the Knowles. The curator has reviewed the book personally and says that it's a true masterpiece."

"Wow!" said Rusty, listening from outside the door.

"Rusty!" shouted his mother. "Go and get the others. We have an important family conference."

"Oh, boy!" Rusty said aloud, but inwardly hoped the meeting was not about him.

As Rusty's footsteps were heard racing down the hallway, Polly turned to Aunt Louise and asked, "Aunt Louise, do you need either Uncle Russ or me to be present at the family conference? If not, I'd like to talk to Uncle Russ about something important."

"Oh, I guess we can manage without you two for a while. I can brief you later, if I must. Off you go then."

With that, the girl was off, racing to see her uncle. In her haste, she had nearly run into Rhonda and Rochelle but deftly managed to dodge the sisters by spinning her body to break her momentum and then running along the opposite wall.

After recovering from their near-collision, the girls turned to each other with puzzled looks, as if to say, *What's got into the princess?*

CHAPTER 15

Adventures in Stoney Lonesome (Continued); Twenty-Four minus One

For the last two hours, Benjamin Bucannon Riser had been unsuccessful in his struggle to escape the nightmarish barrier which prevented him from reaching the light above. He tried to move his arms, to use his massive strength to tear through the darkness that enveloped him, but they were no longer his to command. He tried to call out to someone—anyone—who might be beyond the darkness to come to his aid, but he could not utter a word. Even his mind seemed a prisoner to the blackness which clouded his every sense, preventing his very thoughts from going forth. All the maddening midnight permitted him to have was a realization of paralysis, along with fear and dread of his complete and utter helplessness.

What was that! A sound perhaps? It was faint, almost imperceptible, but he was certain it had been there, nonetheless. Suddenly there it was again, louder, more urgent than before. And then, it came again a third time, still louder, more insistent than the one before. In spite of the black thing which had paralyzed his body, as well as his mind, still it was there, piercing the ebony envelope from somewhere beyond. It was demanding his attention, compelling him to fight the darkness and reach for the light, and it was unmistakably calling his name.

The voice felt as if it were heralding new vitality and purpose. First, Buck pictured in his mind that he was ripping at the envelope, sweeping away the quicksand that entrapped him. Then he was swimming, each stroke bringing him ever closer to the light above.

Dr. Lyndon Mattock stood next to the gurney, writing instructions for the nursing staff on the wooden clipboard it carried. He was just finishing when Buck, fighting off the last effects of the anesthesia, slowly regained consciousness. Replacing the record on its hook at the foot of the bed (and his pencil to his lab coat pocket), he said, "You have just got to be the luckiest son of a gun that has ever lived in the entire state of Kansas. It's a miracle, and I don't cotton to using that term lightly. Of all the machine-gun rounds spitting around that night, it seems that only one of them managed to hit you, and it miraculously passed clean through you without lodging. The only real damage was that after piercing your right upper arm—just missing your brachial artery—it ploughed into your chest, completely severing the last floating rib on the right rib cage. You're in recovery, following close to three and a half hours of surgery to control hemorrhage from both areas as well as removal of the severed rib. The good news is, you had twenty-four of them, and the loss of an otherwise insignificant floating rib will hardly be missed."

"You couldn't save the rib, but you still saved m-my life," Buck said groggily.

"Yes!"

An awkward silence began to ensue, until Buck asked, "Doctor, when can I see Warden Sherman?"

"Not until his wake at the end of this week," Mattock said. Then seeing the grave quizzical look on Buck's face, he added," Apparently Warden Sherman hung himself during the night after his interview and confession. I'm afraid to say it, but a new permanent warden may not be selected for two to three weeks and may not arrive until another thirty days after that. However, if you're anxious to speak to any warden in the interim, the commandant of the military wing, Colonel James "Blackjack" Skybolt, will assume the duties of acting warden of the civilian wings, as well. He will be assisted by US Marshal Babel, along with that inspector general representative…a Mr. Peabody, will share duties of putting this place back together."

"Pettibone!" Buck corrected.

"Huh? Pardon me?"

"His name is Pettibone… Mr. Horace Pettibone. Please, get it right, the man deserves at least that."

"Oh well, Pettibone, Peabody, what difference does it make?"

"To you, probably nothing… Dr. MATCHHEAD."

"No, no! It's MATTOCK… Oh, yeah, I um, concede your point. Pettibone it is."

"Thanks." Satisfied with his first victory of the day, Buck asked, "Did Warden Sherman give any indication he was planning to kill himself?"

"He left a note for Weasel, that was all. Except the switchboard reported that he made three phone calls just prior to his demise. The first call was to the governor. The second call went to an Agent Pete Bartholomew at FBI headquarters in DC. The last call was made at one o'clock this morning to a Mrs. Geraldine Pointer in Wichita. As of yet, I have no idea what any of the calls were about. However, shortly after the last call, he was gone. Now the US Marshals had overheard his confession to Weasel. And you know what? The warden—"

"STOP!" demanded Buck. However, it was not so much the emphasis in his voice but the look of implied threat that flashed through Buck's face that caused Mattock to bite his tongue, to bar the escape of a single subsequent syllable.

Buck continued, "Regardless of an isolated mistake he might have made, or to any extent that the Bull may have dominated his life…in the end, the warden had found his courage and strength again. In the end, the warden had regained his manhood. In the end, the warden I knew was a good man, let me assure you. And a good man is how I want to remember him. Understand?"

"Yes," Lyndon replied, as he felt the conversation becoming more somber. Not willing to leave their discourse on that note, he offered, "I've known Sherman since I first came here as an intern, some ten years ago. He was someone I grew to respect greatly. And you're right, he was a good man. I think I'll never forget the last conversation we had two days ago before his death. He could talk about nothing but you. He talked about what you had done to land you in here, and he talked about how you've changed. I concur with everything he said about you. But there's something that baffles me about you."

"And what would that be?" answered Buck.

"The judge believed your testimony that you had no intention to kill your daughter, and yet you threw a pickax at her. How in hell could you do that?"

"I guess I just wasn't thinking," Buck said, feeling his face flush with anger.

"Don't get angry now, Buck, I'm not here to criticize or judge you. You've already had your day in court. I'm just trying to point out a contrast, a dichotomy if you will…between a man who committed felony assault against a child, explaining that 'I just wasn't thinking…' and a man who meticulously planned a campaign to overthrow the prison terror…placing your own life in jeopardy…all to protect your sodomized cellmate…and all culminating in the singlehanded thwarting of a prison break and assassination attempt on two government officials, as well as yourself and your cellmate. And you thought out and planned your every move, days in advance. It's hard to believe the two stories are about the same man."

Buck shook his head in protest and said, "I just did what I felt I had to, Dr. Mattock. Bettermann was big, too big…too big. He needed to be cut down, like a rotten tree. Please don't make a big deal out of it."

Dr. Mattock raised his hand to object as he retorted, "But that's just it, it is a big deal. When I first performed surgery on you, it was to repair a shattered right knee from a gunshot administered to prevent your rampage against a small child. Today I have labored to repair your arm and torso from entry and exit wounds from a single gunshot, received while you strove to protect others lives from certain death. You've changed, Buck. What's more, you've caused me to change as well."

"That's my point about a big deal," argued Buck. "How in the world can a poor relatively uneducated dirt farmer possibly change a man like yourself?"

Dr. Mattock was thoughtful for a moment, while he deliberately slowed the conversation down for emphasis. "Please, let me explain. At first, I truly hated your guts! Any man who would do what you did to a child deserved to be hung. Mere incarceration is too good for him. Whipping him until he's skinned alive is too good for him."

"You seem to have strong feelings about this," Buck interrupted.

"Yes! Yes, I do!" Mattock answered without hesitation. "My eight-year-old sister was kidnapped from home by the gardener, raped all night long, and then finally decapitated. You're bloody right I have strong feelings about this."

Once again, silence came between the two men, while Buck seemed as if he were about to speak, but the ground was too dangerous. Then he decided to speak, come what may. "And after you found him, what then?"

"Say!" Mattock began in a voice between surprised and wrapped in unbelief. "How'd you know I went hunting for him?"

"Because had she been my sister, I would have. What then?"

"Well," Mattock began slowly. "Despite the FBI warning me to stay out of it, I looked for him, and I found him down in Texas, about to escape into Mexico…just four days before a beleaguered and overworked FBI caught up to me…long enough for the nest of fire ants I staked him facedown over, basted in blackstrap molasses, to leave him fit for any university Science Department. The judge severely reprimanded me for going after him and that the FBI worked hard for evidence to convict him and didn't need a revenge-seeking vigilante. She added, what if I had been wrong and killed the wrong one? In the end, the FBI confirmed the evidence I had gathered and ruled that, though deplorable, I saved the state the cost of an execution and that the suspect's death was justifiable."

"Good for you!" Buck said in genuine sincerity.

"So you see," Dr. Mattock continued, "why I have a real problem with anyone who would harm a child, especially a little girl. Believe me, when you first came here, I had more than just angst against you—I despised you. However, that was back then, but today, I have nothing but respect for you. You've changed, Buck. In fact, I'd say that you have turned your character completely around."

Buck lowered his head, cupped his chin in his massive hand, and wrestled with a thought, a memory which seemed so distant, he wondered if they were truly his or if they belonged to someone else, whom he merely heard about. Suddenly he raised his head and asked, "Dr. Mattock, just what do you attribute this complete change and even reversal of my personality?"

Mattock answered without delay, "Oh, I know exactly why you've changed, Buck, you've been drinking that alcohol so long, it became a part of your body and mind. In fact, every cell in your body craved for the stuff just to allow you to function normally. But when you do drink, your 'normal' is a monster. However, there's no booze allowed in prison, and after I repaired your leg, it didn't take long for you to start going through the hell of sobering up. Believe me, at times, I thought you were going to leave this world, but I guess you were too bloody stubborn to die. But I will say this, the monster you were seems to have died instead, and in its place, you've become a real hell of a man…the man you were always meant to be. And so, I concur fully with Warden Sherman, who said that you are a completely different person when you're sober. Therefore, never ever take another drink, Buck. Don't ever use alcohol ever again…not even beer, lest the old you should return."

CHAPTER 16

An Unselfish Prayer

Days come, and days go. On this day, Mr. Randolph Russell III sat on a wooden rocking chair, near the end of a sprawling back porch, contemplating the myriad of problems confronting him; that is, his wife, the house, and the dust storms. This trio had, of late, ceased to be three separate problems but had somehow melded into a single entity, which mocked and defied his confused and throbbing brain's powers of reason.

"Dear God," he said through clenched hands and through clenched teeth. "Please help me. I don't know what to do anymore. My wife's down and out because she can't keep the house clean. The house won't stay clean because of the dust storms outside, and the dust storms are on account of the drought. I can't control the weather, Lord. Please, please help me."

When Russ looked up at the end of his prayer, there was Polly seated on the floor of the porch next to his feet. She was looking up at him and smiling.

"I don't get it," Russ said, feeling perturbed by Polly. "I'm here, pouring out my heart to God, and you're smiling all along?"

"Oh, Uncle Russ, please don't be cross," she said as she stood before him and placed an arm around his neck and shoulders. "I'm smiling because I was praying much the same prayer just the other day. I'm also smiling because until then, most of my prayers were pretty selfish ones, like, 'Lord, please change Pa and make him like Uncle Russ so I can have my family back together again.'"

"Why do you say that was selfish, Polly?"

"Because it was all about what I wanted for me, not what was best for Pa or for those around him. I could have… I should have been praying that God would bring out all of the best traits that he placed inside of him so that Pa could be a blessing to the town, and not its bully."

"Fine, Polly, but why all the smiles?"

"Oh, yeah, God also showed me that I'm really not in control of anything, but that ultimately, God is in control of all things."

Polly paused and thought a moment before adding, "Last night I dreamed about Paul and Silas, in jail. They were beaten and in chains and certainly unable to control anything that was happening to them. They could have been selfish and prayed for their release. Instead despite all their suffering, they sang and praised God like they were in church, not in prison. And when they lifted God up in praise…when they lifted God up, higher than their problems, God showed that he really was in control of…EVERYTHING."

CHAPTER 17

Farewell to Stoney Lonesome; Part 1: Mr. and Mrs. Pointer

Like the swallows returning to San Juan Capistrano, reporters from every radio and newspaper agency in the state of Kansas suddenly descended on Leavenworth Federal Prison. Even some of the national newspapers and magazines arrived. In airplanes and buses, they arrived. In rented trucks and cars, they arrived. By the scores and by the hundreds, they arrived, and all of them determined to interview Mr. Benjamin Buccannon "Buck" Riser to discover the truth behind the rumors that one man was singlehandedly responsible for putting down a prison break, a kidnapping, and assassination of four individuals, including an agent of the inspector general, the warden of this very prison, as well as a fellow inmate and himself. His actions, reportedly, helped to topple a criminal network which reached throughout the state of Kansas. And so they arrived hungry—hungry to twist and turn any story of the man into that of a hero, a superhero, a legend, an immortal, and perhaps, worst of all, a celebrity.

As hungry as they were, the reporters were anxious to interview the man himself. However, unable to find him, the reporters found plenty of fodder for their stories via a host of fellow inmates who personally witnessed Buck's three attacks on Bull Bettermann, ultimately defeating him each time. And each time, the farmer from Garden City had flatly refused to assume the mantel of Bettermann's successor. This part of the story seemed completely incredulous to them, leaving them skeptical and full of unbelief. Some of them had even decided to return home and declare to their editors that it had all been a hoax but cancelled their departure plans when acting corrections officer, Captain Javier Dumas, opened the prison morgue for them to inspect Bettermann's remains, who further reported that at the time of his death, he was being supported by Buck, a man clearly a foot shorter and over one hundred pounds lighter than his opponent. Any residual doubts some of them stubbornly held onto where assuaged by Federal Inspector General Auditor Horace Pettibone's eyewitness account of the final struggle between the two men, along with his sworn testimony that just prior to this Herculean feat, Buck had been severely beaten by Bettermann using the butt of a twelve-gauged shotgun.

To this last report, Javier Dumas informed reporters that on the night in question, he had been assigned to the guard tower off the quadrangle. He then announced that what he said next would sound crazy; however, he knew what he had seen. He had received numerous awards for expert marksmanship with the Browning Automatic Rifle, while in the military, and still possessed better than 20-20 vision.

"Believe me!" Dumas insisted. "I know what I saw. When the doors to the quadrangle opened, prisoner Bettermann could be clearly seen in the doorway, and I'd swear on a stack of Bibles, the man was floating. I mean, his body was moving forward, but his feet never touched the ground. As he continued to advance, I could see he was being held up by his arms like a baby. Before I opened fire on him with my BAR, Buck pushed Bettermann further into the exercise yard, then disappeared back inside, leaving Bettermann to his fate. That's when I opened fire on the prisoner. Now here's the remains."

Reporters ascribed to Buck's powers and abilities, which set him above and beyond those of lesser humans, to include strength, resistance to pain, and uncanny patience. Of late, a new power had been added to the list—the ability of invisibility. Since they had flocked to this prison, not a single reporter had so much as set eyes on Buck, the reason for the invasion.

The truth was that Buck had not divulged his current whereabouts, even to his cellmate, Weasel, lest he be enticed to reveal it to the news correspondents.

Acting commandant, Colonel James "Blackjack" Skybolt, twisted back and forth in the swivel chair in his new office, chomping repeatedly on an expensive unlit cigar (his habit whenever he pondered a new problem). Looking down the length of the hand-rolled cylinder of the finest tobacco (as if it were the barrel of a gun), he narrowly regarded the man seated on the opposite side of the freshly polished mahogany desk.

"You can't hide from them indefinitely," he said while savoring the flavor of the cigar. "And why the hell would you, son? You're a bloody hero now. There's hardly a corner of this man's country that doesn't know the name of Buck Riser."

"That's just it, sir," Buck replied. "They've already made me into something larger than life."

"What's wrong with that, son?" Colonel Skybolt asked as he finally took the cigar from his mouth and pointed it at Buck to emphasize each word. "Most folks I know would give their right arm for this kind of recognition."

"And they are welcome to it, as far as I'm concerned. All I ever wanted was to be left alone, to do my time in peace and quiet. Is that too much to ask, sir?"

"I'm afraid so, son," he said, returning the cigar to his clenched teeth. "Unless I ban them from this prison."

"Hey! Sounds great, sir!" Buck said as he showed some enthusiasm for the first time during this conversation. "Can we do that, sir?"

"I'm afraid not. It could open a fully certified crap storm for possibly violating the very constitution I'm sworn to protect and uphold."

"Darn!"

"About the most I can do is to deny them access to you by keeping you in the hold. And before you say, 'Great, sir! Let's do just that,' I'll disobey Governor Patton's direct orders. So understand that what I say next…you did not hear from me… I never said it. But just prior to my predecessor declaring a retreat from this world, the FBI discovered that he had made three phone calls. "The first call was to Governor Patton himself, informing him, ahead of the press, of an eyewitness account of your exploits pertaining to the deceased prisoner, Bettermann.

"The second was to a friend at the FBI who quickly found the whereabouts of one Geraldine Pointer in Wichita. The third and final call was to her."

"So what is that supposed to mean to me?" Buck interrupted the colonel.

Without taking offense, Skybolt continued, "It means that she was informed that a Mr. Wayne Pointer was, in fact, completely innocent of any and all crimes for which he was convicted of and sentenced to here, as your cellmate."

Buck's spirits began to rise again. "If Sherman told her, then he also must have told the Governor—" Colonel Skybolt raised his cigar-filled hand to cut him short.

"As a result of that first phone call of Sherman's, Governor Patton himself is on his way here, even as we speak, to publicly announce his pardon of you and Mr. Weasel, along with an expunging of his conviction. Ever the opportunist, he obviously wants to take advantage of the press already present to garner some free publicity for himself. After all, nothing looks better in the next election, than his picture with a genuine hero. That'll be enough of a story to finally get those sharks off you."

*****

As abruptly as they had arrived, reporters from every radio and news agency in Kansas departed hence to return to their various hovels. They departed in Governor Patton's wake in order to digest their meal of raw facts and testimonies, ultimately to produce defecations of libelous contrivances.

In time, Buck's apprehensions over his newfound notoriety would prove as groundless as the myriad reasons people have given for maintaining confidence in the promises of politicians made at impromptu press gatherings. Buck quickly discovered that as the prison settled down and returned to regular boring routine, so his much-feared fame rapidly began to wane and disappear, almost as quickly as the drying of ink in the press releases. And he was glad for it.

Commandant (acting) Skybolt had hoped that Governor Patton would have seen fit to provide transportation for the newly pardoned back to their homes. Unfortunately no sooner had the flash from the camera's receded, that the governor's feigned concern for the two men departed as well. Commandant Skybolt was preparing to order four of his guards to drive them home; however, he remembered to look at their intake forms, then placed a call to their contacts. He reasoned that the prison had just weathered an emergency, which could have developed into a full-blown riot. He would need every one of his correction officers.

Toward noon of the next day, Correction Officer Captain Javier Dumas announced through the bars of their cell that the two cellmates' transportation had arrived outside of the main gate, and that he was personally collecting their belongings at the main security checkpoint.

Buck was anxious to leave but noticed that Weasel had not moved from the edge of his cot but sat there with his head buried in his hands.

"You don't look much like a man being set free to return home," Buck said, with just a hint of sarcasm.

"Buck!" Weasel replied sadly with his head still entombed in his hands. "I'm not sure I have a home to go back to."

"I don't understand. Your wife's in a car, at the gate, all the way from Wichita, waiting for you."

"She's not my wife anymore," he said in anguish. "As soon as the judge said 'Guilty!' Geraldine filed for divorce. When I needed her to believe in me most, she left me, saying, I wasn't a good man anymore. She said I was now a criminal…a bad man and was, in some way, responsible for all the banks failing. She called me a bad man. Then

Mr. Bettermann comes along and sees to it that I'm not even a man anymore. That bastard turned me into his woman...into his whore."

"You're telling me that you don't think you're a man because you were raped by that animal? Believe me, there was absolutely nothing you could have done to prevent that. But you survived that...you survived all that he did, day after day, and have come out of it alive. Bettermann was the Bull of this prison, but he didn't beat me, and he didn't survive me. In the same way, no matter what he did to you, in the end, he couldn't beat you either. From where I see it, I'd say that makes you a better man than Bettermann ever was."

"I hear you, Buck," said Weasel. "But what about faithless Geraldine?"

"You have to understand, Geraldine is like so many others who believe everything they read in the newspaper. They believe their politicians and other officials are infallible, that everyone in prison belongs there, and that bad things only happen to bad people...and if you're here, it must be because you're a bad man. Regardless of all of that, a part of Geraldine must still believe in you. After she received Sherman's call, she wasted no time in getting here. Now I want you to think on this whenever you start to be depressed over your experiences in prison—the man who hurt you is dead. The man responsible for you being here so that you could be hurt is dead as well. Finally you're leaving this hellhole and going back home to someone who once loved you and can easily love you again, but you're going to have to cultivate the land where her love can grow...you're going to have to forgive her. Everything that has happened here is in the past. Let the past go, man! Let it all go! Then reach out...and make a glorious new future happen."

*****

A sense of the surreal flooded Buck's mind as he and Weasel walked escorted, for the last time, toward the last fenced gate of the facility. Just beyond the fence stood an older, much more heavily beat-up, version of Sheriff Pucket's sedan, only of brighter cheerier livery.

As they approached this last gate, their escort, Commandant Skybolt, abruptly halted and performed a textbook perfect about-face maneuver to stand before the other two.

"There's not much point in bringing charges or of even suing those moguls," Commandant Skybolt said as he extended a hand toward Weasel. "They're too big and too powerful. However, our Inspector General Auditor, Mr. Pettibone, has managed to find unreported funds in excess of our budget. He tells me that the law allows for a ten percent finder's fee for discovering Bettermann's secret stashes and ledgers. Therefore, the government of the United States wishes to thank you..." he concluded by placing an envelope in Weasel's hands.

Quickly viewing the envelope's contents, Weasel exclaimed, "OH MY GOD! There's more than—"

Raising his hand as a gesture to cut him off, Skybolt said, "There's no need to say how much it is, Mr. Pointer...EVER!"

"Oh, yes...yes, of course...and thank you." Then turning to Buck, he held the envelope under his arm to warmly shake Buck's hand with both of his. He held his hand for a longer moment than usual before saying (with tears in his eyes), "I...I...d-don't...know how to begin to thank you...you saved my life, Buck, and freed me from that...that...son of a b-bi..."

"Thank me, Weasel, by forgiving your wife and, together, having a good life."

"I-I d-do forgive her...without reservation...with all of my heart. Again, Buck... Colonel Skybolt...thank you...more than I can possibly express."

With this last expression of gratitude, he was past the last gate, past the last barrier from freedom and a new life. As the gate closed behind him, he looked back only once to see the now-closed entrance from the only decent and proper aspect from the outside. Only when he turned around again did he happen to see her in the rear seat behind the driver.

The cabby exited and hurried to her door. As he opened the door with a bit more pomp than circumstances warranted, he said to himself, "Hank, old boy, you've driven a lot of broads in your day.

I think that this is the first time you've been on the road with a real genuine lady." Then aloud he said as he offered his hand to help her up, "Dear lady, please be gracious and accept this hand as gnarled, ruff, and hopelessly unworthy as it is."

"Graciously offered, so graciously accepted," she said, taking the pro-offered hand.

And then, both Wayne and Geraldine stood, nervously regarding each other; no one feeling confident enough to approach the other, each one fearful of the others' rejection. Finally the cabby, still clasping Geraldine's hand, released it while gently guiding her forward. An instant later, she was in the strong embrace of her former-and-soon-to-be-again husband; her legs swung carelessly behind her as she collapsed onto his neck in a torrent of convulsive sobs.

Suddenly the two were now seated in the cab, without any recollection of having moved from where they stood, still locked in their embrace; she snuggled contentedly upon his lap. As the engine of the conveyance roared to life, Wayne reached toward the driver, a large bill in his hand, saying, "How much is it back to Wichita?"

The driver politely waved his hand away and said, "Sir, there is no charge. A Mr. Pettibone hired me, care of the federal government, and has paid for my services in full, including, gas, mileage, fees, and even a sizable tip. Therefore, sir, I must happily decline further remuneration."

"Well, then, let's be gone from this hellhole. But there's no hurry... I'm already in heaven."

CHAPTER 18

The Two Letters

Days come and days go, until one day came, and it was the end of summer.

Although Pastor Knowles was known for almost always being on time, the same could not be said of Polly. Since Knowles wasn't scheduled to arrive for another three hours, at two o'clock in the afternoon, she decided to pack her two old alligator leather travel bags early. She had been at it for a whole two hours and was only halfway finished. It didn't help that Rusty Russell sat on the edge of the bed (keeping her company). As she worked to fill one bag, a small dimpled hand of a cherub would creep into her work area to gently probe the scaly face of the predator on the bag's cover (in the boy's defense, it should be pointed out that all children—even Polly—had always been fascinated by the bags' use of a single whole alligator skin, with the head of the creature prominently displayed on the cover). It was easy to imagine the animal still lived; its lips, though frozen in a permanent scowl, seemed to issue perpetual challenge to all who dared to approach.

Little eight-year-old Rusty was so unaware of his surroundings, he could never find his own clothes to dress himself in the mornings without his mother's help. Upon each embarrassing incident, his mother would always remark that, "I do declare, boy, you'd likely forget your own head in the morning if the good Lord hadn't bolted it on already."

Each morning only served to collaborate his mother's testimony. However, since the day that Polly arrived, Rusty's, as well as all his male siblings', ability to concentrate and to notice the most minute detail in Polly's appearance would give the lie to his mother's complaint. However, though he had not spoken, preferring rather to quietly observe his temporary sister's eyes, as their deep crimson background failed to be extinguished by the copious swollen teardrops which, at first, were content to merely fatten themselves and accumulate at the edges of her equally swollen eyelids. But now, stimulated by his reassuring and understanding touch upon her shoulder, the tears would be content no longer but escaped the ruptured dam. Once free, they plummeted en mass down her cheeks and neck to finally cascade down the front of her blouse, some even daring to venture down the back of Rusty's shirt.

"Oh! That's why Dad taught us to always keep a clean handkerchief in our pocket," Rusty said to himself as Polly accepted his pro-offered token to apply to her draining eyes and nose and to dab at the tears she felt run down her cheeks. However, one look at the strained expression on her host's face told her that her efforts had only worsened her appearance.

"Here!" Polly said, handing back the handkerchief. "You might as well do the honors."

"Gladly, my lady," Rusty said as he took back the instrument and, having folded it neatly, held it under the girl's chin and said, as formally sounding as he knew how, "Madam, a spot of spittle if you please."

A quarter of an hour later, Polly asked if her face was clean yet? To which he responded that it was as clean as they can make it without a basin of water. They both laughed.

"You know something, Angel? When we heard that you were coming to stay, us older kids were trying to calm the younger ones down, telling them it was only for this summer."

"That's strange!" said Polly. "Reverend Knowles told me pretty much the same thing and for the same reason. You see, I was a bit out of sorts on the way up here, even before my father hurt me."

"Hurt you! From the way your leg looked and from what your pastor and sheriff told my mom and dad, he didn't just hurt you—he tried to kill you."

Polly felt her face flush with anger as she said, "That's not true... That's not true! Pa may be a little rough on me sometimes, especially when I make him angry, but he'd never do something...anything like that to me. Daddies are supposed to love their daughters, not murder them."

"Yeah, they're supposed to is right, but that don't mean they always do. You really are a flippety-jibbette. Open your eyes...sometime. Fathers who love their daughters don't throw axes at them or attack them at their mother's funeral or lock them in closets for days without food. Fathers who love their daughters don't do anything like that, only fathers who hate and despise them."

The two children looked shocked. Rusty had never spoken to her like that before, and he instantly regretted it. An uneasy silence ensued between the two, like a cease-fire between two armies, preparing for their next sortie.

Suddenly the dark upstairs hallway erupted with the deafening sound of four bedroom doors, which were snatched open and then released in midsequence, to crash themselves as one against the ceramic-coated wall guards.

Then came the sound of a stampede, reminiscent of the annual running of the bulls through the streets of Barcelona, Spain. However, the sound of this stampede, which invaded Polly's room to assail the ears of the two children within, was the result of nearly the entire rostrum of Russell Sprouts barreling down the hallway and jostling for the front of the herd. Naturally the four oldest children (ages fourteen through eleven, by reason of their increased size, weight, reach, experience, as well as aggression, would always result in the big kids complete domination over their eight younger siblings [aged ten through age three]).

Today, however, would prove different, for as the fates would have it, the cover-all suspenders of the oldest child, Randal, became tangled in the doorknob when it opened, causing the room's three inhabitants to stumble and fall in a heap in the center of the hallway.

Though it took only a moment to extradite the offending suspender, it was long enough to allow the other Russell Sprouts to scramble over them and take the lead.

Now panting from the effort of catching up to the others, Randal stopped in front of Polly's open bedroom door to announce, "Hey, guys, come on! A big delivery truck just pulled up out front with another car. It looks like Reverend Knowles is here."

*****

Reverend Knowles was shocked to see how quickly Polly could run. Even before the car had come to a complete stop, and before the dust had settled on the road, the girl had appeared seemingly from nowhere to deftly weave her way, around, through, and almost over the heads of the assembled Russell Sprouts in order to emerge at the throngs' vanguard. He was also equally shocked to feel how much weight she had gained over the summer when the girl flew headlong into him. He had no time to raise his arms to catch the ballistic child as she hurled herself toward him. However, upon impact, like a mantis, her slender arms snapped up and around his neck, entrapping him in a nigh-unbreakable noose of prepubescent affection.

Rusty watched the girl liberally paint her pastor's face with wet kisses and was equally amazed (and a little bit jealous) that Polly had any saliva remaining after he had cleaned her face earlier, or that her lips could function at all after the way she had complained of facial fatigue from continuously expectorating into his handkerchief.

Polly elected to remain in her pastor's strong arms as the two deliverymen set about their work. It was now her turn to be amazed with the apparent ease with which they picked up such a large and supposedly heavy shipping crate to deposit it, almost effortlessly, on the ground alongside the front porch of the house. Two pry bars were then produced from thick rawhide leather holsters they wore around their waists and, in no time, had forced open the outer crate to reveal the beautifully black-lacquered and brass-accented box within.

After securing the remnants of the shipping crate in the truck, the older of the two deliverymen produced a well-weathered clipboard. "I need a parent to sign the receipt," he said, waving the clipboard for all to see.

"I'll sign for it," said Mrs. Russell, taking the board and a dull stub of a pencil he offered her. Once signed, she was given a copy of the receipt, plus two envelopes. The first envelope was addressed:

To: The Russell Sprouts
From: Polly Quashi'miuoo Riser

Instructions 1: Please DO NOT open the black lacquered box BEFORE reading the contents of this envelope.

2: Please DO NOT read the contents of this envelope UNTIL I am departed and safely down the road.

3: Please, NO PEEKING! Especially you, Rusty!

The second envelope simply read:

To: The Lady Polly Riser.

To be read only after you have departed for home in Garden City ("Do not neglect to show hospitality to strangers, for thereby some have entertained angels unawares" [Hebrews 13:2 KJV]).

The scriptural reference added an air of mystery to the letter that awakened Polly's curiosity, which was unusually strong. However, the cryptic tone of the message gave it such power that it was nigh impossible for the girl to resist. With an effort that would have gladdened all of Olympus, she parted with the letter, surrendering it to Pastor Knowles, who stashed it in his jacket's inside pocket. With its spell over her broken, she noticed the Russell Sprouts standing around the lacquered box, chanting in awe.

Reaching deep into the throng, she grabbed Rusty firmly by the shirt collar, effectively liberating him from the lacquered idol.

"W...Where we going?" Rusty asked sleepily as they entered the big house and began to climb the main stairway.

"I need your help carrying my bags down."

"Oh, okay," was all he would say until they had reached the landing of the second floor, just before stepping onto the final stairway. "What's in the big black box?"

"Now you know I can't tell you. It's a surprise. All will be revealed, just as the pastor and I pull out."

Rusty was silent as he stared at the floor and kicked at the dirt and the dust. Polly noticed his fidgeting, and that it was the same as the first day they had met. Like then, she knew that he would talk about it when he felt ready. She just kept silently praying for him as she collected her things.

Finally when there was nothing left to pack, he opened up; like the sky splitting open to spew forth a torrential rain, he opened up.

"It ain't fair!" Rusty exclaimed, close to tears.

"What ain't fair?" she asked.

"You...you ain't fair."

"Me?" Polly asked, genuinely surprised and a little hurt. "What did I do?"

"No, not you!" he corrected himself. "You ain't done nothing unfair. It's everything else...about you...being here and all."

"Okay. So what's so bad about me being here?"

Rusty's answer wasn't forthcoming, and Polly felt he was becoming evasive.

"Well, Rusty, what's so bad about me being here? And the words 'because all girls have cooties had better not come out of your mouth."

Even if Polly had not issued her challenge, the silence that ensued between them would have been just as palpable and just as uneasy.

Finally Rusty spoke up. "All right, I'll tell you, but you're going to get mad."

"Oh, too late for that now, mister. I'm already mad."

Rusty took a deep breath, closed his eyes, and looked every bit like someone about to jump off a cliff. "When we...us kids...the Russell Sprouts, I mean, heard that you were staying with us for the summer, we all took a vote. And you know what? It was unanimous— not one of us wanted you here. No offense, but with five adults, twelve kids, and a rabbit the size of a horse, coupled with the worst money issues the nation has ever faced, and you can understand..."

"I think I do understand," said Polly, beginning to soften up. "You simply couldn't afford another mouth to feed."

"Yeah, we had no use for you. But that was before we really got to know you...before you became...one of us. And now that you are one of us, it's not fair you're leaving us. You're supposed to stay with me... I mean, us-us forever. When you leave, it's gonna hurt too much. It ain't fair, I tell you. It just ain't fair." Again his young eight-year-old self was close to tears.

Polly thought that Rusty's sentiments were so much like her own when she had first arrived that she wanted to laugh. However, a feeling of warning suddenly came over her, and it was as if a physical hand had been placed over her mouth, preventing any sign of merriment. Instantly she understood. Rusty had never let his feelings be known like this to anyone before (much less to her). He was too vulnerable, and if she laughed right then, or gave any indication of belittlement or rejection, it could hurt him or even break his young heart.

The smile dissipated before it had solidified, freeing up her mouth to say, "You know, Rusty, that was exactly the way I felt on the drive over here. I was miserable for nearly the entire trip. I didn't want to leave the Knowles or Garden City or anything that meant HOME to me. But then, I met YOU...and the others. Now I don't want to leave either."

Another uneasy silence crept in between them but for a different reason. Each felt that there was something they should be doing; however, they were both too young and way too inexperienced in the realm of emotions to know what.

All at once, the silence was broken, shattered like window shield plate glass, by Reverend Knowles's booming baritone voice which said, "All right, Polly, get the lead out! We're burning daylight here."

"Yes, sir, right away!" Polly said loudly down the stairway. Then she returned to the bedroom and said, "Rusty, please take the suitcase closest to you, while I take the one in the closet."

Even while she spoke, she quickly had her assigned suitcase in hand and, after slinging it onto the foot of the bed, sat down next to it. After opening its lid in a manner as to shield the contents of the case from the boy's view, she said to him, "Rusty, what's in the big box outside is for the whole family. However, I have something here that's just for you."

"Something just for me?" he asked, suddenly excited. "What is it?"

"Oh, believe me, you deserve this more than anyone else. So please, Rusty? Please close your eyes."

Rusty nodded his assent. Almost at once, he began remembering other times with other siblings. Back then, he had a well-deserved reputation of being a pest, a peeker, and a punk. However, this time, Rusty felt different, overcome with a desire to *put his best foot forward*, to be the kind of young man his paternal grandmother had always prayed that he'd become. And then, Polly arrived from Garden City, and at first, she had seemed to him to be anything but inspiring.

Then came that terrible dust storm, and he had become hopelessly entangled in an old painter's tarp as it rolled uncontrollably down a hill, further entangling him. Few could understand his tendency to have a panic attack whenever his face became covered. And that evening was worst of all. To him, it felt as if he were being buried alive. His head pained as if it would split, straight down the back, while his heart beat so frighteningly strong, he felt that it would free itself from its confines, and that his soul would leach itself from a body now too weak to retain it.

As Paul and Silas were extricated from prison, or even as the great stone sealing the entrance to Christ's tomb was cast aside (both by the angel sent from God), Rusty was now convinced that God sent an angel, in the form of a little girl, to liberate him from the torturous tarp. From that time, though just a little boy, Rusty became determined to live his young life to cultivate a fertile field in her heart where love for him would grow.

So to follow her instructions, no matter what, he closed his eyes, as tight as he could, and prayed they would not betray him.

"Now no peeking, Rusty, no matter what."

Again he nodded his head, not daring to speak, lest it cause him to lose his concentration. While his mind was focused thus, he could hear her breathing become deeper; the warmth of her body indicated that she was slowly getting closer. Instinctively he raised his arms, waist-high, and turned his hands up, as if to receive something. However, when nothing was placed in his outstretched hands, he suddenly became apprehensive. He was about to ask what the "something" could possibly be, *when suddenly, it happened!*

All at once, a warmth he had never known, coupled with a softness he had never imagined, washed over him, from his neck to his waist. And then, he felt her breath, hot upon his face as her lips gently pressed against his and caressed them.

By the time Rusty had recovered enough to open his eyes, she had already departed downstairs to rejoin the others. And she had taken both suitcases—*both of them!* When the boy had emerged onto the front porch, she had finished her hasty goodbyes to the family and was gone.

*****

As Polly scurried onto the front bench seat next to Pastor Knowles, he chanced to notice her reddened eyes and tear-streaked face but chose to keep quiet about it.

While the Ford Model A sedan quickly pulled away from the others to make its way onto the dirt path leading to the main road, Polly noticed the quizzical look in the rearview mirror and decided to answer Knowles's unspoken question.

"I said all of my goodbyes yesterday. I didn't want to make it any harder to leave today."

"Even so," replied the pastor, "it must have seemed somewhat awkward to the family, to have you run away like that...maybe even downright, rude."

"I know, and I'm truly sorry," she said, sounding genuinely contrite, "but I couldn't chance being seen there when they opened the box... I just couldn't."

Knowles thought a moment before answering. "I believe I understand, so we won't mention it further."

Relieved, Polly pushed herself deeper into her seat and relaxed, as she imagined how the Russells would react when they finally opened the box.

*****

The paper crackled with far more noise than it had a right to, as Louise tore open the plain pulp-embedded envelope to unfold the paper within. She took a moment to look over the letter, and then, she began to read

> To: The Russell Sprouts
> From: Polly Quashi'miuoo Riser
> Subject: The Black Lacquered Box

DEAREST FAMILY: THOUGH I HAVE NEVER OWNED A PET, MY SUMMER WITH ALL OF YOU HAS TAUGHT ME THAT A PET IS MORE...SO VERY, VERY MUCH MORE THAN AN ANIMAL YOU HAPPEN TO TAKE CARE OF FOR YOUR OWN AMUSEMENT. QUITE THE CONTRARY, A PET IS A BELOVED MEMBER OF THE FAMILY. IT MAKES NO DIFFERENCE WHATSOEVER THAT IT HAS FOUR LEGS INSTEAD OF TWO; THE LOVE BESTOWED ON IT BY THE FAMILY IS JUST AS REAL AND VITAL. AND SO, WHEN A FAMILY EXPERIENCES THE DEATH OF A PET, THEIR PAIN AND GRIEF IS JUST AS REAL AND EVERY BIT AS INTENSE

AS IF THE DEATH HAD BEEN THAT OF A BROTHER
OR SISTER...OR OF A MOTHER OR FATHER...

At the mention of the death of a pet being equivalent to the death of a sibling or a parent, the youngest child, little three-year-old Roberta, burst into loud convulsive sobs. Attempts of the two oldest children (Randal, age fourteen, and Rhonda, age thirteen) to comfort their sister proved disastrous, for as soon as Randal picked her up and cradled her in his arms, she became completely inconsolable, her crying suddenly escalated to the intensity of a genuine northeaster, as Roberta screamed with everything her tiny frame was capable of. The little girl's tears, which had been manageable coming only from her eyes, quickly transformed into a gully washer, spewing from almost every orifice in her head.

When Rhonda tried to relieve her brother of his burden, Roberta arched her back and began kicking her legs with such force, Rhonda nearly dropped her. "Oh, this is ridiculous," she said in her frustration. "Why's she so upset now? We're only reading a letter?"

Surprisingly Roberta answered her sister's angry question. Pointing her stubby finger from one to another, she screamed the more loudly, "You all ate our rabbit!"

"Cannibals! Murderers!" Rusty shouted out anonymously from the midst of the other Sprouts.

Indignation blazed in Randal's eyes, while his mind rehearsed the several ways to wring a three-year-old's neck.

By now, a true cacophony was brewing, as all the Russell Sprouts were either crying in grief or crying out in frustration and anger. Then came the booming commanding voice of Mr. Russell, who said, "ENOUGH! Everyone settle down now." Then in a somewhat softer tone, "There, there, Roberta...calm down, princess...that's a good girl. Quiet now, everyone. Your mom's going to continue to read the letter."

He gave a nod to his wife, who ever-so slightly nodded back, then read:

I KNOW THE GRIEF THAT YOU ARE SUFFERING
FROM THE LOSS OF A BELOVED FRIEND AND FAM-

ILY MEMBER BECAUSE I JUST RECENTLY LOST MY
MOTHER, WHO WAS ALSO MY BEST FRIEND.

SO I CANNOT TAKE THE PAIN YOU MUST BE
FEELING FOR GRANTED, AND NEITHER SHOULD
ANYONE ELSE. AND SO, DEAR FAMILY, I HAVE
ARRANGED A SORT OF MEMORIAL IN THE HOPE
THAT IT BRINGS YOU SOME COMFORT.

LOVE ALWAYS,
POLLY
PS, YOU MAY NOW OPEN THE BIG
BLACK-LACQUERED BOX.

Immediately upon the letter's conclusion, all crying, shouting, fussing, fighting—all clamoring—ceased as the children crowded around the box, like wolves cornering a prey. Then they all turned toward their father, bearing the same longing look in their now-angelic faces.

Mr. Russell waded through the throng and saw what prevented the children from gaining their prize. On the front of the box's lid, a large brass disk, the size of a silver dollar, presented itself. The children intuitively ascertained, the disc concealed a locking mechanism of some kind; however, when the disc was swung upward, it revealed a large darkened bronze keyhole, but there had been no key in the letter or it's envelope. And so, they all stood there waiting, confident that their father would perform his usual feat of magic.

Randolph Russell smiled, thinking how fathers were often young children's first hero. Then melancholy threatened to invade his mood when he thought of the day his children's adoration of their *Pa-man* would be short-lived. "But not today!" he said to himself, as he remembered Polly's instructions the night before.

"Let's see now," he said as he inspected the medallion in front of the box. Aloud, he said, "Hmm, metal disk is swung upward… allowing guardian vipers to run free…FREE…to bite off the nose and lips of disobedient children."

At this, all the Sprouts broke out into laughter, while Randal reassured his siblings, saying, "No they won't, kids…biting noses off is my job."

Mr. Russell continued, "Polly said, once the disk is in the raised position, it will reveal itself to be a round silver box, the top of the box unscrews, like a jar of pickles…and…VOILA!" The box opened, and inside of it, a brightly polished brass key.

He held the key high so that all could see, then handed it to Louise, who stooped down and fitted the key into its hole and slowly turned it. Immediately the top of the box moved upward slightly to indicate the box was now open. Randal and Richard lifted the lid, and when it was clear, the sides of the box fell outwards as well.

All at once, the adults and oldest children gasped in amazement, while most of the others looked on as if they were gazing upon an apparition. However, it was the youngest child, three-year-old Roberta, who, eyes awash with tears, flung herself at the box's now-revealed contents and, landing on its fluffy back, wrapped her arms round its neck, her face buried deep in its fur.

"HASENPFEFFER!"

*****

As the Ford Model A sedan quickly headed down the dusty hard-packed dirt road, Reverend Knowles would frequently divert his gaze to his young charge seated next to him.

"Hey, Vashti?" he said as he swerved to avoid a large pothole in the road.

She quickly looked up; her customary curiosity returned. "Why did you just call me, Vashti, sir?"

Knowles smiled, happy to be in a normal conversation with Polly again. "Vashti was queen of Persia, in the book of Esther. She had been greatly wronged by her husband, King Ahasuerus. She reminds me of you and the situation with your dad."

Polly suddenly became defensive. "But 'the heart of the King is in God's hands…'" (Proverbs 21: 1). "God can change Pa's heart!"

"Yes, he can. After all, God can do anything."

"It's nice to hear you say it," she said with a hint of sarcasm.

"Thank you, Pastor Polly!" They both laughed. Then he remembered the moist eyes and tear streaks he noticed a moment ago, and added, "When we came out here, you were crying your eyes out because you didn't want to leave Garden City. However, after an almost five-month absence, you're still crying?"

"I know it's strange. Biddy—oops, Bedelia—always calls me her little flippety-jibbette. I guess it's because there are several folks there I'm really, REALLY going to miss terribly."

Pastor Knowles was thoughtful for a moment before he said, "You know, Vashti, this doesn't have to be the last time you see them. I'm certain that we can arrange to bring you back again someday."

"Promise?"

"Yeah, kiddo, God willing, we'll find a way to make it happen."

After he had said "I promise," Pastor Knowles noticed that the girl's mood instantly improved.

And so did his.

The two remained quiet for the next half an hour; however, this was not the uneasy almost-paranoid feelings she suffered on the drive to Dodge City with Mr. Russell. Today Polly felt nothing but warmth and happy feelings from her desire to be at the new parsonage. To her fanciful mind, being with the Knowles meant that she was soon to be reunited with her father.

So what of the myriad instances of abuse? So what of the fact that Buck had thrown a pickax at her, in full view of the sheriff and her pastor? So what it had been less than six months since that brutal assault resulted in him being sentenced to not less than ten years in the federal prison in Leavenworth. It would take a miracle to bring them back together in the foreseeable future. Then again, she had long believed in miracles.

They drove on for another thirty minutes in relative silence, and Reverend Knowles was enjoying the peace and quiet so much he had almost forgotten Polly's letter. "Hey, Your Majesty," he said as he reached into his jacket's side pocket.

Polly struggled to be polite and kind, despite being anxious, as she took the letter from her pastor. She carefully opened the letter, willing herself to preserve each fold and crease, as well as the embroidered company letterhead, in spite of her strong urge to do otherwise.

"The Living End, Taxidermy Shoppe and Gallery," she said looking quickly over the paper. "But it's not from Mr. Klaus Koe, the owner and proprietor. The letter is written by someone I've never met."

"Are you sure?" Pastor Knowles asked. "I mean, you must have impressed someone there enough for them to commandeer a business's own letterhead in order to write a letter to someone they barely knew."

"Hmm, let me think," she said as she scanned the missive anew. "There weren't that many people there, so…could it be?"

Suddenly her large wondering eyes lit up like a bonfire as her hand moved up to cover her mouth.

"What's the matter, girl? You look as though you've witnessed an angel."

"Well, sir, the letter begins with a reference to 'angels unawares' in Hebrews 13:2. The writer wasn't talking about himself. I think… he was talking…about me. Please, listen to this:

> "To the dearest lady, Miss. Polly Riser. for most of my adult life, I gave little credence to that passage of scripture. that is, until last month, when it was only by a truly merciful God, who caused us to encounter each other at that most miraculous of moments. please, allow me to explain."

Polly paused for a moment and said, "This is incredible! The letter goes on to say that the proprietor of the shop, Mr. Koe, was a former apprentice of the writer, who considered him to be as close as a son. Unfortunately after molding Mr. Koe in the ways of classical embalming and taxidermy, at the most crucial moment, Klaus rejected classical taxidermy, as well as his mentor, in order to escape to America and practice that pseudodiscipline of outlaw taxidermy and never was anything more aptly named."

Polly bit her lower lip and frowned as her eyes ran ahead on the page, occasionally stopping to wait for her voice to catch up. In a while, she continued, "The letter goes on and on about the impetuousness of youth and of how he—the writer—was known as the taxidermist to the royalty and nobility of Europe. In addition, he had been endorsed by the Museum of Natural History in France. That was when he accompanied an exploration of Australia. The quality of the wildlife samples he prepared and brought to the museum were truly astounding, being of a variety never seen by Europeans before. In addition, the selections appeared as if they were still alive, even including such details as moisture, in the form of water droplets, in the eyes and nose. Finally he sent two examples of Aborigines. Though he assured the museum director that the couple's demise was of natural causes, their presence caused enough of an uproar—concerning ethics—that their viewing was closed to the general public and reserved for the scientific community only."

Polly rested from her recital long enough for Reverend Knowles to wonder if it had reached its conclusion. However, just as the pastor was preparing to question the girl to that affect, she announced that here, the tone of the letter changed. She was preparing to continue her reading assignment when Reverend Knowles offered to relieve her. She gladly accepted the offer, and he wasted no time in continuing the story.

He loudly cleared his throat and pronounced, "It goes on to say that Mr. Koe's master had come to America as well in order to somehow persuade his former pupil to return with his old teacher to Europe. He was engaged in that very endeavor, about to present the argument of his own qualifications and honors, as well as how much of an honor it would be for Koe to be reunited with his teacher, when the two of us entered the shop. The letter says that:

"I BECAME INSTANTLY ENCHANTED WITH THE LADY POLLY AND OF HER PLANS TO UTILIZE HER GRANDFATHER'S INHERITANCE IN ORDER TO BRING

HELP AND COMFORT TO OTHERS WAS ESPECIALLY CHALLENGING. AT ONCE, I KNEW THAT I HAD BEEN APPROACHING MY FORMER APPRENTICE ALL WRONG AND FOR THE WRONG REASON.

REPENTANCE CAME TO ME AS WELL AS MY PURPOSE. NOW MR. KOE HAS CONSENTED TO RETURN WITH ME TO EUROPE, NO LONGER MY STUDENT BUT AS MY FULLY INVESTED PARTNER, BRINGING A WHOLE NEW AND FASCINATING FIELD TO TAXIDERMY, THAT IS, TO CREATE A WORK WHERE NO PREVIOUS BODY EXISTED."

Reverend Knowles paused briefly before reading on.

"FURTHERMORE, IN ORDER TO HONOR YOUR SELF-LESS GENEROSITY, WE ARE ENCLOSING WITH THIS LETTER A FULL REFUND OF THE PURCHASE PRICE. AND FOR THE FIRST TIME, A WORK OF PRESERVA-TION WILL RECEIVE BOTH OF OUR SIGNATURES, AND IN SO DOING, I DECLARE THAT THIS MASTER-PIECE SHALL BE THE FINAL WORK OF THE GREAT LEOPOLDO (LEONARDO SAINT KRISPEN POLO), THAT I NOW STAND IN RETIREMENT, AND THAT MY PARTNER, MR. KLAUS KOE, SHALL ASSUME PRO-PRIETORSHIP OF MY SHOP, MY GALLERY, AND MY TAXIDERMY ACADEMY. THANK YOU, POLLY, AND MAY THE LORD LOVE YOU AND KEEP YOU.

LEOPOLDO."

At the letter's conclusion, Knowles handed it to Polly, saying, "I believe I'm familiar with that name, sweetheart. A newspaper article last year referred to him as a maestro and a true creative genius, one of the finest preservation artists in the world…EVER! And likened him to the ancient Egyptians. It just goes to show you, little girl, you never know who you're going to meet."

Polly reverently received the letter from her pastor and scrutinized the name of the writer, picturing the face of the old man in the taxidermy shop in Dodge City. "Leopoldo... Leopoldo... Leopoldo..." she said sleepily as she gently held the precious missive to her chest.

And just like that, the interlude of a dream that was a homestead on the outskirts of Cimarron, was gone, receding into distance and time; its passing marked by the muffled thuds of rubber tires upon dusty bumpy roads. It was also marked by a single tear slowly cascading down a dirty cheek, with a solitary well-defined smudge in the shape of a promise made by the lips of an eight-year-old little boy.

CHAPTER 19

Farewell to Stoney Lonesome; Part 2: Buck versus Skybolt

As the 1928 Ford Model AA heavy-duty truck plodded along the roughly 374 miles between Leavenworth and Garden City, Kansas, Buck had remained largely reticent while the loquacious Sweeny brothers spoke almost incessantly. When they became excited, talking about a recent newspaper article on Buck's heroism, he became absolutely withdrawn, causing Budd Sweeny to remark that Buck was more fun to be with when he was drinking.

Instead of taking offense, Buck smiled and said, "Get used to it, boys. In prison I learned that I'm a different person when I'm sober…a better person…a person I could even come to like, and I'd like to get to know him better."

Budd was preparing to escalate the argument when Doug gestured for his silence, saying that they would continue this in town.

With the only two subjects the Sweeny brothers could enthusiastically or intelligently speak on (Buck's celebrity and drinking, respectively) off the discussion table (for the time being), the Sweeny's became bored and restless. So it remained for nearly the rest of the trip. The Sweeny's conversed noisily among themselves, while pointing out interesting scenery variations and features (Kansas being a plain state, there seemed precious few of either).

Time and again, Buck tried to retreat into slumber; however, each time he was almost successful, he was rudely awakened by the

Sweenys, whose voices would miraculously crescendo to their loudest whenever Buck began to relax and doze off.

The two Sweenys' vain attempts to entertain themselves slowly began to chisel into Buck's consciousness, interrupting his quiet introspection and testing his newfound influence over his temper. Their irritating banter began to strip away his emotional safeguards, defenses, and controls, leaving his nerves raw and his temples throbbing.

Buck thought that his mounting anger was reminiscent of an incident between Colonel Skybolt and himself, the night following Governor Patton's pardon announcement.

He was brought, under guard, to the recreation area of the quadrangle. The commandant was waiting for him, dressed in his old army fatigues, and Buck noted the tense way the colonel stood, as if he were prepared for trouble. Buck was brought to a halt close enough to see the hard angry continence on the man's face, as well as the absence of the ubiquitous cigar.

Colonel Skybolt waved the guards away and then gruffly said, "You may have the press and everyone else here fooled, thinking the biggest bully in Garden City is now the benevolent, self-sacrificing, altruistic hero. Newspapers say how you came here in chains, but now, you walk on water. But I know the truth—you haven't changed. You might have polished up the outside, but deep inside, you're still an ax-wielding maniac, waiting for an opportunity to come and cut loose. Isn't that right, punk?"

Buck's heart began to race as a bead of cold sweat trickled down his back. He stood there, bewildered, but said nothing.

Growing impatient with Buck's silence, Skybolt challenged, "I know men, and they don't change. You're just a blasted animal...ain't that right, PUNK?" He followed this last pronouncement with a sharp backhanded slap to the face. The impact stung, as it rolled his head violently to the side, but Buck kept his hands unclenched and glued to his sides and remained silent.

"I said, you're just a blasted ax-throwing bastard...ain't that right, punk?" Skybolt said as he slapped the opposite side of Buck's face, even harder than before. Still Buck refused to defend himself from the acting warden, whether physically or verbally.

"I'm starting to lose my patience. Now tell me, punk…you want to lay into me, don't you? You want to tear my bloody head off, don't you? Well, don't you, punk?" Skybolt followed this last rant with a hard punch to the gut, which bent Buck over and nearly floored him.

Rising upright again, Buck finally spoke, "Look, Colonel sir, I don't have a beef with you. Why are we doing this?"

"Because deep inside, you're still an animal, and I can't let a monster like you loose on an unsuspecting town. Now show me the real Buck Riser. Show me, you bloody punk! SHOW ME!" Skybolt bellowed as he shot off a massive uppercut, which landed square on Buck's chin, nearly flooring the big man. The blow caused Buck to bite his tongue, almost severing the tip of it. Blood poured like a stream from his mouth, but he somehow managed to regain his footing.

"Why don't you fight me, goshdarnit? I know you want to. Do it now and not later, when folks who believe the lies of the press won't be ready for you. Come on, bastard… Come on! Why won't you fight me?"

"B-because I don't want to. I have changed, Colonel. Be-besides you hit like a weak schoolboy."

"Oh, yeah?" Skybolt said as rage was clearly mounting in his eyes. "How about now?" Skybolt said as he raised a heavy leather boot and kicked Buck mercilessly to his unprotected groin, hard enough to finally floor the man.

The concrete floor came up at him too fast to check his fall. With arms to his sides, and hands over his injury, Buck was as straight and stiff as a well-planed oak plank when he plowed, face-first, into the concrete floor of the quadrangle. Blood burst from Buck's nostrils and his deeply excoriated cheek as he remained on the ground, unable to rise.

Skybolt brought his heavy boot crashing into Buck's diaphragm, forcing the air from his lungs, leaving him desperate to breathe. "Tell me, bastard," he said, as he prepared to strike again. "Was that hard enough for you? Well, was it hard enough for you, punk?" he said, as he let his booted foot fly.

Before the blow had reached its mark, Buck rolled away from its arc while bringing his arm up and out, like a fishing hook, to sweep the surprised commandant off his feet and crashing, stunned, onto the concrete. Faster than Skybolt could react, Buck rolled the opposite direction, using his broad chest to smother his opponent by covering his face. Then he rolled over again, bringing his attacker with him and placing him in a near-perfect chokehold.

Now it was Colonel Skybolt's turn to panic. His eyes bulged, looking as if they would liberate themselves from their sockets, not so much from lack of air as from the sudden realization of the position he allowed himself to get into.

The acting warden slashed with his elbows, first to the right, then to the left, to strike his assailant, throw him off balance and dislodge his hold of his neck, all to no avail. Then Colonel Skybolt began to throw his weight left and right in a further attempt to free himself. His efforts became weaker and weaker, as Buck anticipated his every move and shifted his own weight accordingly. Buck then squeezed harder, incrementally increasing the pressure to his opponent's carotid arteries, until his thrashing subsided, and his arms lowered themselves helplessly to the ground.

"I told you," Buck said as he applied one more ounce of pressure to his victim's neck, not to snap it but to further occlude it, until Skybolt's whole body became limp, and there was no longer any more fight left in him. Only then did Buck ease his grip, allowing Skybolt's lungs to loudly inflate. "I told you," Buck repeated, "I had changed, and I meant every bloody word of it. Now I mean no harm to anyone…not even you, you son of a gun. Remember that whenever you wake up."

Buck released his hold, and Colonel Skybolt tumbled forward to the ground. He then limped over to the entrance and, when it opened to his knocking, said to the guard, "Please escort me to the infirmary and have someone pick up your boss and carry him to his room. I think he has learned all he wanted to about my character and intentions. Good night."

Buck opened his eyes, bringing his mind back into the truck, which was now quiet, except for the sound of the engine, the tires alternately rolling and then bouncing on the road, and the clean-shaven farmer, who gently whistled, while he drove along.

The Sweeny brothers were fast asleep.

A sign on the side of the road, receding quickly into the distance, had read "Now Entering Finney County."

Buck then looked up and noticed the bloated darkened clouds accumulating above. He frowned and remarked to himself, "Hmm! A storm's coming."

PART 2

The Worst Cloud (1935)

And when the thousand years are expired, Satan shall be loosed out of his prison...and they went upon the breadth of the earth, and compassed the saints about...

> —Revelations 20:7, 9 (KJV)

Be not deceived: evil communications corrupt good manners.

> —1 Corinthians 15:33 (KJV)

Polly Quashi'miuoo Riser

Dear God, thank you for all of your blessings. Even the drought and the terrible dust storms cause me to look deeper to see your blessings like Biddy—oops, Bedelia—told me. I'm with folks who love me, but I do so miss a family of my own. You probably get tired of hearing me ask you, but please, dear God, please bless Pa to love me so we can be a family again. And please, Lord, bless my town so the people here will have faith in you again. Your Son sacrificed his life for us all, and he said that a servant is not greater than his master. So, Lord, even if I must be a sacrifice too, please, bless my pa and my town. In Jesus's name…

CHAPTER 20

Return of the Prodigal

Long before the two recipients of Leavenworth's recent gubernatorial pardons had emerged again into the light of day, news of Buck's heroics plastered every newspaper in the state of Kansas and indeed the entire United States as well. Buck winced from a sudden wave of nausea when he thought of the teeming unimaginable plethora of humanity who had read a newspaper and believed every word of the exaggerated tale it told.

As Buck fought to subdue another pang of nausea, he wished that stories reporting of his valor and heroism (along with pictures of his face, for all to recognize him) would disappear as well. It was not that he felt disdain toward the papers and their writers. To the contrary, Buck found the stories entertaining and the pictures of him to be flattering. However, few people (apart from those who knew him best) could possibly understand the conflict those papers were producing in the hero's life.

From his earliest memories of childhood, Buck had been uncontrollably afraid of just one thing. At first, people simply dismissed it as him being shy. But it was more than mere shyness—so much more. It was as if every part of Buck's being capable of feeling fear was predisposed to respond to just one common everyday stimulus—that of being in a large gathering of people in which he was the focus of their attention.

As the truck noisily rolled along the last few miles toward Finney County's county seat, Buck had strong misgivings from the thought of a reception to celebrate the return of Garden City's favorite son. Even so, as the truck came to a dusty halt in front of the town hall, he was surprised to feel relief, as well as melancholia, as the only one waiting to meet him was Sheriff Pucket.

"I don't believe it!" Pucket said, as Buck emerged from the truck and told the old driver to convey the still-sleeping Sweeny brothers back to their home, near the northernmost border of Finney County. "No, sir, I just can't believe it!" he reiterated as he listened to Buck offering to pay the old man for the Sweenys' extra (out of the way) trip. However, like the Porter's cab driver, the old man respectfully declined, saying that a government representative, named Pettibone, had more than generously compensated him for any possible expenses.

At last, the old truck noisily pulled away. Buck turned to the sheriff and asked, "What can't you believe, sir? That I served only two years of a ten-to-twenty-year sentence?"

"No, that ain't it," Pucket replied, scratching his balding head. "It's just so hard for me to believe that the man I arrested for trying to kill a child is the same man I'm looking at now. News reports aside, you don't even look like you're the same man."

"Thanks, Sheriff. That means a lot, coming from you. Being clean and sober now, I feel like a new man. I reckon the other fella died the night of the prison break. May he rest in peace. I like the new one better anyway."

"Amen to that!" Pucket said, and they both laughed.

Presently the laughter died down, and Buck thoughtfully said, "Speaking of new things, has anything new happened here since I've been gone?"

The sheriff was equally cautious as he answered, "Yeah, Buck, there's been some important changes here, mainly concerning you. But the mayor wants to explain it to you himself. He's in his office with Judge Lynch, and Their Honors are waiting."

Buck's thoughts pondered what two of the highest officials in Garden City could possibly want with him as he and the sheriff quickly climbed the cluster of recently swept steps and entered the most imposing building in the entire town.

Buck felt his apprehension crescendo as the sound of the two men's leather soles echoed throughout the otherwise quiet austere palatial corridors. A mounting desire to break and run began to grip the pit of Buck's stomach as he realized that he had never, in his life, been in this area of the building before. The desire to flee intensified until it became almost unbearable, when suddenly, the two men rounded yet another hallway intersection and literally bumped into two smartly uniformed Sheriff Department deputies, standing on either side of a heavy double-oaken door, with a large sign suspended above which read "Mayor's Office."

The two startled guards immediately drew their revolvers but just as quickly returned them to their holsters when they recognized the sheriff, saying together, "Sorry, Sheriff, sir! We'll present you to His Honor's secretary, who'll announce you two."

Mrs. Crestfall sat almost motionless next to the door to the mayor's office, wearing the same style of floral-print dress she had faithfully worn for twenty-six years. She was known to sit so still and quiet, in fact, that visitors often mistook her for a decorative houseplant.

Mrs. Crestfall certainly was not in this anteroom alone. Several (younger) entities moved constantly about the room, performing various general clerical tasks. Because Crestfall was so stationary, the activities of the other occupants resembled worker ants, servicing their queen. In fact, Mrs. Crestfall was so much like the hive queen that she too had but one main function (though somewhat different than that of the ant). In truth, she had grown so old (and indispensable to each administration) that all of her official duties had become the responsibility of the other younger office workers, while she retained the charge of Cerberus—that is, guarding the gates of Hades, or in Crestfall's case, the door to the mayor's office.

Crestfall was so old she had long since passed the age of retirement. However, it was long rumored that she was a distant relative of the mayor, who desired her to be set for life. It was perhaps the most blatant example of nepotism that anyone had ever heard of. However, under the current economic and climatic conditions, there were few who still remembered and fewer still who cared.

No sooner had Buck and Sheriff Pucket entered the room that a deep gravelly contralto voice heralded, "Gentlemen, the mayor is expecting you… Please go right in!"

The room was surprisingly dark, illuminated only by the ambient light coming through the window and by the Honorable James J. Smoke, who was warmer and more congenial than any public servant had a right to be in a nonelection year. His words were unnecessarily flamboyant, his subject unremarkable and unmemorable, and its purpose redundant. Fortunately the only good thing that could be said of Mayor Smoke's welcome-home address was that the event was both intimate and exclusive in its attendance, and the address was mercifully brief in its duration.

After the mayor, the next (and final) speaker was Judge Thaddeus Lynch, who pronounced the following admonishment to Buck, "Since the governor has deemed it appropriate to pardon you from your conviction for felony assault of a child…the court's awarding of permanent custody of the child to court-appointed foster care, along with court-ordered no contact, must now of necessity, be considered temporary in nature. Even so, for the time being, it remains enforced. How long that alternative custody lasts will be solely dependent upon your evidenced good behavior and your ability to properly provide for the child."

Judge Lynch's final statement to Buck, some have criticized, were more appropriately delivered from a church pulpit, or even from a courtroom, instead of the office of the mayor.

"In conclusion, Mr. Riser, I feel I would be remiss if I failed to point out that the undeniable success of your exploits at the federal penitentiary at Leavenworth could not have been possible without your total abstinence from intoxicants, along with your complete avoidance of unsavory influences that might lead you astray. Both elements were involuntarily facilitated in Leavenworth but must now be maintained on a voluntary basis. Therefore, I encourage you, admonish you, and adjure you to maintain your newfound sobriety by all possible means. I leave it with you, sir!"

During the judges' speech, Buck's face and neck became deeply reddened, and his fists were tightly clenched to fight the rising anger he felt. With Judge Lynch's conclusion, Buck turned to leave, saying over his shoulder that, "You can do what you want with her. The brat's probably better off where she is with your foster care appointees. She's none of mine!"

*****

Though not present at the mayor's meeting, Buck's harsh words were swift to reach Reverend Knowles's ears to stab at his heart, as if he had been there all along. The words reverberated in his mind, were just as swift to produce a pounding headache whose intensity had rarely been felt by him. "LORD GOD ALMIGHTY!" he said, fighting a losing battle with pain on two equally unsuccessful fronts. His head felt as if it would split open, like a coconut, while his mind threatened to lose its hold on sanity.

"How can he deny such a beautiful wonderful child like Polly? He must be totally mad, completely out of his mind. But of course, this will break her heart far more than it's already been. Dear God in heaven, what am I supposed to do about this? Please tell me, Lord... what am I supposed to do about this..."

Reverend Knowles prayed in anguish for another two hours, leaving him exhausted and with the feeling his prayers had risen no higher than the ceiling of his parsonage study.

*****

Benjamin Buccannon "Buck" Riser raised the plain ceramic cup to his lips and allowed the hot black pungent liquid it contained to bathe his parched throat.

"That's absolutely disgusting!" said Budd Sweeny as he watched the big man swallow an entire cup of strong coffee, as if it were cold. "In fact, I'll go so far as to say that it's positively revolting, after being a real drinker for so long, to start drinking that crap in here."

"Aw, why don't you leave him alone!" said the bartender from across the room. "It's a free country again. He can drink a sarsaparilla if he has a mind to. Besides your brother's a teetotaler,[12] and you never had a problem with that."

"And why the hell don't you mind your own darned business!" said the younger Sweeny, becoming loud and belligerent as the bourbon whiskey he was drinking began to embolden him.

"Why don't you come over here and make me," said the bartender, reaching for the genuine Louisville Slugger concealed nearby. Placing it on the counter, he continued, "My bar, my business. Now you settle down over there, or do I have to give you a sedative?"

Instantly the barkeep seemed much larger than the 5'11" he was when the three men arrived.

Budd Sweeny turned around and looked sheepishly into his drink before taking another swig of it. Quietly he said to the others at the table, "You all know I don't mean nothing. It's just that if they can create a law forbidding a fella from drinking intox...intox... INTOXICANTS on public streets, there should be a law that ONLY intoxicants can be drunk in a bar."

With this, Budd fell silent and timidly shifted his eyes repeatedly from his drink to his older sibling, as if to say *I'm getting in trouble here...help me out.*

The elder Sweeny merely shook his head. It had always been like that ever since their father, on his deathbed, charged Doug to "take care of that half-wit brother of yours." Whenever Budd's mouth was getting him into trouble, he always looked to his "responsible" big brother to get him out of it.

Budd was always in some sort of trouble, and Doug was always there to rescue him. The routine had long grown old and stale, though Doug continued to be faithful to their father's dying wish.

Doug thought about it awhile. It didn't occur often; however, there was one thing his younger brother had said the other day that made the smarter, calculating, even scheming older brother to remark that truer words had never been spoken. Buck seemed bound and determined to remain clean and sober for the remainder of his life. Budd had remarked that Buck was no fun when he hadn't been drinking, which was to say that when Buck was sober and clear-headed, he was far less likely to be a follower, easily manipulated by the elder Sweeny.

Sweeny smiled a sly smile (as he was known to do whenever a new scheme of his was about to hatch), stood, and reached for Buck's coffee cup. Buck was about to protest when Doug cheerfully said, "Hey, pal, let me freshen that up for you while I'm up." Before Buck could offer further resistance, Doug proved the faster of the two men. Then with cup twirling in his hand, Doug triumphantly walked to the bar.

As Sweeny approached, it was easy to see that the bartender was still angry from Budd's tirade. Mean-looking bloodshot eyes glared in Budd's direction, and his grip on the genuine Louisville Slugger tightened, causing the blood vessels in his meaty hand to grotesquely distend as the older brother came near.

"Hey, Mack!" Sweeny said as he leaned against the bar, too close for Mack to effectively swing. "Mack," he said again, getting the man's full attention. "I've heard a rumor around town that you can make a cocktail so that no one can tell there's booze in it."

"Sure!" the barkeep proudly replied. "Anyone who went to mixologist school can do that. Now what can I get for you?"

Sweeny smiled knowingly and said, "Well, my brother and I would like another round of what we had—that is, a cup of black coffee for me and a whiskey. Neat for my brother. And please, let's forgive him this time, omitting the customary expectoration in his drink. Finally my other friend would like an Irish coffee, without the cream and toppings, and it absolutely must have the alcohol undetectable to him. He must think he's drinking a regular coffee."

"Why not just slip him a Mickey? It's easier."

"Thank you, but no. We don't want him passed out, just moderately inebriated. Do this right, Mack, and I'm willing to pay you double for the entire bill since we walked in today."

"Now you're talking," Mack said as a greedy smile came across his lips. "This will be ready in a jiffy, sir."

Without another word, Doug returned to his table in time to see his brother, Budd, was nodding his head back and forth. As he approached, Budd became agitated and then verbally abusive. "How the hell longer is it going to take to get a drink around here?" A couple of nods more, and his head finally came loudly crashing to the table.

While Buck just shook his head, Doug turned around, even as Mack was arriving with a tray of drinks. Seeing Budd passed out on the table, he said, "You know I cannot serve a drink to an obviously drunk person. After I've served our two survivors, I'll take your brother's drink back and take it off your bill."

Mack sounded so sad and dejected that Sweeny said, "Yes, dispose of it, but keep it on the bill, as per our arraignment. After all, a deal is a deal."

"Gee, thanks, Mr. Sweeny," Mack said, putting down the drinks for the living before hurrying back to the bar.

Doug picked up his cup and literally inhaled its contents. Buck similarly gulped his coffee down in a single swallow. Sweeny gestured toward the bar, and in a moment, Mack had arrived with refills. Doug was glad that he was drinking coffee; the coffee cups were always stored in a closed drawer, and it seemed as if everything else was covered in dirt, dust, and sand.

Two more refills later, and Doug stood, raised his coffee cup high, and said, "To my friend, Buck Riser, upon his homecoming and his heroic release from incarceration. May this year be filled with adventure, happiness, and prosperity for him and his associates." Sweeny extended his neck and allowed the robust bitter liquid to cascade down his throat. Concluding his toast, he listened, but there was no hear, hear coming from Buck. In fact, his coffee cup was held at half-mast between the table and his mouth, as if the big man bemoaned the death of his pre-Leavenworth self.

Doug looked closely into Buck's bloodshot diminished reactive eyes. Their similarity to his brother's all-too-familiar one's were unmistakable.

"Wh-what the h-hell are you lo-looking at?" Buck said, pushing a meaty palm into the older Sweeny's face, throwing him violently across the table skipping over the top of his chair, like a stone over a pond, to land in a bruised heap upon the floor.

Immediately Mack cleared the bar counter in a single leap with Louisville Slugger held tightly in hand. However, one look at Sweeny's quickly broadening smile reassured him that all was well.

"It's all right, Mack," Doug said as he examined the two men left seated at the table. While his brother never stirred from his alcohol-induced slumber, the effort Buck expended to push him away allowed the disguised alcohol in his coffee to finally take its toll. Like a spinning top at the end of its cycle, Buck's head came crashing down to join the younger Sweeny's in a spreading puddle of spilled drink and spittle on the table.

Triumphantly Doug Sweeny declared, "This is indeed a perfect homecoming...AN OLD FRIEND OF MINE HAS FINALLY RETURNED!"

CHAPTER 21

Nowhere to Run, Nowhere to Hide

Time (the determination of a single moment rather than its overall passage) was measured by various ways and means, historically as well as geographically. Prehistoric peoples watched the position of the sun, as it arced across the azure expanse. Later ancient civilizations (in the Western world) viewed this daily journey with the use of a sundial, while water clocks, were employed in the East.

In both the industrial and rural portions of the United States in the 1930s, time was mostly measured with the use of mechanical clocks and watches. However, for a certain little girl living in Kansas, time was determined by the anxiously anticipated late-afternoon broadcast of her favorite radio serial.

"Walk, young lady, you know better!" demanded the woman of the house to the yellow sundress-clad blur that nearly collided with her on the second-floor landing. "And keep the volume down. Pastor is napping in his rocker!"

"Oh, yes, ma'am, Biddy—oops, Bedelia, I'm such a flippety-jib-bette," said Polly as she checked her plan to leap down the entire final flight of steps. Instead she obediently walked down the remaining steps (albeit quickly) to plop down prone on the living room floor, in front of the 1933 Philco Cathedral Radio, Model 18.[13]

"Oh, I'll be so glad when someone invents a radio people don't have to wait for it to warm up before it'll come on," she said quietly to herself, being careful not to disturb the man snoring in the rocking chair, on the other side of the room.

The girl reached up to turn the dial to activate the radio, only to discover it had already been turned on. "Thanks, Biddy—oops, Bedelia." She was thankful that the vacuum tubes contained in the radio were already warmed up and that the pale, ghostly light behind the indicating dial had come to life, showing the proper station already tuned in.

Polly had just managed to turn down the volume when the radio heralded the arrival of her favorite heroine. "Now the National Broadcast Company, Blue Network, and the folks at OVALTINE proudly present, *Little Orphan Annie*..."[14]

So thoroughly entranced by the radio drama that for a moment, each day (only a mere quarter of an hour), the radio was no longer a radio. It had somehow been transubstantiated into the fabulous magic carpet of Aladdin. Indeed, the quaint parsonage, located just two miles south of town, had similarly been changed into a palatial mansion, whose cavernous hallways could easily hold several parsonages. Perhaps best of all, Polly was no longer Polly. Although her body still occupied its place upon the floor, it itself was no longer occupied by her soul. It had, like Mercury, passed through organs, refused the intervention of sinews to ooze unencumbered past skin and raiment, past space and time to meld seamlessly into the life of an adorable orphan, who had charmed her way into the life of a New York billionaire industrialist, giving him the one thing that all his incomparable wealth could not buy...

The passage of time resumed with the voice of the announcer proclaiming tomorrow's journey, while the voice of an angel gently pronounced the benediction.

"Polly, dear, when your broadcast is over, please turn the radio off, tidy up down there, and set the table for supper. But be careful not to wake Pastor just yet."

"Yes, ma'am, Biddy, I mean, Bedelia. Right away."

Polly quickly looked around the living room for anything amiss. Only a pile of crumbled-up pulp newspaper lay next to Knowles's precious rocking chair. As quietly as she could, she busied herself straightening the papers. Suddenly written in large bold print was a headline that caused the blood to drain from her face and forced her to bring her hand to her mouth, trying to suppress a scream that was surely larger than she was.

> FROM PRISON TO PARDON: Local bad boy sentenced to up to twenty years in Leavenworth for the felonious assault of his young daughter with an axe…has been granted an unconditional pardon by Governor Patton, after serving only two years… HERO…thwarted plot to assassinate the Warden… Federal Auditor… Has returned home to Garden City without fanfare.

*****

Reverend Patrick Knowles had often said that the two most enjoyable moments of his day were being awakened in the morning by Bedelia, his wife and the angel of his house and of being awakened from his afternoon nap by another angel, of sorts, the effervescent Lady Polly Riser.

It became rumored in town that Knowles was a man blessed beyond measure. He could never gainsay his neighbors, for indeed, Knowles himself was the source of those tales, and he took a great pride in them, as well as constantly being thankful to God. After all, Bedelia was the absolute love of his life, while Polly had become the child that the Knowles could never conceive. Both women had transformed the parsonage into paradise, and both were indispensable as the joy and comfort of his life.

Except for that moment, at the end of his nap.

Where, in the name of all he loved, were the delicate hands that caressed the knots in his neck? Where, oh where, was the voice of the cherub that brought him back to life? Today his paradise was indeed lost, as the gentle brush of angel's wings had somehow become the relentless stab of a demon's pitchfork, applied with all the skill and dedication of Grand Inquisitor Torquemada himself.

Knowles forced his eyes open and ignored the pain of a sudden flood of light. There next to his chair arrogantly stood the imp of hell, with shoestring-thin arms defiantly resting upon nonexistent hips. Something else was missing as well—she had not spoken a single word.

It was a little known foible of his that whenever he became nervous or apprehensive, Knowles would resort to sarcasm, at the worst possible moment, engendering the worst possible of results.

"So," he said, stepping into his own trap, "the flippety-jibbette is speechless for once. This must be serious."

His cavalier flippancy was instantly regretted, as all the warmth in the room was suddenly sucked into the body of the basilisk standing before him. And still, she remained silent; only her eyes spoke of anger and of condemnation.

Suddenly a page of newspaper he had crumbled up before dozing off was smoothed and straightened and thrust accusingly before his face. He didn't bother to read the headline, his tortured mind had already wrestled with it just before falling to sleep. Instead he noticed her trembling lips as she held her body threateningly stiff and knew that, this was going to be so much worse than the ride to the Russell's farm in Cimarron could ever have been.

Knowles, like his foster child, remained silent for the time being, not from any desire to appear polite, deferring to his opponent the opening salvo of this regrettable but unavoidable melee. Instead he had already engaged another enemy on an unseen front, one which could exacerbate a tense situation into one of harsh words of even crueler intent.

Deep in his mind, he parried aside every calloused unfeeling expression that appeared and waited for her onslaught. Looking into her reddened tearful eyes, Knowles could see that Polly was fighting her own internal struggle—one to hold back the swollen rivers of crushed hope and betrayal. *And her dam was breaking!*

Polly let the newspaper slip from her grasp, like the challenge of a cast-down gauntlet.

"Just when were you going to tell me Pa was back in town?" she demanded, stamping her foot upon the paper.

"I wasn't going to tell you," Knowles said, sounding as calm as he possibly could. Then anticipating her obvious next question, he continued, "Buck may have received a pardon from Governor Patton, but there is a restraining order from Judge Lynch still in force."

"But...but didn't you read the paper? He's a hero now...a HERO!"

Bedelia became alarmed by the rapid crescendo in Polly's voice. Her alarm quickly turned to panic as the cacophony from the girl stamping with all her weight upon the living room floor was ample evidence that this was no longer a simple argument. Still more than a mere tantrum. Polly's outburst was in danger of becoming what the old folks used to call a conniption. The thought of what an angry frustrated Knowles might do to the girl instantly drove her downstairs.

"Buck was a hero while he was in prison. But he's back home now, and the good deeds he did over there, he could undo now that he's back, especially where you are concerned. Remember, there has never been any love lost for you. I just don't trust him yet. I'm just trying to do what's best for you."

Bedelia saw that Polly's small body began to quiver, at first, and then to shake uncontrollably as their argument continued.

"What's best for me? What's best for me? I've been praying for what's best for me...for my pa to love me so we can be a family again. And you and Judge Lynch are blocking God's answering my prayers."

"You little fool! Don't you see, dammit, I am the answer to your prayers. I love you... Me...and you're in my family now."

Instantly Bedelia could see what was coming next. She moved to the girl and tried to wrap her in her arms, to comfort her or to protect her from Knowles's mounting rage, but the girl shrugged off her touch and defiantly said, "BUT YOU'RE NOT MY FATHER!"

"Like hell I'm not! I'm the one who really loves you, not that drunken sot. I would never lock you in a hallway closet for days or even weeks on end without food. I would never beat you until you were unconscious. And I'm the one who would never throw a bloody ax at you. I'm a better father to you than he ever could be."

Bedelia moved to separate the combatants. She knew that Knowles was a good man, an upright man, but he was, after all, a man. And she knew that even as Polly's anger level increased, so too did Knowles', along with a corresponding decrease of his better judgment and self-control. She feared that someone was bound to get hurt and not just emotionally.

"B...but...but G...God can ch...change him...him...hi...hi...hhhhhhhhhhhhhhh."

Knowles was so upset that he was oblivious to the changes in Polly's voice. However, Bedelia could hear, and Bedelia could see. Polly was no longer able to argue or even to breathe effectively as she vainly struggled to fill her tiny lungs; however, it was as if someone had knocked all the wind out of her. Legs, no longer able to bear her weight, gave way, collapsing the girl to the floor.

The sound of the girl's cease-fire was what brought Knowles around to see Polly lying supine on the floor, gasping for air, like a fish out of water. Even her skin had taken on the ashen bluish gray of a corpse at a mortuary.

So suddenly brought out of his own tirade, Knowles was now speechless. But his pleading eyes clearly said, *Bedelia, what do we do now?*

"Knowles, bring your paper from the floor, pour the rest of your tea over it. Get it as wet as you can, then give it to me!"

Pastor Knowles busied himself preparing the newspaper as instructed, grateful to be doing something useful to occupy his mind instead of worry.

"Now, dear, spread them out thick upon the floor and be ready to hand them to me when I ask." Then turning her attention back to the hapless girl, reassuringly said, "Now, Polly dear, this is going to be hard to force yourself to do...but quick, girl, HOLD YOUR BREATH FOR THE NEXT TEN SECONDS! I'll count for you..."

Before Bedelia was halfway through her count, Polly's eyes rolled up into her head, and she collapsed even further into the floor.

"NOW GIVE ME THE NEWSPAPER!"

Cradling the girl in her arms, Bedelia wasted no time in loosely wrapping her entire head in wet paper, then fought to keep Polly from tearing herself free. "No, girl, breathe...BREATHE!"

"Hey! No fair! I want to smother her too."

Bedelia completely ignored her husband's flippancy, as she concentrated on any sound emanating from the makeshift bag. At first, only labored exhalations could be heard, and these were quite faint.

"That's right, girl! That's it...you're doing it...keep going. You're doing great."

Husband and wife held their own breath and waited and quietly prayed.

Finally it came. Small and faint, yes! Nonetheless, it was unmistakable—the sound of an inhalation, followed by an unlabored exhalation. Then another, stronger, more natural. Still another pair, yet another. Quickly Bedelia removed the soggy papers. And still they continued, inspiration and expiration, one blessedly following the other in the dance called breathing.

Big strong arms effortlessly carried a thoroughly exhausted little girl to a former storage room turned ideal foster child's bedroom, at the very end of the long hallway. Upon reaching the room, Pastor Knowles felt as if Polly had suddenly become quite heavy. Even so with one arm, he held her steady against his chest, while he employed the other one to swing the door inward, granting access to the room.

Knowles listened to the heavy door as it loudly squealed against its hinges, loud enough to be heard throughout the entire house. "Oh, that will never do," he said to himself. "I will have to oil those hinges in the morning."

Once in the room, Knowles used the same free hand to draw open the bedspread. Laying her on the bed, he then focused his attention to the removing of her dusty boots.

So worn out from her breathing ordeal that it was only then that Polly was hard-pressed to recall even one word spoken to her since leaving Bedelia to tidy up the living room. In fact, not only had her pastor not spoken to her since their fight, he deliberately avoided all eye contact with her. However, as he placed the blanket over her, she chanced to notice the tears barely being kept in check by him and instantly regretted she had been the cause.

Polly's lips trembled as she struggled to say I'm so sorry, or please forgive me, or some such half-hearted conciliatory statement, only to have her beloved pastor deride her efforts.

"No, don't say it!" he demanded, sounding so much more than merely cross with her; her words had wounded him deeply, and there was nothing she could do to make up for it. "I don't want to hear a word you have to say, young lady. Just stay here until Bedelia brings your supper. You need to cool off...and so do I!"

As soon as the door was closed, a flood of tears soaked her pillow and streamed onto her mattress but fell far short of bringing the relief she needed. It pained her deeply to be the cause of such turmoil for those she loved. However, she was determined that nothing either Pastor Knowles or Judge Lynch did would keep her from seeing her father again. Instantly the thought brought the unpleasant realization that their fight had only begun, and her next actions, willingly or not, would only serve to bring more pain to her beloved foster family.

*****

Bedelia once told Polly that, "Frustration and determination often walk hand in hand." For the last half-hour, Polly felt that no truer words had ever been spoken, as she struggled to silently open her bedroom window. It was almost as much of a struggle as her own confusion over Judge Lynch's decision.

"Lord, why did the judge have to take me away from Pa like that? I feel like an orphan, losing both of my parents now. I do so love Pastor Knowles and Biddy—oops, I mean, Bedelia—and I'm grateful to be living with them. And I know that Pa can be mean when he's drinking. But if I can just get him to come back home, I just know that we can be a family again."

Finally the stubborn window yielded to the fourteen-year-old's determination. Making sure not to alarm the Knowles, Polly slipped through the opening and began to run as fast as she could, down the dirt road leading to town.

The two-mile journey was difficult enough on foot. However, the strengthening winds and choking dust made it doubly so. Three times the girl lost her bearings, and two times she stumbled and fell.

But somehow, Polly managed to arrive at the stiflingly dirty main street, just in time to feel the mercilessly hot noonday sun.

Even in the best of times, the visage that was the town of Garden City bore no aesthetic to its name. Appearing to grow up from the shallow soil itself, the hamlet's buildings shared the subdued rustic colors of red, yellow, brown as well as an occasional green to match the surrounding prairie.

Then the dust storms came. Some lasted only hours, while others proceeded for days. Collectively they sandblasted Garden City until the usually dull pigments used to cover its edifices were stripped away altogether, leaving a town as monochromatic as the now-desolate and denuded prairie.

In 1933, during the early months of the great dust storms, shop owners would periodically emerge from their stores and homes. Armed with brooms, they valiantly fought to protect their dwellings from the onslaught of the pulverized and powdered earth. Two years later, those shop owners have all but capitulated to the foe. Their morale, like the paint that had adorned their shops, was gradually eroded away and obliterated by the pitiless winds.

Polly wanted to get to the bar as quickly as possible; however, twice she had to stop and cough up a wad of charcoal-black soot tinged with bright red streaks. During her second bout of expectoration, she rose up to walk right into Sheriff Pucket.

The two looked at each other in total surprise. When Polly appeared too guilty to speak, the middle-aged lawman took it upon himself to fire the first shot.

"It's always a joy to see you, Polly," the sheriff said as calmly as he could manage. Then the enforcer side of him would no longer be suppressed. Slipping a meaty hand around her delicate forearm, he shouted, "What in hell are you doing out here? You're supposed to be home, with Sister Knowles."

The first impulse Polly had was to tell him that she wasn't alone and that she and Biddy—oops, Bedelia—had taken the bus into town. However, her infantile tendency to lie had long since been prayer-purged by her first Sunday school teacher, Bedelia Knowles. At any rate, the lie was too easy to discover with Bedelia still at home.

Fortunately the sudden arrival of the mayor diverted the sheriff's attention enough for her to slip her slender arm from his grasp. She was saved! In a flash, she was off.

Polly knew that her father would not be at all happy to see her. She even realized that his being in a bar meant that he might be violent. However, she had come much too far to let something like common sense deter her now. All too soon, she came upon the faded red-paint peeling door of the local (and only) drinking establishment. She took a deep breath to steady herself. But it only brought on a new bought of violent coughing, followed immediately by a bloody flux. All in all, the girl felt anything but calm. So be it, she thought, as she turned the tarnished brass knob and entered in.

It had become the habit of the barkeep to look over the rim of his black horn-rimmed glasses, to see whoever walked in. This time, he saw no one. Curious he leaned over the corner of the bar and saw Polly.

"I'm sorry, miss, but you can't come in here."

Acting as if she hadn't heard him (in and of itself, a lie, she chastised herself), she quickly looked around the room to find her father. The air was heavy with cigar smoke, which made it difficult for her to see. It also made it difficult to breathe.

She didn't hear the barkeep's second warning, as she supported herself on her knees, while her body was racked with a new coughing spell. It was not quite over as she walked slowly to a table which sat in a darkened corner of the room. Three men sat at the splintered desk, sharing a bottle of clear liqueur. A tall mountain of a man sat between two others. She recognized them at once. Her father, Buck, bracketed by his hoodlum buddies, Doug and Budd Sweeny.

While Doug nursed his customary cup of black coffee, the other two looked and smelled as if they had been guzzling booze at the table for quite some time.

It took all the courage she had for even her most timid squeaky mouse voice to come from her. She listened to a stranger's voice say, "Pa, please come home?" Immediately the mountain began to rumble.

Rolling two heavily encrusted bloodshot eyes toward her, he said, "Get the hell outta here, brat!"

Her father's voice sounded like a junkyard guard dog. It alone had always caused her to freeze in terror; her mind no longer able to think properly enough for her to answer. Nevertheless, this time she did.

"P…Pa. Please come home. If you did, I know that we could all be a family again. Pa…I…love…"

Without further warning, the guard dog attacked. A mighty backhand flashed from the table, striking the little girl to the ground. Polly raised her head from the sawdust-covered floor. The entire right side of her face burned as a bright-red patch, the size and shape of a canoe paddle, covered it. Her split lower lip hemorrhaged freely, filling her mouth with a foul metallic taste.

Up and over the table, Buck Riser leaped, knocking it over, along with the bottle of booze.

"Get the hell outta here!" he roared. "No narrow-hipped heifer is gonna tell a grown man like me what to do."

Then before she could react, a heavy boot lashed out. The kick to her stomach lifted the girl bodily off the floor. No longer a delicate child, Polly was now a battered and discarded rag doll, which remained airborne as it crossed the room to lie in a heap at the bar's entrance.

As the guard dog moved in for a final assault, strong hands of his drinking buddies withstood him, wrestling him to the ground.

"What is the matter with you?" said Doug Sweeny. "She's your own bloody kid, for Christ's sake."

"She ain't none of mine! She ain't none of mine!" he bellowed as he struggled to rise. Despite the size of his cohorts, Buck gained a foothold and rose to his feet. "That little bastard is Knowles's spawn. She ain't none—"

Buck got no further as a massive fist from Sheriff Pucket smashed into his jaw, leaving him sprawled out on the floor.

"Get out of here, Polly!" Pucket yelled back at the girl who, even as he spoke, was already out the door.

Swimming in and out of consciousness, the girl stumbled out of the bar. The smashing pain in her head was all but forgotten; its place superseded by the excruciating pain to her abdomen. Wrapping her arms around herself, she felt that her lower rib cage was no longer the solid structure it once had been. Raising her blouse, she fought against her blurring vision to inspect the right side of her lower chest. Two, perhaps three, of her ribs felt loose and detached, floating in a slowly expanding pool of dark liquid.

With every step, Polly struggled to breathe. Even so she practically sleepwalked her way to the main road of the town. No longer thinking, she had only one impulse—she must get home.

Stumbling, she slowly began to move toward home. Blinded by pain, Polly was oblivious to her surroundings. She didn't notice the wind, which began to blow so much harder than when she came into town. She didn't notice the rapidly darkening skies. But somehow, she heard it, sounding every bit like an approaching freight train. But why was it running off its tracks? And why was it coming her way? Somehow Polly summoned the strength to turn around.

Living in the great state of Kansas for all her life, Polly was well familiar with the tornadoes that were a regular seasonal phenomenon. She knew their appearance. She knew the sound that they made. The swirling mass that was approaching her from the northwest was somewhat like them, except this was much, much bigger and much, much louder—and the thing was tumbling sideways. She thought it looked like a giant steamroller. It was immense, filling the entire sky with impenetrable darkness. Then like her father, the mass was coming in way too fast to run from, even if she could. Finally Polly saw that there was nothing on the sides of the road to hide behind to shield her from the monster.

"M...Mommy!"

CHAPTER 22

Remember Lot's Wife

In time, the date of April 14, 1935, would be known as Black Sunday. Ironically it took the worst of the black blizzards phenomena of the Plain States to convince the entire nation of the need for federal intervention in what was heretofore considered a regional problem.

Originating in Southwest Canada, the murderous swathe had respect for neither man-made borders nor geographical boundaries but sandblasted and buried everything as far north as Chicago and Boston, to arrive at the nation's capital while congress vainly debated the need to regulate the efficient use of farmlands. The dust storm, which many people thought to be the end of the world, motivated congress to quickly push through the enactment of The Soil Conservation Act of 1935. The storm eventually made its way past America's Eastern Seaboard to properly dust the decks of ships, up to two hundred miles at sea.[15]

In the Knowles's parsonage, dust from another type of storm was just beginning to settle when Bedelia asked her husband and pastor, "Has sending Polly to her room given you a chance to cool off?"

Knowles let out a long sigh of relief as he clasped his hands behind his neck and leaned back as far as his antiquated rocking chair would allow, as he replied, "No argument there, dear, you know me too well. Where'd you learn that little trick with the newspaper earlier?"

Bedelia lowered her head and shyly said, "That last summer before starting college, I had the opportunity to work in the nursing school library. It was fun, and I read everything I could lay my hands on. Didn't get much work done, though, I was let go after the first week."

It was then Knowles's turn to humbly say, "Praise God, you were always a gifted student. I was so angry, and I felt so helpless, and I despise both feelings. Sometimes I even despise myself," he said softly to himself, hoping Bedelia had not heard.

She had indeed heard him but acted as if she had not.

Presently she said softly, "We are all only human. For better or worse, we all carry the image of God in crude imperfect human vessels. It is only human pride that demands we be better or holier than anyone else. And it is that same pride that causes self-loathing when we fail to live up to the lies of our self-image."

Knowles said nothing but sat there contemplating his wife's words, which were gentle and soothing in tone yet sharp and probing in their portent.

Suddenly the ambient light in the room darkened and faded away completely, as if the hand of God had reached out to extinguish the sun. The roar of a freight train pounded throughout the entire edifice where railroad tie had never been laid.

The two clung to each other on the floor, in a corner of the room, trembling, as if the whole structure would collapse around them. Then amid the nightmare of the phantom trains, a singular thought came to them both—*what about the girl?*

Without relinquishing their hold on each other, the couple groped their way into the central hallway. Though the cacophony continued unabated, streams of light escaped into the hall to reveal— dust, dust everywhere. The ceiling and walls were all permeated with the powdery debris, with the greatest accumulations present on the floor. The pattern of infiltration clearly indicated that it was coming from Polly's room.

Panic gripped them both as Knowles, not waiting for an answer, bounded into the room, which was in complete disarray with the lone window in the room gaping wide before them.

Bedelia clutched her hands to her chest in horror, upon seeing the open port towering above the empty bed. "Knowles!" She cried, "The storm, it must have—"

"The storm nothing," he said, his anger mounting within him like a knight upon his charger. "She opened the window herself before the storm. Bea, Polly's run away."

"R...run...away," she said incredulously. "But...why...would she go? Where...would she go?"

Out of the corner of his eyes, Knowles saw the utter wretchedness in Bedelia's face and wanted to pity her. But there was no time. "Bea, your two questions have but one answer, and you well know it. Polly is braving this storm in order to see her father, Buck, and she is in grave danger from either. And there's only one place that he would be."

"But surely, Judge Lynch's injunction—"

"Can't possibly protect her from what she so desperately desires. Come, Bea, I'll lead, you'll drive."

Though the dust storm showed obvious signs of waning, there was yet enough life in it to reduce visibility to little beyond one's reach to stall the engines of vehicles and to smother and choke those foolhardy enough to be exposed. Still the Knowles plodded on. With wet tarp covering the engine cowling and wet bandanas covering their faces, he walked a body's length ahead of the truck, while Bedelia gingerly coaxed it forward.

By the time they reached town, the winds had all but ceased; however, turmoil continued to reign, especially in the direction of the town's only surviving vestige of the days of prohibition.

"Stay with the truck and keep it running!" he ordered Bedelia, as he ran directly to the booze hall, fearing the worst. Bursting in, he saw Sheriff Pucket, the Sweeny brothers, and several others working to restrain Buck in a slowly deteriorating stalemate.

"Where's my little girl, you bastard?" said Knowles, throwing his weight to the throng.

Doug Sweeny answered, "She was in here a moment ago, then disappeared back outside."

"But she ain't got far." Budd chimed in. "Not the way she was banged up and all."

"The way she was banged up?" Knowles repeated, his hands tightening around Buck's throat. "What in hell did you do to her?"

Buck's eyes began to roll up into his head, while Sheriff Pucket fought to release the clergy's stranglehold. "Let go, Pat! Let go! This ain't gonna help her. She's out there somewhere and needs you. So you get on now! I got Buck."

Even as the sheriff spoke, all could feel that, Buck was beginning to regain his footing. "Sheriff!" Doug said, straining against the rising mountain. "I don't think Buck wants to go to jail again."

That's when Mack, the bartender, approached, bringing his preferred "sedative" to lend his talents to the cause.

Seizing the moment, as well as the baseball bat, Knowles pivoted completely around, bringing the genuine Louisville Slugger crashing onto the top of Buck's head. It shattered, sending splinters throughout the room, as Buck's head swiveled, as if on a spring, before rolling backward, taking the rest of his massive body crashing to the floor.

"Well, I think he's amiable to the idea now, Sheriff," Knowles said as he tossed the remnant of the bat onto the floor, then hurried outside to Bedelia.

The Knowles quickly interviewed several people who reported having seen the girl. They all said the same thing—though severely injured, Polly miraculously managed to pick herself up and stumble toward the main road out of town.

Bedelia slowly drove the same route, praying to get a glimpse of her. "You know where she's headed, don't you? As hurt and confused as she is, she is trying to make her way back home."

Knowles offered no reply but took advantage of the improved visibility to concentrate the more. The thought that *she'd never get too far in her condition* turned repeatedly in his mind, driving him to pray, "Merciful Lord, whatever condition she's in, help me to find her and take care of her."

After that, Knowles shouted to Bedelia, "Polly's not back in town, and she's too hurt to make it home, so she must be close by."

Silently he repeated his prayer, *Dear Lord, guide me to the girl… open my eyes and my understanding so that I may find her.*

Sweat from the earnestness of his prayers began to sting his eyes, forcing them shut. Suddenly, with eyes still closed, a new thought dug into his mind with such insistence, his temples began to throb. The words of his last week's sermon flashed through his thoughts like a signal flare—*remember Lot's wife*—along with the indelible image of a pillar of salt standing on a hill, overlooking the destruction of twin cities below would not be denied.

Kansas is a Plains State extraordinaire. Nearly flawless in its featurelessness, the monotonous montage of much of the state had become nothing short of legendary. Anything presenting itself against this palate of nothing would instantly contrast and catch the eye. So it was that as Knowles fought to clear his eyes of the stinging salt of his brow, his peripheral vision barely caught its silhouette as Bedelia drove by.

"BEA, STOP THE TRUCK!" Knowles shouted, and before the vehicle had come to a halt, he tumbled headlong from its cargo bed to crawl on hands and knees through the dirt to reach the object they had nearly missed altogether. There, discarded along the side of the road, lay the very image of the biblical illustration—*a pillar of salt.*

"Oh, Knowles," she whispered, "it can't be…it's not possible…"

But her husband was now beyond all hearing, beyond seeing anything save that which lay before him, beyond all reason save for the singleminded purpose at hand. As one possessed, he ploughed into the column, his bare hands raking it until his nails split and bled. Thus he continued until his excavation was complete. Though revulsion gripped his stomach to the point of retching, he still thanked God that he had found her.

As Bedelia moved to her husband's side, she too fell to her knees, her hands covering her mouth in total shock. "Oh, dear God! My baby!"

"I can hear her breathing…barely," said Knowles. "But, God Almighty…look at her!"

The girl who lay before them had the semblance more of an old worn-out and discarded rag doll than of the vibrant frolicking naiad they had known. The flowing yellow sundress lay in tatters about her, exposing the skin beneath to the scouring forces which left little distinction between the two. Then there was her face, once smooth and beautiful was now well excoriated and scrubbed with various depths of furrows and gashes, like the Grand Canyon. Upon each exhalation, fine dust mingled with frothy blood bubbled from her nose and the corners of her mouth. Her arms crossed her lower chest and, upon gently feeling the area, immediately knew that the blood gurglings were as much the result of multiple fractured ribs, from the force of a heavy leather boot invading the chest cavity, as to any dust that might have infiltrated therein.

Finally the girl's eyes, like the dust and debris which protruded from under her bedroom door that gave a sort of premonition of the carnage within powdered and pulverized sand and dirt, forced itself through the defenses of her eyelids to ravage and savage the delicate structures beneath. Cornea and pupils, once clear with lustra, had been scoured and scored into opacity. Even the liquid lens that lay in front of her retinae had not been spared but were pierced, penetrated, and dried out by the desiccating silicate.

Bedelia was ashen as it was now her turn to say, "Knowles, what are we going to do?"

However, Knowles was already at work, removing his clergy waistcoat to wrap it around the naked body of the girl, as gently as if she were a newborn baby wrapped in its first receiving blanket. Being equally as gentle, he slid onto the passenger side of the truck's bench seat to finally cradle the child in his protective arms.

As Bedelia climbed in next to him, she heard her husband whisper into the girl's ear, "I've got you now, sweetheart, ain't gonna let nothing hurt you ever again."

Bedelia said under her breath, "That's sounds like 'closing the barn door after the cows have all escaped.'" However, she said to Knowles, "Drive back to town or go back home?"

"Neither!" he replied. "Stay on the main road to reach the outskirts of Garden City, as safe and gentile as you can."

"What's there, darling?"

"Saint Catherine Hospital, beyond Polly's old farmhouse and just before the border of Finney County. I know a friend there who may be able to help us."

*****

Benjamin Bucannon "Buck" Riser, once the terror of Garden City, in two short years had transformed himself into the hero of Leavenworth and Kansas's favorite son. However, with skill and cunning, and within a week of his triumphant return home, Buck managed to return to being Finney County's most hated and reviled citizen.

Effigies of Buck were beaten and burned in his honor. Children gathered and played, reenacting "Buck's last stand" when, after a simulated kick from the largest child, the smallest of them would be carried by the others and deposited roughly in the street. Mothers reprimanded their young ones saying, "Be good, or Buck's gonna get you."

In the municipal lodgings, next to the courthouse, Landlord Pucket watched his adult neighbors and friends slowly congregate under Buck's cell, chanting and calling for the reenactment of a "necktie social."

Now it will forever be a matter of debate, among high-brow academics and low-brow rabble alike, as to the circumstances surrounding that peculiar evening. Some contend that Sheriff Pucket's keys were lifted as he passed by Buck's cell, while others dismiss this theory saying that Buck's fingers were too large to possess the manual dexterity needed for such a task. Others postulate that the mischievous Sweeny brothers somehow collaborated in the events that transpired; however, though they were present that night, multiple eyewitnesses report that they were gathered with, and even leading, those calling for social revenge. By far, the most outlandish theory alluded to Sheriff Pucket's possible motivation toward job security by maintaining the viability of his most frequent prisoner.

Whatever the cause, whatever the reason, whatever the mechanism involved, the result was the same. Somehow Buck had slipped through his manacles, slithered from his cell, sifted his way past deputies and lynch mob alike to disappear into the vast surrounding countryside.

Sheriff Pucket stood outside the door of the parsonage and waited, while Pastor Knowles prepared to join him. Throwing on an old corduroy jacket belonging to his father, he happened to notice his wife standing in the archway to the main hallway. Or rather he noticed her dark liquid-crystal eyes pleading with him, *Please, don't go!* Then aloud, she said, "Please, not tonight…not like this…angry and hateful, like the rest. What if SHE wakes up…what if she DOESN'T wake up?"

Knowles sighed but was unflinching in his resolve. For the fifth time since last night, he patiently explained, "Dr. Goodwell assured us that the worst is over, and if we keep her wounds clean and dry, she should wake up. Maybe not tonight or tomorrow, but consciousness should return. When it does, she's to see a colleague of his up north, in Topeka. There's nothing more I can do here, but out there…" He pointed with his thumb toward Pucket and the distant nightscape.

Bedelia fell silent, as Knowles slowly made his way to the mantel place and opened a pressed steel box on its shelf. It stared back at him, mocking him, daring him to reach inside, giving the lie to all he professed. After ensuring a full magazine had been shoved in place and charged, he tucked it neatly away in the side pocket of his jacket, then said, "When Grandpa Clemmons gave this to me, he asked if I could really use it against another person. I wasn't sure back then. But…seeing what he did to her…to that sweet beautiful child…has answered the question for me. I CAN kill Buck Riser. I WANT to kill him…and when I see him again, believe me, I WILL kill Buck."

Bedelia knew, there was no longer any holding back. With an anguished cry from her very soul, she spewed, "But you're not talking about protecting your loved ones anymore. All you're after is revenge!"

Knowles snapped. "Woman, I don't give a good gosh darn which is which anymore. I've prayed long enough for Buck to be out of her life…to be out of our lives. Now I'm done praying."

"P-please, d-don't do this," she said exhaustedly. "Let the law handle this…let a jury handle this…only God can judge a man…"

Knowles interrupted and, in a low rumble, said, "This day… I am the hand of God."

With this, he made his way past the front door, pausing briefly to say over his shoulder, "I agree with Grandpa Clemmons… I should have done this long ago."

Once outside, Sheriff Pucket looked downcast and contrite. He had spent an entire hour that evening receiving gratuitous verbal abuse from the mayor, from the town council, and from the press. Now as Knowles approached, thoughts of a friendship finished filled him with self-recriminations; after all, Buck had escaped on his watch, from underneath the lawman's very nose.

There was much that Knowles could have said as he sauntered alongside the sheriff. Instead all he uttered was, "Leavenworth, hell! Where next we send that bastard, there will be no escape, no pardon, and no reprieve."

CHAPTER 23

A Gift on the Altar

Bedelia Knowles wiped her hands upon the well-worn embroidered apron she wore. She'd been busy cutting up chicken to fry for supper, when she was interrupted by a loud scraping noise coming from the kitchen window above the deep double sink. She sauntered over to it; however, before she could ascertain what it was, the window suddenly slid open. She was surprised to see it was Buck, who glided through the opening, leaving dirty boot prints in and on the sink before, at last, coming to stand before her.

"Buck, you know you're not supposed to be here. It's not safe… everyone's out looking for you," she said, fear tingeing her voice.

Buck Riser spoke; his voice was intoxicated and threatening. "I've been watching the house most of the day till your old man left."

Bedelia averted her eyes to the floor, hoping Buck had not seen the mounting fear in them.

"Relax, woman, and have a seat!" he demanded.

Bedelia quickly obeyed, plopping down onto a chair at the checker-boarded kitchen table. However, she was back on her feet with a speed that belied her fifty-two years of age when Buck turned and walked toward the bedroom at the end of the hall. Bravely, she stood, arms outstretched, in front of the door to the room where Polly lay.

Buck took little notice of the woman's challenge. Instead he said, "I don't mean no harm, to her or to you. I heard the brat got hurt bad in the last dust storm. I come to see if what they say is true."

"She got hurt bad before getting caught in the storm," Bedelia said bitterly, praying all the while that Knowles would return soon.

Buck pushed his way past her five-foot-nothing frame and entered the room. Intimidated as she was, Bedelia still managed to hover close to Buck as he stood next to the bed and peered down at the broken rag doll that lay upon it.

Several deep cuts and scrapes could easily be seen poking from under the borders of her heavy facial dressings. Buck thought they resembled aerial pictures he had seen of the Grand Canyon. However, all the whiskey he had consumed prior to arriving here could not anesthetize him from what he saw as he gently raised the bandages to examine the face beneath.

"So it's true then," Buck said, wheeling back.

Bedelia thought she heard a note of regret in the visitor's voice.

"Yes, it's true. She is blind."

Bedelia hoped her voice was not as heated as she felt toward her charge's father. The truth was quite the contrary; she felt nothing but cold icy rage toward this man who had hurt her baby. And she wanted to hurt him back somehow. "She hasn't been awake since Knowles found her, naked and completely buried along the road three days ago. Seems like every woman you're with ends up caught in storms naked. Doc says it's a wonder she's alive at all after—"

"After what I'd done to her?" Buck interrupted.

"After the dust storm," Bedelia corrected. "Knowles dug her out with his bare hands."

Buck snarled when he heard the pastor's name. The change had not been lost on Bedelia, and it brought her a cruel sense of satisfaction.

Bravely, she asked, "Seems you've always bore some sort of grudge against the pastor for only who knows why! But why do you hate that poor child so much? For god's sake, Buck, she's your own daughter."

Buck Riser turned upon her as she finally pressed upon his festering wound.

He grimaced at her and said, "Woman, that dumb heifer ain't none of mine!"

"Nonsense!" she replied. "Why of course she's yours."

"You're wrong, woman!" Buck said, spewing his venom over Bedelia's bespectacled face. "I know she was sired by Knowles."

"That can't be!" Bedelia said matter-of-factly.

"Darn right it is. I know those two had a thing going on, long before Penny and I got hitched."

"I remember," Bedelia admitted. "He was a young assistant pastor, and she was the choir directress. Everyone was just sure they'd be together forever. But Pastor Knowles eventually married his childhood sweetheart, and you married—"

"I know who we all married!" Buck said, his anger mounting. "Trouble was, Penny couldn't stay away from Knowles. Every time we had a spat, she'd run to him for 'pastoral counseling.' I ain't stupid, woman. I know what the 'laying on of hands' in prayer means where those two were concerned."

Hot sweat, which had begun to soak the severely tied hair bun behind Bedelia's head, now freely cascaded down her wrinkled face. However, with growing courage, she intended that the truth be finally said, no matter the consequences to herself.

"Buck, every time Penny was with Pastor Knowles, I was with them, ALWAYS!"

Buck glared at her, like a rabid dog, but Bedelia wouldn't back down. "No matter how you might feel about Polly, the truth is, Penny had never, NEVER been unfaithful to you."

"Never?" Buck asked suspiciously as he leaned against a bedroom wall.

"Never, Buck," Bedelia insisted. "I know what those two had meant to each other. But I'm a pastor's wife, who never trusted human nature. Knowles and I just couldn't afford a scandal. So I watched them like a hawk...ALWAYS. There was never...EVER a time I allowed those two to have even the slightest moment alone together."

Buck looked as if he were beginning to understand when a tangent thought ignited his angst anew. "But, woman." He spat. "All those months with you...she came back to me pregnant...with that jacklegged preacher's baby."

"Buck," she said, looking deep into his eyes, "she WAS pregnant…WITH YOUR BABY. Penny told me all about that night and your fight. You came home drunk and demanded to know where old man Clemmons kept his cashbox. She wouldn't tell you, so you did what you always do…you started smacking her around—"

Just then, Buck's anguished howl cut her short. But Bedelia would not back down now. With renewed courage, she continued, "When she would no longer be intimidated by you, you decided to dominate her in a different way."

"STOP!" Buck howled like an animal, rather as one possessed as he raised his massive hand, ready to strike her down.

But as his hand commenced its deadly downward arc, she shouted, "In the name of the Lord Jesus Christ, you can no more harm me than you can erase the truth!"

Buck screamed, this time not in anguish but in pain, as his bludgeoning arm became locked in paralysis, the veins in his temples distending as if they would explode. And as the searing, piercing pain in his head forced eyes to bulge and pupils to dilate, Buck could see the grimacing face of Grandpa Clemmons stare into his, the old man's overwhelmingly powerful hand locked in a crushing death grip around his arm, the pain driving Buck to his knees.

Suddenly Clemmons spoke, but it was Bedelia's voice which was heard to say, "When she would no longer be intimidated by you, you decided to dominate her in a different way. When she ran out of the house, naked into the night, she was already carrying your child…because…you had forced yourself upon her. Buck, YOU RAPED PENNY!"

"YES, YES, YES!" Buck vomited the words, as well as his stomach's contents. "That was what happened… I raped Penny."

"Believe me, Buck! I swear by all I hold holy, that little girl is your daughter. Polly is your own flesh and blood, Buck." In her mind, she prayed, *Oh, Lord, please help this knucklehead to finally understand.*"

Buck looked thoughtful for a moment. Then anxious to escape Bedelia's barrage by changing the subject, he said, "You know what the last thing she tried to tell me was? 'I love you, Pa.' Goshdarnit,

'I love you, Pa.' How the hell could she possibly feel that way, after what I'd done to her and her mother?"

Bedelia, not wanting her answer to sound easy or cliché, softly said, "Buck, all those days and weeks where you kept her locked in the hallway closet, with nothing but bread and water to eat…and sometimes not even that…do you know what she was doing? Do you know what she did? She spent each moment in there praying and fasting for you. Beaten and abused, she never ceased to pray and fast for you. Because she loves you and wants you two to be a family again."

She paused to allow what she had said to catch hold. At length she said, "Buck, the answer to your question is that little girl loves you because God is love, and he fills Polly with himself. Buck, God is also forgiveness."

"It's too late, woman," he exclaimed. "Judge Lynch took her from me. It's too late now."

"I don't believe that, Buck. There may still be time…to be the father…to be the man she needs. Buck, be someone she can look up to and be proud of."

"I've never been someone that anyone could be proud of," he said as he knelt on one knee beside the bed. "Not for some time now."

Buck tentatively reached for Polly and then stopped.

"Go on," said Bedelia. "You won't wake her."

Buck felt uneasy as he combed her matted hair through his gnarled fingers.

"I'm sorry, kid," Buck said, as if she really could hear him. "I never meant for anything like this to happen to you. I know, it sounds hypocritical coming from me, after all I've done. I hardly believe it myself. But somehow, kid… I swear… I'll find a way to make this right."

He rose from Polly's bedside and walked to the door. Then he abruptly stopped and turned around. Bedelia looked puzzled as he opened the room's only window. Taking out his hipflask, he opened it and poured its contents onto the ground below. Then closing its top, Buck placed the empty bottle on the pillow next to Polly's head.

"Whenever she wakes up, she'll know what this means."

Without another word, Buck left the room, and the house, and walked into the dry night air without seeing Pastor Knowles Model A Ford as it drove up.

By some miracle, Knowles had failed to see Buck as well. However, what he saw was the front door ajar. In a near-panicked state, Pastor Knowles burst into the house and immediately saw the boot prints in the kitchen, recognizing their unique size and owner.

Drawing his pistol, he saw Buck's whiskey flask in Polly's bed and the strange contented look on Bedelia's face. He looked back and forth between them both, feeling alternately confused, concerned, scared, and finally, thankful that God had watched over his family while he was ill-advisedly away, seeking anything but God's will.

Knowles held Bedelia close in his arms and wept.

In the bed below, almost imperceptibly, Polly smiled.

CHAPTER 24

Topeka Iron Horse

Polly Quashi'miuoo Riser lay supine and unmoving for the fourth day following the great dust storm. Though her body remained still and unresponsive, her thoughts, like salmon eggs during spawning season, swam back and forth in a stream which coursed its way between recovery and release, between consciousness and chaos, and between time and eternity. Yet even in this state, her mind remained in prayer.

Dear Lord, please forgive me complaining that Judge Lynch's ruling made me feel like an orphan. You let me live with Pastor and Biddy—oops... Bedelia... I'm such a flippety-jibbette—and I love them to pieces. But I wonder, who'll take care of Pa while I'm gone? Please, Lord, you take care of him until I can do it again.

Bedelia Knowles had not left the parsonage since the girl arrived unconscious but spent her days happily moving about, attending to her foster daughter's every unspoken need. "My dearest," she said as she finished putting a fresh nightgown on the girl. "It is a true miracle that you're still among us. So I promise, I'll be patient, and I'll be right here until you come back to us."

Though the Reverend Patrick Knowles still carried the Luger in his pocket, he no longer was a part of those involved in the manhunt for Buck. As he distanced himself from the mob, so the desire for revenge and murder had distanced itself from him, leaving only a need to stay close to home. Partially from a renewed sense of purpose toward his family, but mostly from a sense of guilt and shame from his attitude and actions of the night before. The words "Vengeance belongeth unto me, I will recompense, saith the Lord" (Hebrews 10:30 KJV) chastised him throughout the day.

Though the Knowles were unaware of it, the stream of Polly's thoughts had changed during the night, from the back and forth, side-to-side ramblings that kept them bound to this temporal plain, to a more up and down, rise-and-fall pattern, from subtle beckoning stimuli, drawing it to a patch of light of amethyst hue, hovering in the distance above.

The persistent image of the approach of a tunnel of light troubled Bedelia out of a sound sleep and would grant her no rest. Alarmed, she hastily threw on a well-worn housecoat and ran to the girl's room. Though Polly's breathing could still be seen and felt, it was becoming slow and sporadic. There was more; her skin gradually grew cold, and Bedelia imagined it felt as if her spirit were leaving her body.

Immediately Bedelia was down upon both knees, crying out, "Oh, Lord! Don't take this girl, not yet…not like this. Not for me, Lord…not for my sake, but for the sake of your promise to her. This girl is your beloved servant, and she once told me of a promise in a vision you gave her that, 'Her father would not see death until his name had been added to your kingdom, and that Polly would not die until she had seen the fulfillment of her prayers for him.' I thank you that a change is going on in him… but he's not quite there yet. Oh, Lord, perfect your word to her and send her back to us. Cause her to dwell again among the living…in Jesus's precious name…"

As Bedelia continued in prayer, Polly's soul continued its upward journey toward the purple light, while a part of her mind was back at her family's old farmhouse.

Ma always told me that, whenever I am sad or confused, to look up at the clouds and tell them whatever it is ailing me. Since she has been gone, I spend a lot of time on the grassy hill behind the house. I lie on my back and talk to the clouds passing by and pray. I know the Lord always hears me, but I make-believe that the fluffy clouds can hear me too. It is a fun game. I pray a lot that Ma is happy now. I do so miss her terribly and long to see her again. And I pray for my pa to stop drinking, to not be so mean, and to love me so that we can be a family again. Sometimes I think I hear the clouds talking back to me...calling me. It is very hard to understand what they are saying...there is so much going on here, it is hard to hear them.

Though the presence of the amethyst light above called to something familiar in her, and filled her with a sense of happiness, heretofore unfelt by her, it remained in the distance. However, she now felt the existence of another—another presence, another voice, louder, more persuasive, and so much closer than the purple presence receding to the stars. Surrendering to the new impulse, she made her way toward it. As she drew near, the voice became both understandable and recognizable.

"B-Biddy?" Polly weakly asked, for once, unapologetic for the use of the nickname. "Is that you?"

Bedelia, for once, unperturbed by its use, said, "Yes, pumpkin, it's Biddy. Praise God, you're back! I've been waiting for you."

Just then, Knowles came into the room, eyes full of wonder and surprise. "I thought I heard her talking. Why didn't you tell me Polly was awake again?"

Bedelia pondered it in her heart but did not say, *Because you were too preoccupied...feeling sorry for yourself.*

*****

It was no secret that Polly had always possessed a fascination with the iron horse. In fact, her love affair with the billowing behemoths began when she was just a toddler as she sat on the farmhouse hill, with Grandpa Clemmons, and listened to them chugging away in the distance. Boxcar and flatcar, hopper and caboose, along with rolling passenger stock of both wood and, later, of corrugated steel. Clemmons had told her about them all, and it sparked her affection as well as her imagination. Yet Polly had never, in all her fifteen years of life, ridden on one of them or even seen one up close. That was about to change.

On the day of her "accident," Dr. Henry Goodwell (who had previously saved her ax-mangled leg) wrote a letter of introduction for her to see a colleague of his—a specialist in a new medical science known as ophthalmology—whenever she had awakened and was safe to travel. For the last two weeks since Polly had come out of her coma, she had grown increasingly excited; not so much because of hope of regaining her sight but because Dr. Goodwell's colleague was in the city of Topeka, farther north than she had ever gone, necessitating her very first train ride.

Atchison, Topeka, and Santa Fe's pride of Wichita departed on time, for the 312-mile trip to the state capital.[16] Polly sat between her foster parents, reveling in each sound, scent, and sensation, but especially in the clickety-clack of the wheels as they passed along the tracks.

All too soon (for Polly), they disembarked the train in Topeka, and she marveled in the sheer size of this "true city" compared to the county seat township that was Garden City.

Dr. Steven Hillcrest seemed, to Polly, a younger man than Dr. Goodwell back home. And though he was a physician, she thought that his gentle mannerism and demeanor where more like those of a nurse. She instantly liked him. He spent a long time in his examination and testing of his young patient. When he was finished, Polly thought that his mood had saddened, as he left her in the exam room while he took the Knowles to his office next door.

Always curious, Polly strained to hear the adults talking through the wall behind her. Much of the conversation was unintelligible to her altogether. Though she could just make out words, like *lens*, *mucus membranes*, *corneas*, and *surgery can't repair*, she had no understanding of their combined meaning. Whatever it was, Polly clearly heard Bedelia start to cry inconsolably, and this made Polly sad as well.

The return trip home was spent largely in silence, with Polly and Bedelia held in each other's arms. Just who was comforting who was purely a matter of conjecture.

CHAPTER 25

Angel Has the Blues

On the northwest corner of town, a deserted dilapidated red brick building is all that remained of the Sweeny family's pre-Prohibition-era small-batch brewery and distillery.

Predicting the passage of the Eighteenth Constitutional Amendment, the patriarch, Douglass Pressman Sweeny, abandoned the sight in favor of moving operations to Canada. Though Prohibition ended with the passing of the Twenty-First Amendment, the site of the Garden City facility remained vacant. That was common knowledge among the townsfolk.

What no one knew was that it was not altogether abandoned but served as a home to the town's two more odious citizens, Doug and Budd Sweeny. Recently the brewery took on another more clandestine role—that of hideout for Buck against Sheriff Pucket's posse, as they continued their search for the fugitive.

The three comrades had spent the last hour discussing the matter of a certain locked strongbox, which had belonged to the late Saint Peter Clemmons, who willed the entirety of its contents to his granddaughter, Polly. What was envisioned as a meeting to draw up plans for its heist had begun immediately in a heated dispute, as Buck decided not only to back out of the project but to abandon those plans completely.

"Doug," Buck said, trying a second time to ease the brother's tensions while disappointing their hopes. "I once asked you how you could work in your family's old brewery and still be a teetotaler. You told me that—"

"Someone had to think straight around here," Doug impatiently finished the story. "Yeah, I remember. What of it?"

"Well, stealing the loot and splitting the country was your plan. And it was a great plan, but things have changed. I'm sober now, and I'm thinking straight, and I'm telling you straight—there's not going to be a heist."

Though resolute, Buck's pronouncement was without malice. Nonetheless, it amounted to a declaration of war to Doug and Budd Sweeny, who suddenly found their hopes of a better life (far removed from the drought, dust, and Depression of the Plain States) shatter like fine china hit with a howitzer.

Normally the more levelheaded of the two brothers, Doug, was livid, his face as red as if he had stepped out of an oven; its features twisted and contorted with rage, bordering on madness.

"You…you…you can't do this to me," Doug bellowed, choking on his own words. "Not now, after all the plans we've made."

Buck listened patiently as the older Sweeny brother ranted on. Doug's words and his demeanor caused Buck to mourn the calm quiet collectedness of his friend's sanity, feeling that it may never be present again.

"Boys, you don't understand," Buck began. His voice was conciliatory in his attempt to explain the changing situation. "I just found out…the kid… Polly really is my own flesh-and-blood daughter. As such—"

Buck got no further as Doug exploded out of his chair. "It's you who doesn't understand. I don't give a good-gosh-darn whose brat she is. I only care about the money. That strongbox is my ticket to a new life, and no son of a brat farm boy is going to keep me from it."

Doug rushed forward, brandishing the chair he had been sitting in. Holding the chair menacingly high, he prepared to bludgeon Buck with it but was suddenly held back by a frightened yet determined Budd Sweeny.

Darkness shone on Buck's face as he relieved Doug of the chair, tossing it across the room. Buck warned, "Let's not lose our heads over this, but I've thought about it, and my mind's made up. I'm clean and sober again, and that's how I'm going to stay. No matter what it takes, I'm going to be the kind of man that little girl can be proud of. From now on, I swear, I'm never going to hurt her ever again, and no one else is ever going to hurt her either. That means you ain't going to touch her or her inheritance. Who knows, if we ask nice, she might just give us the money we need. Heck, after I finish making things right with her, she might even go with us. But that's a long time off, and I got a lot of proving myself to her to do. So the heist is off. It's over, understand? Now don't make me tell you again."

Stillness enveloped the room as the color returned to Buck's face. Only then did he realize that he had been holding Doug Sweeny by his severely twisted jacket collar, his feet dangling just above the floor, as if Buck had been holding a child. Embarrassed Buck released his prisoner into the hands of his brother, Budd. The two then stormed from the room and continued out the building, heading back into town and their favorite watering hole, the speakeasy.

Once there, the barkeep immediately brought Budd his usual drink of whiskey but was surprised when the teetotaler Doug Sweeny ordered the same. Doug massaged his smarting throat until the drinks arrived. When they finally arrived, Doug downed his in a single lustful guzzle, then ordered another.

Holding his next drink in one hand he used the other to grab his brother by the arm and draw him close. "Say none of this to Buck, but it's not over, not by a long shot, it isn't. That money is still going to be ours, only now, we're going to do the job without that fool."

"But how we gonna do that after what Buck said. He ain't likely to just let us get away with it, is he?"

"Oh, don't you worry about him," Doug said, taking another huge drought of whiskey. "That posse is still looking for Buck. I figure it might just be about time they and the good sheriff found him."

*****

199

Polly was hard at work—pretending to be hard at work—in the kitchen, while Bedelia busied herself preparing supper. Throughout her work on the stove, Bedelia kept one eye on Polly, discreetly watching the child's half-hearted hit-and-miss performance. At length, Bedelia could take no more of it. Wiping her hands on her apron, she said, "Child, stop washing the dishes, you're done, Polly."

"Thank you, Biddy—oops, Bedelia. I was starting to get tired."

"I can't see how you can be tired, child. You've been standing there a whole hour playing in the water, but you haven't washed one dish yet. Do you really think those dishes are clean, when all you've done is swish them around the water without ever feeling them to 'see' if they're clean or not?"

"Sorry," Polly sullenly responded.

"And that's not all, young lady. You used to be so fastidious making up your bed each morning. Now your bed is made up haphazardly at best, if it's ever made up at all."

Polly sat down at the kitchen table and said, "Again sorry!"

"Oh no, young lady, you're not getting off that easy. I don't want an apology. I want to know why."

"Biddy—oops, Bedelia—I don't know why. I think my heart just wasn't in it anymore."

"Child, that's all right. I used to resent Biddy, thinking it made me sound old, but I don't mind anymore if you call me it." Bedelia paused and thought a moment before adding, "Dear child, I believe you're depressed."

Caught off guard, Polly tentatively replied, "But that can't be, Biddy. I AM happy, ma'am, really, I am… I'm okay."

"No, child, you're not. I watch you closely. Day by day, little Miss. Vibrant Sparkle is slowly becoming weighed down in gloom and sorrow—"

Polly said in protest, "I may have some low days in my life… I mean, everyone does sometime. But that doesn't mean I'm depressed. Besides isn't depression a sin, when God tells us to rejoice? I thought the Bible said that, 'Why art thou cast down, O my soul? And why art thou disquieted within me? Hope in God…'" (Psalm 43:5 KJV).

Bedelia said, "Child, depression is just a type of pain. It's not a sin to be in pain, and it's not a sin to say OUCH when you are. Depression, anger, sorrow, they're all just emotions common to all people. It's not a sin to HAVE an emotion. It's only a sin if you ACT upon what you're feeling outside of God's will. Remember, the Bible says, 'Be angry, and sin not'" (Ephesians 4:26 KJV). "Child, God knows that—"

Suddenly Bedelia stopped talking and began to weep. Wiping her wet hands upon her oversized adult apron, Polly came over to her foster mother. "Whatever's the matter?" she said with genuine concern, encircling the woman's waist in her slender arms.

In between sobs, Bedelia said, "Child, I thought we were going to lose you for sure. The fight between you and Knowles…those things tend to damage relationships beyond repair. Then there was you getting caught in that dust storm. I'm so sorry for your eyes, but blind or not, you're still alive, and nothing is better than that. I only wish…"

"Wish what, Biddy?" Polly said, trying to get used to saying the name.

"I wish that I knew some way to help you, now that you've lost your sight, to really enjoy life again and to do more than merely keep up appearances for everyone. You know, the pastor's tea party celebration is happening in two days. I know you probably won't feel like going, but I hope you do come. I've been praying and expecting something to happen there that'll start you getting back to your old self again."

Polly asked, "Isn't that a bit much to hope for?" And instantly knew she had walked into her own trap.

"Child," Bedelia began, "I don't believe I just heard that come out of your mouth. Weren't you the one who scolded the sheriff, telling him that God can do anything? Weren't you the one that believed God would bring your pa home early from prison? And weren't you the one who prayed that God would do something to take away your pa's desire to drink? 'Is there anything hard to God? Is anything too hard for Yahweh?'" (Genesis 18:14 KJV). "Well, you believed God would, and he has always come through for you. I believe I'll do the same for you. Now off you go, dear, and let me finish supper."

As Polly obediently left the kitchen and made her way to her bedroom, she thought she heard a muffled giggle from Bedelia. Dismissing it from her mind, she entered her room and plopped down on the quilt Bedelia had handmade for her while she stayed with the Russell family in Cimarron. There she pondered Bedelia's words, over and over. Weary of thinking and in need of a conclusion, Polly decided that her foster mother was right; Polly had little desire to attend the Knowles's tea party celebration.

Just then, though Polly could no longer see, nevertheless, she was instantly aware of the presence of others in the room. Vanity alone propelled the girl to the chest of drawers to adjust the bandages on her face and to don her dark glasses. Then feeling herself more presentable, she turned and said, "Is anyone there? You can come out now."

A voice said, "I was wondering if you'd ever detect us here." Then toward the kitchen, the voice called out, "Bea, it took her almost eight minutes to find out we were here."

"Give her a break, Randcine, she's lately had a lot on her mind."

"Aunt Randie!" Polly called out in surprise and delight. "Who else came with you?"

"You hoping for anyone in particular?" teased Rhonda, the oldest girl of the Russell Sprouts.

Immediately Rusty's voice broke in, "Don't listen to her, Polly. It's only me, Rhonda, and Rochelle with Mom. We heard you weren't feeling well, so we came over to try and cheer you up."

For the next hour, and then well into supper, the conversation went on. After Polly had been pulled from the mound of dust from the great storm, Bedelia lost no time in telephoning Louise with the news, asking for prayer on behalf of the girl. Now that they were reunited, Polly felt that nothing could have been more of a surprise or more welcome.

While the others gathered in the living room, Polly and Rusty finished cleaning the kitchen. Presently he lightly touched the bandages on Polly's face and simply said, "Let me see."

Polly shook her head frantically and tried to wave him off, saying, "No, you mustn't, it's too ugly."

Rusty gently but firmly held her flailing arms to her side, then held all of her in his arms, saying, "Angel, you could never be ugly... can never be anything but beautiful."

Polly's resistance melted away as she felt that much of her insides had as well. She thought, though only three years had passed, and Rusty still was not quite a teenager, still much about him had matured. His voice had deepened, his stature became taller, and his arms (Lord, those arms) had become more muscular. Even his mannerisms had grown more likable. She allowed his probing fingers to lift the bandages.

"See, Angel, I was right. You can never be anything but beautiful...to me."

Polly was about to say, "No, Rusty, I can't see," but she never got the chance. Suddenly her mouth had become—preoccupied.

The next day, the Russells where gone. Miraculously so too was a good deal of Polly's melancholy.

*****

Though inspired by author Lewis Carroll's *Alice in Wonderland*, Pastor Knowles's get-together had a dual purpose. First and foremost, it was a church social, a chance for the congregation to relax and get to know each other and their pastor better. Second, it provided an opportunity for congregants to vocally critique their pastor's performance and to recommend areas of change.

Though Polly loved tea, this second function of the event seemed to Polly to be nothing more than an elaborate business meeting. Even when she had her sight, she had always found business meetings to be detestable and boring, something to be avoided at all costs. Nevertheless, Polly could never deny her beloved Sunday school teacher anything, and so reluctantly, she decided to go to the event. After all, she thought, Bedelia was expecting something from God.

As everyone spilled into the social hall located in the basement of the church, they were greeted by a rustic interpretation of an actual tea party worthy of author Lewis Carroll. Long tables were covered in various homemade cakes, pies, jellies, jams, and preserves, much of it imported from outside Kansas. Large carafes of either hot tea or coffee appeared as sentries on each table.

Soon enough, it was time to begin the question-and-answer period. Adorned on both arms by Polly and Bedelia, Pastor Knowles quickly stood up to gain everyone's attention.

Clearing his throat, he said, "I think, I'd like to start. You see, on the day of the great dust storm…that day Polly was hurt so badly by… I should have, as your pastor, been an example of trust and obedience to God. Instead I let another spirit take hold…one of hatred and revenge, and yes, even murder. I was ready to murder Buck Riser that night. Not as an executioner for the state and certainly not as a duly deputized citizen under lawful authority of the sheriff. No, I wanted to kill him because he had hurt someone I love. Vengeance belongs only to God, but I was ready, in my arrogance, to usurp the Lord. My actions and my attitude were reprehensible that night because I was of a wrong spirit… I was wrong. I've asked God to forgive me, but… God help me… I-I can't seem to forgive myself…"

Knowles could go no further but wept bitterly before his congregates. A shout of, "Heck, Reverend, had she been one of my daughters, I know I'd done the same," could be heard. Presently he felt Polly's comforting hand on his arm as well as the warmth of Bedelia on his other arm. He looked down at her. She subtly nodded her head in approval, saying, "Man of God…this day, they have a pastor."

Suddenly a congregate from upstairs burst into the room, shouting for everyone to come up and see this. Once upstairs, he pointed to the rustic clock-and-barometer combination in the foyer outside the main auditorium. The barometer read 28.46 inches. While they watched the level of the indicator decrease, a few people complained of old knee and other joint injuries starting to ache. However, when the level of the barometer dipped below 27 inches, most of those present began to complain of headaches.[17] That's when everyone heard *it*—the low rushing sound of a freight train approaching.

Racing outside the church building, the people looked in the direction of the sound, just in time to see *it*—the touchdown of a tornado to the northwest of them whose base seemed to go on for miles. While they watched, as if tripping over its own feet, the giant column suddenly fell over to its side and began to pick up dirt and debris, as it began to cut a murderous path of destruction toward them.

The horizontal tornado's base continued to pick up greater quantities of solid particulate matter, until its height completely occluded and eclipsed a bright noonday sun, extinguishing its light, until the daylight had become darker than midnight.

"Come inside, everyone!" shouted Knowles. "Back downstairs, it's the safest place." No one had to be asked twice. Once downstairs, Knowles told everyone to stay away from the windows but to gather along the opposite wall to the storm's approach and pray that the storm would quickly pass.

Though inside the solid wood-framed brick-and-mortar edifice, the deafening roar of the approaching dust storm reopened emotional wounds, leaving Polly to feel just as exposed and defenseless as she had been on the main road of town not long ago.

Suddenly as the gale-propelled sandblaster neared the edge of Garden City, a scream was heard above the cacophony of the storm. Everyone turned and saw Polly, lying in a fetal position, rocking back and forth on the floor.

"Please, God...not again...not again!"

PART 3

The New Cloud (1935)

CHAPTER 26

Dust Storms and Purple Nebulae

As the people of Garden City kept an anxious vigil of the massive cyclonic meteorological event bearing menacingly down upon their town, so too had others kept watch of the singular cosmic cloud on approach to their world. When it was first sighted just two years prior, its size alone (or rather lack thereof) made it unique among other known similar astral phenomena. Two years hence and everything astronomers had observed of its behavior only served to challenge, frustrate, and even turn into assumptions nearly every bit of knowledge about the universe they had considered canon.

In order to minimize panic, the media at large said little about its existence, preferring instead to generate daily reports purposed to give people hope during the worldwide economic downturn. Now they needn't bother. As soon as the mysterious cloud of amethyst hew had left Saturn in its wake, it had become visible to unaided eyes of the general population. However, what could not be readily detected by the common citizenry was that immediately upon passing through the orbit of Mars, it had nearly doubled its speed while simultaneously reducing its already diminutive size.

Observations and calculations discovered that it's decrease in size was not due to sloughing off material (as was the case of asteroids and meteorites entering the atmosphere) but apparently was the result of it contracting its borders, compacting its substance, and even concentrating its mass. By the time the cosmic cloud had finally reached Earth's outer atmosphere (sooner by weeks than predicted), it had become smaller than Earth's moon. As it continued its descent, it continued to become smaller—smaller than the continent of Africa, smaller than Alaska, even smaller than the continental United States.

Suddenly the cloud halted its descent, its base a scant twelve thousand yards above the ground, its top fluctuating between five and seven thousand feet above its base. Remarkably its diameter was now smaller than that of Pennsylvania (or even of Texas, which some have said is as large as the world itself).

Though the mysterious cloud's vertical movement had ceased, it's horizontal course crossed the border between Oklahoma and Kansas. As it drifted in a northwesterly direction, it slowly continued to shrink.

*****

Although the citizens of Garden City had been forced, during the last two years, to deal with the tremendous dust storms that would later be known as black blizzards, they had hardly become used to it. The chaos outside the church filled all inside with fear but more so for Polly, who was absolutely petrified with terror. Though Bedelia did what she could to calm and comfort the child, her efforts were poor at best as the black cloud of dirt, dust, and debris continued its merciless assault on the edifice.

All at once, those complaining of headaches and joint injury flare-ups reported that the pain had abruptly ceased as another cloud, one of amethyst hue, came to rest over Garden City. It was amorphic; like some impossibly huge amoeba, it pushed and pulled itself until it completely overshadowed all of Garden City. Its comparison to an amoeba continued as it sent forth pseudopods of its own substance, which moved above the geopolitical border until it now covered Finney County in its entirety. The amethyst cloud extended its southwest corner to encompass Cimarron and Dodge City, then extended itself to the northeast, as far as Topeka.

As the strange purple apparition took up its final position, any portion of the horizontal tornado which passed underneath it was suddenly checked of its onslaught. First, the storm's forward progression halted as if it had been a wool blanket striking a patch of molasses in February. Though its forward movement had ceased, it continued to turn over and over around its own skewed axis. As it did, it quickly began to vibrate and unravel, casting its captured dirt and debris in all directions, until finally its winds blew, naked and impotent, to die out altogether.

Although dust storms in the region abounded, none could endure under that cosmic umbrella. Even the noonday sun triumphantly appeared, filtering through the amethyst expanse.

*****

A PARADOXICAL REACTION OR PARADOXICAL EFFECT IS AN EFFECT OF A CHEMICAL SUBSTANCE, MOSTLY A MEDICAL DRUG, OPPOSITE TO THE EFFECT WHICH WOULD NORMALLY BE EXPECTED. AN EXAMPLE OF A PARADOXICAL REACTION IS PAIN CAUSED BY A PAIN RELIEF MEDICATION.[18]

Though *paradoxical reaction* is a term predominantly reserved to a medical phenomenon, it could easily be applied to matters of psychological and human behavioral importance as well. For instance, it has often been noted that people are strange, having demonstrated during a period of stress, a time of testing, or otherwise a moment of moderate to severe temptation, an almost unerring tendency to do the exact opposite of what they have been told is right, what morals, mores, and taboos have traditionally shown them to be right, or even what an inane sense of personal logic indicates what is right and proper to do.

In the same vein, when faced with a situation whose outcome potentially is death, it is normal, right, and proper and even expected that whatever entity rescues, saves, or otherwise brings relief of that situation would naturally be regarded with gratitude, thanks, and welcome instead of suspicion and fear.

Case in point, when the black blizzard descended upon Garden City, it was a force of nature bringing death and destruction in its aftermath. However, though the mysterious cloud of amethyst hue had protected the people of the town from the threat of the invader, it was by no means a familiar natural phenomena but was unknown in its origin, purpose, and potential for harm. At best, it could be expected to produce fear in a handful of easily influenced people in town. Paradoxically it had the potential to generate the more extreme effect of overwhelming widespread panic. *It did!*

With everyone in the congregation outside, gazing up at the cloud, either in awe of it or cowering in fear of it, they were ill-prepared for the human stampede of townsfolk scrambling in blind terror to get out of town. In the confusion, Polly was torn from Bedelia's hands, to be carried away by the wave of terror-stricken bodies and eventually lost to sight.

"KNOWLES!"

Like Polly, Bedelia's scream was drowned out, carried away by the din, and lost.

Like a felled log caught in the rapids, Polly was helpless against the irresistible force of the throng. Her neighbors were all oblivious to her frantic cries for help, her feeble futile struggling, and even to her very presence. All her neighbors, that is, except for one.

Usually preferring to work alone, or from darkness, he paradoxically found the crowds and daylight an excellent opportunity to maintain his anonymity. Snaking a long lean arm through the river of humanity, he blindly felt for her. It didn't take long to find Polly and, on making contact, wrapped his arm around her slender waist and liberated her from the throng. Tucking the struggling girl under his arm, he sprinted from the main road, turned sharply, and headed down an alley attached to the bar. Unrolling his arm, he deposited Polly indignantly upon the dusty ground.

Scrambling to her feet, Polly began to rub the painful bruises that were debuting throughout her body, while she cocked her head and sniffed the air. The pungent odor of stale days'-old dried whiskey was unmistakable.

"Sweeny?" she asked. "Mr. Doug Sweeney? Thanks for getting me out of that jam."

"You!" Sweeny said accusingly, pointing a drunken thumb in her direction, while he struggled to focus bloodshot eyes on her. "You little brat. You're the one who ruined Buck for us. You're the reason we can't trust him anymore."

"But what did I do?" Polly asked innocently enough. "All I ever did was pray for him."

"All I ever did was pray for him," he said mockingly. "LIAR! All you did was change him…all you did was stop his drinking…all you did was make him think for himself. That's all, nothing much, really. Stupid useless girl, all you did was ruin everything."

"That's not true," Polly said, feeling her timidity replaced by temerity. "All I ever did was to pray for my pa. It was God who did all the rest." She thought that her part in the conversation was over. Instead she felt she had to go on by adding, "Sorry my prayers to my God interfered with your prayers to yours."

Polly braced herself for Doug Sweeney's inevitable response. It came quickly with a sharp backhanded rebuke, which opened the corner of her mouth, followed by his words, "Stupid useless girl." The blow sent her reeling backward. She tripped and fell, striking the back of her head against the unyielding ground beneath. The impact sounded as if the pavement were cracking and not her skull. Polly lay silently upon the ground, her mouth wide open to emit a scream of pain, which would not come out.

Doug Sweeny towered above the sprawled-out girl below and gloated, "Humph, serves you right. That'll teach you what to do with that sassy mouth of yours. Stupid useless—"

Suddenly Sweeny's gloating was cut short as his own face was savagely pimp-slapped,[19] first on one side, then the other, in such rapid succession, it felt as if they were but a single blow. Sweeny collapsed to one knee but rose quickly to see who had hit him.

"Ugh, what the hell!" he exclaimed as his fingers instinctively reached into his pants pocket, grasping the ivory-handled switchblade stiletto he always carried. "Whoever you are, you just bought a world of trouble." Quickly, like a jungle animal, he surveyed the alley. The narrow causeway was empty, save for Polly and himself. Or so he thought.

All at once, it happened again, two more pimp-slaps descended on him, so quickly, Sweeny felt the blows were one and the same. They left him feeling dazed and frightened. Brandishing the switchblade, he challenged, "All right, come on out wherever you're hiding. Me and Sammy Slicer here want to have our fun too."

Sweeny's heart pounded wildly as he readied himself for any attack. However, all his experience still left him unprepared for the two disembodied hands that suddenly appeared before him. Faster than he could have dreamed of reacting, they struck.

The older Sweeny was helpless as one hand encircled his throat, lifted him bodily off the ground, to slam him against the side of the bar. The other hand extended its index finger to touch the blade of the stiletto. Immediately his entire hand and forearm became gripped in mind-numbing pain as the blade's mirrorlike finish dulled, frosted over, became as blue as a corpse, then shattered into splinters, leaving the knife handle nothing more than an empty hollow threat.

Terror gripped Doug Sweeny as strongly as the hands which pinned him to the wall. Although he was more afraid now than at any other time in his life, his fear quickly doubled as the outline of a young lady, not more than twenty years old, materialized before him. He could identify no facial details in the apparition, for it was transparent. But what he could make out clearly was the waves of anger and hatred emanating from it.

A voice as cold and distant as the grave came from somewhere beyond the outline, saying, "You and I both know that the only 'fun' left to you has been by molesting little girls, like the Hines girl from last year."

Fear of a different sort now gripped Sweeny. He bellowed, "How can you know about her? No one knows about her. No one will ever find her."

"She knows and I know." The voice waited for the full impact of the revelation to take hold. "I know your secrets. Now learn one of mine. Though you may escape the judgment of this world, you can never escape that of the next. In time, all things come to an end. Touch the child Polly again, and I will personally bring about yours."

The voice, the hands, and the outline melted away, and Doug Sweeny slid down the wall. Once his legs stopped shaking, he scrambled out of the alley and, screaming, joined the river of people blindly stampeding down Main Street.

Strong but gentle arms picked Polly up and cradled her. Though Polly could by no means see it, she instantly knew that she was outside the alley and was now occupying a position in the very center of Main Street, even as countless tons of humanity bore down on her.

Polly's rescuer sat cross-legged on the ground with the girl securely nestled on her lap and gently palpated the back of the girl's head. "Hmm, nothing seems to be broken, but you are going to have a splitting headache for the next two days," she said, whispering in Polly's ear.

The new girl's voice acted like a sedative, both relaxing and distracting Polly as the new wave of loving neighbors approached.

In her current state, Polly was unable to figure out why she felt there was something both safe and familiar about the new girl. However, like meeting someone new and feeling you've known them all your life, Polly only knew that she was instantly drawn to her.

Strangely enough, when the onrushing townsfolk reached the girls, instead of trampling them underfoot, they parted to the left and right, like a rushing stream going around a boulder in its path.

Ever since Polly was swept away by the masses, Pastor Knowles and his wife, Bedelia, had been frantically searching for her. Paralleling the throng from shops that bordered Main Street, they thought they had gotten a glimpse of her. A feeling of alarm gripped them when it appeared their foster child was being trampled. Their panic quickly turned to confusion when they realized that she wasn't.

Observing the human stampede, the Knowles wondered why, if their neighbors were truly reduced to an unthinking mob, would they move right and left to avoid a lone girl sitting peacefully in the middle of the street, as if she were safely at home.

Now with the crowds thinning out, the couple headed into the street, shouting Polly's name.

Slowly waking up, Polly said, "Wow, that was a strange dream," and marveled at the faint floral scent in the air.

CHAPTER 27

Closer than a Heartbeat[20]

As Garden City's latest arrival to their unwelcomed black blizzard pageant had turned day into night, so too had the mysterious cloud of amethyst hue turned night into day. Those who had complained of having a long and difficult day (and who hadn't?) were subjected to an equally torturous night. The people quickly discovered that the window shutters and door bulwarks that had proven ineffectual at keeping out debris from the dust storms were an even more pitiable deterrent to the light show outside.

Those townsfolk brave enough to venture forth from their hovels became witnesses to a fantastic cosmic display lasting throughout the night. In addition to the soft-purple glow of the cloud, there appeared from deep within the cloud what was later described as gold-colored will-o'-wisps. They appeared both singularly and in pairs at first. Then groups of three, four, and even five or more individual will-o'-wisps floated to the underside of the cloud. There the various groups coupled with others nearby to form long chains comprised of between thirty and forty-five orbs. Once formed, each strand (or ribbon, as they came to be called) would begin to rapidly move about the cloud, twisting, turning about, and even somersaulting in wild, uneven loops, never colliding with another ribbon. Those who watched the display thought it resembled the movement of roller coasters at an amusement park.

Though the citizens of Garden City, who remained huddled in their various abodes, were spared the intensity of the display outside, they were hardly ignorant of it. Like a pestering child who raked for attention, the dancing lights shining through the cloud, upon encountering the solid structures of homes, would not be denied but probed their way past holes and fissures and even through gaps in fabric to bathe those inside with its presence.

Variations of "Hey, Edna! Turn off the lights and come to bed!" would be heard throughout the town, throughout the night.

Remarkably in addition to the lights, both those within and those without later commented on the sounds emanating from the cloud. Most who heard it dismissed it as the sound of the wind from distant dust storms echoing along the underside of the purple expanse Still a few—a precious few—thought they heard the cloud *singing*.

Yesterday the strange purple cloud arrived, and its sight drove most into a panic, while for only a few, it drove to their knees. Pastor Knowles, with so many of his congregates plagued by fear at the cosmic cloud's arrival, was at the church conducting an impromptu all-night prayer vigil. However, Polly and Bedelia remained at the parsonage.

Seated at the kitchen table, the two discussed the strange events of the other day.

"Sorry I screamed so much," Polly said as she sipped on her second cup of tea. "I don't like to make a fuss and disturb people, but I was so afraid."

"Child, don't apologize for being scared. Believe me, everyone there was scared, but God knows you got more reason to be than most."

"Thanks, Biddy," said Polly, still trying to get used to the name. "By the way, does tea really take away a headache?"

"Some say yes, some say no. But tea does have a mild sedative in it, so it'll help you to relax and hopefully get some rest. And just how did you get that lump behind your head anyway?"

Polly took another sip of tea, then said, "Well, after we got separated, I tried hard to get away from the crowd, but I just couldn't. That's when someone grabbed me and pulled me free from the crowd and carried me between some buildings on the side. It was Doug Sweeny."

Bedelia listened without letting the girl detect her growing misgivings, despite her knuckles having drained themselves of all color.

Polly continued, "I thought he was trying to help me, then I found out he was really sore at me for something."

"What was he mad about?" asked Bedelia, desperately attempting to ease the tension she felt.

"I'm not sure. But he said that something about my pa was all my fault. I think he said I had stopped Pa's drinking and that he was no longer letting Mr. Sweeny make his decisions for him. But it really wasn't my fault. I just prayed a lot, and God answered me. I told Mr. Sweeny that, and it made him even sorer at me. Then somehow I fell and hit my head. I don't remember much of what happened after that until you and Pastor found me in the middle of the street."

Polly had deliberately omitted from her story her feisty remarks being a catalyst for Sweeny's attack. However, when she heard Bedelia rise from the table and go to the telephone, she nervously added, "It's all right, Biddy, please don't call the sheriff. In the morning, I bet his headache will be bigger than mine."

"Child, what are you talking about. How do you know he'll have a headache?"

"I could smell he had been drinking a lot, and Mr. Sweeny never drinks. He's a tea-tootler."

"That's teetotaler, dear, and it's never all right to bring harm to a child. In the condition he was in, who knows what that man might have done to you. You don't seem too bad off, though. I'll have a talk with Knowles in the morning and see what he wants to do."

Polly quickly agreed. Desperate to change the subject, she said, "If it's okay with you, Biddy, I'd like to try doing my chores again. If I try hard, I bet I can do them. I'm just so tired of feeling helpless."

A muffled click indicated to Polly that Bedelia had returned the telephone to its cradle. Almost immediately, the girl was swept into Bedelia's arms and felt her foster mother's salty tears cascade down her cheeks.

Early the next morning, Bedelia's sleep was interrupted by a loud knock on the front door.

"Land sakes, Knowles must have forgotten his keys again," Bedelia said, perturbed at the inconvenience of prematurely ending her slumber but relieved that her husband had finally returned home. Quickly throwing on an old housecoat, she reached the door just as the knocking repeated itself, louder and more insistent than before.

"Oh my goodness" said Bedelia, surprised that, upon opening the door, there stood not her husband but a young woman who appeared to be not a decade older than Polly. She wore an old faded-yellow sundress, which Bedelia thought must have belonged to her mother, along with an equally old faded-green cardigan sweater. She said nothing at first but smiled shyly, as she handed Bedelia the large official-looking envelope she carried.

"Land sakes, girl," said Bedelia, "I didn't see you carrying anything." Bedelia, now more curious than apprehensive, beckoned the visitor to come in.

"Please wipe your shoes off, and have a seat," she said, opening the door wide and stepping to the side to allow her to enter. It was then she noticed that there were no shoes to wipe, only bare feet, with skin that looked as new as a newborn baby. However, most striking about those feet was that despite the more-than-generous coating of dust and dirt, over everything (courtesy of the periodic dust storms), not a bit of it could be seen on them. Not a gram nor a grain of it had clung to her feet or to any part of the woman, for that matter.

The visitor entered and instinctively veered away from Pastor's "sacred" chair to gracefully deposit herself in a corner chair and waited patiently.

That was when Bedelia noticed something else that seemed strange about the newcomer; that is, though the living room curtains had been drawn tight, as proof against the dust, making the room seem dark all around, the new girl had not removed the thick dark-green sunglasses she wore, whose oversized lens covered much of her face.

Without comment on the spectacles, Bedelia studied the envelope.

From the desk of Dr. Steven Hillcrest, Hillcrest Eye Institute, Topeka, Kansas.

To the Reverend and Mrs. Patrick Knowles, Garden City, Kansas.

Gently, Bedelia opened the envelope and drew out the missive it contained. It read:

> DEAR REVEREND KNOWLES: I AM MOST PLEASED TO INTRODUCE TO YOU MISS. BOO ASTROPHEL FROM BRITISH COLUMBIA IN CANADA. RECENTLY A FORMER PATIENT OF MINE, HER HISTORY SHARES SOME REMARKABLE SIMILARITIES WITH YOUR FOSTER CHILD, POLLY. CAUGHT IN THE GREAT DUST STORM THAT ORIGINATED UP THERE, SHE WAS DECLARED TO HAVE EXPIRED. SHE WAS PLACED IN A COFFIN AND WAS BEING LOWERED INTO THE GROUND WHEN SHE MIRACULOUSLY REJOINED THE LIVING. SHE COMES TO YOU IN MY EMPLOY, AS A TEMPORARY COMPANION AND MENTOR TO POLLY, IN ORDER TO FACILITATE HER ACCLIMATION TO SIGHTLESS LIFE. PLEASE RECEIVE HER, AS YOU WOULD RECEIVE ME.
>
> WITH WARMEST REGARDS, STEVEN HILLCREST.

Just then Polly slowly felt her way into the room, asking, "Who was there, Biddy? Anyone we know?"

"Umm, pumpkin, this is Miss. Boo Astrophel, sent by Dr. Hillcrest. She's here, I believe, as an answer to our prayers."

Polly reached her hand out toward the newcomer, who took her hand in both of hers, drawing her close. Gone now was the half noncommittal grin of before, in its place, a full genuinely warm smile, which lit up the darkened room, as if the gesture alone had ushered in the sun.

"Ah, Polly, at last!" Boo Astrophel said, as she stood to her feet, still holding Polly's hand in both of hers. "I have been so anxious to finally meet you."

"It's, umm, it's really good to meet you too, Miss. Astrophel." Polly was certain she had heard the young lady's voice before, two days ago in fact, but she could not clearly remember; it had all seemed like just a dream.

Just then, Bedelia opened the living room curtains. Polly felt the warmth of the new sun, which hovered only two miles above, as it flooded the room and instantly remembered all that had transpired the day prior to yesterday. However, she made no indication to Bedelia that the two had met before.

All at once, Polly felt a new and different kind of warmth pulsating within her, as the young lady leaned in close to Polly's ear and whispered, "You do not know this yet, but you and I are going to be best friends…together…FOREVER!"

*****

Though at the time, Boo's use of the term *forever* brought a sense of alarm to an overly protective Bedelia (though she had no idea why), in the few short days following her sudden arrival, her words were proving quite true, nonetheless. The two went everywhere together, each one never seen outside the company of the other. This too became a matter of concern for Bedelia but for a different reason. Initially Bedelia was worried for Polly's safety in the light of this total stranger coming into their lives. However, the new issue for Bedelia was less easy to identify because it was more personal, more visceral in its nature. She prayed that God would give her understanding.

One day, she watched Boo and Polly walking together around the parsonage, discussing who knows what, when the issue suddenly became quite clear to her—*jealousy!* The Knowles had always been a childless couple; however, Bedelia's dream from her early adolescence was to be a mother. Thanks to Buck's irresponsibility and Judge Lynch's wise jurisprudence, she had finally gotten her chance. Even if she was only a foster parent, in her heart, Polly was her very own daughter, the child that she and Knowles were always meant to have.

Now in Bedelia's heart, Boo, as mysterious and as charming as she was, had become a threat to Bedelia and Polly's relationship.

Bedelia felt that the more time Polly spent with Boo, the less time she and Polly could enjoy together. The closer Polly and Boo became, the more distant she and Polly were becoming.

In her mind, she knew that jealousy was darkness, not light. In her mind, she could see that Boo (like an older sister) was good for Polly. In her head she knew that with each passing week, Polly was becoming more confident, more independent, more capable (even her daily chores had improved). And when tasks and expectations became difficult, Boo would never allow Polly to give up, relying on her sightlessness to become an excuse for underachievement but would insist on the same level of accomplishment that would be expected of the girl had she not been blind.

Of course, all of that knowledge was in Bedelia's head. The problem was not in Bedelia's head but rather in her heart, and her heart prompted her to act, to preserve what remained of hers and Polly's relationship.

One day, she imitated a father confronting his daughter's suitor. She sauntered up to Boo and, in her deepest voice, demanded, "Sir, just what are your intentions toward my daughter?"

Though Bedelia had meant her probing question to be half in jest, she was totally unprepared for the answer the mysterious girl returned. Boo's eyes narrowed as a frighteningly mischievous smile came to Boo's lips, as she said, "Why, sir, my intentions are nothing more than to love your daughter to death."

At once (though she still could not logically understand why), every alarm of danger in her head went off. With lack of concrete evidence, Bedelia could override her sense of fear and go on as if all were right in their little world. However, she said to herself that, "Understanding is of the head, knowing is of the heart."

As Bedelia repeated Boo's words, "I INTEND TO LOVE YOUR DAUGHTER TO DEATH," Bedelia's mother instincts took over, and again, her heart won out in the debate. Something must be done.

Bedelia had, of late, developed the habit of pushing a portion of her meals to the side of her plate to wrap it up later in a clean kitchen towel and bury it deep in the pocket of her apron.

Late one evening, as supper was over, and Knowles had retired to the living room to read, she dismissed the girls, saying she would finish up in the kitchen. Once alone, she made her way to the door of the root cellar and quietly entered. On a low-lying shelf, she placed the dishtowel bundle she carried, then rummaged deeper in her apron pocket to produce Boo Astrophel's letter of introduction, placing it on top of the towel. Then as quickly and quietly as she had entered the cellar, she was gone.

No sooner had the door to the root cellar been secured that a beefy hand shot forth from a shadowy corner to snatch away both dishtowel and envelope in a single grasp.

*****

It was now forty days since the entity known as Boo Astrophel came to stay with the Knowles. Forty days in which Polly had not listened to her cherished radio drama, *Little Orphan Annie*, and had neither longed for nor missed it. It had been replaced with Boo Astrophel who had totally consumed her. Her thoughts, her feelings, her speech, her time, even her hopes and aspirations—they now all bore the stamp of Boo Astrophel.

Even Bedelia, who still did not completely trust Boo, found that she was not immune to Boo's spell. Like Polly, Bedelia had become almost mesmerized by the strange girl's insights of matters both natural and spiritual, from around the world, as if she had studied the whole world from the vantage point of God's lap.

One evening, the Knowles's new extended family were all gathered for supper. Curiosity or jealousy notwithstanding, suddenly Knowles flippantly blurted out, "What happens when you die?" The question caught everyone by surprise, except perhaps for Boo.

Knowles, expecting the deep cliché answer of "A baby born into the world feels as if it were dying to the only world it has known, in the womb..." was shocked as Boo closed her eyes, her head lowered, and with a voice tinged with hurt and pain, she addressed him, "Oracle of God! Some souls are taken so quickly out of time, into eternity, they have no knowledge that they have passed. The world appears the same, for their memories are locked in their time. There they wander alone, fearful their loved ones have been taken from this world, when in fact, it is they who have been taken from their loved ones. This wandering about continues until the soul is taken in hand by others who…"

Boo came out of her reveling to finish the rest of her meal in silence. However, once everyone was finished, it was Boo and Polly who volunteered for kitchen duty. That's when Boo began to speak to Polly again. She spoke of things no one else could easily comprehend, but somehow, Polly could understand, and it filled her with wonder.

Presently she confided that when she was feeling at her lowest, her blindness made her feel as if she had lost everything.

Boo said, "But, sweetness, you have gained so much. Though others have eyes, most people go through their entire lives practically blind to the world around. They depend on their eyes so much, they almost completely ignore the other senses God gave them in order to appreciate the world he had given them. Oh, sweetness, do not lament your eyes. I will show you how truly useless they were, and how much better off you are without them."

"Oh, Boo," Polly said. "The Knowles expect that your teaching will, at best, only allow me to just barely get along. But to be better off than when I was sighted, how is this possible?"

Boo laughed genuinely before saying, "Sweetness, it's a secret, but where I come from, most have no eyes, yet we get along just fine. We rely on our other senses and on each other."

"You rely on each other to get by. Again how can this be?"

Boo smiled and said, "I will show you tomorrow, but for now just know that it was the others that kept watch on you and told me where to find you when Doug Sweeny had…"

The two of them talked and laughed far into the night and even into the predawn morning.

The morning was now in full bloom, and when Bedelia emerged from her bedroom, she discovered that Boo had already been up and dressed for quite some time. Boo had arranged with her yesterday to allow Polly to sleep in, while Boo busied herself arranging odds and ends she had picked up in town into a wicker basket she borrowed from Bedelia. Now neatly packed to the top, a self-satisfied almost-childish grin came over her, as she fastened the basket shut.

At a quarter to noon, Polly awakened to the presence of Boo in the room and smiled.

"Get dressed, sweetness," Boo said. "I have planned a special afternoon, just for us."

"Where are we going, Boo?"

"Shh, no questions...but you will see."

The term *you will see* was so preposterous (given Polly's new circumstances), it caused both girls to laugh wholeheartedly.

When Polly was ready, Knowles drove the four miles to Polly's old farmhouse and deposited the girls there before driving back into town to work at the church.

Once they were alone, Boo led Polly up the lone hill to stand at its apex. A solitary apple tree stood like a beacon on the hill's summit. Though a mature specimen, it had ceased to bear fruit shortly after the drought had begun.

Scattered about were other vegetation as well. Shrubs, patches of bleached saw grass, and even a few low-lying bushes were there, giving ample testament to the ecological disaster that had befallen the Plain States.

Still the view from the hill of the surrounding area was nothing short of breathtaking. Though the purple cloud was suspended thousands of feet above, it seemed close enough to be touched by those on the summit.

While Polly sat close by, Boo worked on the contents of the basket. First she spread out a large square tablecloth in front of the only genuine tree atop the lone hill. Then she neatly arranged the other items in the basket to form a perimeter around the edges of the spread. Satisfied at last with her setup, Boo sat Polly next to her, their backs propped against the tree to partake of the repast.

For the rest of the morning and well into the afternoon, Polly and Boo sat. On the little hill overlooking the family's farm, the two were completely relaxed in each other's company as they finished the tidy picnic lunch Boo had brought.

Presently Boo sat Polly down on the tablecloth in front of her, on the flowing skirt of the yellow sundress she wore. Reaching into the wicker basket, she produced a tortoiseshell brush and sang softly while she brushed the girl's hair. Polly listened as each stroke of the brush, followed the rhythm of the song, the mysterious girl sang. Polly marveled that the song was instantly familiar.

"You're singing 'Great Is Thy Faithfulness," Polly said at length. "That was my mother's favorite hymn."

"It's my favorite too," admitted Boo, never losing the rhythm of her brushing.

Polly sat and thought carefully before saying, "Boo, seems to me you do a lot of things like my mother used to…before she passed."

"Why, thank you, sweetness. It is a great compliment to have so much in common with someone you loved so dearly."

After that, a great silence descended over them. Boo noticed that Polly gestured as if she were about to say something; however, the girl merely continued to stare, with unseeing eyes, at the grass beneath her. The silence between them was almost as palpable as the ground they sat upon.

Finally Polly raised her head and said, "I think that Boo Astrophel is such a strange name."

"Not nearly as strange as Quashi'miuoo, little Miss. Vibrant Sparkle."

"Hey!" Polly excitedly exclaimed. "How do you know my middle name? I thought that only my mother knew what it meant."

Boo continued her rhythmic brushing of Polly's hair, completely ignoring the girl's question.

Presently Polly asked, "What does Boo Astrophel mean anyway?"

Boo chuckled softly. "Sweetness, Boo is Irish for 'star,'[21] and Astrophel is Greek for 'star lover.'"[22]

Polly thought for a while, then added, "Hmm, 'star, star lover.' I still think it's a strange name, but pretty, though."

Suddenly Boo stopped brushing and laid the tortoiseshell brush aside. With the slightest hint of impatience, she asked, "You were going to say something a moment ago. What did you really want to tell me?"

Another wall of silence ensued between them. Boo felt as if she had pushed too hard, pushed too soon, and had lost the moment.

When Polly finally spoke, her words were mingled with self-conscious nervousness. "You really are an awful lot like my ma was. You even brush my hair the way she used to." She stopped briefly to think, then added, "Ma was my best friend. I could talk to her about anything…tell her…anything."

The uneasy silence returned, and Boo thought that this time, it was not so much as a wall as it was a chasm. She was wondering how to breech it, when slowly, guardedly, Polly spoke, her empty gaze never veering from the ground.

"Are…you…my…friend, Boo? Can I…tell you…anything…anything at all?"

Boo Astrophel suddenly grew apprehensive. Something was deeply troubling her young charge; and the wrong word or gesture might serve only to insurmountably widen the gap between them.

"Of course, sweetness. Go on. What is ailing you?"

"Oh, Boo, please…don't…hate me…but…I…" She trailed off, her hands cradling her stricken face. When next she spoke, it was with all the trepidation of one walking upon a frozen lake. "Sometimes… I think that… God…made me blind…to punish me."

Boo reeled backward, as if she had been struck to the face. Quickly regaining her composure, she tenderly replied, "Do not say that, sweetness. You know that cannot be true. God does not—"

Suddenly Polly interrupted, "But you don't understand, Boo! I… I did…something terrible…something…horrible."

Boo felt Polly's body convulse under a weight of guilt and sorrow, much too deep for tears to express, much less through eyes that no longer bore the means to do so. Tenderly, compassionately Boo lifted the distraught girl and placed her on her lap. After encircling Polly in her arms, Boo said, "Oh, sweetness, what could an angel like you possibly do that is so bad?"

"Don't call me that!" Polly said, her words full of self-reproach. "I'm not an angel. I'm bad. I'm…a…terrible person. I'm…a monster… I KILLED MY MOTHER!"

CHAPTER 28

Communion of the Purple Nebula

At the parsonage, Bedelia was at work, tossing grain among the chickens in the back. It had been saved and accumulated over the years by the departed Grandpa Clemmons, who was obsessed with the biblical story of Joseph in Egypt. As she approached a load of rough-hewn bricks lying under the very tarp she and Knowles used during the great storm, she turned her head to the side and said offhandedly in its direction, "What did you think of supper the other night?"

As if by some miracle, the tarp replied, "A little salty but good, just the same. As for the information you wanted, neither the eye institute nor Dr. Hillcrest himself had any knowledge of this Boo girl's existence. No municipal records from here or Vancouver attest to her existence. It's as if she were born the day she arrived at the house. Whatever she is, she's a liar and an imposter, and I don't trust her."

"Is that because of jealousy…because she has the sort of relationship with Polly that you could have had…should have had all along?"

"Of course I am, woman. But a greater question is one you harbor as well. That is, if Boo Astrophel is not who she says she is nor is here for what she says she's here for…then who in the world is she, and more importantly, what does she want with Polly?"

Bedelia didn't argue the point, knowing they were exactly the questions she wrestled with.

Presently the tarp spoke again, "You may not see me for a while, woman. I have to keep an eye on that Boo creature."

"Be careful, the posse's still out to get you, except for Knowles... he doesn't want to kill you anymore."

The tarp chuckled, but there was no mirth in its voice. "No, woman? Well, he should want me dead. Because he loves that kid as much as I do, and given the chance, I'm going to take Polly away from him."

*****

"I killed my mother!" Polly repeated, sounding more wretched than before.

"No, you did not," Boo said calmly. "You had nothing to do with your mother's death."

"But I did!" Polly insisted, her body beginning to shake uncontrollably. "Ma was so tired of Pa always beating us that she finally decided we were going to run away. I always planned things better than she did. So I told her that to keep Pa from thinking anything was out of the ordinary, she should take the tractor and plow the last few rows he had told her to do the week before." She paused and buried her face against Boo's chest. When she continued, her voice was eerily cold. "So you see? I told Ma to ride the tractor that day. She wouldn't have been on it except for me."

Boo Astrophel cradled a distraught Polly in her arms, waiting for the girl's storm to subside. Then at last, her quaking, shaking body began to calm down.

"Oh, sweetness," Boo said as she gently lifted the girl's head. Though Polly's eyes could no longer exude tears, her nose remained unaffected and viable. Boo produced a red cotton handkerchief from the pocket of her dress and attended to it. Satisfied Boo continued, "You did not cause your mother's death. It was an accident, which no one could have foreseen."

"How can you say that?" protested Polly through tearless sobs. "You weren't there."

"Yes, I was..." said Boo patiently.

Suddenly Polly exclaimed, "But that can't be true. You couldn't have been there. You're just saying that to make me feel better."

Boo tightened her grip around the girl's waist ever-so slightly. "Oh, sweetness, believe me, I was there. I watched as Buck chose that day to remove the tractor's front wheels so he could lubricate them with axel grease. I watched as he continued to drink while he worked, becoming so drunk he almost forgot to replace the retaining cotter pins on the wheels. Although he did remember to remount the pins, he was too inebriated to see that they had nearly rusted through with age. They came off when your mother was ploughing the field."

Boo paused to allow her words to settle in the girl's mind. Then she said, "Believe me, sweetness, your mother died as a result of an accident, and though tragic as it was, it really was no one's fault. But take comfort in that she was killed instantly. She did not suffer. Nor does she suffer now, for she is in a much happier place."

"Now I know you're just trying to cheer me up," Polly said despondently. "It's not possible for you to know what goes on after someone dies."

"Oh, sweetness, I have seen and known so much more than this. You heard the letter Bedelia read. Like you, I too was caught in a great dust storm, and everyone thought I had died. It was then that I was allowed to visit the afterlife, if only for a brief moment. However, it was enough time spent in eternity that caused me to see everything and everyone, in this world and the next. That is how I know of when you were eight years old, you fell and cut your knee on a rusted nail. You yet bear its scar…there…on your right leg. Believe me, I see and know all things, as if I had witnessed them from on high. That is how I know of a certain that your mother is happier where she is now than she has ever been."

Boo briefly paused again, then slowly continued, "It is also why I know that, just as you were tormented with undeserved guilt over your mother's death, so too has your father. When he sobered up, he found and examined the worn and rusted cotter pins and has cursed himself ever since. I know how your father's own guilt and shame drove him to drink even harder, trying to forget his perceived culpability…or to find solace in death."

"Please, Boo, stop," Polly said. "You're frightening me."

Polly, genuinely affected by Boo's tale, scooted closer to her, placing her head once again on Boo's chest. Boo, in turn, wrapped her protectively in her arms. There the two remained, silent, until Boo said, "Please understand this, sweetness. Long before they are taken in death, everyone requires mercy, certainly and ultimately, from the Creator, but assuredly from others here on earth as well. It is especially needed now, from a dear little girl toward her pitiful father."

Polly was thoughtful for a moment. "Boo, I think that when I die, I'd like it to be like Ma's. I'd like it to happen so quickly, I wouldn't know what happened."

"Wish not for that, sweetness," Boo said, looking pensively toward the cloud of amethyst hue in the distance and beyond. "The things I spoke of at the supper table that evening were in earnest. Some souls are released in death so quickly, they do not know they are dead. Their tortured souls wander in the world they remember, alone and afraid, without family or friends, for a season. Oh, do not wish to share that fate."

"I remember the other evening," Polly said thoughtfully. "I think the last thing you said was, 'They wander about until taken in hand by...' By what, Boo?" she asked, both curious and a bit frightened at Boo's story.

"Why, sweetness, they are found by those souls who have gone on before. Gradually they are able to convince the newly departed that it is they who are departed in death, inviting the soul to join them."

Polly's young mind filled with a million questions for Boo. She found that though her mind struggled against believing everything Boo told her, her heart still trusted in their friendship, allowing her to be more at peace. Thus they remained together, wrapped in comfort and silence.

Presently Boo asked, "Oh, sweetness, when you look to the skies, telling them all of your deepest longings and feelings...your greatest hopes and dreams, you believe that something...someone there actually listens. Or was it all make-believe? Was it all a child's fanciful game of pretend?"

"Ma always told me that whenever I was troubled or confused to come to the hill, look up to the clouds, and tell them everything. She always said that someone would hear me."

Boo placed her hands on Polly's shoulders for emphasis. Polly felt that her touch, once gentle, warm, and tender, had become heavy and discerning.

"And what of you?" Boo asked. "Can you...will you believe that, as you look to the skies, they, in turn, see all that you do and all that happens to you? They hear all that you say. They feel everything you feel. They listen to everything you say in prayer. And sometimes... they answer them."

Polly wanted to ask if Boo spoke of God or of anything, or anyone else, when suddenly, she fell still and quiet and listened. Had she imagined it? Music, music which seemed to emanate from deep within the strange cloud above. It was then Polly noticed that the birds were no longer singing and that the flies had stopped their insidious buzzing. Strange, she thought, as she felt all of them—birds and bees alike—land upon the ground around her and point their bodies toward the cloud of amethyst hue.

At that moment, a light, bright enough to illuminate the whole of Kansas, came from the midst of the cloud to bathe the entire hill. Polly certainly could not see that light; however, she felt its warmth upon her cheeks. What's more, she felt its peace. The light caused Polly to "see" that her long familiarity with the hill had suddenly become meaningless. Bending down, she touched the grass. Once sparse and parched from rain's long neglect, each blade suddenly became full and robust. She imagined that like the birds and the bees, the grass too rose in salute of the strange billowing mass above.

Sniffing the air, Polly discovered that instead of the usual smells propagated by a farm (hay, manure, etc.), the air suddenly became rich and fragrant, like the air just after it rains, fresher and sweeter than she had ever known. Even the old apple tree the girls sat under had somehow changed as well. Showing signs of blight and decay, it now literally burst forth with new life, as if in the height of summer before harvest.

All the while Polly was lost in reverie, Boo was no less affected by the light. With arms raised to the sky, she sang a bizarre melody, both soothing and haunting, in words Polly could not begin to comprehend. Nonetheless, the great mass floating above them began to respond to the mysterious girl's chant. As it continued to slowly revolve around its axis, it slowly began to descend. Not the whole of the strange cloud, which covered much of the state, but only the area immediately over the hill, slowly, gracefully came down until it was so close, a harvester upon a ladder may have caressed its underside.

Then there appeared orbs of gold, the will-o'-wisps seen on the cloud's arrival, scattered randomly from deep within, smoothly organized and melded into a single pulsating ribbon, which twirled and looped, dancing in rhythm to Boo's song.

Suddenly the cloud boomed with thunder that reverberated throughout the surrounding sky. Its roaring calmed into a low rumble, which started and stopped periodically in a most curious pattern. Boo would frequently nod her head or mumble in acknowledgment to the cloud's strange rumblings.

Polly listened to it all and wondered, was Boo actually talking to the cloud? Had the cloud really spoken to her?

When the strange mass once again grew silent, Boo gently lifted Polly to her feet, taking the girl's hands in hers.

All at once, Boo stopped and said, "Sweetness, yesterday I promised I would show how my people help others of us to get along without sight. Well, it is happening now. The cloud sees everything below. It has just told me something." Then Boo, inclining her head toward a nearby bush, said, "I know you are there, for we have watched you since before you arrived. Foolish man, come out at once!"

Buck Riser stumbled out of his place of concealment and snarled threateningly. He had lurked about all day, seeking opportunity to "rescue" Polly from the newcomer with no past and with dubious motives, as well as from the Knowles. A new sense of alarm and urgency overcame him as he became witness to Boo's interplay with the mysterious cloud of amethyst hue.

"You… You!" he said, pointing a grimy calloused thumb toward Boo. "Get away from Polly, impostor. I checked around…you're not from the eye clinic, and Dr. Hillcrest never heard of you, and there's no record of your birth or of you ever living here in Kansas or in British Columbia. So you're not who you say you are, so you're certainly not here for the reason you said in that phony letter. So who are you, and what do you want with my daughter?"

Polly, who had until now been silent, could hold back her excitement no longer. "Pa, is that you? Are you really here?"

Irritated by both Buck's interruption and by Polly's display, Boo said, "Go to sleep now, sweetness, you do not need to hear this."

Immediately like turning off a light, Polly became limp as a rag doll and collapsed on the ground, asleep. With anger radiating from her as palpable as heat from a nearby fire, the creature known as Boo Astrophel answered, "Who am I? I am one far removed from your natural laws and far more than your mortal mind can comprehend. I am here to give Polly more than you ever have and far more than you possibly can—a life free of your cruelty and pain."

Buck, his anger dangerously mounting, said, "Look, I don't know how much you think you know about me, but I've changed. I'm not the same guy who hurt Polly in the past. Now all I want is to love and care for her like a father should. Now get out the way."

"It is much too late for you to play at being a father. Besides Polly is no longer your concern."

Buck menacingly approached, fist clenched in hatred and fear. "I told you to get out of my way. So long as I live, that girl will always be my concern." And then Buck lashed out.

Seemingly having no time to react, Boo stood unmoving. Then as Buck's fist reached his victim's face, it passed right through, like it was passing through old man Clemmons' smoke rings from his cigar. The momentum of Buck's attack brought him into Boo's reach. As his hand passed harmlessly through her, so too did her hand pass effortlessly into him. However, unlike Buck, Boo's hand did not come out but remained inside to clutch at his heart and squeeze.

Almost at once, Buck's breathing became laborious, his skin became pale blue, and his powerful legs had turned to rubber. As

Boo slowly applied pressure, she said, "So long as you are alive…personally, I relish your terms. However, I am constrained to do otherwise. Therefore, know this, man of brutish nature, the heavens have witnessed your abuse of this innocent child, and the heavens have shaken with rage over it. Now the heavens are here to shake you with this message. We are here to grant this child a new and better life. Get in our way again, and I will grant you OBLIVION. Now be gone… BUCK-WILD."

With Boo's hand removed, Buck tumbled headlong down the entire height of the hill. Upon reaching its base, he scrambled to his feet, then tore off down the dusty road leading into town. Where anger had once been his motivation, his encounter with the Astrophel girl caused a distant memory to surface and terrorize him.

"Only SHE called me that… Only SHE called me that."

PART 4

The Rue Cloud (1936)

CHAPTER 29

Town without Faith

In the not-so abandoned brewery in the remote northwest corner of Garden City, the two Sweeny brothers listened intently, as Buck relived the events at the hill on the Riser Farm.

"I'm telling you what I saw," Buck said, trying to catch his breath. "That bloody thing up there ain't natural, and neither is that Boo Astrophel thing that runs around with my daughter, Polly. She must be some sort of a witch or something."

"Umm," Doug said thoughtfully. "Something, indeed. I think we may be able to use this Boo, whether she likes it or not."

"You can do whatever you want to that Boo thing, but I have to get Polly away from her, but how?"

"Let me figure that out. If all you say is true—and I don't doubt it—we can take advantage of it to 'rescue' Polly and then use Miss. Astrophel's influence with that strange cloud to perform a boon for the town."

"What should I be doing in the meantime?" Buck asked.

"Why nothing, of course, except to get something to eat, then get some rest. We're going to need you later. Remember, everyone's still out looking for you. But whatever you do, stay away from Boo and Polly. We'll settle that account later."

As Buck stood up to leave the room, he was haunted by something Boo Astrophel had said, something he deliberately omitted from his report to the Sweenys, where Boo had called him Buck-Wild. To Buck, the mere fact that Boo and Polly had grown so close

239

in so short a time was ample enough reason for him to feel threatened by their relationship. However, the only person in all the world to refer to him by the name Buck-Wild was his wife, Penny. This remembrance brought a new sense of urgency to his need to separate the two girls. Urgency and parental fear. It would have been hard enough to contend with Boo because she presented herself as a rival for Polly's affection. However, Buck doubted that even his new reformed self was enough to compete against the dead.

Doug waited as Buck left the room. Satisfied that he would not be overheard by the departing Riser, Doug turned to his brother and said, "I have spent a good deal of time studying our dear Mayor Smoke, whose family owns the First Bank of Garden City and where resides the strongbox containing Polly's inheritance. Of late, this public official has developed the habit of entering the vault, just before closing, and making personal withdrawals from old man Clemmons' cashbox."

Budd was indignant. "Hey! That's our loot he's stealing."

"Quite right, but we're coming away with the lion's share of it. To do this in a few days from now…"

The clandestine meeting continued throughout most of the night, with the older Sweeny repeating instructions over and over, until he was certain Budd knew his part.

Satisfied, he reassured Budd, saying, "Now don't worry. Tomorrow I'm going to make a call to someone who can help."

The meeting being adjourned, Budd departed as well, leaving Doug to brood all alone.

"I promised our father, I'd take care of that half-wit brother, of mine. I'm going to do just that, only not as he envisioned."

*****

Early the next day, Doug and Budd were up and about at the local drugstore. Doug picked up the ear bell, then cranked the phone to life. "Yes, operator. Please connect me to Miss. Lilly Marz, at BAR-5, 3605, in Oklahoma. Yes, I'll pay the charges."

Doug waited until a voice on the other end said, "Yes, who is this?"

"Lil, this is Doug… Doug Sweeny."

At first, the person on the other end almost hug up. "So what!"

"So I need you to get a message to your brother for me. This concerns that favor I still owe him. Tell him that the apple tree will be ready for picking in two days. You got that? The apple will be ready—"

"Yeah, yeah, I got it," said Lil, the irritation in her voice was unmistakable. "Now buzz off and stop bothering me."

When the call ended, Budd said, "I didn't know you knew a burlesque queen named Lilly Marz."

"That's not her name, and she's not with any peep show. Her real name is Lillian Marie Barrow, the youngest sister of Clyde Barrow,[23] a true expert in robbing banks."

Budd scratched his head. "So that's the help you talked about. Where do you know Clyde Barrow from?"

Doug answered matter-of-factly, "I used to date his sister."

"So why do you owe him a favor?" Budd asked innocently.

"I broke her heart…he let me live."

*****

Pastor Knowles stopped the truck at the end of Main Street, allowing Boo and Polly to get out, with instructions to meet the Knowles at the church in time for prayer.

As the two walked leisurely together, Polly asked, "Hey, Boo! What are we doing walking through town?"

"For my part, sweetness, I am observing your townsfolk, listening to what they are saying about the cloud up there."

"Boo?" Polly asked, somewhat concerned. "That sounds like it's going to take awfully long. Will we be able to meet the others at church in time?"

"Not to worry, sweetness, we will not be walking all over town. I should be able to get everything I need right here."

"Where's 'here?'" Polly asked.

"We have reached the drugstore in the middle of Main Street." Boo guided Polly inside and directed her to sit at a small table and chairs set up in front of the large shop window.

"Wait here, sweetness, I will only be a moment."

Boo left Polly and walked up to the counter. She returned shortly with a cup of tea and a donut for Polly and a cup of black coffee for herself.

"From here," Boo said, "I can listen to people from all over town. Let me see now… Mr. Carruthers across the street is speaking to his wife. They are wondering whether to leave Garden City and move further West, like his brother did.

"At the end of Main Street, in the old schoolhouse, Miss. Alice has no pupils but still sits alone. She is angry at God for forsaking her town and for the embarrassment of having to move back in with her parents back East in Boston. She is saying that her parents never believed she could make it on her own…now she has just given them enough proof to fuel a lifetime of ridicule and subtle insults."

Astonished, Polly asked, "But, Boo, I don't understand, how do you know everyone's name, and how can you hear what the whole town is saying?"

Boo laughs, taking another sip of coffee. "Oh, sweetness, remember when I said that where I come from, most have no sense of sight and that we help each other whenever needed? And of course you remember our picnic, when I danced and sang to the cloud, how it sang back to me? Well, my friends are up in the cloud, and it is the cloud that hears the townspeople's words and even their very thoughts. The cloud then tells me whatever it is I need to know."

"How can the cloud hear folks' thoughts?" Polly blurted out, nearly choking on her donut.

"Be careful, sweetness! Do not talk and eat at the same time."

"That's what Mom always told me."

"Every mother says that to her child," Boo said as she took another sip of coffee. "Your favorite broadcast is carried to your radio on a signal made up of electrical energy. The thoughts of people are made of nearly the same energy…" Boo's voice trailed off. She frowned as she cocked her head to one side and listened.

"What's wrong, Boo?" Polly asked, her voice tinged with apprehension.

"Most of your neighbors are afraid. They marvel how the cloud can keep the dust storms away, but it frightens them as much as the storms. Others think that, if the cloud can do that, what else can it do? However, I am sorry to say that for the majority of your neighbors, who still pray, their words are only a pretense—empty, hollow, without substance or power—because they are without faith. Still others hate the very God they pray to."

Slowly Polly's head drops to her chest, and had she been able, she surely would have cried.

"What is wrong, sweetness?" asked Boo, knowing full well the girl's answer.

"I know I shouldn't be sad or upset, Boo, but I've been praying for my dad and for this town every day. It bothers me that—"

Boo interrupted, "Oh, sweetness, your prayers are full of beauty and are precious to God...and to others. But know this, though you may be full of faith, you cannot force others to believe. Your neighbors lack the faith you covet for them because they have chosen to cling to their fear and unbelief, thereby rejecting the faith of God."

Polly sat quietly and wrestled with Boo's words. Likewise Boo sat and pondered, her continence darkened as she listened to the almost-imperceptible low rumblings emanating from the cloud.

Suddenly Boo shot up from her seat. Taking hold of Polly's hand, Boo hefted the girl clear of her chair and over the table. Almost before her feet had touched the ground, Polly's arm stretched out, compelling her to scramble to keep up with her friend and mentor.

Boo said without looking back at her charge, "Come with me, we must hurry to the church. I think there is going to be trouble."

The girls hurried along in silence. Twice Polly stumbled and would have dived headfirst to the ground had it not been for Boo's strong wiry arm upholding her. Finally the church loomed into view. They had almost reached the sanctuary doors, when Boo chanced to notice a moderately sized group of neighbors approaching the edifice from the opposite direction. Ignoring them, the two scurried inside the building just as the prayer meeting drew to its conclusion.

"Oh, Lord!" Pastor Knowles said, sweat pouring down his back. "We thank you, with all our hearts, for the relief from the murderous dust storms the strange apparition in the sky has brought. Whether it comes from you or not, we cannot know. Still, Lord, whatever it is, grant thy servants may put their trust in you, looking only unto you, the author and finisher of our faith... Amen."

Prayer let out, and as the congregates departed, they were met outside by Doug Sweeny and a growing band of townsfolk. Immediately Doug challenged Boo before the whole congregation.

"We know you have a certain influence over that thing up there. That being the case, you can influence it to make it rain and relieve us of this drought. Isn't that so... Witch?"

"You call me witch, then seek a boon as if I were your servant. You beseech God, as if he were your servant, as well. He is not YOUR servant, neither am I. Further, if I be a witch, then I would be the enemy of God. Why call upon God and call upon me as well? Call on the One that you serve."

Doug Sweeny persisted, growing louder as the number of those gathered began to increase. Soon they were close to becoming a mob.

"Witch! Right now, I'd pray to Satan himself if I thought he would end this bloody drought."

While the Doug Sweeny-Boo Astrophel interchange continued, more and more heated with every passing moment, Pastor Knowles began to usher his parishioners back into the church.

Boo looked about to address all those gathered. "Foolish desperate people, I have seen your hearts. Many of you pray against hope. Even more of you have lost your hope altogether. Still there are those of you who curse God, as well as the day you were born. Faith alone is pleasing to God, but you have long since lost yours. Therefore, there shall no relief come to you until you have learned to bless the Lord and to serve only him."

As Knowles was leading Polly into the church, the hand of Budd Sweeny reached out from the crowd to snatch her away. Placing the point of a switchblade knife to her throat, he shouted, "You will do this thing, or I'm going to take away much more than her eyes."

Polly, afraid to inhale, held her breath, trying to keep the knife from her throat. She felt Budd's grip tighten around her. She felt the knife press harder against her quivering throat. Then she felt his knife hand go slack as he dropped the knife onto the dusty ground. Finally Polly heard Budd scream in terror and in blinding searing pain.

Gone now was Astrophel's accustomed quiet even disposition. In its place, a burning wrath ignited, while above, the mysterious cloud of amethyst hue darkened until it was the color of coagulated blood.

"How dare you threaten this innocent child whose prayers alone sustain this miserable hovel. You are not worthy to even gaze upon her. Therefore, the hand of offense shall touch her no more."

Budd Sweeny stared in shock at his hand; even as he watched, from his fingers to his elbow, the flesh on it shriveled and desiccated until it resembled a skeleton's arm, the whole of which was locked, as if from a palsy.

Ominous thunder, like a thousand kettledrums, split the ears of those gathered, as lightning from the cloud struck the ground repeatedly in a pattern that surrounded all those in the crowd. Wherever it had touched the parched earth, long tendril-like fingers moved just under the ground's surface, reaching for the mob at their center.

The townsfolk jostled and pressed against one another to escape the tendrils, which, as they approached, grew closer and closer to the surface. Those who piled up on one another to flee watched as the fingers reached ground level, pushing the soil up in long fingers as they continued to get ever closer.

Suddenly all the phalanxes burst open lengthwise, spewing forth hordes of locust, who attacked those gathered, biting them repeatedly, mercilessly. Wherever one was bitten, burning boils the size of fava beans erupted.

As the attack began, Knowles reached out from the doors of the church, drawing Boo and Polly back inside. Then as God himself closed the door of Noah's ark, Pastor Knowles closed the doors of the church and locked them.

The agonized wailing of the townsfolk persisted throughout the night and well into the next day.

CHAPTER 30

And a Man's Enemies

And a man's foes shall be they of his own household.

—Matthew 10:36 (KJV)

Buck watched Doug Sweeny pace up and down the floor of the basement in the abandoned brewery, like an animal about to strike. "You idiot!" he said to his brother. You almost got yourself and almost all your neighbors killed. Just what possessed you to jump the gun like that and threaten Polly?"

"You threatened my little girl?" Buck said, anger rising in him, even as he rose from his seat to approach the hapless younger Sweeny brother. "Why, you sorry sleazy bastard, I'm gonna—"

Budd looked at Doug with his help-me-brother look. The older Sweeny wanted so much to allow Buck to have his way with Budd, thus conveniently relieving him of the millstone around his neck. Instead Doug stepped in between his brother and assured parental judgment and retribution, saying, "Buck, we still need him. Besides he wouldn't really harm your daughter, not now, not after you let us all know how you felt about her. Why don't you go upstairs and blow off some steam, while I straighten him out? Believe me, this will never happen again."

Doug Sweeny waited as Buck, for the second time, left the brothers Sweeny alone together at Doug's insistence.

"Sorry, Brother, but I thought I could make that Boo person make it rain," Budd said contritely.

"Don't think! It's never been one of your strengths."

Budd held his right arm up for his brother to see, his voice was close to hysterics. "Look what that Boo witch did to me...look at it."

"It's far less than you deserve. Let it serve as a reminder, you have but one concern in life...that's to do what you're told to do, by me. Now pull yourself together, man. You're no good to me like this. Rest assured, though, she won't get away it, but we're going to need more than a few angry citizens. We need to arm them, and I know how to do it. We will help ourselves to Sheriff Pucket's armory and distribute the weapons there to those bitten by witch Astrophel's locust plague. Fortunately because of your blunder, their pain and their lust for vengeance will make them only too easy to lead."

Budd fought to regain his composure. At last, he stood before his brother and asked, "What do you want me to do now?"

"From here on out, you have just one job to do. Get over to the bank, as we rehearsed, and hide in the janitor's office until the bank closes at two o'clock in the afternoon. Come out and let the Barrow Gang in. When you have the cashbox, rendezvous back here. The Barrows can help themselves to everything else. Get started now!"

As Budd turned to leave, Doug said, "One last thing...don't get caught!"

*****

Reverend Knowles and his congregants spent an uneasy night of prayer vigil, listening to the lamentations of their neighbors. In the morning, after ascertaining the streets were sufficiently clear, he released his congregation to their several homes. With the church emptied of all, except for his own brood, Boo Astrophel took him aside.

"After all you have seen, you are not afraid of me. Why?"

Knowles looked her in the eyes and said, "Scriptures say to 'be careful how you entertain strangers, for in doing so, some have entertained angels unawares'" (Hebrews 13:2 KJV). "Besides Polly truly loves you, and that's good enough for me. Lastly you remind me so much of someone I loved dearly, Polly's mother, Penelope." As he spoke Penny's name, tears came to his eyes. Embarrassed, he quickly wiped them away.

"Thank you for telling me."

Knowles then called everyone to him. "Listen, people, this isn't over yet. I think it may only be the beginning, and this place won't be safe anymore." He turned to Bedelia and continued, "I want you to take the girls and head down the main road toward the parsonage. Make sure that you are seen leaving by some of the townsfolk. Just after you leave town, turn off at the old railroad access road and take the back-country shortcut to Polly's old farmhouse. I'll catch up with you there."

Bedelia asked, "What are you going to do?"

"We're going to need some help, so I'm going to go find the sheriff."

Bedelia shook her head in protest. "I don't like the idea of separating. What if something should happen—"

"It has to be this way. Don't forget, the old railroad access road."

As Boo led Polly away to the back of the church, Bedelia turned to Knowles and said, "Before I go, there's something I have to say to you...something I have to confess."

"There's no time, Bea."

"There may not be another time, later. In short, I've been hiding Buck from the search parties...and from you. I know you must be angry with me, but he's changed. He's not the same Buck anymore. I had to give him a chance to prove himself."

"I could be angry...but in truth, I'm relieved. When I saw the footprints in the kitchen and his whiskey flask on Polly's pillow, and that you hadn't been harmed, I knew something was different. Then when I noticed you saving a portion of your supper, I thought you might be helping him."

"Why didn't you stop me? Why didn't you stop him?"

"Because of Polly. I love that little girl with all my heart, but she clings to the love for her father, Buck. I didn't want her to have to choose between us... I just couldn't bear to lose her...again. So I'm relieved when I think what I might have done, if I had seen him. I thank God...and I thank you for not letting me see him. Now for goodness sake, get going."

They embraced, as if it were the very first time—as if it were the last time. Then she was gone.

Knowles watched the women drive off until they were out of sight. "Godspeed, my love."

*****

Budd Sweeny remained out of sight in the locker room of the bank's small janitor's office, reciting over and over his part until his head began to ache. Time passed slowly until finally, it was closing time, and the bank was at last empty, except for an aging night watchman and himself.

Budd watched from the small slit in the partially opened door and waited for the guard to leave for his security rounds. Sweat accumulating on his short sharply sloping forehead gave evidence to the younger Sweeny's mounting impatience. The desire to rush out and attack the aging guard tempted him to leave his place of concealment. Fortunately, however, the bank watchman chose that very moment to push himself away from his security desk and, defying gravity and his arthritis-plagued knees, stood and slowly shuffled his way out the customer service area to begin his late-afternoon rounds.

Budd gave a loud sigh of relief as he scurried from the janitor's closet, crossed over to the teller supervisor desk, and hid behind it. The new hiding place allowed him space to relax. This, in turn, caused him to remember, he had been instructed by his elder brother to overpower and tie up the guard prior to Barrow's arrival. However, the stress of waiting and of thinking for himself made him wish that Doug was there, even if he was still angry with him. But Doug was not there, and with the absence of his brother to personally direct him, inevitably he had completely forgotten those instructions.

Nervous sweat rolled down his back onto the cluster of boils. A piercing fiery pain ensued, prompting him to use his withered hand as a backscratcher. Lacking feeling in it, and so preoccupied with intense scratching, he failed to feel or hear his elbow striking the metal table. However, the deteriorating hearing of the night watchman was just acute enough to pick it up.

"Put 'em up, mister, an' come on out!" he said with revolver drawn and pointed directly at the suspect's heart. As Budd stood up with raised hands, the guard took one look at his cursed hand. "What in the world is that thing?"

Suddenly the front of the bank exploded in a shower of brick, mortar, and glass, as the front end of a Packard sedan came crashing through. The automobile came to rest upon the chest of the guard, killing him instantly.

"Budd Sweeny, your brother was right," Clyde Barrow said, as he stepped over the body of the guard. "You really can't do anything right. Now show me this cashbox."

Budd led the way to the bank's vault. Though closed and locked for the day, Clyde had no trouble at all spinning the huge middle-of-three wheels until all three wheels were properly aligned and opened.

"Your brother, Doug, managed to persuade the mayor to share with him the combination to the bank's vault. Good thing he noticed the mayor was embezzling funds almost every night. He even had pictures to confirm the accusation. In the end, His Honor, the Mayor, was only too happy to purchase a silent partner. Now let's get to work."

It took the Barrow Gang almost no time to clean out Clemmons' strongbox, as well as quite a few safety deposit boxes and place their contents into canvas sacks.

"Good," Clyde said, "now let's be off."

"Where to?" asked Budd.

"Why, back to Oklahoma, of course."

"Hey!" Budd protested. "Brother said to hang out at the abandoned brewery, until he rendezvoused with us."

"I know," Clyde said with a sardonic smile. "Doug changed the plan, at the last minute. He threatened to expose the mayor, unless on one of his embezzlement trips, he withdrew all that your brother would need to start a new life outside the US and away from his two ex-partners. He said we could have the rest."

When Budd moved to further protest, Clyde said, "You should know, I've never received high marks in school for sharing."

"Huh!" a bewildered Budd said, as Clyde slipped a 1911 Colt .45 automatic pistol from his shoulder holster, twirled it in his hand only once, and took aim.

"Doug also asked me to give you this…"

As the Barrow Gang piled into the Packard, Clyde stood upon the running boards and shouted into the air, "Thank you for the favor, Doug Sweeny! Now we're even!"

*****

Doug and Buck walked over to Sheriff Pucket's office. His three deputies were out about Finney County, gauging reactions to the mysterious cloud of amethyst hue, leaving Pucket alone to catch up on paperwork. Buck stood beside the door to the sheriff's office, while Doug entered alone.

"What can I do for you, Sweeny?" Pucket said without looking up from his desk.

"Sheriff, we would like to file a complaint."

"Who's 'we' and against whom?"

With lightning speed, Doug's deft fingers reached out to expertly lift Sheriff Pucket's gun from its holster. Buck entered the room.

"We would, and against you," Doug said, pointing the gun at Pucket. Tilting his head toward Buck, he said, "When you shot my partner in the knee, he swore that no matter how long it took, he was going to make you pay. Well, Buck, now's your chance." He handed Buck the gun.

Sheriff Pucket cursed himself for having been caught with his guard down. He looked Buck in the eyes, not pleading and not begging but waited bravely, figuring it was finally his time, after all.

Buck regarded him and discovered, to his surprise, that he no longer harbored any malice toward the sheriff.

"No…no! I won't do it. I just decided to be the man my daughter can look up to. I don't want to hurt anyone anymore…especially him. He was just doing his job." Buck handed the gun back to Doug.

Doug trained the revolver back on the Sheriff, saying, "Well, Pucket, this looks like your lucky day. Now where are your keys?"

"Top desk drawer."

"Good! Buck?"

Buck went and retrieved the keys, handing them to Doug.

"Now, Sheriff, which one's for the door to the armory?"

"No!"

"Very well, we'll figure it out ourselves. Now this way, if you please."

Sheriff Pucket walked toward the first jail cell in the adjacent passageway. When he reached its door, Doug used the gun to deliver a mighty backhand plow to the back of Pucket's neck. He fell unconscious onto the cell floor.

As they were about to leave for the armory, Buck announced, "I wanted help to get Polly away from that Boo witch, but not like this. She could get hurt. And by the way, I'm not stupid. I know you and Budd have been planning to steal Clemmons' strongbox without me, and I still can't go along with you or anyone else stealing my girl's inheritance."

Doug Sweeny gave out a disappointed sigh. "I thought you might say something like this. You know, I was wrong about you. You really are no bloody fun unless you've been drinking. And for the record, you really are stupid for handing Pucket's gun back to me." He brought the pistol down hard onto the top of Buck's skull once, twice; finally it took three blows for Buck's hard head to become tenderized enough for him to get the message.

Doug Sweeny dragged Buck's limp unconscious body to the same cell as Pucket and threw him in next to the body of the sheriff. Doug locked the cell door and hurried out back to the patrol car lot and armory.

*****

Three years ago, Pastor Knowles's closest friend, the sheriff, reluctantly convinced him to register the church as an emergency shelter and command post should anything happen to his office.

Allowing a police radio to be placed in the pastor's study, it had remained unused in the closet ever since. However, upon hearing a single gun report from the direction of the bank, he was on the radio now, trying to reach the sheriff, but no answer could be heard.

Quickly he walked up to the bank. Climbing through the gaping hole in its front wall, he immediately saw the bank guard, lying crushed on the floor. Then he saw Budd Sweeny, eyes still open, though quite dead, with a third eye nestled between and slightly above the other two. He vomited and looked up in time to hear a police megaphone blaringly calling the bug-bitten townsfolk to action.

"FELLOW CITIZENS...FELLOW VICTIMS...COME OUT...COME OUT!" shouted Doug Sweeny, as he slowly drove the multiple-prisoner wagon through town. Wherever he went, droves of townsfolk covered in festering fava bean-sized boils moved like zombies and followed. When their numbers had risen upward of five score, Doug brought them all to a halt in front of the church, where he had first clashed with Boo Astrophel the day before.

Still utilizing the megaphone, he challenged, "ARE WE GOING TO LET HER GET AWAY WITH DOING THIS TO YOU...YOUR NEIGHBORS... YOUR FRIENDS? ARE WE GOING TO ALLOW THIS BOO WITCH'S INSULTS TO US TO GO UNANSWERED? I SAY, HELL NO! WHAT SAY YOU?"

"Hell no! Hell no! Hell no!" chanted the crowd.

"I SAY, EITHER THAT BOO WITCH RELIEVES US OF THIS BLOODY DROUGHT, OR WE WILL RELIEVE HER OF HER LIFE. WHAT SAY YOU?"

"Relieve the drought, or we relieve your life... Relieve the draught, or we relieve your life."

"I SAY TO THAT BOO WITCH, STAY THIS DRAUGHT OR BE STONED! WHAT SAY YOU?"

"Stay or stoned... Stay or stoned... Stay or stoned!"

Doug opened the back of the wagon. Filled with armloads of Thompson submachine guns, Browning Automatic Rifles, and Remington pump-action shotguns, there were enough weapons and ammunition to equip a small army. Doug now had a small army. He distributed the wagon's contents severally until the wagon had been emptied, except for a large canvas drawstringed tote bag on the floor next to the driver's seat.

Just then, Pastor Knowles emerged from the midst of the crowd to stand in front of Doug. Turning to face the others, he said, "Neighbors and friends, I know you're all hurting... I know you are in pain. But I tell you this, it will get better...it will go away. But if you do this thing...if you take a life...your guilt will remain...it will never go away."

Suddenly the butt of a shotgun, wielded by Doug Sweeny, struck Knowles hard in his temple. Like a marionette puppet whose strings were suddenly cut, down he went to lie in the middle of the dusty road.

"Check the church!" Doug ordered. "She was seen here last."

Several townsfolk went into the church, then soon reappeared, shaking their heads. No one was inside. However, one of those bitten had remained huddled in the doorway of the barbershop across the street, throughout the night, sauntered over to Doug, saying, "I saw her... I saw her light out, down the road, headed for that preacher's house, not more'n an hour ago."

Still using the megaphone, Doug said, "THEN THAT'S WHERE WE'RE GOING. GRAB ANYTHING THAT DRIVES AND FOLLOW ME! I SAY, EITHER THAT BOO WITCH BOWS TO OUR WISHES, OR SHE WILL BURN!"

*****

A blinding headache woke Knowles from a torturous sleep. Still lying in the middle of the road, a trickle of blood stung his eyes. Struggling to his feet, he moved, with drunken gait, toward the sheriff's office at the south end of Main Street.

Looking around, the office looked deserted. He shouted, "Dale Pucket, are you in here?" The effort made his head throb until he thought that he might lose consciousness again, when he heard the voice of the sheriff. It came from behind a set of heavy doors, which read above, "PRISONER DETENTION HALL."

"Pat... Pat Knowles, is that you out there?"

Knowles followed the voice, through the doors and down the long corridor, until he came to his friend's cell. The irony of seeing the sheriff behind the bars of his own jail tempted him to laugh, if it didn't hurt so much. Instead he asked, if the prisoner needed anything, which hurt enough.

"Very funny," Pucket said. "You still carrying Clemmons' hog's leg in your pocket?"

"Yes!"

"Well, get over here, son, and use it on this lock!"

Knowles complied. Three shots rang out, as Buck and the sheriff shielded themselves at the corners of the cell. When the door finally swung open, Knowles reported how Doug Sweeny was leading a mob, armed with stolen weapons, looking for Boo and the others. He also reported that the bank had been robbed, and finally, Budd Sweeny had been killed.

Exiting the cell, Buck spoke out, "Sheriff, I'd like to come too. I know I've done wrong so many times. But Polly is my daughter, and if she's in any danger, I'd really like to help...for a change."

Pucket replied, "When you had the opportunity to do harm, you didn't. So you're in. The more the merrier. Before we go, I must get on the horn and call someone."

"Who?" Knowles asked.

"Captain James Masters, Kansas State Police. We're gonna need all the help we can get."

*****

Doug Sweeny's mob reached the parsonage. Like the church, they found it to be deserted. Frustrated and more incensed with each new setback, they continued down the road, declaring that there was only one place left where they could go—the old Clemmons/Riser farmhouse.

Bedelia, Boo, and Polly, thanks to Knowles's shortcut, had arrived at the farmhouse with just enough time to spare to ensure every door and window was properly boarded or barricaded before the dust cloud from the Sweeny mob's caravan was spotted in the distance, rapidly approaching.

"Stay inside," ordered Boo. "And don't open the door for any reason!"

"What will you do?" asked Polly, her fear mounting.

"I am going out to meet them, greet them, and make them wish they had never been born."

"Be careful," said Bedelia.

"We are far beyond careful now, Auntie Bea."

As she neared the front door, Polly called out, "I love you, Boo."

"I love you, too… Polliwog."

"Hey! That's what my mother used to call me."

"I know," said Boo. And then she was gone.

Boo stood on the front porch and waited as the vehicles of the murderous mob skidded to a halt, forming a wide crescent in front of the house. Doug Sweeny was first to alight from his stolen wagon and stand before her.

"We asked you politely before. Now we're telling you, witch… MAKE IT RAIN, AND END THIS DROUGHT!"

"And I told you, NO! But you will not accept it. Well, can you accept GO STRAIGHT TO HELL for an answer?"

Boo waved her hand to summon the locust as before, and suddenly—*nothing happened.* "I was too lenient with you before, I see. Now may the earth swallow you up and have done with you."

Again she waved her hand, and again—*nothing.* Then she felt it. Waves of disappointment and displeasure radiated from the cloud, directed not at the blasphemous gang facing her but at herself.

Boo Astrophel looked up at the mysterious cloud of amethyst hue and said, "You cannot do this to me. Not now when—"

All at once, a shot rang out from the crowd. The leaded projectile grazed the side of Boo's forehead. Though not fatal, it was enough to drive Boo to her knees.

Doug raised his arms in triumph, as he faced his posse. "See, she can indeed know pain." Then upon turning again to face Boo, he said, "I will give you this one last chance. EITHER YOU STAY THIS

DROUGHT, OR I SWEAR, BY HEAVEN ABOVE OR HELL BELOW, I WILL DESTROY YOU AND THAT LITTLE GIRL YOU HOLD SO DEAR."

"Kill you all… Kill you all… Kill you all…" the crowd chanted while Doug reached into his canvas satchel, producing from it an incendiary grenade. Pulling the pin, he turned to Boo and said, "Now, Boo witch, YOU ARE EITHER GOING TO BOW TO OUR WISHES, OR YOU WILL BURN!"

Even as the mob chanted, "Bow or burn! Bow or burn…" the front door opened, and Bedelia quickly dragged Boo back into the house. Simultaneously Doug threw the firebomb through a sec-ond-floor window. It landed in the master bedroom and detonated. Soon billows of toxic vapors began to waft downstairs, reducing those inside the farmhouse to a choking panicked state.

"YOU ARE EITHER GOING TO BOW TO OUR WISHES, OR YOU WILL BURN!" Doug said as he tossed another incendiary into the already well-involved house.

Inside there seemed to be no escape from the deadly fumes. With the girls lying as close to the floor as possible, Bedelia tore three strips from her petticoat and, feeling her way, crawled to the kitchen to wet them, to afford some protection from the smoke. When she failed to return, Polly asked, "B-Boo, w-what shall we do? W-Where can w-we go?"

"We must go to the centermost room in the house. We may find some relief there."

Polly answered, "But, Boo, that doesn't make any sense. Wouldn't being near the outside walls make it easier to make it out-side the house?"

Unperturbed, Boo said, "Trust me this once, at the center guar-antees we will leave this place sooner." Then leaning close over Polly, Boo tenderly kissed her on the forehead before adding, "Polliwog, you must be brave for only a little while longer…this will be over soon."

Crawling, Boo was leading Polly by the hand when suddenly, inexplicably, Boo's handhold was broken, and Polly was all alone. She was too frightened to move or even to think clearly. All she could do was lay prostrate and listen to timbers cracking and splitting above her.

Though the vaulted ceiling above had always seemed impossibly high to the girl, the distance afforded no respite, no protection from the searing heat it generated, making Polly feel as if she were in an oven. Suddenly it seemed to the frightened girl that the oven was growing hotter, more intolerable every moment.

No, not hotter, she thought, but closer, as if the blistering heat had become a vicious creature from the underworld reaching down to snatch her away. All at once, without enough substance left to hold it up, the ceiling came crashing down over her.

"Mommyyy!"

PART 5

The Bright Cloud / The
Right Cloud (1936)

AND GOD SHALL WIPE AWAY ALL TEARS FROM
THEIR EYES, AND
    THERE SHALL BE NO MORE DEATH, NEITHER
SORROW, NOR CRYING,
    NEITHER SHALL THERE BE ANY MORE PAIN:
FOR THE FORMER
    THINGS ARE PASSED AWAY.
                    —Revelation 21:4 (KJV)

CHAPTER 31

Into the Purple Nebula

As Moses parted the Red Sea, so the "peaceful" citizens of Garden City gave way to Sheriff Pucket's' blaring siren. Suddenly, before the patrol car had come to a stop, Buck Riser exploded from the passenger door. He took no notice of his neighbors, some of whom yet retained their stolen police firearms. Instead Buck concentrated on the door that loomed before him, willing himself to see through the smoke and flames beyond that tried to keep him from "her." Buck kicked open the front door and disappeared into the inferno that he had once called home.

When the patrol car came to a complete stop, Pastor Knowles came out and ran to the back of the house. Climbing up the trellis there, he managed to reach an attic window. Punching out the boards covering it, he crawled inside.

Heat and smoke from the floors below rose quickly, willfully speeding upward to attack the intruder. Pastor Knowles was instantly overcome, yet he willed himself onward and downward, desperately seeking Bedelia and the others. Instinctively he moved in the direction of the kitchen. Though he could no longer see anything but a red hazy glow all around, his hands and feet were now his eyes, searching the bright darkness before him.

Suddenly his foot discovered a gaping hole that had once been the second floor hallway. Feeling his way to an adjacent passage, he remembered there was another narrow stairway at its end, which descended to the kitchen. Coughing and gasping, he had almost reached the stairs when he suddenly stumbled over a large soft object at the edge of the steps. Instantly he recognized it as Bedelia, even as he fell headlong down the stairs, the dislodged body of his wife tumbling close behind.

Unable to move further due to multiple fractures to his arms and legs, and unable to breathe due to the choking billowing smoke, Knowles had, at last, succumbed to both. His body lay at the base of the stairway, with Bedelia's head resting serenely upon his chest.

When Buck entered the house, immediately smoke blinded his eyes and assailed his lungs. Unable to see, memory alone guided him forward. "Oh god!" he said as he groped his way along. "Help me to find her. I just have to find my little girl."

He had not gone far before he stumbled over something in what had been the kitchen. Dread smothered his thoughts, even as smoke smothered his lungs. Kneeling in the absolute dark, he felt for whatever it was that had tripped him. Though unable to see in the dense smoke, he could easily tell that it was an adult body—no, two adult bodies. "Not Polly...thank God."

He would have breathed a sigh of relief had he been able to breathe at all. Laboriously Buck reached down to the bodies and gathered their jacket collars in each of his massive fists. Then through force of will alone, he began to drag them both behind him as he managed to backtrack his way in the direction he had entered the house from. Nearly an eternity later, he emerged into light and fresh air. With his lifeless burden in tow, Buck tumbled headfirst down the rickety front porch steps.

Quickly the mob gathered around to morbidly gaze upon the two victims. The crowd was amazed at what they saw sprawled at their feet. The cleric and his wife were not charred nor were they smoldering. In fact, apart from the fact of where they were both found dead, there was no evidence to suggest their having died in the blaze. And there was something more—the two were smiling.

Even as state police cars encircled the rioters, Buck scrambled to his feet.

"Buck! Buck! Don't go back in there!" Sheriff Pucket warned. But it was already too late. Just as he did in his football years, Buck deftly spun around, breaking Pucket's precarious grip on his arm. Then as if bounding over the goal line, he barreled headlong back into the billowing hell.

Ignoring the heat and the flames, Buck desperately groped his way through the suffocating blackness, searching for redemption in the form of his daughter.

A single-minded urge to find Polly consumed Buck as surely and completely as Hephaestus's flames consumed the residence. Still oblivious to danger and destruction alike, Buck forayed deeper into the inferno, even while burning timbers fell, and walls gave way all around him. Finally the flames took their toll on the highest structures of the house, and like the last leaf on a tree in autumn, the roof relinquished its purchase, and with a deafening roar—collapsed.

*****

Polly gasped as her cries were suddenly snatched from her throat. Then she realized the truth—it was she herself that had been snatched away from her body.

Like flour in a sieve, Polly's spirit sifted itself through what little there was left of her body and continued to float up, passing through the remainder of the farmhouse.

Though no longer possessing eyes, Polly could "see" the crowd below, receding away, as she rose higher and higher. She could see Doug Sweeny try to pass unnoticed through the throng, only to be caught by Sheriff Pucket, who roughly handcuffed him and stuffed him into his patrol car, saying, "I know you must miss your brother, but don't you worry none, you'll be joining him soon enough."

Faster and faster she rose until she became bathed in cool purple light and no longer able to see anything about her.

Presently Polly felt as if she were no longer rising but gently falling and falling, while unable to reach the ground. Still she was grateful to be out of the burning farmhouse.

Polly marveled that though she actually no longer possessed a body to interact with a physical environment, that fact was no longer relevant as her mind became bombarded by a variety and depth of senses she was never aware existed.

Flashes and specks of light danced before her "eyes," which were not. Music and song filled her "ears," which were not. Sensations of gentle breezes and of gentle touches from others caressed her "skin," which was not. Smells so wondrous they could make any flower or perfume seem dull and lifeless enticed her "nose," which was not.

All these new and wonderful sensations gave her the impression that she was somehow swimming through them (instead of them coming to her). The heady thought that the fires, which had consumed her body, only served to free her mind to directly experience an alternate more glorious reality filled her with a joyous wonder she had only dreamed of. This realization left her feeling as if she had been unable to see or hear or touch or smell, or even taste, for her entire life, and that she had only begun to truly be alive this very moment.

"Boo... Boo!" Polly's nonmouth called into the expanse. "Boo, where are you?"

"Everywhere, sweetness." Boo's voice came from all around her, like a thousand-voice choir singing in unison.

Puzzled, Polly asked, "Boo, where are we?"

There was no reply. Instead Polly felt as if a door had opened close by, and someone brushed by her to step through it.

Presently the voice returned, only different somehow. It was still the thousand-voice choir, only now, the all-voice had the quality of a child.

"Why, sweetness, we are in the cloud, of course."

"Oh, of course," Polly repeated with a hint of sarcasm, as if those words from her beloved Boo somehow explained everything. Of course they did not. Bewildered, she asked, "But, Boo, I don't understand...what is it? What is the cloud?"

A palpable silence enveloped Polly, and for the first time since entering the farmhouse, the girl felt truly alone.

Presently the all-voice spoke again, "Listen carefully! In the world, regular clouds are formed when the heat of the sun turns water into vapor, which rises into the sky. That's called *evaporation*.

There the droplets bind with other vapors still rising. Called *accumulation*, the resultant form continues to ascend to form the fluffy clouds you are familiar with. It continues to gather still more vapor until it reaches its saturation point, that is, *condensation*. Eventually it releases its moisture in precipitation to begin the process anew."

The all-voice paused; then it was Boo's voice that continued, saying, "Human souls behave in the same manner. Once released from the prison of their mortality, souls rise and accumulate in the heavens. When a great number of them have joined, they appear as gaseous cosmic clouds, which have been observed by your astronomers. They call us nebulae. We call ourselves Antecedents."

"All right, Antecedents it is," Polly said. "Why have you come here to Garden City? And why am I here?"

"We felt a kindred energy in your prayers for your town and your father. It sounded of music to us, and it drew us closer. When we descended upon your world, we chose a soul of your clan…one newly set free, who had not been with us long enough to be fully one. We chose them and sent them to closely observe the people of the town, to ascertain if they were worthy of your prayers for them being answered."

"Hmm," Polly said to herself. "Souls released from their mortality…"

Polly wanted so much to find out more; however, apprehension bordering on dread suddenly gripped her. It was more than just a fear of the possible answer to her next question, the very question itself held a certain terror for her. Still she had to know. Cautiously, as if her very life was at stake, she asked, "But, Boo, in order to be here, wouldn't I have to have…died?"

"Yes, you do."

"And…am I…dead then?"

"Yes… Yes, you are."

Polly paused to think again to prepare herself to ask the unthinkable.

"B-Boo, d…did…you kill me?"

"Yes, sweetness," Boo's voice said proudly. "Yes, I did."

*****

Somehow Buck made it out of the burning remains of his house alive, almost. Large patches of blistered flesh covered most of his head and chest. However, on his back, portions of flesh were missing altogether. Then there were his arms and hands. Those watching gasped in horror at the sight of raw meat and sinews showing through where his skin should have been. The charred skin had not been burned away but rather had detached completely from his fingers to roll up, like a glove, to his elbows. Each rasping, labored breath he took expelled a plume of smoke. Then like the unfortunate roof, Buck collapsed.

*****

The degree of apprehension Polly felt about asking her dire question was nothing compared to the absolute revulsion it replaced, now that she had her answer. Quickly the revulsion was substituted by anger, which was immediately superseded by loathing, directed toward her erstwhile mentor and best friend. Had Polly possessed legs, she certainly would have paced back and forth across the floor (had there actually been one).

"Stand right here, she said… Right in the middle of the house, she said… Smack-dab beneath a burning ceiling… Trust me, she said… We'll get out sooner, she said…"

"Oh, sweetness," Boo said, ignoring the girl's tirade. "If you really must know, I actually managed to kill you three times."

"Don't you dare call me that, ever again!" the girl screamed. "You don't have the right to call me that."

Still unaffected by Polly's tantrum, Boo continued, "There was the time your father threw the ax at you. He was going to miss you, so I sort of corrected his aim before he released it. Then there was the great black blizzard that blinded you. You were supposed to be dead…both times…but somehow, you always managed to pull through. Finally there was the house fire started by your loving neighbors. Well, I guess the third time really is the charm because here you are, at last."

Polly was hardly amused. "Boo, how could you? I thought you were my friend… I thought you loved me. Well, true friends don't let their friends die in fires. True friends don't repeatedly set up their friends to be killed. Tell me, just what in the HASENPFEFFERIN world would possibly possess you to—"

"Because you asked me to!" Boo interrupted, at last growing impatient with their exchange.

Boo's words cut through Polly's emotional storm and brought her up short, as if she had struck a wall, as if she were a dog whose leash had been yanked upon.

"HUH!"

"That is right, child…you are here because you asked to be here."

"B-but I don't understand. How could I—"

"When you pray, you always talk about how much you miss your mother, how much you long for her, how you cannot wait to see her again. I was merely answering your prayers… POLLIWOG."

For the second time, Polly was taken aback. Meekly she said, "Polliwog was the private nickname Ma gave me. Not even Pa called me that."

"I know."

Suddenly, with unaccustomed sternness, Polly asked, "Boo Astrophel, who are you really?"

Exasperated, Boo said to no one in particular, "People have eyes, yet they are easily fooled by appearances. Their hearts know what their eyes fail to see…what their minds refuse to accept." Then to Polly, she said, "Oh, Polliwog, have I not already told you? Have I not already shown you? Believe your heart, for it knows the truth."

A flash of both recognition and alarm gripped her. Polliwog was a nickname known only by herself, her grandparents and her mother. It didn't make sense that anyone else could know of it. Then she remembered other things that didn't make sense. There was the way Boo always smelled of Chanel No. 5 without ever wearing it. There was the way she walked as if her feet never touched the ground. Then again, there was the way she held Polly as she brushed her hair. Finally there were the feelings of closeness and warmth she had whenever Boo would hold her. It was as if they were the only two people in the world, and time had stood still, leaving a perfect moment. Separately each seemed merely coincidental. However, when viewed together—

Pleadingly, Polly asked, "Boo, who are you, really?"

The voice answered, sounding far younger than Polly's fifteen years of age.

"You wouldn't understand, silly, you are too old."

You're not getting off that easy, Polly thought. She recalled an impression she had that day of the picnic. Since then, she had suppressed it, thinking it was too fanciful. She had almost dismissed it altogether; however, the thought would no longer be denied.

"Boo," Polly asked shyly. "Are you…my mother?"

CHAPTER 32

Temptation of the Purple Nebula

Buck struggled to rise to his knees; his every movement caused him to spew forth smoke and soot, like a chimney. In vain he tried to raise his hands, only to again fall prostrate to the earth.

"Lord," he said, his face buried in the dust. "I can't find her, Lord. I can't find her. I know that wherever she is, she's close to you, whether down here or up there. But, oh God, please don't let me lose her again. I lost her when her mother died. Then I lost her when I drove her out the bar and into the dust storm. It's my fault...my fault she's blind."

He coughed again, hard, scattering the loose dirt and dust beneath his face. A crowd of those not arrested by the state police gathered around him, but he was oblivious to them.

"Please, God," he begged. "I deserve whatever I get. But in this whole bloody town, only that little girl was faithful. Only Polly was true to you. Lord, please, let her still be alive, but take my life instead. Take me instead."

No longer able to speak or to remain conscious, Buck plummeted once again, facedown, into the grimy earth.

*****

Polly anxiously waited for Boo to answer. Finding her answer was not forthcoming, she timidly asked again, "Are you my ma, Boo?"

269

Polly prepared herself for Boo's answer. Presently, however, it was the all-voice which said, "We believe that we once were the entity you call Ma and Penelope."

Polly knew that she should be happy she now had her answer, and that she was at last reunited with her mother; however, this was not the reunion she had envisioned. All she could manage to feel was crestfallen. "But, Boo, why couldn't you have told me earlier?"

Again it was the all-voice which answered, "Kindred spirit, HERE IT IS WE!"

"Sorry, but I don't understand."

"HERE IT IS WE!" the all-voice repeated matter-of-factly, as if it was the easiest thing to grasp. Suddenly Boo's voice rang throughout the ether.

"Antecedents, I will explain it to her." Boo/Penelope paused to direct her attention to Polly. "Polliwog, here—this place—this cloud is a phenomena composed of a single mind, and there are no longer any individuals who can be addressed...usually. We said that souls released from mortality's bondage ascend and accumulate with other souls, other souls of like clan...souls belonging to the same ancestral strain...family. No longer possessing bodies to separate one from another, they all meld...that is, they combine to form a collective entity or a communal mind, so to speak. Hence, 'Here it is we.'"

A thought suddenly came to Polly. "Boo. You're not the 'we' yet. You're still Boo Astrophel, an individual...your own separate and distinct entity. How can this be if the Antecedents are a group mind?"

"Thoughtful, clever girl," Boo said with a voice tinged with pride. "Very true, I have not been here long enough for the Antecedents to fully absorb me into the group yet. And the reason is you."

"Me?" Polly asked incredulously. "What did I do now?"

"You have not let go of me yet. My memory is still so fresh in your heart, I am still alive there. So I literally exist in two worlds—in the nebula and in your heart. This dual existence made me the perfect candidate to come down and observe the town...and to see you again."

Suddenly Polly felt a ripple cascade throughout the cloud, as if someone had "snapped" a sheet open, preparing to make a bed.

Immediately she became aware of the myriad of soft illuminated spheres dance around her, only to scurry off in all directions throughout the cloud.

"What was that?" Polly asked, a new sense of alarm taking hold of her.

"Those are the various elements of the nebulae positioning themselves to lend their life energy to the collective. We are preparing to leave earth and return to our proper place.

"Nonononono!" Polly blurted out in a panic. "I can't stay here. I have to get back down to earth again. I still have too much to do down there."

The Boo/Penelope voice became unmistakably perturbed. "Miss. Polly Quashi'miuoo Riser, this is not a vacation town, where you come and go as you please. Nor is it the corner of that board game you like so much that says 'Just Passing Through.' Whatever life you had down there, whatever you think you still have to do down there is over. Understand this, you are dead now, and there is no going back. Get used to it!"

Polly was surprised to find that instead of the panic she had felt, a sensation of calm and peace seemed to wash over her. The new feeling was not one of resolving herself to her fate; rather it was one of courage and hope brought on by a renewed sense of purpose.

Calmly Polly said, "But, Mother, you did."

"I did what?"

"You died, then you came back into the world of the living. Why can't I?"

"Because I do not wish it so. Now that we are finally together again, I am going to keep you here with me...FOREVER!"

*****

Though some time had passed since the Kansas State Police arrived and disarmed the mob, no one had been carted away yet. Indeed aside from forming a makeshift corral with their squad cars, to keep the rioters in check and seated upon the ground, no further move was made against them. One look at the festering putrid boils

271

on the townsfolk, coupled with their zombielike movements convinced law enforcement that nearly the entire town of Garden City had somehow been stricken with leprosy overnight. They didn't want the people carried in police cars, much less to even touch them. For the time being, law enforcement was satisfied to sit and wait for the competent medical authority they had requested to arrive and assess the situation.

With the evening beginning to wane, Kansas State Police began to wonder when medical personnel would arrive. Unbeknownst to them, medical relief would not be forthcoming. An impressive caravan from the local hospital had spent the last three hours only a mere seven miles from the police encampment and unable to proceed further. The mysterious cloud of amethyst hue, which miraculously had proven a bulwark against the deadly black blizzards, now proved a curse to those in the relief party.

Unexpectantly, inexplicably, the cloud which had originally taken on an umbrella-shape, sheltering the land below from the dust storms, had altered its shape, becoming fluid, more irregular, resulting in patches of land, previously protected by the cloud, to suddenly become exposed to the relentless winds and blowing dust. So it was that the caravan which had comfortably traveled in calm air, all at once, became assailed by blowing debris which choked out engines and battered personnel who had begun to venture forth on foot to the rescue theater, forcing them to take shelter in their stalled and stranded vehicles.

*****

Polly could feel the weight of the entire collective consciousness of the Antecedents had now become focused on the conflict taking place amid their own ethereal world. Though up to now she had remained resolute in the possibility of her getting back home, Boo/Penelope's logic was beginning to chip away at the wall of obstinacy she had erected.

Gradually Polly was becoming aware that the Boo/Penelope creature was employing a new tactic as she continued her attack in the form of the cloud's atmosphere becoming inundated by a strange floral scent. While the Antecedents seemed unaffected by the scent, it had the ability to sedate her mind, relax her resolve, and make her susceptible to her opponent's suggestions. Even the very sound of Boo/Penelope's voice now had a subtle hypnotic quality, causing Polly to believe that even if her cause were right, she would need help to escape her mother/warden.

"Now you understand that you cannot leave this place. You had no choice in your birth or in your death. Why should you believe you have any power to change your destiny in eternity? Besides even if you somehow had the ability to go back to that dismal world, why would you? Why would anyone be willing to, for that matter?"

"But, Ma," Polly protested. "It's not that I want to leave, but I just have to leave because—"

"Because down there, you have troubles and sorrows. The beauty of this place is that all of the pain and bad times of your life are left behind in time. Here in eternity, only your memories of all the good times of your life remains. Stay with me, Polly... Stay with me."

The hypnotic effects of both the perfume and her mother's voice were taking their toll on the girl. Sleepily, Polly said, "I want to stay here with you, Ma...but I have to..."

"Stay right here with me, Polly, where the best thing here is that in eternity, time has no meaning. Backward or forward, it does not matter. In eternity, thoughts become destinations, and memories become your reality. Just think, Polly, here in eternity, you can think of the best moments in your life and then relive them. Not watch them like a movie but actually experience them again, over and over, for all eternity. Stay with me, Polly... Stay with me."

"Yes, Ma, I want to stay with you."

Polly instinctively knew she had to break away from her mother's tightening grip of her mind, but how? It was then that the Boo/Penelope creature's words came back to her. *In eternity, thoughts are destinations...and memories are reality.* Polly now began to cling to the hope that somewhere in her past events, something would appear to break her mother's hold.

"Ma!" Polly said, attempting to hide her feelings from her Mother, if not her thoughts. "If I can truly relive any memory and go to it as if it was an actual place, tell me…just where should I go first?"

The Boo/Penelope creature caused more of her floral scent and more of her charmed voice to waft toward the girl in order to increase the hypnotic influence over her. Satisfied she answered, "You can go wherever you would like to go. The choice is entirely up to you."

Polly considered the matter carefully, grateful she really did have a choice in the matter.

"Well," she said, "I would like to go to…"

The little girl squealed with delight as the wooden board she sat upon was pulled back, until all the slack was out of its two support chains, allowing her to be propelled into the sky. Was that her voice screaming with delight, Polly wondered.

The puddle splashed in all directions as mother and child frolicked in the pouring rain.

The hastily built fort barely withstood the latest barrage of hastily made snowballs launched against it.

Then she was in her Uncle Fred's old truck, playing the game slam on the brakes and watch the kid rocket forward. It was amusing to adult and child alike, until once, she failed to bounce back to her place on the bench seat. Instead she continued forward, smashing into and beyond the windscreen, which transformed into a hundred lethal stilettos, falling all around her. The girl, emerging unhurt, delighted in the look of impending heart attack upon her uncle's face. That was the last time they played that game.

As Polly revisited all her most-cherished memories, cloudiness overtook her mind, engulfing it in a dense haze. The haze deepened to a thick fog. At first, Polly tried to withstand the fog. But she soon found that she was helpless against it, as she became cast adrift on a sea of her memories.

All the while, Boo/Penelope's lilting voice deepened its hypnotic quality, at first captivating, then tempting, and finally ensnaring the girl. "Stay with me, Polly…please, stay with me."

"I want to stay with you, Ma," Polly said, her voice sounding to her as if it were coming from a great distance.

"Stay here with me forever."

"Yes, I want to stay here with you."

Like quicksand, Boo/Penelope's voice pulled Polly deeper and deeper into the fog.

It was her first (remembered) Christmas, and her three-year-old self delighted in climbing the "tree" that was her pa's leg to finally hang from his outstretched arms.

That time in 1928 was special for father and daughter alike. Buck laughed with her, played with her, rolled around the floor with her, and loved with her. He was truly a child with her.

That was the last Christmas before the worldwide economic downturn of the Great Depression began the very next year with the stock market collapse, on October 1929. Hard times descended on the nation as a whole; however, those living in the Plain States were affected by it the hardest.

As the decade of the 1930s wore on, Polly watched as the Dust Bowl (Robert Geiger, *Associated Press*, April 15, 1935)[24] swallowed up the precious farmland as well as her father's spirit. That was when her father's drinking began. That was when her father's violent rages began. That Christmas was the last time they would ever be happy as a family again.

"Stay with me forever." Boo/Penelope's haunting Siren's call persisted.

Even as Polly responded, "I want to stay with you, Ma," a tiny hotly contested part of her consciousness called out, *Oh God, help!*

"Yes, dear," Boo/Penelope intoned. "Everyone you have ever loved is here with us, Polly."

Suddenly a small hole pierced through the fog. Though seemingly insignificant, it was enough to bring the girl a singular word, portending a singular thought—*Pa!*

"But…Ma," Polly said as she felt the fog begin to clear. "Everyone I love is not here. Pa's not here yet."

Though the disembodied Polly had no eyes, she had no difficulty detecting her mother's soothing demeanor change into one of anger and spite.

"How can you possibly continue to hold any hope for him after he has hurt you so?" she asked, her threatening persona rising like the tide.

"I love him," Polly said simply. "In spite of everything Pa has done, I still love him."

"There is no place here for that drunken sot." The mother spat out the words, like venom. "His destiny lies elsewhere."

"But, Ma, that can't be," Polly calmly said. "That's not what HE told me."

"Who told you what?" the mother challenged.

"God did, when I looked into the sky one night and prayed. He said that Pa wouldn't die until he was added to God's kingdom."

Polly waited for her mother to reply. Instead like a predator, the fog pounced upon her, not gradually as before but full force.

All at once, she heard the loud crack of a leather ball (fired in anger) being punished by a Louisville Slugger. Amid the deafening roar of the crowd, the offending orb sailed up and up, out of the reach of any possible hope of retrieval. The smell of steamed hotdogs and fresh-roasted peanuts filled the light breeze that barely brought relief from the noonday sun.

There were other smells, still more wonderful. Cherry and bourbon-flavored pipe tobacco, along with that aftershave in the porcelain bottle with the clipper ship on it whose name she could never remember.

"Grandpa, I've missed you so much," she squealed.

Then yet another scent came to her—fried creamed corn, fatback, and biscuits.

"There you are, Grandma. I've wanted to be with you two for the longest..."

"Now that you are here," the mother's charm voice said, and the fog became heavier still. "You do want to stay with us FOREVER?"

Polly was helpless, being washed away, not by her own memories as before but by the opiate of her mother's voice. "Yes, Ma, I want to stay with you," said Polly, her voice sounding to her as if she were in a dream.

"Here, Polliwog, there are no more heartaches or troubles. But you want to stay here, with me."

"Yes, Ma, I want to stay with you."

"No more dust storms and drought. But you want to stay here, with me."

"Yes, Ma, I want to stay with you."

Polly fought to retain her own mind, her own soul. However, the current of her mother's will was too strong for her to resist.

"No more sickness, and you will never grow old. But you want to stay here, with me."

"Yes, Ma, I will stay."

"After all, dearest daughter, did you not desire to be here when you prayed toward the heavens? But you want to stay here, with me."

"Yes, Ma, I will stay."

"You said that you missed me terribly and longed to be with me. But you want to stay here, with me."

"Yes, Ma, I will stay."

"You said that you would give anything to be with me again. But you want to stay here, with me."

"Yes, Ma." It was no use. Polly was powerless to escape from Boo/Penelope's grip.

"Well, I missed you too," Polly's mother said triumphantly. "And now that you are finally here, in eternity, time has no more meaning. We can both experience nothing but the very best events of our lives, with the very best of people…TOGETHER…and nothing is going to take you from me ever again. We'll be together, for all time."

"TIME!" the all-voice boomed throughout the cloud.

Immediately Polly could no longer hear her mother's chant. Indeed, Polly found that she could no longer hear her own thoughts. She could hear nothing except the all-voice.

"TIME!" it said again, and Polly imagined she had heard her mother scream.

"TIME!" the all-voice said thrice, and all at once, the fog was swept away, and Polly's mind was free again.

*****

Having been placed in an improvised body bag by the police, Buck was left to lie undisturbed. The torn, burned, and melted flesh over much of his body gave everyone the impression that the villain-turned-hero-turned-villain-turned-hero-again bore little hope of surviving the evening. However, he was still breathing. Labored breathing? Intermittent shallow breathing? Soot-exhaling breathing? Yes, but breathing nonetheless, having been confirmed by the most junior peace officer present being assigned canteen duty. Leaning in close to allow the victim to sip water as he was able, the officer overheard Buck repeating three simple words, "Take me instead... Take me instead... Take me instead..."

*****

Struggling to retain this last chance at sanity, Polly boldly said, "But, Ma, you don't understand. When God told me Pa would not die until his name was added to the kingdom, he also said that I would not see death until I had seen his promise be fulfilled. Being here, with you, is what I've wanted most in life, but it's too soon. God's promise to me must come to pass, and it's not time yet."

"It...is...not...your...time!" the all-voice intoned.

"Nooo..." the Boo/Penelope entity cried, sounding of mortal pain and terror. "Don't listen to them, Polly!"

"It is not your time," the all-voice repeated, the words declaring liberation and condemnation alike.

Polly had a strange feeling of warmth spread throughout her, as the Antecedents spoke. Suddenly the feeling altered to one of cold hard judgment, as the Antecedents' attention focused on the now-contrite Boo/Penelope entity.

"As for you." The Antecedents rumbled. "You were sent down to earth because you were not deceased long enough for you to have assimilated with us entirely. You were sent to examine the people of Garden City, to determine whether they were worthy to have answered the many prayers lavished upon them by this girl. Instead you seized the opportunity to indulge in your past life. Your transgression knew no restraint as you murdered an innocent in order to fulfill your own selfish design."

As Polly listened intently to the proceedings, she knew that the "trial" was not going well for her mother. It was then that Polly decided to speak up in her mother's defense.

Cautiously Polly asked, "What will happen to her... Boo... I mean, my mother now? Can she...will she be expelled from you now?"

"Child, even for an offense such as hers, she will not be entirely cast aside. However, know this, once relieved of her mortal shell to rise and enter us, there remains naught but the fellowship of the Antecedents. As such, to know the separation of displeasure from us, even for a season, is to experience the pain of the rending of a soul far more intense...far more complete than what can be revealed to mortal mind."

"Antecedents," Polly said timidly, "is it true that for those who die too suddenly, to know they are dead, they grieve for the loss of their family?"

"It is, sweet child," the Antecedents answered. "Their grief too is beyond mortal comprehension."

"It's probably no excuse," Polly cautiously continued. "But I believe that Ma did those things because of her love for me. When she lived down there, on earth, the two of us were close like sisters. When she died, she must have been so very horribly confused and lonely. Then she saw a chance for us to be together again. The temptation must have been more than anyone could bear."

Polly paused a moment and waited for some sort of response from the Antecedents. When none was offered, she decided to press her way on her mother's behalf.

"Couldn't you...could you please find some way to forgive her?"

This time, Polly didn't have to wait for an answer. Almost before she had finished asking, the Antecedents sent their reverberating reply, "No!"

At once, Polly's spirits became shattered, dashed to pieces like discarded pottery. She turned toward her mother's presence, not to receive comfort (as she had done on earth) but to offer it somehow.

Then the Antecedents spoke again, "We are powerless to forgive your once-mortal parent of her transgression. Pardon may only come from the one who had been transgressed against. Only the injured party may tender forgiveness."

At once, Polly knew what she must do. Quickly she returned her consciousness in the direction of her mother's presence. Then trying to sound as formal as she could, said, "Mother, I hereby forgive and absolve you of all harm done to me, both in the mortal world and in this one. I declare that now and forever, I hold you blameless."

She had considered the matter closed, when there came to her mind something she had almost overlooked. "And in like manner, I fully and completely decree forgiveness to my father for each and every wrongful act performed against me...especially the one in the bar the day of that terrible dust storm."

"That was well-spoken, kind and loving child," said the Antecedents.

Polly wondered what would happen next, when suddenly, a new tune reached the cloud. The Antecedents had never encountered it before, but their communal attention became instantly attracted to it, as a moth is irresistibly drawn to darkness-piercing light.

With their collective will, the Antecedents opened a ring-shaped aperture in the center of the cloud and listened, as the hauntingly beautiful melody from below invaded their ethereal world. "Take me instead... Take me instead... Take me instead," permeated every-thing and everyone within the cloud. Though the Antecedents made no comment concerning the strange song, Polly could tell that the whole atmosphere within the cloud had suddenly changed.

"Polly of a true heart," said the Antecedents. "Because you have been brought here before your time of summons, it now falls on you to decide and choose. You may return to your mortal life below. Or you may remain here, as one with us, until the One who has created all things brings all things to an end. So now, Vibrant Sparkle, choose well."

Polly considered the matter for only a moment. Then, taking care not to upset her mother further, said, "Ma, you WANT me to stay with you always. And I WANT to stay here with you and Grandpa and Grandma. Lord knows I would have wanted to stay here, even without the tricks and schemes."

Polly paused, as powerful conflicting emotions washed over her, as a wave assaults the beach, then retreats into the sea.

"Seeing departed loved ones again is what I've longed for almost all of my life. And now that I'm finally here, I want ever so much to stay with all of you, but especially with you, Ma. I have missed you so very much."

Polly waited and silently prayed that God would guide the decision she must now make, as well as to give her courage and strength.

"Ma, I WANT to stay…but I can't. I must go back. Pa really NEEDS me now. He has lost everything and everyone. He's all alone. Besides what I said to you before was true, when the Lord told me that Pa wouldn't die until he was added to his kingdom, he also said that I would live as well until I had seen it happen. So, Ma, I just must go back. If time truly means nothing here, couldn't you wait just a little while until I've lived the life God has designed before I come to be with you, for good?"

Without waiting for the Boo/Penelope entity to respond, the Antecedents spoke, "So be it! Child, return to your mortality until the One for whom it is meant decrees your end. And know this, sweet girl, because of your willingness to sacrifice your place among us, preferring instead to return to earth to help your father in his distress, we grant you the lives of those below, whithersoever our shadow has touched the earth. Fare you well, mortal child."

No sooner had the Antecedents concluded their pronouncement, Polly felt herself being pushed and pulled at the same time and that her mother was moving further and further away from her. Or was it she who was moving away from her mother?

"I will see you again, Ma," Polly said, struggling to be heard over the rapidly increasing distance.

"When it is your time," the Antecedents said.

"Oh, Ma, you will always be here with me, in my heart, until—"

"It is your time."

Now Polly had the sensation that she was not moving away from her mother as much as she was fading away, becoming nothing altogether.

"I love you, Ma…"

*****

Like the eye of cyclops, the center of the cloud opened to allow an ever-widening area of shower to reach the parched earth. The "eye," as if surveying the land below, slowly moved in one direction, then the next. It continued thus, until its life-giving precipitation had made contact with and inundated the whole of the region over-shadowed by the cloud.

The townsfolk of Garden City all witnessed it. They were also witness to an even-narrower stream of glistening rainbow-colored droplets, which occupied the very center of the larger one. Once on the ground, each of the individual rainbow droplets danced upon the ground as a hot skillet would affect beads of water dropped thereon. They continued their dance; drawing closer and closer, they merged and began a vertical accumulation as more rainbow drops were added. The growth spurt abruptly ceased as the rainbow conglomerate congealed into a semisolid pillar not more than five feet in height.

As if being formed by an unseen sculptor, the column expanded in some areas while simultaneously contracting in others. The process continued, until a rough likeness of a child stood in the larger cascading stream. All at once, as soon as the child-form evidenced itself, the entire cloud burst forth in a massive downpour. It was no standard ordinary shower but a genuine gully washer.

The rushing waters dissolved the police body bag and bathed the prostrate Riser, whose body began to let off steam as the burnt, charred flesh was dissolved and washed away by the sudden deluge. In its place, pink flesh, without a blemish, looked as fresh as a baby not one hour old.

As for those once bitten by the locusts, whose bodies erupted in festering boils, whether at the farm or remaining in town, whether outdoors in the rain or indoors, the effect was the same. The boils steamed and foamed, as hydrogen peroxide poured over an open wound, then were either sloughed off or washed away until all exhibited the clear tender skin of the newborn.

The child-form in the center of the stream continued to be refined until a perfectly formed little girl could be seen. As it began to slowly move toward the older Riser, a baggy full-length cotton slip materialized over its naked features. Buck would later report that it was the close-fitting half-slip his wife, Penelope, had worn the night before the tractor accident, which took her life.

The child, now clearly Polly, glided on, coming to rest in front of her father. The same Polly Buck had always known. But wait, this Polly was not quite the same. The sandblasting scars around her face were gone. Most importantly, her dried scoured-out sockets were now occupied anew. Not with the root-beer-brown eyes she had before. These were white pearlescent ones, which mimicked the cloud in that they bore the cloud's dancing gold flecks.

Buck cried unashamedly as Polly approached. Without a single word spoken by either of them, the father rested his head upon his daughter's chest and continued to weep.

While the people of Garden City reveled unabated in the rain, few, if any, noticed the cloud of amethyst hue slowly begin to rise into the early evening sky. Higher and higher it rose until the people of Garden City could no longer see it, had they been observing it at all. However, for those occupying the various observatories around the world, the cloud held their collective attention, as if spellbound.

As it arched through the immediate interplanetary expense, its atmospheric form melted away, regaining the amorphic amoeba appearance they were accustomed to. Thus it continued to expand and grow until it was the puny size (as far as nebulae were concerned) it had been when it arrived, perhaps five souls larger.

Though the mysterious cloud of amethyst hue had departed, its rains continued for the rest of the night and through most of the next day. The cloud left the solar system of Sol far behind, rejoining all the other nebulae, formed from all the clans that have ever existed anywhere.

EPILOGUE

The loss of Polly's inheritance, bequeathed to the citizens of Garden City, though tragic, was a matter of almost-complete indifference to Polly. Once she had prayerfully decided to release the monies, in her heart, it no longer belonged to her. However, the most devastated, by far, was Mayor Smoke who, while serving as the grant's executor, viewed its theft by others as a personal loss.

As for the one who orchestrated the bank robbery, in which his brother and a bank guard were murdered, incited and lead a mob, assaulted an officer of the peace and started a fire in which three people were killed, Judge Lynch lived up to his name by ordering Doug Sweeny to pay for all he had taken from the town with the forfeiture of his own life. Governor Patton himself presided over his execution, while Sheriff Pucket pulled the lever to the gallows door. Mayor Smoke was not in attendance.

One day, Polly received a letter from her old friend Mr. Klaus Koe, informing her that Leopoldo had, at last, passed away. Having no natural issue, he had in his will named two people as heirs of his estate. First his protégé and partner, Klaus Koe, was given Leopoldo's taxidermy shop, his artistic academy, as well as the associated gallery.

Second "the most gracious lady, Polly Riser," was to receive the sum of the amount agreed upon for the taxidermy restoration of the Flemish giant rabbit, known as Hasenpfeffer, multiplied by her age at the time of their meeting, to be paid from the estate upon each anniversary of Leopoldo and Koe's reunion, in perpetuity.

It surprised no one when she declared it to be a grant to the people of Garden City as well, only this time, it was to be administered by her father, Buck. As was the biblical tale of multiplying of the fish and bread, the monies were used to preserve the people of Garden

City, covering their mortgages and protecting their homes, farms, and businesses from foreclosure until the end of the worldwide economic downturn, known as the Great Depression.

As for Benjamin Bucannon "Buck" Riser, the church congregation unanimously established him as head deacon, where he tirelessly worked as an undershepherd for three years, until the diocese ordained a new and permanent pastor. After that, Buck continued to serve faithfully, never straying, and never wavering until he peacefully departed this world, just one week prior to his seventieth birthday.

Many attended his funeral, most notably a Mr. Johnny "Mack" Mackenzie, former owner of the only speakeasy/bar in Garden City. Witnessing Buck's transformation and subsequent heroism, he joined the church and immediately closed the bar. When interviewed as to why he remodeled and reopened it as the largest ice cream parlor, Soda Fountain Emporium and Sweet Shoppe in all of Finney County, Mr. Mackenzie simply remarked, "If Buck can change, then so can I."

History records that "In the Fall of Nineteen Thirty-Nine…the return of regular rainfall to the region,"[25] ended the worst continuous drought in the annals of the United States. However, for the citizens of Garden City, Kansas, the "miracle of the rains" occurred a full three years before then.

In time, the Great Depression became past tense. In time, the Dust Bowl subsided. In time, crops returned. In time, people returned. In time, life returned to Garden City, Kansas, as well as to the other Plains States.

Since then, tales of the Great Depression, along with the black blizzards, would be told by parents and grandparents to their children and grandchildren, from one generation to the next.

In Garden City, it became a treasured tradition that on every New Year's Eve, the entire town, young and old alike, would gather at the town hall to be regaled with the story of the miracle that saved their town, told by their oldest citizen.

And this year (2020), eighty-four years later, at age ninety-nine, Mrs. Polly Quashi'miuoo Riser Russell *Golden* still does.

THE END

ACKNOWLEDGMENTS

The love of reading is indelibly in my family's blood as surely as the erythrocytes, leukocytes, and plasma of which it is composed. One of my fondest childhood memories is of my siblings and I gathered in the living room to hear my father's annual yuletide reading of Charles Dickens' *A Christmas Carol*. Later that tradition was expanded upon by those very siblings gathering together in order to take turns reading aloud a selected novel from a favorite author. This became the seed for my desire to someday have my siblings, our children, and even grandchildren gather for a reading of a literary work of my own.

There is an African proverb which states, "It takes a village to raise a child."

As I undertook this journey, I soon discovered that it takes an entire world to write a novel. Let me explain. Hollywood director Cecil B. DeMille's films were reputed to have "a cast of thousands." Well, I do not personally know that many people; however, almost everyone in my world, i.e., my personal circle of family and close friends, in one way or another, bore a hand in bringing the story of *The Cloud People* to life.

From encouragement to criticism, from sounding boards to shoulders to cry on, all were helpful, and all bore a hand in my first (completed) novel. However, there are some who deserve special mention.

Mrs. Brown (my first-grade teacher), Rosedale Elementary School, Cleveland, Ohio—Long before dyslexia and attention deficit had entered the cultural lexicon, she bravely rejected the educational assembly line and refused to advance a student challenged by both until he successfully learned to read.

Dr. Anita Bryant (formerly of John Hay High School, Cleveland, Ohio)—She was instrumental in facilitating my induction into The National Honor Society and Who's Who in the Cleveland Public

School System. However, perhaps most important of all, she genuinely believed in me.

Curtis Wright, my best friend—Proved to be as enthusiastic about the book as I was and became a constant reminder to finish it in this lifetime.

Nedra Vashti Moore, lifelong friend and beloved sister—She provided inspiration for much more than this work.

Karsten and Shyquandria Reynolds, extended family—Their critique of the book, as well as their moral support, proved invaluable.

Dr. Carl Barham, psychologist, counselor, author, and personal friend—Whose prompting for constant progress reports kept the work goal-oriented and progressing and whose advice facilitated its publication.

Susan Moger, author, instructor (beginning and intermediate fiction writers course, Anne Arundel Community College, Arnold, Maryland)—Her knowledge, instruction, and encouragement not only introduced me to the art of writing, gave me confidence to believe in the light within me, but amounted to nothing less than true mentorship (I still use her notes to this very day).

The doctors and nurses at Johns Hopkins Hospital, Baltimore, Maryland—For three weeks during the spring of 2019, they patiently put up with my writing obsession while facilitating my receiving and recovery from transplant surgery, allowing me to complete the first draft of the manuscript.

To all my older relatives who, throughout my childhood, told me stories of their experiences during the Great Depression. Their stories became the primary inspiration for this book.

To my wife, Mae, for her patience, impatience (at times), encouragement, and intense personal motivational speaking, the value of which can never be overstated.

Last but certainly not least, a special heartfelt thanks to all who, by the purchase of this work, gave a newbie author a chance, as well as the incentive to launch out in pursuit of future literary endeavors.

Please never forget, *I am truly a fan of all of you.*

M. Samuel Golden

References

1 The Holy Bible (King James Version), (Pennsylvania: The Online Parallel Bible Project, 2018).

2 Larry Sanger and Jimmy Wales, "The Dust Bowl," Wikipedia Online Encyclopedia, retrieved 2017, https://en.m.wikipedia.org.

3 Joe Defazio, "Black Blizzards, Black Sunday," Ancestry.com, retrieved October 28, 2015, https://www.ancestry.com.

4 "Nebula," Wikipedia Online Encyclopedia, retrieved January 9, 2020, https://en.m.wikipedia.org.

5 "Girl Baby Names," JustMommies, retrieved 2017, https://www.justmommies.com>girls.

6 "Slang Words for Jail," Your Dictionary, retrieved 2018, https://grammaryourdictionary.com.

7 "Henri de Toulouse-Lautrec," Wikipedia Online Encyclopedia, retrieved January 24, 2020, https://en.m.wikipedia.org.

8 "Animal Cognition," Wikipedia Online Encyclopedia, retrieved January 22, 2020, https://en.m.wikipedia.org.

9 "M1918 Browning Automatic Rifle," Wikipedia Online Encyclopedia, retrieved January 24, 2020, https://en.m.wikipedia.org.

10 Ibid.

11 Ibid.

12 "Teetotalism," Wikipedia Online Encyclopedia, retrieved February 20, 2020, https://en.m.

13 "Radio Sets of the 1930s, The Golden Age of Radio," Wikipedia Online Encyclopedia, retrieved 2017, https://en.m.wikipedia.org.

14 Little Orphan Annie, Wikipedia Online Encyclopedia, retrieved October 10, 2020, https://en.m.wikipedia.org.

15 Larry Sanger and Jimmy Wales, "The Dust Bowl," Wikipedia Online Encyclopedia, retrieved 2017, https://en.m.wikipedia.org.

16 "Distance Between Cities," Google, retrieved February 31, 2020, https://distance-cities.com.

17 Susan Sherwood, "Ways to Predict a Storm With Air Pressure," Seattle PI, retrieved February 19, 2020, https://education.seattlepi.com>way.

18 "Paradoxical Reaction," Wikipedia Online Encyclopedia, retrieved February 18, 2020, https://en.m.wikipedia.org.

[19] *Pimp-slap*, Wiktionary, retrieved February 19, 2020, https://en.m.wiktionary.org/wiki/pimp_slap.

[20] Mylon Lefevre and Broken Heart, "Closer Than a Heartbeat (Crack The Sky)," Wikipedia Online Encyclopedia, retrieved October 03, 2020, https://en.m.wikipedia.org.

[21] "Names That Mean 'Star,'" retrieved 2017, https://www.meaning-of-names.com.

[22] "Behind the Name Astrophel. Meaning, Origin and History of Names," retrieved 2017, https://www.behindthename.com.

[23] "Barrow Revisited," Babyface Nelson Journal, retrieved February 15, 2020, https://www.babyfacenelsonjournal.com.

[24] Christopher Klein, "10 Things You May Not Know About the Dust Bowl," The History Chanel, retrieved September 27, 2020, https://www.history.com.

[25] "Dust Bowl," Wikipedia Online Encyclopedia, retrieved February 22, 2020, https://en.m.wikipedia.org.

About the Author

A native of Cleveland, Ohio, Mr. Golden is a graduate of John Hay High School, where he was inducted into the National Honor Society, Who's Who in the Cleveland Public School System, and served as student council president. Simultaneously attending Cleveland's Aviation High School, he was one of the first graduates from its class in air traffic control.

After successfully completing the paramedic training program at Cuyahoga Community College, he enlisted in the United States Coast Guard, serving with distinction as a health services technician (hospital corpsman) until retiring after twenty years of service in 2003.

Married to his high school sweetheart for the last thirty-eight years, they reside in a suburb of Baltimore. A graduate of the University of Maryland, Baltimore County, *The Cloud People* is his inaugural published work.

CPSIA information can be obtained
at www.ICGtesting.com
Printed in the USA
FSHW021626090222
88199FS